W9-BNF-241

RED MESA

Also by Aimée & David Thurlo

Black Mesa
Second Shadow
Spirit Warrior
Timewalker

ELLA CLAH NOVELS
Blackening Song
Death Walker
Bad Medicine
Enemy Way
Shooting Chant

RED MESA

AIMÉE & DAVID THURLO

A Tom Doherty Associates Book
New York

This is a work of fiction. All the characters and events portrayed in this novel are either fictitious or are used fictitiously.

RED MESA

Copyright © 2001 by Aimée and David Thurlo

All rights reserved, including the right to reproduce this book, or portions thereof, in any form.

A Forge Book

Published by Tom Doherty Associates, LLC
175 Fifth Avenue
New York, NY 10010

Forge® is a registered trademark of Tom Doherty Associates, LLC.

ISBN 0-312-87060-4

Printed in the United States of America

To Linda Maestas—friend, neighbor,
and possibly the best cook in New Mexico

RED MESA

ONE

✖ ✖ ✖

It was already dark before Special Investigator Ella Clah, head of the major crimes unit for the Navajo Tribal Police, was able to call it a day. As she stepped out the main entrance of the Shiprock station, the cool September air made her realize how stuffy her office had been.

A relatively uneventful afternoon working on reports had made the passage of time excruciatingly slow, and Ella was looking forward to seeing her daughter and playing with her tonight. The time she spent with Dawn was always the best part of any day.

Ella shook her long black hair loose from the confining silver barrette and looked across the cobalt blue sky to Ute Mountain northwest of Shiprock. The image was said to be that of a sleeping warrior, and tonight, in the light of a bright full moon, it appeared peaceful. Yet, as the wind blew a gust of cold air against her, Ella couldn't quite rid herself of the feeling that the Rez was due for a change.

Adjusting her dark brown leather jacket, Ella walked down the steps toward her vehicle. Her young assistant and cousin, Officer Justine Goodluck, had just pulled out of the station's parking lot. Justine had only recently started dating again after a failed relationship, and from her rush, and the scent of her perfume still lingering in the station lobby, was apparently going out again tonight. They'd not even crossed paths today because Ella had been wading through paperwork, and Justine had been in her small crime lab, conducting tests and writing reports.

It was probably a good thing that they hadn't spent any time together today, because Justine had been a bit testy lately. The fact that they were shorthanded was a major cause of the stress, undoubtedly. Justine had been forced to do a lot more of the work formerly done by Harry Ute, who had resigned the department to become a federal marshal. Cutbacks had prevented the department from finding a replacement.

Ella settled into her dark blue Jeep and backed out of the parking space. She always had a slot close to the entrance because she was one of the first cops at the station every morning. Of course, with all the funding problems, and the closure of their only branch station, there were fewer cops these days. Even the last officer to arrive had a close space available in Shiprock.

As she drove through the small reservation community, the lights of the supermarket's parking lot shone on her hands. It suddenly occurred to her how much they looked like her mother's, not old, but familiar and strong.

Families. They were at the core of everything she valued these days, though as a single, working mother she couldn't say that much else about her lifestyle was traditional. Yet, despite that, she still felt strongly connected to everything on the Rez. All things were interrelated, particularly here. Justine, for example, was her second cousin as well as her assistant at work. That family connection was why Ella couldn't help but feel a little protective about her at times.

Admittedly she also saw a bit of herself in Justine. That drive to succeed, to become better at her job and make a difference to her people, also defined Ella's years in law enforcement.

Ella thought about Justine and the endless possibilities still before her. A woman needed more in her life than her job. In that respect, she was glad that Justine was dating again.

Ella remembered the last time she'd been on a date. It was when she'd told Kevin that she didn't want to go out with him anymore, that their relationship had been a mistake. She hadn't known she was carrying his child at the time. Of course, when she'd told him she was pregnant, Kevin had asked her to marry him, but she'd refused, knowing that they were too different in the ways that mattered to make a marriage work. Kevin had accepted her decision, but had been faithful about coming to see his daughter, a right Ella would never deny him.

Although Kevin was a good weekend father to Dawn, Ella was glad his interest in Dawn was limited. She wanted to follow the Navajo tradition that said children were the mother's property, in a very loose sense of the term, and belonged with her. She had a gut feeling that Kevin's ambitions and his desire for success would someday create no end of trouble for him and everyone who was a part of his life.

Ella brushed those thoughts aside and instead focused on seeing her eighteen-month-old daughter's smiling face when she got home. Dawn was growing like a weed, and Rose, her grandmother, was the most loving sitter Ella could have found. Rose still disapproved of Ella's job and would have rather seen her married and settled, but for the most part, the three of them had become a tightly knit family.

Ella passed the new housing area where the old helium plant employee houses had once stood, and now Ship Rock was visible to her right, standing several miles from the highway.

Hearing her radio crackle and her call sign coming through, Ella focused on the transmission.

"This is dispatch, requesting assistance for Officer Goodluck at the Cortez Highway Food N' Fuel. A 2-11 is in progress. Go Code One. Be advised that the officer reports one perp armed with a handgun. Perp is wearing a stocking mask, jeans, and a dark leather jacket."

"Dispatch. This is SI One. I'll respond to the 2-11. ETA five minutes." An armed robbery was in progress and the PD wanted a silent approach. Ella clicked on her high beams and glanced ahead and then into the rearview mirror, verifying that no vehicles were close. Braking with a practiced amount of pressure, she turned the steering wheel with the skills honed on FBI training courses and spun the Jeep around in a one-eighty. With another officer and civilians at the store in danger, she couldn't afford a wasted motion or a second's delay. Keeping her siren off but switching on the flashers, Ella raced back north again.

Fortunately most of the traffic was heading her way, so she was able to pass through town quickly. Turning off her flashers, Ella drove another mile across the top of the mesa. The convenience store was only a bit farther up the road. Ella purposely held off on using her radio, not wanting to compromise Justine's position if her partner was still undetected by the suspect.

Suddenly a frantic radio call broke her concentration. "Ten thirty-seven at the Food N' Fuel! Officer needs help. Ella, what's keeping you?" Justine's voice came in loud and strong.

Shots had been fired. Ella could now see the convenience store ahead on her right, and she turned on her flashers and siren, letting both Justine and the perp know that more cops were approaching. The element of surprise had already been lost.

"I'm almost there, Justine. What is your 10–10?"

"I'm heading around the building in pursuit of the suspect. Leather jacket, jeans. Tall, with long hair and a stocking mask, according to the clerk. I haven't gotten close enough to see his face yet. He headed around the back. Ten-four?"

"Hold your position, Justine. Which side of the building are you on, north or south?" Ella didn't want the perp to get away, but she also didn't want any confusion in the dark. Any officer would be on edge and quick to fire after being fired upon. Ella waited for a response, but all she got was static on the radio.

"Justine? Confirm your location." Ella looked ahead anxiously as she pulled into the dimly lit parking lot. The sides of the building were cloaked in shadows as black as velvet. Ella tried to raise Justine again, but the static was even louder than before.

Ella looked around and saw that Justine's car was parked in a space to the left of the entrance, a strategy most of their officers used when approaching a convenience store during peak robbery hours, usually from dusk to dawn. When exiting the vehicle, officers would have their own car for protection in case they encountered an emerging, armed robber.

Ella pulled up directly behind the only other vehicle there, a beat-up pickup. If this was the perp's transportation, her position would deny the driver a getaway.

Slipping out the driver's side, keeping her car's engine block between her and the gunman in the building for protection, Ella gave the scene a quick survey—from left to right there was an ice machine, double-door entrance, and newspaper rack. Inside the store, no heads or bodies were visible. If the clerk was alive, he or she was staying on the floor. She listened for the sound of footsteps, but the night was silent.

Ella tried her radio again, but heavy static still prevented her from reaching dispatch or contacting Justine. Pistol in hand, she ran to the store entrance and crouched down low, peeking around the doorframe and listening.

On the floor beside the dairy case was a clerk in the store's standard red shirt. "Police officer. Are you alone?" she whispered, watching for movement elsewhere in the store.

"The guy's gone. The other officer ran after him. He took a shot at her, but I think he missed."

"Which direction did they go?" Ella half turned and looked out toward the ice machine.

"To your left out into the dark. That's all I saw." The man started to sit up.

"Stay down till we catch this guy, but get behind the counter. More help is on its way." Ella heard footsteps on the cement outside. She looked out and saw someone in a stocking mask peering around the right side of the store. Seeing the barrel of the person's gun from where she stood, she dove flat and brought her own pistol up and around, but by then her target had disappeared. Rolling quickly to her right, Ella sprinted out, using Justine's car for cover, and looked in the direction the perp had gone.

Not knowing if her partner was lying wounded somewhere out in the darkness, Ella hurried quickly to the corner of the building and looked down the side wall. The perp disappeared around the corner just as she came into view.

Fearing an ambush, Ella moved away from the building and circled wide, slowing to move as silently as possible through the darkness and across the rocky ground. The perp would probably assume she'd hug the wall, and her approach from farther out might throw him. She kept her pistol trained on the corner as she inched forward, the faint radioactive glow of her special tritium sights giving her an edge in the darkness.

As she approached the rear of the store, Ella caught sight of the perp flattened against the side of a Dumpster by the back door, underneath a single dim, flickering light. She took aim and walked slowly forward, hoping he wouldn't notice her until she was close enough to guarantee a hit in the uncertain light if she needed to fire.

Suddenly Ella heard a familiar voice. "Police Officer! Drop the gun!" Justine's voice was hard and sharp.

Startled, Ella turned her head to verify Justine's position and saw a figure approaching from the darkness on the far side of the Dumpster. Instinctively she turned, her aim shifting slightly toward the approaching shape as she did.

"Drop it!" Justine ordered.

Realizing that Justine was mistaking her for the perp, she instantly shifted her aim back squarely on the perp in front of her and called out loudly, "Justine, it's me!"

But it was too little, too late. Warned by instinct, Ella spun away and dove to the ground just as a muzzle flashed. A bullet passed inches from her right shoulder.

"No!" Justine cried out, realizing her mistake and running toward Ella.

Ella rolled and came up to a shooting stance to bring her aim back on the perp's position, but he'd already taken advantage of Justine's misidentification and raced back into the store through the rear entrance.

"I'm okay, Justine. Circle around front and cut him off if he tries to get out that way." When Justine didn't respond, Ella turned and saw the frightened look in her partner's eyes. "Really, I'm okay. You missed me by a mile. Get moving. I'll follow him through the back door. We don't want a hostage situation."

As Justine ran off, Ella hurried to the back door, flinging it open while hugging the doorjamb. The clerk was on the floor beside the counter, his hands clasped over his head as if he were expecting an artillery attack, or immediate arrest.

"He ran right out the front! Get that SOB!" the man yelled, his voice an octave higher than before.

Hearing another two shots out front, Ella raced down the aisle toward the front entrance. Before she could get there, headlights blinded her and she heard the loud squeal of tires. Knowing this was one battle she couldn't win, Ella dodged to the left. Sliding on the waxed floor, she crashed into a display rack, causing dozens of paperbacks to rain down upon her.

A heartbeat later, glass flew everywhere as the old pickup she'd parked behind came up on the sidewalk and crashed through the convenience store's glass front wall. The building shook and the smell of car exhaust filled the store. In a frenzy of screaming tires, the vehicle veered into a hard turn and raced away.

Ella raised her head and looked up at the chaos. The perp, unable to back out of the parking lot because Ella had blocked his vehicle, had gone forward instead, jumped the concrete barrier, and plowed through the glass front of the store to gain the space he needed to turn and flee.

Ella heard Justine yelling and cursing outside. Picking her way out of the store across broken glass and scattered merchandise, Ella managed to reach the sidewalk. "Which way did he go?"

The static that had disrupted communications earlier was gone and Justine was on her handheld radio now, calling dispatch to request additional units to handle the pursuit. After a few seconds, she put the radio into the pocket of her blue athletic jacket. "Look what that sack of manure did to our units." Justine pointed out a flat tire on her own vehicle, and on Ella's Jeep.

Her voice was as unsteady as her hands, and Ella considered, as she often did, how young her cousin looked. Maybe it was her petite size and delicate features, but if it hadn't been for the over-sized-looking handgun in the holster high on her hip, Justine could easily be mistaken for a high school student. "Jeez, how many things can go wrong in one night?"

Ella knew that Justine was still shaken by the realization of how costly her earlier mistake could have been. It was a miracle that Ella had escaped serious injury, despite wearing a bullet-resistant vest beneath her blouse. But all that had to wait. "Since we can't follow the perp, we need to question the store owner while everything's still fresh in his mind."

Ella turned and looked back at the damage done to the store.

The clerk was standing up now, on the phone to someone, perhaps his boss. He was staring at the debris, rubbing the back of his neck and shaking his head as he spoke.

After they went inside, Ella looked around and realized that the small, family-run store had no videotape security. She asked the clerk about it anyway, hoping she'd missed something.

"Nope, never got around to it. Except for the alarm, my dad can't afford any of that fancy stuff. And to be honest, it hasn't been needed, not in the thirty years he's run this place." The clerk, a man in his early twenties, looked around and cursed. "Look at the mess they made."

"Do you have insurance?" Justine asked.

The young man shrugged. "My dad will know. We've never spoken about that."

"What's your name, and what happened here tonight?"

"I'm Juan Benally. The guy came in and the second I saw the mask and gun, I reached down and hit the silent alarm. Then he came right up to me, aimed the gun at my head, and told me to empty the cash register into a paper bag he handed me."

"The suspect was working alone? There wasn't anyone waiting in the truck?" Ella prodded.

"I don't think so, but I can't be sure. I only saw the one who held me up."

"Describe him."

Juan gave her a long look. "He was about your height, had long hair, too. Shoulder length." He scowled. "Heck, he was even dressed like you. A dark brown leather jacket and jeans. Of course, he had a mask, but from the voice, I knew it was a guy."

Justine pressed the clerk for more answers, but after a few minutes, it became obvious that there was nothing further he could tell them, except how much money had been stolen.

After warning him that he'd have to stop by the station and sign a statement, they walked back out to the parking lot. Ella went to her Jeep, opened up the back, and started to bring out the jack and spare tire.

Justine went with her. "Ella, about what happened . . ."

"It was just an accident. These things happen. It was dark, you were expecting someone with a gun, and there I was," she said quietly. "But from now on, make sure to get a positive ID before using deadly force. That's basic, Justine."

"I know, but I had every reason to believe you were the suspect. I'd pursued him out into the scrub brush beside the store and lost sight of him for a moment. When I heard someone in back of the store, I headed that way. Then I came around the corner, saw a figure who looked like the person I'd been chasing. He turned and pointed a weapon in my direction. I fired just like I'd been trained to do.

"Ella, you know that it's not just an excuse, it's a conditioned response. I'd chased the perp to that spot, then the next thing I saw was a gun aimed at me. I hadn't lost sight of him for more than a few seconds, and in the dark you looked just like him."

"You knew I was around."

"Yes, but I didn't expect to run into you back there, or have you point a gun at me."

"Justine, how long had it been since you'd lost sight of the perp?"

She considered the question carefully before answering, ignoring a strand of shiny black hair that drifted back and forth across her face in the breeze. "Less than ten seconds. When I saw you, I thought it was him," Justine replied. "Or maybe it was you I saw all along."

Ella shook her head slowly. "Something's not right about this. He couldn't have moved that fast. I'd been chasing him for more than ten seconds before he went to ground beside the Dumpster. He couldn't have gotten away from you and all the way around to the front of the store before I spotted him in that small amount of time, much less gone all the way to the back of the store where we met. Are you sure we're talking about the same guy?"

"The only way to explain this otherwise is if we say that there were two perps involved, who looked and dressed the same and also happened to be wearing clothing similar to yours. Do you realize how ridiculous that sounds? And nobody saw more than one perp." Justine shook her head. "But something is definitely fishy. Several minutes passed between the time I responded and you arrived on the scene. Why didn't the guy make a run for it sooner?"

Ella nodded. "Good point. Yeah, something about this entire thing stinks. We'll have to keep going over it until we can figure this out." She looked directly at Justine. "But look, let's not make a big deal about the near accident, okay? As long as we're both careful that it doesn't happen again, we'd be better off moving on to the real issue here, which is catching the perp."

Ella knew an incident like this one could cost Justine plenty if it went in her permanent file, and she wanted to give her cousin a break. Justine had worked hard to get to where she was in the department, and a mistake like this would follow her for the duration of her career. Whatever had almost happened, when it came down to it, Ella still trusted Justine's abilities as a cop.

"Tone down that part of what happened today in your report," Ella continued. "Otherwise Big Ed's going to have a bazillion questions and it's going to divert everyone from the work we have to do. All things considered, I'd rather focus on the crime, and I think you would, too."

"All right. And, Ella, it will *never* happen again."

"I know."

"How about if I start by asking around about the robbery and the damaged pickup? Someone out there knows this perp. There aren't many secrets here on the Rez, and if the robber is a local, we should hear some talk right away."

"Go for it. By the way, I noticed your radio is working now. What happened before? When I got here I couldn't hear a thing through the static," Ella asked.

"It just quit for a while. As far as I know, it's okay now."

"I can't figure out where all the static came from. Reception is not usually a problem in this area, and we were pretty close to each other."

"That's true. And I could barely hear you."

"Walk around the side of the building and let's see if that's what was causing the interference." Ella got into her car and tried calling Justine. This time Justine's voice came through crystal-clear. Ella then did a radio check with dispatch, which also came through as normal. The inconsistency just added another level to the puzzle.

Ella put her radio away and shifted her attention to changing her damaged tire, weighing what was the most likely explanation for the radio problems, and not liking it one bit.

Justine came back around to the front of the store, then leaned over, resting her elbows on Ella's driver's-side window. "You realize what this means, don't you?" She continued, not waiting for an answer. "Somehow, the perp must have jammed our radio signals. I sure don't like any of the other questions that raises, like how he did it, and why he went to all that trouble. This whole thing comes across as more than just a 2-11 if you accept that as a possibility."

Ella nodded slowly. "It's getting late. Give me a hand with my tire, and I'll help with yours, then let's both go home. We can fill out the reports first thing tomorrow. Maybe things will be clearer then."

"Don't worry about my flat. Let's get you on the road. Maybe you can still see Dawn before she's put to bed."

"It's too late already," Ella said, checking her watch and trying to hide her disappointment. "She'll be asleep by the time I get there. It's always that way when we get a call around the end of the shift."

Justine started to say something, then changed her mind.

"What's on your mind?"

"I just wondered . . . I've been avoiding serious relationships because I've been afraid they'd add too many complications to my life. But is it a lot harder for you these days, now that you have Dawn?"

"Yes and no. I love my daughter more than I ever thought was possible. But being a single mom with a full-time career is really frustrating. I try to spend as much time as I can with Dawn, but it's never enough. It can tear you in two."

Justine nodded slowly. "I had a feeling that's the way things would work." She stood up and moved around to help Ella get her spare into position and secured.

A few minutes later, Ella pulled out onto highway, notifying dispatch of her status as she headed south. The events tonight had unsettled her far more than she'd allowed Justine to see. Deliberate jamming of police radio transmissions spoke of an operation far more complicated and deadly than a simple armed robbery of a convenience store.

Although experience told her that her questions would be answered as the investigation took its course, instinct warned her that things would get a lot worse before they got better, unless they found those answers in a hurry.

TWO

——— ✖ ✖ ✖ ———

Ella reached home fifteen minutes later. It was after ten and all the lights were off except on the porch. She walked inside silently, locked up behind her, and before doing anything else, peered inside the baby's room. The nursery was her brother Clifford's old room, next to her own.

Ella stood in the doorway and watched her eighteen-month-old daughter sleeping. Dawn's bed these days was a plain mattress placed on the floor against the wall. She could no longer be kept in the crib because she'd learned how to crawl out of it, and it was a long way to the floor. Ella shook her head. She'd wanted to get her a bed with a guardrail, but Rose wouldn't have it. Traditionally, babies Dawn's age slept on sheepskins placed on the floor where they'd be safe from falls. Had Rose had her way completely, Ella was pretty sure she would have opted for that.

The one totally modern amenity Ella had insisted on was the child's gate they'd set up at the doorway. The door would remain open, but if Dawn decided to move off the mattress and play, she'd still be confined to that one room, where everything had been child-proofed.

Ella slipped off her boots and stepped over the gate, sitting down on the floor beside Dawn. She leaned over and brushed a strand of soft black hair away from her daughter's eyes, enjoying the scent of soap and her baby's breath, which never ceased sending a feeling of pride that only another mother understood.

Dawn's tiny arm, which had been tightly wrapped around her stuffed dinosaur, was now relaxed, and Ella gently removed the toy, placing it a foot away on the mattress, so Dawn could find it again if she woke up.

Ella sat there in the dark, listening to Dawn breathe for a while, marveling at the contrast between the dead-to-the-world child of the moment and the fireball that could empty her toy box in seconds or find a new way to get into mischief in the blink of an eye.

After five minutes, Ella adjusted Dawn's blanket, pecked her on the cheek, took another whiff of baby scent, then left the room. It was on days like these, when she arrived too late to put her own child to bed, that she regretted having such a demanding job, but it was the career she was meant for, and nothing else would ever give her the satisfaction that came from being a cop.

Ella closed the door to her own bedroom, then switched on the computer. She was too keyed up now to sleep, so she decided to check her electronic mailbox. Seeing a letter from Wilson Joe, she smiled. It was too bad she'd never been able to see him as anything more than a friend. Wilson would make some woman a great husband someday.

She was in the middle of replying to his invitation to meet for lunch when a tone sounded and an "instant message" flashed on the screen.

The message was curt and simple.

> Ella, keep that .22 Davis in your boot loaded. A
> conspiracy is growing on the Rez, and friends could
> become enemies. Don't try to track me, I'm undercover.
> Tell no one. I'll contact you when I can.
>
> Coyote

When Ella tried to reply, Coyote had already logged off. She read the message over again, then quickly reached for the printer to make a copy.

Puzzled, she studied it more closely. Many people used aliases on this computer network, so having no other name on the 'from' line except Coyote didn't surprise her. But her curiosity was working overtime.

It was possible that someone was just messing with her mind, but somehow she didn't think that was it. The mention of the .22 Davis derringer in her boot was the key. Only a friend would have known about that. It wasn't uncommon for officers to keep a backup weapon in their boot, but the make, model, and caliber of her weapon was something very few knew about. It was a weapon of last resort, and the few times she'd been forced to use it on an enemy, the criminal had not lived to tell the story.

Ella put the printout of the brief message in her wallet. If it really was from an undercover cop, and there was some kind of conspiracy, all she could do was keep her eyes and ears open. But one thing worried her. The comment about friends turning into enemies made her stomach tighten until it ached. Justine had almost shot her earlier that night.

She forced the thought away. That had been an accident, nothing more, even though the circumstances of the armed robbery had been unusual, to say the least. She wouldn't get carried away with thoughts about conspiracies that could turn out to be nothing more than someone's weird sense of humor, or the product of an overactive imagination.

Ella's sleep was restless that night, but instead of waking, she just seemed to drift from dream to dream. She tossed and turned as the faces of her old enemies came back in a haunting procession of the evils that had touched her life.

Thankfully her daughter brought her out of the last nightmare. Dawn's first loud squeal of the morning woke her up just after sunrise. As Ella opened her eyes, she saw her mother standing by the door, trying to hold Dawn back. Rose, a slender but slightly shorter and older version of Ella, was still in her red flannel robe, her graying hair a bit disheveled, but her eyes bright and wide awake.

Ella smiled at her daughter, who was by now wearing a fresh sleeveless cotton top and training pants, then held out her arms. Dawn ran toward her and, with a little help from Ella in front and Rose behind pushing, managed to haul her chunky twenty-five-pound body up onto the bed.

"*Shimá*," she said.

"My mother" was one of the first few Navajo words Dawn had

learned from Rose, her *shimasání*, maternal grandmother. Since Ella spent her days and evenings working, Dawn was being reared by Rose, but it wasn't that unusual a situation on the Rez.

Many children on the reservation were traditionally raised by the mother's sisters or by grandparents. The father normally only played a small role, if any, in the upbringing of a child. A mother's brother often paid a larger role than the biological father. It was his duty to instruct and to discipline, along with the grandparents and the mother. Yet, despite this, Ella felt a twinge of disappointment that she couldn't be the one always home to instruct and take care of her own child.

Tickling Dawn and playing with her in the early morning hours, after she'd been to the potty, was one of the rituals Ella had established with her daughter. They both enjoyed the game and looked forward to it each day.

Once Dawn had enough, Ella let her catch her breath. "She actually slept later than I expected," Ella said, glancing at the clock on the nightstand, then back at Rose. "Did she get to bed on time?"

"On time," Rose scoffed. "Babies know what's best for them. She sleeps when she's tired."

Ella exhaled loudly. "Mom, a kid needs a certain amount of sleep in order to grow up healthy."

"That's the Anglo thinking you can't seem to leave behind, daughter. Children sleep and eat when their bodies tell them to."

They'd had this argument frequently, and Rose was not going to budge. Rather than force a hopeless issue, Ella let it drop. As Dawn crawled off the bed and padded over to Rose, Ella climbed out of bed.

It was actually her day off, but despite that, she still had work to do this morning. She'd have to make out her report on the convenience-store robbery, and talk to Justine about the particulars to make sure their stories matched the facts and events. After that, she'd finally be off the clock.

Ella showered and dressed quickly. As she brushed her hair and tied it back in a ponytail at the base of her neck, she could hear Dawn in the kitchen. Rose refused to use the high chair. Instead, she sat Dawn on her lap and allowed the little girl to eat whatever she pleased. Dawn liked her small cup, but more often than not, Ella would find her daughter drinking tea.

At least it was herbal tea, which wouldn't harm her, but Ella still would have preferred for Dawn to drink milk. Unfortunately, that was an Anglo practice that wasn't followed by many traditionalists. They believed that cow's milk was good—but only for calves.

Ella walked into the kitchen and picked up a tortilla her mother had just made. It was still warm to the touch.

"Wait until I can fill it with some beans for you, daughter."

"No time," she said, pouring honey on it and folding it in half. "I've got to go into the office for a while."

"It's your day off. Why are you going to to work? Didn't you make another promise?" she reminded, looking at Dawn.

"I'll be back in plenty of time to take her to play by the river," Ella whispered.

Dawn clapped her hands. "Want to play!"

"I'll be gone for a little while, then I'll come back and we can go."

Rose's gaze was penetrating. "Something bad happened last night, didn't it?" Before Ella could even answer, she sighed loudly. "It's starting again. There's going to be another cycle of trouble for us."

Her mother's intuitions were not to be scoffed at. Many said it was a gift. Others claimed it was a curse. Only one thing was for sure. Her predictions were amazingly accurate.

"Some unusual things happened, but I don't know what's at the root of it yet," Ella said slowly. "I don't think we're dealing with any of our old enemies, though."

"Be careful, daughter."

Dawn wriggled out of Rose's grasp and ran into the living room. Ella looked at her mother as she slowly got to her feet. "Mom, you're still having problems moving around with your bad leg. Why don't you let me hire someone to come in and at least help you with her," she said, gesturing toward Dawn.

Rose's expression grew firm. "She's my granddaughter. I don't need help taking care of her."

"But she's constantly on the run, and these days she can go almost anywhere. It's got to be exhausting for you."

"I can handle an active child. I'm not a useless old woman."

"I never said you were." Ella knew that Rose was determined to see this through on her own. She'd turned it into a matter of pride, though it was the last thing Ella had wanted.

"And I don't want strangers in my home," Rose added.

"We could pick someone you know. The daughter of one of your friends, for example."

"No."

Ella decided not to pursue the matter for now. Sooner or later Rose would have to see that it had nothing to do with admitting age, but rather accepting reality.

Glancing at her wristwatch, Ella rolled up a second tortilla, then went to find Dawn and gave her a kiss. The little girl's attention was now focused on the rag doll Rose had made for her, and she barely looked up.

Ella smiled, admiring her daughter for one last moment. Dawn was fiercely independent already, and was developing a mind of her own. Though she was still just a baby, Ella knew Dawn would be a leader, never a follower. Dawn, like most children, feared nothing, but there was something special about her child. She wanted to learn about everything around her, and her intelligence allowed her to grasp things kids her age seldom could. But then again, maybe that was just the pride of motherhood talking.

"*Shimá* work too hard," Dawn said.

Ella chuckled softly, recognizing Rose's words despite the fact that they were coming from her daughter. "*Shimá* is needed by the tribe."

Dawn nodded solemnly, then turned her attention back to her doll.

Saying good-bye, Ella walked out, waving back at her mother. Unlike many of the non-Indian kids she'd seen, Dawn seldom cried or made a fuss when Ella or Rose had to leave. Dawn was always with a relative, and that support made for a very extended family. If anything, she missed Dawn far more than Dawn ever missed her.

Ella had driven the route so many times, the trip was almost automatic. The closer she got to Shiprock, the more focused on work her thoughts became. One of her priorities for the next few weeks would be to find time to work with Justine on her shooting discipline. Justine's training as a cop had conditioned her to respond to deadly threats with an automatic response—deadly force—but her decision-making process in a shoot/don't shoot situation needed work. Despite the danger inherent in hesitation, Justine had to relearn some skills she'd lost to ensure she'd always identify the threat and verify her target before pulling the trigger.

As she strode inside the building, Ella passed Joseph Neskahi in the hall. The stocky young sergeant, with closely cropped hair and a round face, was one of her most trusted co-workers, and had played key roles in several cases.

"The chief wants you, Ella, and he's not in a good mood."

"Maybe I should go to his office right now," Ella said.

"I'd give him a few more minutes. Justine is there now."

Ella suppressed the disturbing sensation that rippled down her spine. "Any idea what's going on?"

"No," he said.

Ella knew from experience that Joseph hated to speculate without facts, but right now something told her that he could have made a very accurate guess had he chosen to do so.

On the way down the hall to her own office, Ella had to pass by Big Ed's door. It surprised her to see the door was closed. Before she could pass by, the door flew open and a red-faced Justine stormed out.

Seeing Ella standing there, Justine's eyes narrowed into a hateful-looking scowl.

"What the heck's got you so upset?" Ella asked.

"You stabbed me in the back, Ella. How could you do it?"

Ella stared at her in shock, but Justine whirled around and walked away, disappearing into her small lab and slamming the door behind her.

Before Ella could gather her wits, she noticed Big Ed was now standing in his doorway. The fifty-something-year-old police chief was a head shorter than Ella, but with his broad shoulders and barrel chest, was probably twice her weight.

"Good. You're here. In my office, now. And close the door behind you."

Big Ed sat behind his desk, rocking his chair back and forth, staring at her. He said nothing, allowing the silence to stretch.

If it was meant to unnerve her, it was working well. Ella forced herself not to fidget, but it was taking all her energy to stay still.

"I read Justine's report. She, unlike you, filed hers last night."

"I was too exhausted to come back to the station, and since dispatch had the initial report, I decided to come and do the paperwork this morning," she said, waiting for the other shoe to drop.

"Tell me something. How were you going to explain the communications problems and the gunfire?"

Ella couldn't imagine Justine coming in here and telling the chief how close she'd come to shooting a fellow officer. Yet she knew from the look in his eyes that Big Ed knew precisely what had happened.

"There *was* a communications problem and a problem in identifying the perp," Ella admitted, "but fortunately we resolved that before anyone was injured."

Big Ed stood up so suddenly his chair fell over with a crash. "I will not have my officers trying to BS me, especially ones in a high-profile unit like the Special Investigations team. *Is that clear?*"

Ella couldn't figure out how Big Ed had learned all the details from last night, but this wasn't the time to ask.

"Were you planning a con job? Did you think I wouldn't find out?" he roared.

"We reported the shooting incident from the very beginning. Dispatch has it on tape."

"Your assistant almost shot you last night. Isn't that right?"

"I was dressed like the perp, and in the dark, all she could confirm was that I was armed. I shouted a warning, and her shot wasn't even close," Ella said.

Big Ed glared at her.

"The incident was the direct result of a technical problem. Something interfered with our radio communications. I suspect that we were deliberately being jammed so we wouldn't know each other's position."

"And that's why your partner almost shot you?"

"What it came down to was this. I saw the perp going in one direction and followed. Justine had done the same earlier, but lost track of him in the dark. Then she ran into me, thinking *I* was the perp. The fact is that the perp appeared to be in two different places at nearly the same time."

"So you're saying that there might have been *two* suspects, both dressed the same as you?"

"Unless one of us is having memory problems, it's the only way our differences in timing and location of the suspect make any sense at all. I haven't found evidence that it was a two-man job yet, but I intend to pursue it from that angle. In the meantime, I think Justine deserves a break. We've all been trained to react automatically to certain situations, and I believe that she was manipulated into doing exactly what she did."

Big Ed regarded her thoughtfully for what seemed an eternity. "I trust your instincts. I always have. But this time . . ."

"Justine's a good officer, and she had a difficult, split-second decision to make. She had already been fired upon, and was really pumped up. If we ride her too hard before we have all the facts, we'll ruin what's left of her confidence, and without that, she'll be no good as a cop."

The chief said nothing, staring at a daddy longlegs spider crawling up the wall. "Okay," he said at length. "But I want her out at the range going over target selection and lethal-force procedures twice a week until further notice."

"Done."

"By the way, isn't this supposed to be your day off?"

Ella nodded, then shrugged. "We debriefed last night, but I came in to make sure Justine was okay, and to make out my report. Officially, I'm not here."

Ella walked toward her office and on the way stopped by Justine's lab. Justine wasn't there, so Ella left a note on her desk asking Justine to call her at home. She wanted this straightened out.

She also wanted to try and figure out where Big Ed had gotten all the details. Only four people had been there. Ella, Justine, the perp, and the clerk. It was possible that Justine had inadvertently said more than she intended, or the chief had caught her in an inconsistency, but that didn't seem likely. The perp was long gone, and the clerk hadn't seen anything. He'd been inside the store. Of course, it was very possible that he'd overheard their conversation outside. But would he make it a point to talk to the chief about it? That seemed like a stretch.

After making out her report and dropping it by Big Ed's office, she left the station. She'd told Dawn she'd take her to play by the river's edge today, and she wouldn't break the promise.

Remembering the cryptic warning she'd received on her computer, Ella stopped by the Totah Cafe and picked up the latest issue of the tribal newspaper and a copy of the Farmington daily, the biggest paper from the area. She wanted to reacquaint herself with the latest news in and around the Rez. If there really was trouble brewing, she had no intention of being caught unawares.

THREE

✖ ✖ ✖

On the way home, Ella listened to a Navajo radio station, and in particular to the hourly news. If there was a major conspiracy going on, maybe it was connected to an event or an institution, like the tribal government. Major elections were coming up in another year, and already many politicians and wanna-be politicians were starting to position themselves to run for elected office.

Mrs. Yellowhair, the late state senator's wife, would be running for the office her husband had held. An interim appointee held the seat now, an Anglo car dealer no one outside Farmington supported. Abigail Yellowhair, seeing that as a sign to move forward and accomplish her own goals, was gearing up her campaign.

After the terrorist incident last year, the tribe's faith in their elected officials and the tribal government had plummeted. Corruption allegations and scandals continued to rock the hierarchy on the Rez, creating even more unrest.

Ella thought about Coyote and what he'd told her. That instant message had rattled her more than she wanted to admit, even to herself. She suspected it had to be a cop, but Ella didn't think it could be any officers working out of the Window Rock or Shiprock stations. She knew all of the experienced officers, and as far as she knew, no one was undercover now.

That left officers in the county sheriff's department, Farmington PD, and a few other departments, not counting the few Feds she knew from the area, and a couple in California whom she'd worked with years ago. From what he'd said, Coyote knew her well, but she had no idea who he was, and that bothered her.

As a Navajo, she'd been taught that to be in harmony, all aspects of her life had to be balanced and ordered. She wasn't a traditionalist, but she'd always liked to keep things neatly sorted in her head. It was a habit that had served her well as a cop. One of the reasons she was so successful with her cases was that she never disregarded unanswered questions. But to press on Coyote's identity might compromise an undercover cop. Not to mention that to access the real name behind that account, she'd need a court order. Since he hadn't threatened her, or committed any criminal offense, it was extremely doubtful she'd get one even if she were willing to try.

By the time she arrived home, Dawn was playing in the front yard in the sandbox Ella and her daughter's father had constructed for her, wearing her denim mini overalls with the lamb in the center, plus matching sneakers. She was pulling a dinosaur on wheels across the sand by a short length of nylon rope. The toy was being dragged, since it was nearly impossible for it to roll in the soft, dry sand, but Dawn didn't seem to mind.

The moment she saw Ella, Dawn squealed and climbed over the low board of the sandbox, then ran toward her in her wobbly gait. "Go play now?"

"If you're ready, I am," Ella said, nodding to Rose, who'd been nearby working in her herb garden.

All the way to the river Dawn tried to discover a way out of the car seat. She wasn't crying and fussing, though, just trying tirelessly to find a way to defeat the straps and web mechanism that kept her in the seat.

Ella watched her daughter, proud of the way she never gave up. She'd need that stubbornness to survive. Many in the tribe would never accept Dawn, no more than they did her, because of the legacy that followed their family.

It was part myth, part history, and part legend, and Ella herself wasn't sure how much of it to believe. The story centered around Mist Eagle, a woman of their clan, who'd fallen in love with Fire Hawk, a member of her same clan. In spite of the taboos that strictly prohibited such an association, Mist Eagle tricked Fire Hawk one night and, in the dark, posed as his wife. She'd become pregnant, and shortly afterwards her deception was discovered and she'd been banished from the tribe.

Shunned by everyone except the skinwalkers—Navajo witches who were no strangers to incest—Mist Eagle learned from them and became a powerful healer. Despite their efforts to corrupt her, she never used her powers for anything but good. But as the years passed and Mist Eagle's daughter grew, so did her anger and resentment toward the tribe that had banished her mother. She eventually became a powerful evil force among The People.

Since that time, Mist Eagle's direct descendants, particularly those apparently born with special abilities, had been watched carefully by specially appointed members of the tribe. It was said that the gifts they inherited would either bless or totally corrupt them, and if they turned to evil, they would pose a danger to the tribe. For that reason, Mist Eagle's descendants had always been encouraged to have at least two children. If one turned to evil, it would be up to the other child to restore harmony.

Clifford's healing gifts, her own remarkable intuition, something that often gave her the edge on her investigations, and her mother's ability to sometimes predict what was about to happen were all believed to be part of a dark legacy connected to their ancestor Mist Eagle.

In all fairness, none of their abilities was so remarkable as to be considered astounding. Ella's intuition could have been attributed to other things, like the powers of observation police work demanded, or in Clifford's and her mother's case, talent, coincidence, and plain luck, but the rumors persisted.

Ella parked near the river and unfastened her excited child from the car seat. As they walked down to the narrow, sandy banks lining this section of the San Juan River, she began to feel the presence of something or someone nearby. She looked around her, peering into the saltbush and willows, and past them into the cottonwood trees that comprised the bosque, but no one was about.

This isolated area south of Shiprock was deserted, not an unusual occurrence for the middle of the week. But something niggled at the back of her mind, and Ella kept a firm grip on Dawn's tiny hand. The birds were quiet, and the only sound was that of the murky water twenty feet away. The damp sand where they were standing reminded her of the smell of catfish, but there was something else around that kept nature at bay.

She couldn't shake the feeling that she was being watched, but at the same time, she didn't feel any sense of imminent danger. Reaching up to touch the carved badger fetish resting as a pendant around her neck, she discovered it was cool, not warm as it normally was when something bad was about to happen.

Unwilling to take any chances with her daughter along, Ella turned around and started heading back, promising Dawn an ice cream cone instead. It was then that she heard a soft whistling to her right. She smiled, recognizing the habit if not the tune.

"Hello, Harry."

She heard a deep-throated laugh as the former tribal cop and member of her investigative team stepped out from behind a large salt cedar, a wide grin on his face. "Hey, Ella. How have you been?"

At first all she could do was stare. Harry Ute had always been cadaverously thin, but in the past year he had put on at least twenty pounds of muscle. Clad in jeans and a dark blue western shirt, he had the build of a rodeo cowboy. As far back as she'd known him, Harry's expression had been so serious, almost glum. But although the man before her still retained that familiar intensity of purpose, gone was the perpetually gloomy expression.

"I hope you're here to tell me that you've decided to leave the Marshals Service and come back to us."

He crouched down and smiled at Dawn. "Hey, little one. You're already getting tall like your mother."

Dawn smiled, then looked up at Ella. "Can I play now?"

"Yes, but stay here where the sand is damp, and don't go near the water."

Dawn sat down a few feet away and began forming a mound of damp sand into something only she could identify.

"No, I haven't come back for good," Harry said, squatting down and sifting sand through his fingers. "I'm where I belong now. My new job suits me."

"Then what's brought you back, and why haven't you stopped

by the station? There're lots of people who'd love to say hello to you."

"Can't do it. I'm undercover right now, tracking a fugitive. I followed you down here so I could catch you alone and advise you to stay on your guard. Remember Samuel Begaye, who was sent up for murder when he beat a guy to death in a bar fight? He swore he'd get you and Justine for bringing him in."

"I remember," Ella said. "He was one mean drunk. He nearly took off Justine's head with a shovel when we caught up to him. It took the both of us to subdue and cuff him."

"He hates you and Justine with a passion. He believes that if it hadn't been for you showing up when you did, he would have made it up into the hills and no one would have ever found him."

"Tough," Ella said with a shrug.

"I have reason to believe he's come back to New Mexico, and is here in the Four Corners area."

"Do you think he's going to try and even the score?" Ella asked, glancing at her daughter. Dawn had given up making shapes in the sand and was now trying to bury the small stuffed donkey she'd brought along.

"Dawn, no," Ella said. "You'll get Blinky too dirty to sleep with." She picked up the animal, shook it free of sand, then glanced over at Harry. "Sorry."

Harry smiled, and they both watched Dawn for a moment as she made lines in the sand with a small piece of driftwood, then stood there fascinated as water seeped into the tiny ditches.

"It's hard to say what Begaye is up to with any degree of certainty," Harry said, resuming their conversation. "My guess is that he came back here because his father, John, was murdered. Thomas Zah was arrested and will be facing trial in Window Rock eventually. But that's probably not Samuel's only reason for returning. This is a big Rez with a lot of empty spaces where he can hide or blend in far more easily than he could anywhere else. He's got friends here and family, too, people who'd help him without question. But if he sees a chance to even the score with you two, I'm almost certain he'll take it—unless I catch him first."

"Just how close are you to doing that?"

Harry exhaled softly. "I'm not sure. I've had a few leads, but

MONROE COUNTY LIBRARY SYSTEM
MONROE MICHIGAN 48161

he always seems to stay at least one step ahead of me."

Ella studied his expression, wondering if Harry could be "Coyote," her mysterious contact. "Seen any coyotes lately?"

"Huh?"

Harry puzzled expression was genuine enough. There had been no sign of recognition on his face. "Never mind," she said with a thin smile. "I'll tell Justine about Begaye."

"Oh—one more thing. Whatever you do, don't tell anyone else I'm back, not even Justine Goodluck. If word gets around that there's a Navajo deputy marshal looking for Begaye, his relatives will band together, close their mouths, and I'll never find him."

"If that's what you want, you've got it. But if you need help, anytime, come by the house or give me a call. You remember my home number?" She saw him nod and continued. "Mom can keep a secret, and no matter what, I promise to cut through the red tape and give you all the backup you need."

"Thanks. I appreciate that."

Seeing him glance at Dawn, Ella shook her head. "Don't worry about her. You're not as interesting to her as the river or her stuffed pal. By the time she gets home, she'll forget all about you."

Harry laughed. "Women everywhere seem to feel that way about me."

Ella laughed, then looked at her daughter, motioning her back farther from the water's edge. As she turned to look back at Harry, he'd disappeared into the reeds, and all that remained were boot tracks in the sand.

Ella exhaled softly. Harry was one of those men who was born for surveillance and undercover work. He could blend into a crowd of three and go unnoticed virtually anywhere. Although she admired him for following his dream, she found herself hoping that he'd return to Shiprock and the Navajo police in a few years.

Ella used her cell phone to contact Justine, but there was no answer. Leaving another message on her phone mail, she hung up. Either Justine was incredibly busy in her lab, or she was ducking Ella's calls. The thought annoyed her. This was work, not personal, and Justine had professional responsibilities. When she told a member of her team to get in touch, she meant it.

Ella spent another hour with Dawn by the river, but when

Dawn tried to make a pillow in the sand to sleep on, it was obvious that her daughter was ready to go. By the time they were home, Dawn was already asleep, so Ella put her down for her nap. After watching her daughter for a while, Ella joined Rose in the living room where her mother was crocheting a woolen hat for Dawn.

"You seem preoccupied, daughter. I was hoping that spending time with your child would help you relax. But it hasn't. Not that I can see."

"I'm worried about Justine," Ella said, and explained about the incident with the police chief. "I've left two calls already, asking for her to contact me, but so far Justine hasn't even tried to reach me. I know she's angry, Mom, but I can't let her get away with this kind of nonsense. It's part of her job to stay in touch."

"Give her time to cool off, and she'll remember her responsibilities. Then it'll be easier for both of you to talk. Do what you have to, mind you, but you'll get farther if you don't force the issue until she's ready to listen to reason. Justine has always been stubborn, like her sisters."

Ella nodded. "You're right, but her attitude lately is getting me pretty ticked off, too. Right now I just want to get in her face and chew her out real good."

"And what would that prove? That you're her boss, and she has to listen whether she wants to or not?"

"Right or wrong, she owes me some respect because I'm head of our SI team. Any good law enforcement officer knows how important discipline and mutual respect are when working as a unit."

Rose nodded. "She's your assistant, and you have a right to expect her to follow your orders, but you need her loyalty, too, and that can't be forced."

"I don't know, Mom. If she can't deal with what's happened and move on, then maybe she shouldn't be part of the team. If I can't count on her without question, I'll have to find somebody to replace her. I know there's been a lot of stress at the station because of cutbacks, but Justine has been handling it a lot worse than the rest of us."

Rose nodded slowly. "All I'm telling you is that if you move slowly, and carefully plan your actions, you'll be less likely to do something you might regret later."

Ella glanced at her watch. "I'm going to go back to the station and see if I can catch her there. I need to know why she's not answering my calls. Will you stay with Dawn?"

"That's not a problem, but I sure wish that you could learn to really take time off. Your work consumes you, daughter. You're never away from it, even when you're with your family. I can see it there behind your eyes all the time. You need time for yourself as a woman and a mother. Dawn needs you, too."

"She has me. I'm always there for her. But I have to earn a living, Mom. You know my job's never been eight to five. Criminals don't keep regular hours, and the department is still shorthanded."

Rose shook her head. "What I want for Dawn is what I gave you. A girl needs time to be with her mother. I breast-fed you and your brother when you were little. Not the bottle on a schedule like the Anglos. Whenever you cried, or you wanted comfort, you had it. Dawn's being raised on Anglo time and feeding schedules, like with some TV family."

"It's not as bad as you're saying," Ella said with a tiny smile. "You feed her whenever she wants to eat, and she sleeps when she's ready, like it was with Clifford and me. She's not being raised strictly traditional, true, but the Rez isn't strictly traditional either. Dawn will be a product of her time. Someday she may even be proud of me for the work I do for our tribe."

"I just wish . . ."

"That I were more of a traditionalist, like Clifford," Ella finished for her, looking at her mother's long maroon skirt and colorful blue blouse. The top was worn outside the skirt, and bound at the waist with a silver concha belt. All very traditional, she noted, and unlike her own slacks, boots, and jacket.

Ella felt the sting the truth always brought. Rose loved them both, but Ella had always known her mother's heart was closer to Clifford's, and that was something no one could deny.

"And if Dawn someday chooses to be a traditionalist like your brother instead of a modernist, will that hurt you? Will you be disappointed?"

For the first time Ella understood what her mother must have gone through. "I won't be hurt, not as long as the path she chooses is one that she can give her whole heart to. Without that, her life would only be a passage of days, and *that* would hurt me. I want far more for her."

Rose nodded slowly. "We'll see, daughter."

"But we're a *long* way off from all that, Mom. Dawn's just a baby learning about the world around her. Everything right now is a grand adventure."

"Which you'll miss seeing with her unless you're very careful."

Ella sighed. This was an argument she didn't want to continue. If she'd been independently wealthy, she would have loved to stay at home with Dawn for at least the first few years of her life, but reality had forced her to make a different choice.

Ella drove to the office, wondering if maybe she should have waited until tomorrow before approaching Justine. But her young assistant needed to know about Begaye right away, especially if the escaped killer was in the area. Justine's feelings at the moment were not a priority. Her safety was.

Ella walked into the station a short time later, and as she walked down the hall, Sergeant Joseph Neskahi came out of one of the offices.

"Hey, if it isn't our celebrity," he said with a teasing grin.

"How's that?" Ella looked behind her, wondering what was going on, and if Neskahi was referring to someone else in the hall.

"You haven't heard the radio ads?"

"What ads?"

"You know that Mrs. Yellowhair is trying to get her party's nomination for her late husband's senate seat, right?" Neskahi asked.

"I'm voting for her," Officer Philip Cloud said as he passed them in the hall. "That seedy Anglo car dealer who got appointed by the county commission has been giving The People a hard time for years. He won't sell cars to Navajos because he can't repossess them here on the Rez. That guy makes me sick to my stomach."

Ella laughed, sharing his sentiments as did many Navajos, then looked back at Joseph.

"As I was saying," Joseph continued, "Mrs. Yellowhair is running a few radio ads. In one she answers questions about what she stands for. She then points to you as a role model for our tribe because you keep your identity as a Navajo without shying away from progress."

Another cop came down the hall, saw Ella, and held out his notebook. "May I have your autograph? It's for my son, of course," he assured her.

"Oh, cut it out," she groaned, already suspecting that she'd never hear the end of this.

Neskahi chuckled, but seeing the look Ella gave him, tried to wipe the grin from his face. He didn't have much luck. The corners of his mouth continued to twitch.

"Don't worry, Ella. You'll have your fifteen minutes of fame—until that shock jock George Branch hears about it. Then the character assassination will begin. He doesn't like the Yellowhairs or you."

"Something else to look forward to on what used to be my favorite radio station," she muttered. Seeing Big Ed motioning for her, she excused herself quickly and went to the chief's office.

"I heard about the radio spots," Big Ed said.

"I had nothing to do with that," she said quickly. "You know I try to keep a low profile. It's a lot safer for a cop."

"I figured that wasn't your style." Big Ed paused, then continued. "By the way, I had another talk with Justine a few hours ago. I've ordered her to report to Sergeant Hobson twice a week. They can work out which days. He's going to review our lethal force policy and threat evaluation strategies with her."

"Chief, there's something I better tell you right up front. I was the one who recommended that Justine downplay the misidentification incident on her report. I didn't want anything on record until we were able to figure out exactly what went down."

"Understood, but she'll still have to undergo some refresher training. By the way, when I spoke to her about that, she was very short-tempered and defensive, and that doesn't speak well for her. Those are character traits I don't want to see in any officer."

"Let me talk to her. Right now she's upset because she thinks I told her to do one thing, and did another myself," she explained.

"To the best of my knowledge, Justine's never been quick-tempered before, though she's sure been sensitive lately. If there's a personal problem I need to know about, make sure that I do. I don't like surprises, Shorty," he said, using the nickname he'd given her, though she was actually almost a head taller than he was.

"Justine will come around. She just needs a little time to get herself together. We've been understaffed, and it's meant a lot of extra responsibility for her."

"She may also be getting a little cocky and overconfident. Let's face it, she's been on a winning team for some time now, and has helped take down some real heavy hitters. Maybe that's what happens when you meet so much success at the start of your career. A few setbacks may be just what she needs to bring her down a peg or two, Shorty."

"Let me look into things, and I'll let you know what I find out. I came by to talk to her."

"Then you'd better go by her home."

"What? It's not her day off. Besides, it's payday. I would have thought she'd hang around at least until the checks were handed out."

"So would I. But she took off sick this afternoon."

In all the time Justine had worked at the department, Ella couldn't remember her missing even a half day's work. The news surprised her. Something was going on in her young cousin's life, and now it was affecting her job.

Saying good-bye to the chief, Ella headed down the hall to the side door. One way or another, she intended to find out what was going on. Justine would have to either deal with whatever was bothering her and leave her personal life at home, or take a leave of absence until she could work things out. A cop with only half her mind on her job was a corpse waiting to happen.

FOUR

———— ✖ ✖ ✖ ————

She was about to walk out of the building when Dwayne Blalock, the FBI agent assigned to their area, came walking up to her. A few years ago, Blalock, known by Navajos as FB-Eyes because he had one blue eye and one brown, could have posed for a recruiting poster for the Bureau. The Anglo was tall and athletic, good-looking in a suit, and possessed an attitude of arrogant competence.

Over the years, Blalock had learned the hard way about working with the Southwest cultures and respecting ways different from his own. However, he had mellowed considerably and was pleasant enough most of the time these days. But Ella still wouldn't go as far as saying that she actually liked him, at least not out loud.

"Hey, Ella, are you in a hurry? I have someone I want you to meet," Blalock said, then glanced back at the parking lot. "He'll be here in a minute."

"What's going on? Am I going to regret this?"

"Only time will tell. The Bureau, in their infinite wisdom, has decided we need another agent in the area. I've been assigned to an office here in Shiprock, and the new man will take over my desk in Farmington."

"Is this because of the terrorism incident we had here?"

"Yeah, that and the state senator's murder. The Bureau likes things nice and neat, and neither one of those went down well back at headquarters. Of course, they're citing the growing population in the Four Corners area as a reason for the extra agent, but that's just a smoke screen. The older I get, the easier it is to see past the politics."

A moment later a short, stubby-looking young pueblo man with neatly combed black hair, an easy smile, and a new-looking dark gray suit walked in. "Okay, I'm ready to meet this crack Nava-Joe team you spoke so highly about," the man announced to Blalock in an eager, high-pitched voice.

"Agent Lucas Payestewa, this is Special Investigator Ella Clah. Her crime unit is the primary group you'll be working with when you investigate crimes on and around the Navajo Nation."

Ella stared at the agent. The man was Hopi unless she missed her guess, but why on earth would anyone assign a Hopi to investigate crimes on the Navajo reservation? The animosity between the tribes was generations old. It had its roots in issues still not resolved. They all centered on land disputes compounded by the fact that the Hopi reservation was completely surrounded by the Navajo Nation.

Seeing the surprise on her face, Payestewa chuckled. "Yep, I'm Hopi. But don't worry, I'm the soul of diplomacy. You'll love me."

Ella nearly choked. "Okay. We've learned to believe everything the FBI tells us," she managed with a straight face. Ella then looked at Blalock, who rolled his eyes but said nothing.

"I've been looking forward to meeting you in particular," Payestewa said. "I've heard a lot about the legendary Special Investigator Clah."

Ella shrugged, then as Officer Ralph Tache passed by, she introduced him to Payestewa. Sergeant Neskahi hung back, watching the proceedings, apparently unable to make up his mind about the man.

"So you'll be stationed pretty close to home," Ella said, making conversation when everyone fell silent. "Most agents end up halfway across the country, or farther," she said, leading all of them to her office and inviting them inside the small room.

"Yeah, but I doubt I'll get many calls to go to the Hopi mesas. They don't have much need for an agent with a law degree there. Crimes are usually pretty straightforward, and they already have enough tribal police to find any lost Navajos or run a snoopy Anglo out of a kiva." He smiled broadly, indicating he was joking.

"So you're an attorney, then?" Ella asked

"Yeah, I've got the sheepskin and everything. The tribe paid for my schooling, naturally. I think they wanted someone they could trust to represent them, so I ended up specializing in civil rights cases for minorities. Then, after a few years, I realized that I was spending almost all of my time waiting for a case. There just wasn't enough work for me there. The tribe didn't need really me, so I applied to the Bureau. When the Farmington position came open, the Bureau decided to take advantage of my background. With the large Native American population, Farmington has a continuing problem with civil rights violations, especially between the Navajos and the Anglos." He grinned. "Hey, if you ever want to hear any lawyer jokes, I've heard them all."

Ella smiled, but she wasn't at all sure how to take him.

"I think the Bureau made the final decision after the local politicians chose that car dealer, Marvin Riley, to take over for Senator Yellowhair until an election could be held," Blalock said. "There was quite an uproar on the Rez. I know tribal officials wanted Yellowhair's wife to get the appointment, or at least another Navajo."

"And now you get the honor of being the first FBI agent to open a Shiprock office. That's going to put you under an even bigger microscope. Is that a step up or a step down?" Ella asked.

"Officially I've been promoted," Blalock said with a scowl. "Because of our history of successful joint operations with your PD, they felt I should open an office here with a two-person full-time clerical staff. Up to now, the only staff I've ever had was the infectious kind," he muttered.

Ella knew that it was a dubious promotion. The PD would not like having the FBI so close at hand. Although their help had come in handy in the past, the PD preferred to maintain control over all criminal investigations on the Rez. To make things even worse for Blalock, he'd be Payestewa's supervisor and would have to keep more regular office hours. He'd also have to use office space provided by the tribal government and be forced to rent tribal housing unless he wanted to drive back and forth every day from his current apartment in Farmington.

Payestewa looked at Ella. "So, is there anything interesting going on around here right now? You guys really made the news about this time last year. Maybe you'll get a new gang of terrorists plotting to blow up one of the coal power plants."

"Things are pretty quiet right now except for a recent armed robbery. But something else will turn up," she answered vaguely, recognizing the eagerness in his voice as inexperience. "How long have you been working in the field?"

"Two years. I can't believe that I'm finally back in the Southwest. They started me out in South Dakota, then sent me to New York because someone thought I'd be good at gaining the trust of some South American immigrants getting pushed around by one of the unions." He gave her a confused look. "Don't ask me how they came up with that one."

Ella remembered her first few years in the Bureau. She'd always been eager to work the complicated, exciting cases. The FBI had been a totally different world for her, one she'd wanted to leave her mark on. She suspected it was the same for Payestewa.

As a young clerk about Justine's age came in and began distributing paychecks, Payestewa held out his hand. "It must be eagle day. Where's mine? I'm new here. Did I forget to fill out all the paperwork?"

"Who are you?" the young clerk said, totally confused.

"Payestewa, Lucas. New, good-looking, armed and dangerous when I'm low on cash."

The clerk sorted through the envelopes in her hand, then looked at Ella. "Should I know who he is?"

Ella shook her head, letting her know Payestewa was pulling her leg. "Don't worry. He's here on the merit-pay program. We just don't know if he's worth anything yet."

"Oh, now you're in trouble, Investigator Clah. Here I am, ready to dazzle you with my new, improved FB-in-your-eye training, and you're disrespecting me already."

"Clah was in the Bureau, working undercover, when you were still in high school," Blalock muttered.

"So you left your poverty-level job in the FBI for a high-paying career in Navajo law enforcement?" Payestewa grinned. "That's the problem with federal employees today. No dedication."

Ella looked at Blalock. "Is he always like this?"

"I don't know. I never listen to him," Blalock answered sourly.

Ella put her paycheck into her back pocket and studied Payestewa, who was now introducing himself to Neskahi. She just couldn't get a clear handle on him.

"Hey, in comparison to us, the Bureau agents are wealthy," Officer Tache said, looking at his check before putting it away.

"I'll bet our take-home is about the same," Payestewa said. "I had more spending money in college when my tribe was footing the bills. In fact, I'm thinking that maybe I could afford a better apartment if I started taking a few college classes."

Tache gave Ella a totally confused look, and that same expression was on Neskahi's face and the clerk's. Did he ever say anything without including a joke somewhere in there?

After Blalock and Payestewa left to visit with the chief, Tache looked at Ella and Sergeant Neskahi. "There's more to that man than meets the eye," he said. "I've never trusted a friendly Hopi."

Neskahi shook his head. "No one who takes life so casually could get by for long in the FBI. He bears watching."

Ella nodded. At the heart of everyone's distrust, including her own, was the uneasiness between the Hopi and Navajo tribe. She wasn't kidding herself about that. Yet, as she thought about Payestewa, she had to admit that something about the guy seemed off-center.

"What was his name again?" Tache asked.

"Payes something," Neskahi answered sourly.

"Paycheck's more like it," Tache answered.

Neskahi laughed.

Ella smiled. Navajos often used nicknames, and Payestewa had just been given his. She had a feeling that before long, the entire department would know him as Paycheck.

Ella stopped by Justine's house after leaving the station, but no one was there. Ella's cousin and the rest of the family worked during the day, but she'd expected Justine to be around, particularly if she'd gone home sick.

Puzzled by her cousin's behavior, and trying not to see more to it than there was, Ella drove home.

From the moment she walked inside, Ella knew something was wrong. She could hear the TV going in the nursery, something Rose never allowed during the day unless she was in there too.

Hurrying, she went down the hall. Even before she entered the room, she heard Dawn coughing.

"What's going on?" Ella asked her mother, who was sitting in a chair beside the window, crocheting. Ella kneeled down beside Dawn's side.

"Toons!" Dawn said, then coughed again, standing to give her mother a big hug.

Ella could smell the familiar herbs that her mother had always used for throat ailments and colds. "Hey, short stuff. Looks like I better go to the drugstore and get something for that cough of yours."

She gave Dawn a little peck on the cheek, then checked to see if her nose was red or runny.

Rose sighed. "All those cough medicines treat too many things and make her sleepy and cranky. Take her to your brother instead. Our herbs don't have the side effects Anglo medications have."

Ella nodded, agreeing, then felt Dawn's forehead. Her daughter didn't appear to have a fever, and with the exception of her cough, looked to be in pretty good shape. "I can drive over there right now. Do you know if my brother's home?"

"He is. I spoke to my daughter-in-law briefly. She's in a bad mood because my son has been in the hogan every waking hour for two days preparing new medicines for some of his patients. She wants him to find more time to spend with her and Julian."

"I've never gotten along with her, Mom, but this time I can see where she's coming from. The mother's brother is supposed to assume a lot of responsibility for raising the child, but her own brother lives in California now, and hasn't seen her son much at all. She sees her husband spending some time with my daughter, and that only reminds her that her own brother is away. She can't raise her son in the traditionalist way that she would have preferred, so she demands more of her husband, wanting him to take a greater part, like in the ideal Anglo family."

"It would have been easier on my daughter-in-law if her mother lived a little closer," Rose said.

Ella picked up Dawn. "Okay. I'm taking her to see my brother. We'll be back soon."

Ella parked next to her brother's medicine hogan rather than beside the Anglo-style house to signify she was there to see Clifford in his capacity as *hataalii*, medicine man. She hadn't been there long when she saw Clifford pull back the blanket that covered the entrance and wave at her. As tall as her but two years older, with long hair and a bandanna tied around his brow, Ella's brother looked very traditional, as he indeed was.

Clifford had the high cheekbones and broad face characteristic of their family. His eyes were coal black, deeply set, and sparkled with intelligence and intensity.

Ella took Dawn out of the car seat and, as she walked to the hogan, saw Loretta, clad in a faded yellow dress, standing at the side window of the house. She waved, but Loretta didn't wave back.

Clifford met Ella at the entrance to the hogan. "My wife's had a bad day," he said, apparently having seen the one-way greeting. "My son is nearly four now, and he's very independent. He wants to do things on his own, but she wants him to stay her baby."

"She wants to feel needed, brother," Ella said quietly. "I'll probably be the same when my daughter no longer needs me as much."

"Maybe, but you have other things that demand your attention, like your career. My wife has chosen to devote her life to our son, and because of that, the inevitable changes that'll take place as our son grows up and away from us will be difficult for her to take," Clifford said, taking Dawn from Ella's arms.

As Dawn began to cough, he set her down on a sheepskin blanket, then reached for a pouch of herbs atop a wooden shelf. "Give this to her as a tea when you get home. It'll help. It's Apache plume root. Boiled and prepared with sugar, it'll help with her cough. This other is anise and you can make this into a tea as well." He glanced up at Ella as he prepared an herbal infusion for Dawn to drink right away. "I have to admit that I'm surprised you brought her to me."

"I thought about getting some cough medicine at the store, but Mom's right. Those always have side effects, especially for the very young, and some of the formulas treat symptoms she doesn't have. Often the old ways have distinct advantages."

Clifford nodded as he heated water on the potbellied stove in the center of the hogan. Once it began to boil, he poured it into a small pottery bowl. A pleasant minty scent filled the hogan. "Something else is bothering you, sister, I can feel it."

"Hey, intuition is supposed to be my thing," she teased.

Clifford gave her an easy smile. "Don't try to sidetrack me."

Ella nodded. "I was wondering if you've heard anything about any of our old enemies. Is anything going on these days?"

"Not that I know of," he said. "And I *would* know. Why do you ask?"

"It's been a long time since we've had major trouble here, and I'm feeling a bit concerned. We're due for something, I can almost sense it."

He nodded, straining the herb tea into a small plastic cup, then handing it to Ella. "Have her sip it, if she can."

As Ella held the cup for Dawn, Clifford answered her question. "Like it is with nature and everything else, the Rez has cycles of rest and unrest. I'll keep an eye out for signs of trouble. But there's more on your mind. I can see it in your eyes."

Ella hesitated, concentrating for a moment on the task of holding the cup so Dawn could sip. It must have been pleasant enough, because she didn't shy away from drinking.

At last Ella continued, but measured her words carefully. Police business was always confidential and she had to tread carefully, even when speaking to family. "There's some trouble at work. It's making me a little uneasy," she said, then stopped, hearing a vehicle pulling up outside.

Clifford pulled back the blanket. "It's an old friend and a new one."

"I better leave, then," she said, reaching for Dawn.

Wilson Joe walked in a moment later, followed by another Navajo man she didn't recognize. Wilson was dressed in a western-cut shirt, blue jeans, and boots—the uniform of the well-dressed Navajo gentleman.

Wilson was taller than the newcomer, nearly Ella's height, and broad shouldered. His eyes lit up when he saw her, and he smiled.

"Don't leave on our account," Wilson said. "We're just here to beg a favor from your brother." He turned around, ready to introduce his friend, then out of respect for a traditionalist's views, left out names. "This is our new professor at the college."

As was customary, they didn't shake hands. Ella nodded and allowed them to continue.

"We'd like you to speak to our after-school club about traditional Navajo medicine," Wilson asked Clifford.

"Not only that, but the philosophy behind traditional medicine," Wilson's co-worker added. His speech patterns and lack of Navajo "accent" suggested he'd spent a lot of time off the Rez, and his knit sport shirt and gray slacks supported that notion. He had a narrow face for a Navajo and sharply defined features that gave him an intense look.

The new professor continued. "Our kids just don't get enough of that part of our culture. They learn biology and life sciences in middle and high school, but they don't hear about herbs and Navajo medicine, which has been practiced for hundreds of years. We want to expose the kids to our ways, not just what's in the Anglo textbooks."

Clifford gave them a puzzled look. "But you're both modernists. Whatever's new that seems to benefit the *Dineh*, The People, you see as progress."

Wilson's companion spoke slowly. "I believe, and I think my colleague will agree, that in order to choose their own paths, the children have to know both ways. The kids are under constant bombardment from television and magazines and they're learning about the Anglo world all the time, but our ways are harder for them to understand. We need to make our traditions known to young people, and expose them to our beliefs and customs, or we're going to lose our children."

"I'll be very happy to talk to the kids, but I'd prefer not to do it in a classroom setting," Clifford said. "Bring them here. Let them see a *hataalii* at work, not just be lectured by one. They should experience The Way, not just hear about it."

"That's a great idea," Wilson said. "But there are nearly thirty of them. Are you sure you're up to that here?"

"Let me think about it, then I'll let you know for sure."

Hearing another vehicle outside, Clifford went to the entrance. "I'll have to ask all of you to excuse me now. I have a patient coming." He handed Ella a small bag containing more herbs for brewing tea. "Let me know how my niece does."

"Thanks, brother." Ella picked up Dawn and led Wilson and his friend out of the hogan.

FIVE

✖ ✖ ✖

Wilson and his friend stopped by Ella's Jeep. "This is Professor Jeremiah Manyfarms," Wilson said now that they were outside the medicine hogan and not in the *hataalii*'s presence.

Ella still didn't shake hands, but nodded. "It's good to meet you."

"I've heard a lot about you, Ms. Clah," Manyfarms said. "Your background sounds similar to mine."

"How's that?"

"We walk a difficult line between the old and the new. I received some emergency medical training in the army, but I see the advantages of Navajo healing, and I use it sometimes in tandem, and at other times exclusively."

"I'm that way too. It just depends on the situation." She told them about Dawn's cough, then added, "The tea my brother gave her has worked. She's stopped coughing."

Jeremiah smiled at Dawn as she squirmed, anxious to be put down. Ella complied and watched her daughter tottering clumsily after a lizard who'd darted into some bushes.

"I'm glad we've finally had the opportunity to meet. I hope things will get better around the station soon," Jeremiah said.

Ella's radar for trouble went up. "Excuse me?"

"Well, I understand you and your second cousin Justine have been having problems at work. It must be difficult to work with someone when trust is an issue," Jeremiah said offhandedly.

"I trust Justine implicitly," she said coldly.

"I'm glad to hear it. I'm sure you'll be able to work things out with her then."

"How did you hear about this?" Ella asked pointedly.

"Justine hasn't kept it a secret to her close friends," he answered easily. "Was it supposed to be one?"

"Depends how much you know."

"Well, the shooting incident is common knowledge, Ella," he said, calling her by her first name, something that for some reason she couldn't explain bothered her. "But some people have said that it was a bit of confusion that got blown way out of proportion."

"Who said?"

"The clerk at the convenience store, for one," Jeremiah responded. "Don't be so surprised. People talk. When you're troubled, I'm sure you have your own circle of friends that you trust and confide in. A beautiful woman like you never lacks for friends."

Professor Manyfarms was annoying her. Ella glanced at Wilson and saw that he shared her sentiments.

"We better go back to the college," Wilson said, gesturing back to his SUV.

"I'll catch you later, Ella," Jeremiah said with a casual wave of his hand.

Ella watched them go. Wilson had floored the vehicle, leaving a trail of dust behind him. There was nothing except friendship between Wilson and her, but he still didn't like it when a man paid too much attention to her.

There had been a time when Wilson had hoped a romance would develop between them, but the spark had never been there. Romantic love was not something any Navajo expected, but a match between them had seemed a bad idea to her. Wilson would have expected more from his wife than she, as a full-time cop, would ever be able to give him.

Still, there were times when she wished it could have been different. They'd grown up together and were as close as friends could be. She'd always been comfortable around Wilson.

She pushed the thought aside. At times she could barely cope with the demands her mother made, let alone the ones a husband would make on her. What she had in her life was enough.

Ella headed home, trying to force herself to relax, and taking care not to bounce the truck around on the dirt track. Dawn, as always, no matter how bumpy the road, fell asleep. She envied her daughter's ability to shut out the world and relax so totally.

After hitting the main road, Ella glanced in the rearview mirror. It was an ingrained habit drilled into her after a decade of police work. Off in the distance she could see one vehicle leaving a thin trail of dust on the graveled road. Employing the aggressive caution she'd developed over the years, she avoided taking the turnoff that would lead her straight home. When she reached the next side road, running parallel to a natural-gas pipe line, she chose it immediately.

The vehicle stayed with her, even after she'd changed roads again, this time back toward a small lake. Despite that, she wasn't sure if it was a threat. The driver was certainly not trying to narrow the gap between them. She considered calling in, but with the department's current manpower problems, she didn't want to take another cop away from his patrol for what could turn out to be nothing more than coincidence or joyriding teens.

Ella had to make sure that someone was really tailing her, not just heading in the same direction. Trying to ditch it with so few road choices made things tough. She headed east back to the paved highway, devising a plan.

The vehicle remained half a mile behind, and from this distance she couldn't even be sure of the make and model. Ella slowed her speed, proceeding at half the posted limit. Then, suddenly, after she went around a sharp curve in the road, she slammed down on the accelerator and roared down the road.

Ella raced over the next hill, then lost sight of the vehicle behind her momentarily. Slowing down, she inched along, waiting for the vehicle to clear the hill and come racing after her, trying to catch up. She'd get a good look at him then.

Seconds went by and her pursuer failed to appear. With no other traffic around, Ella turned around and raced back in the opposite direction, hoping to still catch a glimpse of the car. After a moment she saw it off in the distance, heading toward Shiprock.

Even if she floored her truck, she'd never catch it before it reached town. Reluctantly she decided to head home.

Ella looked at her daughter, who was still sleeping in the car seat without a care in the world. The thought that someone might come after her for real when Dawn was with her worried Ella. Maybe it would be better if she stopped taking Dawn on outings for a while. She hated the thought of making any concessions out of fear, but she wouldn't risk Dawn.

Ten minutes later, Ella put her daughter to bed, and sometime during Ella's reading of *The Little Lamb*, Dawn fell asleep again.

Rose met Ella out in the hallway. "Why do you make the child sleep when she doesn't want to?"

"I don't think you can *make* a child go to sleep if she's not sleepy. But if she takes a nap now, she won't be as crabby later. Kids get tired, but they don't always know it until they're put to bed."

"Spoken like an Anglo."

Ella closed her eyes and opened them again. "Mom, if you don't start agreeing with me on some rules, she's going to be hopelessly spoiled."

"You and your brother seem to have turned out all right," Rose shot back, annoyed.

Ella smiled grudgingly. "But we're not talking about me or Clifford. Mom, Short Stuff's a very active kid. If you'd set regular hours for her, it would be easier for you, too."

"I know what she needs," Rose said flatly. "That child needs to be raised like a Navajo."

"She is. But learning a few things from the Anglos wouldn't hurt."

Rose sat down slowly, and grimaced as she settled against the chair cushion.

"Mom, are you okay?"

"Some days are better than others. My legs can still ache from time to time." Rose reached around and removed a crocheted shawl from atop the back of her chair and draped it over her legs.

Since the accident when a drunk driver had smashed into her mother's old pickup, Rose often had difficulty getting around. She could go for several days without pain, but when the weather turned cool as it was doing now, her joints seemed to give her a lot of problems.

"You really have to let me hire someone to come here to help you with my kid. She's almost too much to handle some days, Mom."

"I'm perfectly capable of taking care of her when you're at work. Don't insult me."

Ella knew that to Rose, bringing someone else into her home to help with the work was tantamount to admitting she was growing old. Ella had no desire to hurt her mother's feelings, but she had to find a way to get her to face facts.

"Mom, we could hire a young woman from a traditionalist family."

Rose shook her head. "They would never come to work for us."

Ella took a deep breath, then let it out again. Rose was right. Their "legacy" had made them pariahs to many. "But not all the traditionalists feel that way. Many of the clans see our family as a force for good."

"Since the time of Mist Eagle, our family has been feared and shunned by others. But now that you and your brother have each had only one child, many are afraid that both children will turn to evil. It was always believed that two children in each family would keep the scales balanced. With only one, the balance is gone, and they're afraid of what two evil forces will do if they combine. They're watching all of us carefully to make sure we don't attempt to hide anything that could endanger the tribe."

"I'm not evil and neither is my brother, so why do they think the kids will be?"

"That's just it, daughter. They believe one of you has already chosen evil, and the remaining one might be persuaded to follow. If that happens the children will be corrupted. They already know what gifts you and your brother have, but the children still represent an unknown, and that terrifies many. Just be careful what you do or say."

"Are you sure about this?"

Rose nodded once. "It started when people saw you push your

brother off the roof during the confrontation with those terrible people. Since no one could prove your actions saved your brother's life, people are waiting and watching, looking for a clearer sign. They haven't passed judgment yet, but that could come at any time."

Ella nodded slowly. "That will complicate things. Finding someone to come and help you won't be as easy as I'd hoped."

"I'll take care of my granddaughter. I don't want a stranger in my house."

Ella said nothing, but decided to go ahead with her search anyway. Rose needed help, and not just with Dawn.

Ella watched her mother stare at her cane. "It's no shame to use that, you know," Ella said.

"It slows me down."

"I'm home today, Mom. I'll take care of things. Just relax."

She saw her mother trying to get up, then slipping back into the chair cushion. Ella handed her the cane, then held out her hand, but Rose pulled away. "I am not helpless."

"Mom, you were hurt in a really bad car accident, and for a while we didn't know if you'd ever be able to walk again at all. This isn't about being helpless. This is about being human. We're family, and it's okay if we help each other. How many times did you help me when I got the flu, or when I sprained my ankle one time trying to beat Clifford in a race?"

Rose smiled. "You were only twelve, but even then you were the most stubborn child I'd ever seen—until now. My granddaughter is a lot like you in that way. When she decides that she wants to do something, that girl acts like nothing in the world can stop her."

Hearing Dawn moving around in the nursery, Ella left her mother and went to her daughter.

Hoping to get Dawn to expend some of her excess energy, Ella took her out for a walk along a path leading to an old pasture, holding her tiny hand and letting Dawn set the pace. Two, the family mutt, ambled along beside them. As they reached the shelter made of cottonwood branches that had once served as a lean-to for sheep, Two suddenly stopped and bared his teeth.

Ella picked Dawn up instantly. She'd expected Dawn to start crying or show fear, but as if she, too, had seen or sensed danger, Dawn became very still.

Ella only had the backup .22 derringer in her boot. She made it a point not to wear a holster when she was with her daughter, afraid that the little girl would reach for the weapon.

Now, as she watched the bushy terrain ahead, she couldn't sense or see anything other than a few sparrows and a mourning dove. But another look at Two convinced her that something or someone was nearby. The animal's hackles were raised and his deep-throated growl signaled he was ready to fight.

Ella backed away, listening and visually searching the area around her, then turned and jogged back to the house. Leaving Dawn with Rose, she retrieved her service pistol and went back outside. Two hadn't moved, nor had he sat down.

Ella went on ahead, moving carefully and searching for tracks. The dog finally joined her and stayed at her side, sniffing the air.

Ella was thorough, but she found nothing. As she glanced down at the dog, she saw that Two had relaxed and his hackles were back down.

"I wish you could talk, Two. I'd love to know what it was you saw, or what your nose told you about who or what was here."

They returned to the house without incident, but Ella was still tense. As she looked at Dawn, she tried to make sense out of her child's reaction. Dawn normally would have loudly protested being picked up quickly like that. Yet she'd remained quiet, her eyes glued straight ahead.

Ella sat down on the floor with Dawn, who was sorting her plastic blocks by color. "Daughter, when we went for a walk, did you see anyone out there besides Two?"

Dawn looked up, her dark brown eyes wide as she shook her head.

Rose watched them for a moment. "What happened?" she asked as Ella sat back, lost in thought, idly handing Dawn one block at a time to place in the proper pile.

Ella recounted the events. "It was really weird, Mom. But there were no tracks at all."

"At least not where you looked," Rose said slowly. "Maybe you just didn't search the right place. The only thing that will set Two off like that is when he thinks one of us is in danger."

Ella nodded. "I agree, but I found nothing." She regretted not having checked to see if the badger fetish around her neck had felt warm at the time. That was always a certain sign of trouble.

Ella considered everything carefully. First there was the vehicle she'd suspected had been tailing her. Now this. She might have been able to discount one of those events as her imagination, but not both, particularly in light of Two's reaction. Of course, it could have been a wild creature that Two wasn't overly fond of, like a snake, but she'd certainly seen no evidence of one anywhere.

The remainder of that afternoon, and throughout the evening, Ella remained restless. She went outside and looked around several times, and then one last time before going to bed.

Alone in her room, with Dawn tucked away and asleep after having to read two stories tonight, Ella turned on her computer and checked for mail. It was a comforting ritual, but tonight there were no letters waiting, just ads for things that held no interest for her.

Hoping for another instant message, she hung around on-line visiting some of her favorite Internet places, like a site she'd recently found devoted to herbal medicines. After a while she began a search on-line and tried to locate "Coyote," but a message on-screen said that there was no such member. Whoever Coyote was, he or she knew how to cover his tracks. She tried an Internet search using the key word *Coyote*, but only got listings for wildlife sites and a Web page for an actor.

Thirty minutes later, frustrated and having nothing to show for her efforts, she turned off the computer and crawled into bed. The wind had come up outside. Gusts blasted sand and gravel against her window, and a mournful wail filled the room as cold air seeped through a crack in the casing. The almost human sound made her skin crawl. She hated dust storms, but it seemed a fitting end to a nerve-wracking day.

With a muttered curse, she turned on her side, closed her eyes, and drifted off to a troubled sleep.

SIX

—— ✖ ✖ ✖ ——

Ella came into the substation early the following morning hoping to talk to Justine before they got down to work. As she was walking down the hall toward the small forensics lab where her assistant spent much of her time, Big Ed appeared in a doorway and waved her toward him.

Ella stepped inside the chief's office, and was surprised to see Justine there, looking restless and uncomfortable in her best corduroy jacket and slacks. Both she and Ella were always dressed in civilian clothes except during special department ceremonies. Ella looked from one to the other, but it was impossible to guess what was going on.

"Why don't you fill Shorty in?" Big Ed asked Justine, waving Ella toward a chair and taking his place behind the desk.

Justine looked at the floor, then finally up at Ella. "I received a letter from my aunt Lena yesterday afternoon. She lives right on the border between Navajo and Hopi land, west of the community of Steamboat. My aunt believes that the nearby Hopis are stealing her well water and vandalizing her pump. She wants us to put a stop to it."

"I've spoken on the telephone to the tribal officer that patrols the area," Big Ed said. "He verified that the pump had been vandalized just recently. He'd found vehicle tracks and some footprints, but so far he hasn't been able to catch the perp. His territory is so large, he's having a problem keeping a close watch on the place." He paused for a moment, as if trying to choose his words with care. "Do you know Lena Clani, Shorty?"

Ella shook her head. "Not personally, but I know her by reputation. Justine's aunt is said to be one of our most gifted stargazers. I understand she's been able to find things people have considered hopelessly lost."

He nodded. "She's an important member of our tribe. That's why this could be a touchy situation."

"I want to help my aunt," Justine said, looking at Ella. "But Aunt Lena wants me to go arrest the Hopis who are doing that, and as you know, I can't arrest a Hopi unless I catch him inside our boundaries doing something illegal."

"I don't want Justine down there on her own because she's personally involved, so I want you to accompany her," Big Ed said. "I'll also have the officer in that district meet you. That way Lena Clani will see that we trust our uniformed cops as much as our plainclothes officers. Give this as much of your time as it requires."

"Chief, almost anyone can go with Justine," Ella protested. "Can you assign someone else? That's a long trip, and I've got work to do here." That wasn't quite the truth. The fact was she just didn't want to be far from Dawn and Rose now that she suspected someone was sneaking around the outside of their house. If she told Big Ed, he'd probably let her off, but she didn't want to raise a false alarm and she had no proof anything was going on.

"Your work can wait a bit longer," Big Ed said flatly.

As they walked out of the chief's office, Justine glared at Ella. "I'm sorry this is such an inconvenience, Ella. If you want, I'll go by myself, and just omit that detail from my report. You can do the same and no one will be the wiser. Oh—I nearly forgot. You tend to go back on agreements like those."

"Believe what you want, but I never said a word to Big Ed until *after* he met with you. Since the only people at the convenience store were you, me, the perp, and the clerk, I have to assume that the clerk was the one who told the chief. Maybe he's a friend or a relative."

Justine hesitated, but wasn't quite ready to capitulate. "Maybe so. But if you still think my aunt and I are just wasting your time, perhaps I can get the new Hopi FBI agent to come with me."

"You've heard about him?"

"Of course. Everyone's talking about Paycheck."

"You can't take Payestewa, Justine, without going through Blalock. And this isn't a federal matter. The reason I don't want to go is not because I think it's a waste of time. It's because I'm worried about Dawn and Mom right now."

"Is there a problem at home? You know I'll do whatever I can to help you," Justine said quickly, although her voice was still taut.

"I'm not sure what's going on yet. It's complicated," Ella said, shaking her head. "I'm not quite ready to talk about it."

"Is it because after what happened the other night, you don't quite trust me?"

"Justine, that's bull. You're blowing this whole thing way out of proportion." Ella recognized the expression on her young cousin's face. Justine had made up her mind to assume the worst. It seemed like the incident had affected her a lot more than Ella had imagined. Combined with the growing tension several officers had also observed Justine was exhibiting, it made things unpleasant nowadays.

"I just don't know why Big Ed was so insistent that *you* come. He could have easily assigned Sergeant Neskahi to this, or even Ralph Tache," Justine said.

Ella shrugged. She'd wondered the same thing, and the only answer she had was that maybe the chief was aware of the tension between Justine and her, and had decided the long drive would give them time to hash things out.

They got under way a short time later, taking Justine's unit. It was going to be a long trip, and for over an hour neither spoke. Justine kept her eyes on the road, occasionally fiddling with the volume on the radio. As time went by, she seemed to grow even more agitated. Chuska Peak was already fading in the distance to the northwest when Justine finally glanced over at her.

"I heard talk around the station that Mrs. Yellowhair is using you as an example of a role model for our tribe on some radio ads. Since when did you two become such good friends?"

"We're not, though I do respect the woman for the way she's handled herself through all the difficult times she'd had to face."

"I was really surprised that she chose you instead of me," Justine said pointedly.

Ella looked at her in surprise. "I hope you don't think I had anything to do with that. I don't like being in the public eye."

"Even if it might help counter some of that stupid gossip going around about you turning to evil?"

"So you've heard it too?" She saw Justine nod. "The only way that's going to die is if people get bored and go on to other things. But if I'm being held up as a public role model, it's just going to fuel a lot more talk, not stop it. I really wish Mrs. Yellowhair hadn't mentioned me."

"I wonder why she didn't pick me. My mother would have been so proud! You know how she values everything Abigail Yellowhair says. But no, she had to go with the star of our team."

Ella noted how Justine's hands were gripping the wheel so tightly her knuckles were white. "You're not the type to be envious of anyone, let alone jealous. What's really bugging you?"

Justine shook her head. "I admit I've been in a really bad mood, but I've got some legitimate gripes."

"If they're work related, take them to the chief, or talk to me about them at the station. When we're in the field, it's dangerous to let our minds wander."

"I know my job." She glared at Ella.

"One more thing, Justine. Don't ever let me hear that you're discussing police business with anyone outside the PD. Is that *very* clear?"

Justine gave her a puzzled look. "Who said I was?"

"I spoke to Jeremiah Manyfarms and he knew about the shooting incident and the misunderstanding that followed, including us not getting along."

"That's not going to jeopardize any investigation," Justine snapped. "Jeremiah happens to be a friend of mine, and I needed someone to talk to. I couldn't exactly discuss this with the chief. Or you."

Ella was getting really annoyed with Justine, but she forced herself not to overreact. "Do *not* discuss anything that pertains to the police department and especially our morale problems with any outsiders. It undermines us with the public."

"Jeremiah won't blab it around. I trust him."

"I'm not willing to join in with that trust, so don't let me hear about the department's dirty laundry from him again."

A long silence stretched out as they reached the turnoff to Window Rock, entering some of the more beautiful piñon and juniper hills and rock formations on the reservation. Soon they would pass through the Navajo capital on the way to their Arizona destination.

At long last, after Ella's temper had finally subsided, she spoke again. "By the way, Samuel Begaye is at large. I got the warning from the Marshals Service yesterday. They suspect he's in the area and may come after us. Remember the threats he made when we tracked him down?"

Justine nodded. "He's stupid enough to come after us instead of going underground. I'll keep a sharp eye out." Justine paused. "Is that why you didn't want to leave Rose and Dawn?"

"Partly." The truth was, she didn't see Begaye as one who'd watch their house before striking. He acted first, then thought about it later. But there was always that one chance in a million.

"Why did you wait to tell me about Begaye?"

The question irritated Ella. "I left half a dozen calls for you yesterday, but you never called me back, though you know members of our SI team are required to stay in contact. And today we haven't stopped arguing long enough for me to say anything."

Instead of apologizing, Justine lapsed into silence, playing with the radio volume again. Ella glanced at her assistant, then back out the window. There had to be more to Justine's attitude than the shooting incident and the aftermath. She was wound tighter than a drum all the time these days, like she was drinking too much coffee, or was on uppers. But Ella knew Justine well enough to rule out anything such as amphetamines. She barely even drank beer, except at social events.

Hoping to get her to relax a bit, Ella tried to speak in as casual a tone as possible without appearing patronizing. "What can you tell me about your aunt? I know that she's a traditionalist, of course, but I don't recall anyone in your family ever saying much about her. It would help to know a little bit about what she's like before talking to her," Ella said.

"I really don't know much about Aunt Lena. I haven't seen my father's sister since I was about Dawn's age, and my mom has only seen her a few times at ceremonials."

Ella nodded. It wasn't unusual. The father's family usually didn't play an important role in a kid's life.

"I know that my mother's side of the family believes she's gifted at stargazing," Justine continued. "But most of them think she's a little strange, too. These days she lives in a really lonely part of the Rez. From the way I've heard her home described, I can tell you that she doesn't live at the end of the world—but one can see it from there."

Ella laughed. Finally the old Justine was returning, at least a little bit.

Justine smiled hesitantly. "I sure wouldn't live so far away from town. For Aunt Lena, even going to the trading post for a can of pork and beans must take an hour or so, even by pickup."

"They don't usually buy cans of beans," Ella said with a chuckle.

"Yeah, yeah. They cook them from scratch, for hours. But I've got to tell you, I tried it once, using my mom's pressure cooker. Maybe it's just because I'm used to eating the ones from the can, but mine tasted really gross."

Ella laughed. "At home Mom's the one who can cook. I just warm things up."

"Do you ever feel that if you don't get your own place soon, you'll go crazy?" Justine asked. "Every time I make plans to move out, something happens like Mom getting sick, and I end up staying home."

Ella began to suspect that this was the source of Justine's tension. "It's different for me, Justine. I lived off the Rez for several years, the last few in Los Angeles in an apartment."

"While you were working for the FBI," Justine finished.

"Yeah. When I came back I realized how much I needed my family. Returning to the Rez wasn't easy for me."

"Particularly because of the circumstances," Justine said.

Ella recalled her father's murder and shuddered. "It was a very hard time for all of us." She decided to keep their conversation on the present. "But these days, Mom takes care of Dawn while I'm at work, and we're all pretty happy."

"Your life has been a lot different from mine," Justine commented. "I need to get my own place soon. I've been reluctant to leave Mom alone, but Ruth and Jayne are always over, so Mom should be okay."

"Have you been having a problem getting along with Angela?"

Justine shrugged. "I'm too old to have to tell anyone where I'm going and when I'll be back. It's annoying."

Ella heard the edge in Justine's voice. "Parents and family have a difficult time adjusting to the fact that police work has no real hours, especially when you do fieldwork. You burn the candle at both ends working on several cases at a time. Then, for no reason at all, things will slow down and days will go by when all you do is paperwork and pray that something will happen soon."

"It's hard to find anyone outside the PD who can understand that and put up with it, isn't it?" Justine asked rhetorically.

Ella nodded. "That's one of the reasons why there's a high rate of divorce in our profession."

"It may be hard for a cop to find a way to keep from being lonely, but what we go through is nothing in comparison to my aunt Lena's life," Justine said. "When I got this letter, I couldn't help but wonder if she hasn't gone a little crazy living out there all these years. Mom agreed."

As their car radio crackled, Ella picked up the mike. Dispatch came through, though the signal wavered from the distance and terrain. The Navajo cop who patrolled the area would not be able to meet them at Lena Clani's on time. Someone had flattened all his tires when he'd stopped for coffee in Chinle. It would be a couple of hours before he was up and running again.

"I don't remember hearing about much vandalism on this area of the Rez," Justine muttered.

"Nor I," Ella answered, "though Chinle has had some gang problems, like Shiprock." She remembered the words from Coyote warning her of a conspiracy. Having police officers become targets for harassment could turn out to be a sign of that. She thought of discussing it with Justine, then changed her mind. Her cousin's state of mind was barely back to normal. Until she was more sure of her, she wouldn't risk bringing up any new topics.

Ella had never been to this particular part of the Rez, west of

Ganado and bordering the southeastern corner of the Hopi Reservation south of Keams Canyon, Arizona. She studied a detailed map, and motioned for Justine to turn up a dirt track listed as a primitive road.

They continued up the bumpy path for an eternity when Ella finally spotted a solitary hogan off in the distance. At least two miles to the west of it, in a small valley on Hopi land, was a small wood-framed house and a metal water tank. Although the wooden house was within sight of the hogan, it was miles away culturally.

Both on the Navajo and the Hopi side, the land was filled with sagebrush and stunted junipers, and it seemed as inhospitable an area of the Rez as she'd ever seen. It was certain that the people living there were often snowed in during winter, or trapped by mud when the thaw came.

The bad road forced Justine to proceed slowly as they approached the hogan. White smoke flowed easily from the metal pipe protruding from the center of the roof. Ella looked around, getting the feeling that something was wrong, though she couldn't see anything out of place or even remotely suspicious. A small split-log corral was fifty feet away from the hogan, and several sheep could be seen a hundred yards farther in the brush, grazing, along with two shaggy ponies. A large water barrel rested on a platform of cinder blocks at the end of the two ruts they were following.

Looking around for signs of trouble, Ella suddenly saw a figure race around the side of the hogan and scramble down into an arroyo, dropping out of sight.

"Did you see that?" Justine said. "That can't be Aunt Lena."

"Yeah, get as close as you can, then I'll go after him on foot while you go check on your aunt," Ella said.

Justine drove another fifty feet closer, then slammed on the brakes. Ella leaped out. "I'll try and track him. If your aunt's okay, come back my direction and honk if you spot him."

Ella looked down the arroyo and saw the tracks of the running man leading toward the fence separating Navajo and Hopi land. She began jogging along the top, following the tracks below as they led along the sandy bottom of the narrow wash. It didn't take long to verify where the man was going. After running at least a quarter mile along the top of the arroyo, Ella stopped.

Just ahead was a fence line, and parallel to it on both sides was a dirt track. Ella looked around for Justine's police unit. Justine was now away from the hogan and driving in her direction along the Navajo side of the fence. But it was already too late. Ella could see a running figure on the other side, safe on Hopi land, after having crossed through a culvert beneath the fence line.

Her prey looked and ran like a man, but other than knowing he had dark hair and was wearing jeans and a plaid shirt, no other description was possible at that distance. Ella jogged up to the fence, considered climbing it, then changed her mind. She didn't need the kind of trouble that would bring.

Justine pulled up in her car seconds later. "I never saw him. Did he cross over the fence?"

"Yes, and he's probably headed toward that house. All I caught was a glimpse of him about fifty feet into Hopi land. If I'd have gone after him, I would have been the one in trouble because that's out of our jurisdiction. The guy would have brought in the Hopi cops for sure and that would have created no end of trouble."

"For the chief, too," Justine said, agreeing. "Let's go back to my aunt's hogan. Maybe she'll know more."

Three minutes later as they pulled up to the log hogan, Lena Clani came out and waved at them. Justine got out first and approached her aunt, who was dressed in a long, heavy skirt, long-sleeved blouse, and a blanket draped like a shawl.

The woman was approximately Justine's mother's age, and wore several turquoise rings on her fingers, and a silver bracelet. Her hands were long and delicate, and there were orange stains on her fingertips.

Ella followed a few steps behind, deciding to let Justine make the initial contact. Signs of trust might help Justine regain some of her self-confidence.

Both niece and aunt seemed guarded and cautious around each other, just what Ella expected from a traditionalist facing a member of the family who was in such a modernist profession.

Lena invited Justine and her inside and then offered them metal mugs of hot coffee as they sat on sheepskins inside the hogan.

"We saw someone running away when we first drove up. Did you see him?" Justine asked.

"No, I was playing the radio while I was chopping up some carrots for a pot of mutton stew. The only sound I heard was you approaching. But I'm not surprised. The Hopis have been trying to make things difficult for me."

"Would you tell us about the water problem you've been having, Aunt?" Justine asked.

Lena walked to the entrance of the hogan. "Do you see that water storage tank beside the house across the way?" Seeing Ella and Justine nod, she continued. "Behind the tank is a big water pump that runs on electricity. It all belongs to the Hopi family who lives there. They didn't have that well or pump last year. My water was fine then. I think what started all this was that the Hopi began pumping too much, lowering the water table. I'm not the only one with a shallow well that's starting to run dry."

"But why would someone from that house come over and vandalize your little hand pump?" Justine asked. "They're getting all the water they want."

"They don't want to share, and they want to force me out. But I was here first."

"So you believe the trouble is caused by that Hopi family?" Ella asked.

"Yes, but also from the other families who live over on the next mesa. The Hopi consider all this land theirs, despite all the arguing and lawyers and politicians. They want the Navajos gone. But it's not going to happen. This is *my* land and I'm not moving. So go arrest them. If you put them in jail, maybe that will scare them and they'll stop vandalizing my pump and using up all the water."

"We don't have jurisdiction over the Hopi unless we catch them doing something wrong on this side of the fence, Aunt. We'll have to go through the legal system." Justine started to explain, but her aunt shook her head.

"Don't give me fancy excuses, niece. My water level drops every time the Hopis start their pumps. You can hear them running at night. The water I need to live is being stolen from me faster than the rain can replace it. And they keep breaking my pump so I can't even get my share of what's there."

"What your niece has just told you is true. We have to catch them doing something wrong," Ella tried to explain, but again Lena interrupted.

"But you're police officers, and you're supposed to protect the *Dineh*," Lena added.

"We still can't break the law," Justine said.

"But it's okay for them to break it?"

"We'll file a complaint with their police department. That's what Justine meant about going through the legal system," Ella pointed out.

"*Then* you'll arrest them?"

Ella sighed and looked at Justine. "Here's the way it has to go. We'll tell the Hopi Police Department what's going on, and who we think might be responsible. But if any arrests are to be made, they'll have to make them."

"The Hopis aren't going to arrest their own people," Lena protested.

"They might. We do, when one of the *Dineh* breaks the law," Justine said. "But we just can't go over and arrest a member of the Hopi tribe."

"This is shameful. My own niece is telling me she won't help me!" Lena said.

"We *will* help you," Ella said. "We'll take a look at the pump. If it's been vandalized again and needs repairs, we'll be glad to drive you to the trading post so you can order or buy what you need to fix it."

Lena shook her head. "That's not necessary. I have a neighbor at Steamboat who comes by once a week and gives me a ride to Ganado."

"Okay. In that case, we'll go check the pump, and if there's a problem, we'll try to rig up something for you," Ella said.

As Lena led them outside to the pump, Justine studied the area. "Start keeping a written record of the times you can't pump water, Aunt, or when you notice that the flow is low. You might also consider getting yourself a couple of mean-looking dogs to watch over your place when you're asleep or away from the hogan."

"And that's the best you can do for your own relative?"

"I'll try to talk to the tribal authorities and see what else can be done but legally, our hands are tied." Justine sighed.

"I'm your father's sister. Isn't helping family important to modernists like you?"

"This doesn't have anything to do with that," Justine answered patiently.

"Didn't your mother raise you to stick up for your own, even your father's side of the family? I'm not only a member of the tribe deserving protection, I'm your aunt. I bring you a problem that threatens my home, and my entire life, and all you can do is tell me about the law, like you would for a stranger."

"I'm truly sorry, Aunt. I can't do anything else. Family or not."

"This isn't the last you'll hear about this. I *will* tell your father and mother and all the members of your clan how little respect you've shown me today."

Lena motioned toward Ella. "I heard stories about this woman. She's a modernist like you, but when her family was threatened, at least *she* helped. She returned to her home when her mother needed her. You should be more like her."

Ella stared at Lena, shocked that Justine's aunt would say that about someone she'd never even met, but Justine's reaction was even more pronounced. Her young partner looked stunned.

Justine's voice was strained, a pitch higher than normal. "I came as soon as I received your letter, and I even brought my supervisor. That should tell you that I do have respect for you. But I can't give you what isn't mine to give. The law is the law, and this isn't just the Anglo way. These rules are from the Tribal Council, and I can't break them."

Justine looked at Ella, who nodded in approval.

"I just don't understand you, niece," Lena said, and strode back to the hogan.

"You could have *said* something," Justine grumbled.

"There was nothing for me to add. You were absolutely right about the law and the procedures we have to follow. But maybe we should talk to Kevin. He's an attorney for the tribe, and he'll be up on things like this. He may be able to suggest something else you can do to help your aunt."

Ella and Justine studied the pump. A connecting bolt had been removed and stolen, and the handle was on the ground. After looking around a moment, Ella found a big nail they could use to reattach the handle. Using a rock, they bent the nail so it wouldn't fall out, then trying the handle, were able to pump water.

"That should hold temporarily. But it won't last for long." Ella looked at Justine, who nodded.

"I'll write down the pump brand and make a quick sketch of the handle, showing which part is missing. I'll give it to my aunt, and she can get a replacement bolt or something that will be more permanent than that nail." Justine pulled out a small notebook from her shirt pocket and began to sketch the pump handle.

A few minutes later, Justine took the sketch to her aunt in the hogan while Ella walked back to the unit.

Justine came out several moments later, anger on her face and hurt in her eyes. "I just can't do anything right as far as she's concerned," Justine muttered, opening her car door. "You just have the magic touch, Ella."

"What do you mean?"

"First Abigail Yellowhair, and now my own family. I really should have brought Agent Payestewa with me instead of you. At least I wouldn't have been compared to him and could have avoided the humiliation of being second-rate."

"Justine, a lot of things are going wrong for you right now and I understand that you're testy. But stop taking it out on me. I'm far from everyone's favorite child and you know it. I've spent a lifetime being compared to Clifford. He was the charismatic one everyone respected. I got married and left the reservation because I couldn't get out of Clifford's shadow any other way. Even to this day, he always manages to get people's respect, whether they agree with him or not. I have to explain myself and hope people will understand."

Justine nodded thoughtfully, but said nothing.

"And as far as Abigail Yellowhair goes, she chose me as a role model only because I'm in a leadership position and it makes me look more important."

"It's easy for you to dismiss this, but I'm constantly compared to you by just about everyone. It gets old, you know?"

"Justine, you've been through an awful lot in a very short time. Why don't you take a week off? Relax and give yourself time to work things out in your head before you come back on duty."

"You're kidding, right? If I take time off now, everyone in the department will start thinking that I can't take the pressure." She shot Ella an icy look. "That's a brilliant idea."

Ella was about to answer that it was obvious Justine couldn't take the pressure, but then decided against it. Something was wrong with her cousin, and it wasn't just from overwork. Justine had never complained before or been the jealous type.

"Justine, calm down. I don't know what's going on with you. The issues you've brought up and that have you so upset are things that would have never gotten to you before. What's going on in your life that's making you so edgy and defensive?"

Seeing Justine about to protest, Ella held up one hand. "You and I go back to our childhood, but lately all I get from you is distrust and an attitude. It's really hard to be patient with you when all you're giving back is venom."

"You just haven't been paying attention, and that's the worst part. I've been in a pressure cooker for months, and you haven't even noticed. Ever since we lost Harry, I've had twice as much work and no help. I guess since the budget cuts, everyone just figures 'Justine will take care of it.' You sit around pushing a pencil and waiting for the next case, but I'm in that lab running tests for every cop that comes in. No one seems to care how many hours I put in—except when the work isn't done."

Justine had a point, but Ella knew it was far more than that. "You've handled worse, Justine. I think you're still holding back on the real issue. There's something at the core of all this."

Justine started to answer when they heard their call sign come over the radio.

Ella picked up the mike. Dispatch wanted them to stop at Window Rock and pick up a prisoner who needed to be transferred to Shiprock to stand trial.

"The situation is escalating fast," the dispatcher informed them. "The PD is gearing up for a confrontation with an angry crowd. The suspect's been charged with killing a man, and the prisoner's family is there as well as the victim's relatives. You'll have to work up a plan with the officers there to avoid running a gauntlet out of the station."

"Ten-four."

Justine switched on the sirens. "It sounds like the sooner we get there, the better off we'll be."

Ella knew that her cousin didn't want to talk about personal matters anymore. And, for the moment, she was going to let it pass. "We've got to focus on business right now, but let's try to talk later."

Justine nodded, her eyes focused on the road.

Ella pursed her lips. With Justine in this frame of mind, she was an unpredictable partner. She'd have to keep an eye on the situation and her as well.

"Stay alert and on task," Ella warned. "We go in, retrieve the prisoner, and come out."

"Of course. I'm a cop. I know what I have to do."

Ella stared out the window. The words sounded good, but the presence and control that would have been needed to make them believable were absent. The truth was that the trust that had existed between them was missing now, and without it, the very heart of their partnership had been compromised.

SEVEN

✖ ✖ ✖

The station in Window Rock had called in off-duty officers and those from surrounding patrol areas to deal with the crisis. Six cops stood in pairs outside in a loose line, monitoring the gathering while more police officers remained inside the building in riot gear.

"You'd better take the prisoner out through the back," a lieutenant from tribal headquarters told her. Ella could tell by his uneasiness and the way his eyes darted toward the door every few seconds that he normally served from behind a desk. A crisis like this, however, required every available officer. "There's a TV camera crew in the front, and there's no telling how that'll affect the intelligence of people protesting."

Ella nodded. About thirty people were outside, though she didn't know how many more relatives of the accused and the victim were on their way to the station. Things could have been a lot worse, but with less than a third that number of officers present, it would be hard to control the crowd without someone getting hurt.

"Tempers are running high on this one. Half think the guy's been set up by the victim's family. His brother has been here since dawn, taking his case to every person trying to enter the building. The other half think he's guilty and want him tried right here—or worse, they want us to turn the prisoner over to them so they can deal with him themselves," the lieutenant added.

"We'll take him off your hands, but we'll need some backup

getting him to the unit," Justine said, eyeing the crowd. "Some of the signs calling out for justice are attached to what look like axe handles or clubs."

"I have an idea," Ella said. "Let's dress the prisoner in a cop's uniform and take him out the side door. The crowd won't be expecting that, and we should be able to get him to the car before he's recognized."

"The cuffs will give him away," Justine pointed out.

"I'll cuff him to me," Ella said, "and you can go a few steps ahead to take care of unlocking and opening the doors. Then, as a diversion, we can send some officers out the front with a cop dressed in the prisoner's overalls."

It took a few minutes to get everything ready and notify the officers outside of their plan. Once set, Ella, Justine, and the prisoner left using the side door, a few seconds ahead of the four officers who exited the main entrance guarding the fake prisoner.

Ella held their prisoner, Thomas Zah, by the arm, making sure he stayed in step with her. She didn't want anyone to see the handcuffs that kept her left hand attached to his right.

They were barely out of the building when he suddenly started yelling out his brother's name.

"Shut him up, Ella!" Justine said.

"Just get to the car so we can throw him in the backseat!" Ella answered, grabbing Zah's free hand and bending his elbow around behind his back. Zah ducked down and yelped, trying to pull Ella away from the parking lot.

A man ran around the corner of the building, spotted them, and yelled to the others. "He's over here!" Immediately there were shouts and the sounds of running footsteps.

"Keep going," Ella told Justine, who'd started to come back to help her.

As Ella forced Zah forward in a crouch, a rock whizzed by her head.

Justine was at her unit now, holding the back door open. "Hurry, Ella!" Justine jumped back as a chunk of asphalt bounced off the side of the door.

Ella felt a blow to the small of her back that knocked her forward a step, but the bullet-resistant vest beneath her shirt prevented any injury except a future bruise. Coming in the opposite direction, from the front parking area, were several people carrying signs calling for justice. The last thing she wanted was to get caught between two rival groups. Pushing the reluctant prisoner hard, Ella shoved him into the back of the vehicle, and landed on top of him.

When Justine didn't shut the door behind her, Ella turned her head and was surprised to see her partner swinging her nightstick at a man trying to shove a sign in her face.

"Damn!" Ella reached for her key and slipped out of the cuffs within five seconds, attaching it again to the front shoulder harness. Pushing off the prisoner and jamming him facedown onto the floorboards, she dove back out of the car.

"Forget about him. We've got to leave," Ella ordered Justine, blocking a blow with her nightstick, then kicking the man before her in the groin. When, instead of obeying, Justine turned to face the others coming up, Ella grabbed her by the belt and swung her around to the open back door. "Keep him down!" Ella pushed Justine inside and slammed the door shut.

Whirling around, she spotted three angry men and a young woman rushing up from the passenger side. Pulling out her Mace, Ella sprayed a stream of the chemical at the face of the closest person, a large man with an axe handle.

"Yow!" The man fell back, grabbing at his face and dropping the club.

As Ella aimed the spray at the others, they scattered. In an instant she jumped into the driver's side, closing the door.

"Here," Justine shouted, handing the keys over the seat back.

Ella concentrated on getting the unit started and trying to ignore the thump of rocks against the side of the vehicle. The engine roared to life just as she saw several officers approaching from two directions, armed with Mace and nightsticks.

"We're out of here," she said. "Hold on!" Ella flipped on the siren and emergency lights, and swung the vehicle out away from the curb. People scattered and she gunned the accelerator, speeding past the row of parked vehicles toward the main road. Behind her in the rearview mirror she could see the officers, Mace canisters out, wading into the troublemakers. The crowd gave ground quickly rather than encounter the unpleasant chemical.

Once on the highway, Ella switched off the emergency equipment. "Are you okay, Justine?" she asked, concentrating on putting distance between them and the station.

There was a pause, and Ella looked back to see Justine rubbing a bruise on her cheek. "I guess so. The guy hit me with the sign, and I lost my temper for a moment. Sorry."

"The main thing is we got out of there without any more damage done." Thomas Zah, a short, overweight man in his early thirties, was cursing now and kicking the back of the seat. "How's our prisoner? Can you settle him down a bit?" Ella waited a moment, and after she heard Zah grunt, the kicking stopped, but his cursing picked up in volume.

"I handcuffed his wrist to his ankle on the opposite side. I'll switch back to both hands once he decides to calm down a little. How about it, potty mouth?" Justine said sarcastically.

When Zah's expletives finally ended several minutes later, Justine cuffed the prisoner's hands together again. Ella kept the vehicle at a fast pace as she drove back to the station. The incident had rattled her considerably. She'd expected some kind of trouble, but not like this. Justine's reaction, to stay and fight, had taken her by complete surprise. She'd been prepared for the possibility that they'd have to defend themselves, but she'd never expected her partner to stop and attack. Not wanting to discuss it in front of Zah, she kept silent.

Mercifully, Justine did the same. At the moment, the silence between them was easier to cope with than attempting to communicate.

"You seem to be in a hurry to get back," Zah commented dryly. "Hot date?"

Ella didn't turn around, but she heard a thump, and Zah exhaled with a grunt. Could Justine have slugged him in the stomach?

"Oops, sorry about that," Justine muttered. "Guess my baton slipped when we went over that bump."

Zah didn't say another word, and for the moment, Ella decided to be thankful for the quiet.

———

"He's booked and in a cell," Justine said, coming into Ella's office a few hours later.

"I need you to clear up something for me," Ella said slowly. "When we got caught outside your unit, was it your strategy to make a stand right there and fight it out?"

"Just long enough to show them they had to back off."

Ella studied her cousin's eyes, and realized that Justine had enjoyed that confrontation. "Maybe you need to go to the gym and work out some of that hostility, Justine. You're wound too tight these days."

"I'll choose my own workout schedule," Justine snapped. "I'm in shape and I make sure I stay that way. When's the last time you went jogging?" she countered.

"I wasn't talking about physical fitness," Ella said, her voice as taut as Justine's now. "You need to work on your anger and hostility. If you don't want to talk about what's bothering you, then fine. But deal with it, Justine. Since the shooting incident, you've been off the wall with almost everyone you meet, and you've had a bad attitude for days. In order to save your career, I may have to recommend you go on administrative leave for a while."

Justine grew incredibly still. "You would do that, wouldn't you?" She shook her head. "I thought we were partners."

"Find out what it really means to be a cop's partner, then compare it to the way you've been acting. I think you've forgotten what it means to behave responsibly," Ella said, then turned her back on Justine to look in the file cabinet. The gesture had been one of dismissal, and when she turned around, Justine was gone.

Ella finished up preliminary reports on Lena Clani and Thomas Zah, then headed home. By then it was dark outside. Seeing a car tailing her, she felt herself tense up. But then the other driver flashed his lights.

Ella pulled over and waited inside the Jeep. As the sedan parked just in front of her, she recognized Harry's face and turned off her headlights. Knowing he was undercover, she left her vehicle and walked over to meet him.

Harry smiled and opened the door on the passenger side for her. "Transferring Zah sure got complicated for you today."

"Were you there?"

He nodded. "I figured Begaye might show up in Window Rock and try to connect with his family, taking advantage of the confusion. I told Blalock I'm around, and he's helped me keep an eye on Samuel Begaye's older brother, Jimmy, but Samuel hasn't made a move to contact him yet. I think he knows his family is being watched."

"I'm surprised Samuel didn't show up when we were transferring Zah. It was total chaos and a perfect opportunity for him."

"I didn't see him there, and believe me, I was looking hard. So far Begaye's managed to stay out of my grasp, but I'll get him," he said, his expression determined.

"What can I do for you now, Harry?"

"Blalock's man lost Jimmy Begaye as of an hour ago. If you see hide or hair of him, call me. I'm staying at Rob Brown's house in Farmington."

"The state cop?"

Harry nodded. "He and I have been friends for a long time."

"I'll keep an eye out," Ella said. She started to get out of the car, then stopped. "Hey, since you're already here, why don't you come to the house? Mom would love to have you over for dinner, and you know she won't breathe a word to anyone."

"I hear she's getting around pretty well now."

"Some days are better than others. Dawn's a handful for her, so I wanted to hire someone to help her with the cooking and the chores, but Mom wasn't having any of that."

He laughed. "Did you really expect anything different?"

"No," she conceded, "I know she loves taking care of people. It makes her feel useful. But I had to try."

"Purpose gives us direction," Harry answered. "I don't blame Rose for the way she feels."

"So, what do you say? Join us for dinner?"

"I'll be right behind you."

Several times on the drive to her house, Ella lost sight of the deputy marshal. He hung well back, making sure he didn't call attention to himself by appearing to be following her. Most local residents recognized her car even though it was unmarked.

When Ella arrived in front of her home, she was surprised to see that all the lights were out and her mother's pickup was not in the driveway. Rose and Dawn should have been home, unless her mom had needed to run a last-minute errand. But she didn't see Two either, and that was very unusual. He always came running up whenever any vehicle approached the house.

Whistling, she waited to see if he was off in some arroyo trying to dig out a rabbit. Ella stood beside her vehicle as Harry Ute pulled up. "I guess Mom must be running late. You didn't see her dog beside the road as you came up, did you?"

"The long-haired mutt named Two?" Seeing her nod, he added, "No, I sure didn't. Maybe your mother took him along for the ride," Harry said, looking around casually as he walked with Ella toward the back door.

"Not Mom. She leaves him here to watch the house." As Ella got closer to the house, a chill passed up her spine, and she stopped in her tracks. "Something doesn't look right, Harry. I think the back door is open. Let's handle this like a break-in."

Ella reached down and slipped her pistol out of its holster. As Harry did the same, she noted that his pistol had been hidden in the small of his back, covered by his denim jacket. Harry moved away from her so he could approach out of view of the door.

Ella reached the screen door and, despite the dim light, could see that the solid door behind it was open about a foot. She reached for the stone badger fetish her brother had given her years ago and it felt cool to the touch, a sign that there was no immediate danger. Yet instinct still told her something wasn't right. Signaling for Harry to cover her, Ella swung open the screen door and slipped inside the kitchen, crouching down after she flipped on the light switch.

The room became bright and clear with the quick flicker of the fluorescent light fixture, but everything inside looked normal. All the drawers were closed, and no cabinets appeared to have been rifled.

"Ella. Did you see this?" Harry was inside now, his pistol down by his side. He pointed to the doorjamb, which was splintered around the lock. They both turned for a closer look and saw the dirty smudge of a boot print scratched into the white paint next to the knob. A large crack in the wood showed where the dead bolt had been forced to give way.

"Kicked in for sure. But where are my baby and my mom? Did this happen after they left or before?" She moved quickly into the living room, pistol ready, and switched on a lamp.

"Ella! Careful and by the book! Remember?" Harry followed, covering her. "We need to make sure the bad guys are really gone."

He touched her shoulder, which was shaking slightly along with the rest of her. She looked at him, hoping he hadn't noticed, but there was an uncharacteristic softening in his eyes that told her he had. She tried to calm down and take a breath. "Harry, she's my daughter. I've got to know what happened here, and fast."

"Then cover me, and we'll clear the house." He crouched down and inched around into the hall. Ella followed close behind, ready to take on the intruder with deadly force, if necessary.

Two minutes later, they returned to the kitchen. "Nobody is in the house now, that's for sure," Ella said. "And there's no sign of anything missing or a struggle. If we'd had an intruder while Mom and Two were here, one or both would have taken him on," Ella added.

"Rose would have used her cane, I'll bet." Harry nodded. "Maybe your mom took Dawn and drove away in her truck, and the thief broke in after he saw them leave. Burglars do that a lot. Your family is probably safe, doing some shopping."

"That still doesn't explain Two's absence. Let me look around for Mom's purse or Dawn's diaper bag. If that's gone, it's a good sign that Mom and Dawn left under normal circumstances. Would you take the flashlight from the drawer beside the refrigerator and check outside for Two? I just hope nothing happened to that mutt. He'd die protecting my family."

"If he's outside, I'll find him. You check around one more time. Maybe your mom took a sweater for Dawn, or like you said, her diaper bag."

Harry left for the kitchen, and Ella went into the nursery. The diaper bag was on a chair, but the zipper to the diaper storage was open, and two disposable training pants were in there instead of the usual three. That could have meant that Rose grabbed a pair as she left, not expecting to be gone long, but making sure in case Dawn had an accident. Checking in her room, Ella noted that

Dawn's toy dinosaur was gone. Moving quickly through the house, she couldn't find it on the floor or in any other room.

As Ella reached the kitchen, she saw the beam of a flashlight outside. "Here dog, here boy!" Harry called from near the shed.

Ella checked in the refrigerator and saw an empty space where they normally kept one of Dawn's child-sized water bottles for when they went out. Rose must have grabbed it, too, when she left.

Looking around to see if there were any other clues, Ella glanced over at the hook by the door where the dog leash was kept. The phone rang just as she realized the leather lead was gone.

"Hello, Mom?" Ella grabbed the receiver before the second ring, knowing somehow who it was.

"Hi, daughter. I'm okay, and so is my granddaughter. We're at the vet's in Shiprock. It's Two. He became really sick all of a sudden, and I thought that mutt was going to die unless I did something right away. I tried to get hold of your brother, but he was away visiting a patient."

Ella couldn't speak for a moment, her heart was still pounding so hard. Harry walked in just then, and she smiled at him. "They're okay!"

"Is he okay? Yes, the vet says Two's going to be fine," Rose said, unaware that Ella had been speaking to Harry. "They pumped out his stomach, and they're going to run tests on the contents to see what made him so sick."

"That's great, Mom." Ella mulled things over in her mind. The problem with Two and the break-in could have been linked to whoever had been hanging around outside the night before. "Make sure the vet checks for poison. I have a feeling somebody put something in his food, or left some bait outside for him."

"But why would anyone do that? We don't have any close neighbors, and Two wouldn't harm anybody's lambs or chickens."

"Did you notice anyone hanging around the place today, Mom?"

"Two barked a few times, but that's all. Is something wrong at the house? You've got that tone in your voice," Rose said.

"Somebody kicked in the back door after you left, but I still haven't found out why. You just take care of Two, and Dawn, and I'll see you when you return. When do you think that'll be?"

"I'm about to leave now. Two is coming with us. The vet

doesn't need him to stay overnight, though he's still pretty weak. What else happened to the house? Is anything missing?"

"Except for a little splintered wood, nothing else seems wrong. Don't worry about a thing. By the time you get here, we'll have gone over everything one more time." Ella looked over to Harry, who nodded.

"You have company?" She paused, then continued quickly. "I hope you're not going to tell me it's my granddaughter's father." Rose still wasn't much impressed by Kevin. "My day's been bad enough."

"No, but it's someone you know." She looked at Harry and he nodded, understanding what Rose had asked. Ella knew that her mom liked Harry and knew his family from way back, but she wasn't about to announce his name over the phone and explain why Rose couldn't talk about it. "You'll see, Mom."

"So everything's okay with Rose and Dawn?" Harry asked as soon as Ella hung up. He put the flashlight back into the drawer. "I assume the dog is with your mother."

"She took him to the vet's. Mom thinks he may have been poisoned, but she couldn't get my brother's help because he'd gone to tend a patient."

"Is Two going to make it?"

"Yeah, he's even coming home now. Did you notice anything outside that would help us ID the person who broke in here?" Ella knew Harry was an expert at spotting evidence. She'd hated to see him leave her crime team to join the Marshals Service because of that.

"I found a place where it looked like a man had crouched and waited behind the shed. My guess is that he stayed there until your mom left. The tracks lead to the back door, and the prints seem to match the impression he made on the finish of the door when he kicked it in." Harry pointed out the marks on the door again. "It looks like the whole thing was planned."

"Poisoning Two made it easy for him to break in. With Mom and the dog out of the way, he had a clear field. I wonder what he wanted. I still haven't spotted anything missing." As Ella looked around the kitchen curiously, something suddenly occurred to her. "Do you suppose he broke in to leave something behind?"

"You mean like a bug or a hidden camera? Or maybe a bomb?" Harry's eyes narrowed at the thought. "You *have* made some enemies, Ella, like the guy I'm tracking."

"I don't think he's the bomb type. That's too cerebral for him. And where would he get the materials needed?" Ella looked under the sink, noting the pots and pans, which had replaced the cleaning solutions in the prechild housekeeping setup.

"I agree that it doesn't seem to fit Begaye's profile," Harry said. "If he was ready to attack, he'd probably come up behind you on a street corner or try and run you off the road. A bomb would be too impersonal for someone who enjoyed using his fists and feet to kill someone. But if he wasn't the one, then who was, and why?"

"Let's take another slow, careful look around. If you see anything that doesn't look right, check it out or let me know. Let's go from room to room and look for a subtle trap of some sort." Ella walked over to the refrigerator, opened it up slowly, and looked inside while Harry checked the fittings on the gas stove.

"Here's something, Harry. He took my last diet cola." Ella checked the trash can and shook her head. "Must have grabbed it when he left. My mom won't drink the things, and neither of us would ever give one to Dawn. And there should be two more apples in there."

"Unless your mom had a hungry and thirsty guest earlier today," Harry suggested.

Ella looked in the small plastic, lidded container between the cupboard and the refrigerator. "Then the apple cores and the can would have been here in the trash. She insists I use a glass, and wouldn't serve the drink still in a can to any visitor. I'll ask anyway, but I think we got off lucky if that's all that's missing."

"There's got to be more to it than that. Let's keep looking, and have your mom double-check. I doubt this guy went through all the trouble of poisoning the dog and breaking in because he was hungry. The fact that he brought poison along implies a plan being enacted. Anyone breaking in for food would act spontaneously out of hunger." Harry finished looking into the cupboards and moved into the living room.

On impulse Ella checked her bedroom, but found her father's old deer rifle and extra ammunition she kept in a locked drawer still there. All her and her mom's jewelry seemed undisturbed as well, though the only expensive items they owned were old silver and turquoise squash blossoms and rings.

Moving over to her computer, Ella spotted immediately that her CPU was still warm to the touch, though it had been switched off. "Harry, I'm going to start searching for fingerprints."

He called back from the hallway, where he was checking a closet and the heating unit. "Dust the refrigerator and the door, too. Do you have your kit in your Jeep?"

"Yes, and my old one is here on the top shelf in my bedroom closet. I'll get both and you can dust the kitchen for latents."

A half hour later, they gave up. All the surfaces they checked had been wiped clean, probably with window cleaner and paper towels, which they found, damp, in the trash. Ella put on a pot of coffee and heated up some mutton stew while they tried to guess the purpose of the break-in.

"Let's go over what we have," she said. "We've found no evidence of tampering or vandalism except for the door, nor was anything of any significance taken from the house."

"Yet the perp was very careful not to leave any physical evidence that could help us identify him," Harry pointed out. "And we've pretty much ruled out Samuel Begaye as a suspect. Who else might have it in for you at the moment, Ella?"

"Except for any of the relatives involved in Zah's transfer, I really can't think of anyone. And I think those people would have trashed the place, not just kicked the door open and had a light snack." Ella shook her head, stirring the kettle of stew. Seeing the flash of lights, she turned toward the kitchen window as a pickup came up the driveway. "Here's my family. Let's see what my mom can add to the mystery."

Thirty minutes later, Ella had no more answers than before. Rose had already given her the details of earlier events. She'd left with the sick dog and her granddaughter in a hurry, but hadn't noticed anyone hanging around outside.

As Rose looked at the scraggly brown-and-black-haired mutt,

who was now curled up on his folded quilt in the kitchen, she reminded Ella that he'd been barking earlier in the afternoon.

"When will the vet be able to tell you if Two was poisoned?" Ella asked as she sat with Dawn at the table, helping her eat small chunks of stew with a spoon. Nowadays Dawn managed to keep a high percentage of food off her chin and the front of her shirt. She hated bibs.

"He sent samples of the dog's stomach contents to a lab in Albuquerque. He'll get a call back probably tomorrow or the next day."

"I noticed the dog dish was only half-empty when I went out looking for him earlier," Harry mentioned. "You might want to save what's left just in case the vet needs more to go on."

Ella started to hand Dawn to her mother, but Harry stood and held up his hand. "I'll bring it in. You make sure your daughter has a chance to finish her dinner." He walked over to the kitchen counter and picked up the flashlight he'd used earlier, then slipped outside.

"You told me that the criminal the deputy marshal is hunting could be hiding in this community somewhere," Rose said. "But you still don't think he was the one who poisoned the dog or kicked in my door, do you?"

"No, and until I can figure out what our intruder was doing here, identifying him will be almost impossible. I'll mention what happened to my brother and my daughter's father and see if they have any ideas, or have seen any strangers around lately. In the meantime, I better fix that lock."

"Wait until tomorrow, and maybe your daughter's father can do the job. He's coming over to visit her anyway. At least that's what he said. Just let him know ahead of time so he can bring the right tools. He's always looking for an excuse to stay a little bit longer. You notice when he comes over it's nearly always around a mealtime?" Rose gave her a wry smile.

Harry came in just then, holding the dish of kibble, which was still more than half-full. Ella took it from him, then put the food in a plastic bag. "This didn't turn out to be the relaxing evening I'd planned for you."

He grinned at her. "Then ask me again."

Rose smiled at him. "You have an open invitation."

Ella looked at her mother in surprise. Her hopeful expression said it all. She'd found a new candidate for a son-in-law. Ella barely managed to suppress a groan.

"I better be heading back, but I'll stay in touch," Harry said, then wishing them good night, went to his car.

"He's a very nice man, daughter, and he's even better looking now that he's finally putting on some weight. Don't you think?"

"Mom, don't start."

"You two seem to understand each other so well, too."

"We're cops."

"Which gives you something in common." Rose stood and picked up Dawn. "I'm very glad you brought him by."

Alone in the kitchen, Ella looked at Two. "She'll never stop now. First it was Wilson and now it's going to be Harry. What have I started?"

Two looked up at her, yawned widely and slowly, then put his head back down.

"Well said, dog," Ella replied.

EIGHT

———× × ×———

Ella stayed up late fixing the back-door trim with two steel mending plates and some screws she found in the kitchen drawer. She then attached an old barrel bolt on the inside to serve as a temporary lock until it could be repaired or replaced.

It wasn't until that task was done that she felt safe enough to go to bed. Yet, even though she was exhausted, sleep eluded her. Ella continued to think about the break-in as she lay in bed, staring at the ceiling. Harry's search for Begaye and its ramifications, coupled with the conspiracy warning she'd received from Coyote, circled endlessly in her mind.

It seemed that she'd only just fallen asleep when Two woke her up, sticking his nose right up against her face. He was a big dog, and could easily rest his head on the mattress when standing next to the bed. She tried to push him away, but he'd go to the window, growl menacingly, then return to her bed. Ella grudgingly opened her eyes and watched him. The dog still wasn't feeling up to par, but he was clearly agitated about something.

Reaching for her pistol and the flashlight in her nightstand drawer, she crept out of her bedroom without turning on the light, clad in her long nightshirt and wearing fuzzy slippers. First she checked on Dawn, but the baby was sound asleep, curled up in a fetal position under her blanket. A moment later she entered the kitchen and opened the back door, letting Two out.

The dog ran a few feet, then stood beside Rose's herb garden, the hair on the back of his neck standing up straight. His deep growl was relentless, his eyes glued on something farther away from the house.

Ella moved forward cautiously, the bright moonlight a help as she tried to figure out what was spooking the dog. She checked the ground for footprints and made a visual search of the area surrounding the entire house, but saw nothing new or unusual that could explain Two's behavior.

Finally she went back to the kitchen door. Twice she tried to get Two to come inside, but the dog insisted on remaining on the back step, determined to guard the house from something only he could see.

As Ella went inside, she saw Rose standing in the dimly lit hallway, wearing her flannel robe and old moccasins.

"Something's not right, daughter. Two doesn't get upset for no reason."

"I know," Ella answered. "I get the strong feeling I'm missing something. But I looked carefully and nothing's out there now."

Almost in response, Two scratched on the screen. Ella let him in and the dog trotted to the end of the hallway and lay down.

"Danger seems to be pressing in on us," Rose said quietly.

Ella felt it, too. Her instincts told her that the dog *had* been poisoned, and that the incident was only the beginning of the bad times that lay ahead. "I'm going to call the station. If there's something going on in this part of the Rez tonight, I need to know about it."

Ella picked up the receiver and after several moments hung up. "Nothing unusual," she told her mother. "Just the regular number of DWIs, driving while intoxicated, arrests. I've asked that the patrolman in this area make additional passes around here, just in case."

"We might as well go back to bed," Rose said, unsatisfied. "If there's trouble, it'll find us soon enough. In the meantime, maybe we can get some rest."

Ella didn't get much sleep, but by seven she was ready to get up. Using the phone in her room, she dialed Justine's home number. All night long she'd thought about how to mend the rift between them. Things were starting to get busy again at work, and they had to find a way to pull together as a team.

"Good morning, Angela," Ella said, recognizing Justine's mother's voice. "I'm sorry to call so early, but I need to talk to Justine."

"She's already gone. Lately she's been having an early breakfast with a friend of hers."

"Is she at the Totah Cafe?"

"No, I believe they meet at his place."

The news surprised her. She hadn't known that Justine was seeing anyone that regularly. "Thanks, Angela. I guess I'll talk to her later at work."

Ella went into the kitchen and saw Rose was already fixing Dawn breakfast.

"Hi, Mom," Ella said softly, then went to give her daughter a hug. Dawn was sitting in a small wooden rocking chair Kevin had made for her, wearing her blue toddler-sized sweatshirt and matching sweatpants. She loved to rock back and forth, but the motion usually moved her around on the linoleum floor, so she could start by the sink and soon wind up halfway to the living room. When Dawn rocked, Rose would sometimes sing to her in Navajo, and Dawn was picking up some of the Navajo words already.

Ella grabbed a tortilla, smeared it with butter, then gave Dawn a bite from the tortilla, and a big hug and kiss, and headed to the door. "I'm going to get an early start today. There's a lot of pressing business I need to look into."

"If you find out what's going on, let me know," Rose said.

"I will, but I don't expect any simple answers." She shook her head. "I don't know why I'm saying that. I have nothing to go on."

"Of course you do. Your intuition is a gift, daughter."

Ella shrugged, then, with a wave, stepped outside. The fact was that this was more than just intuition, but she didn't want to alarm her mother. A cop learned to put little, seemingly unrelated incidents together and weave them into a whole until things became clear. She'd been doing that slowly, and the picture that was emerging made her skin crawl. Something big was happening, but she had no idea what it was or how to stop it.

Though it was out of her way, Ella stopped by the vet's in

Shiprock first. She would start by checking on what had happened to Two. The doctor, a young, enthusiastic-looking Anglo working off a student loan by working on the Rez, confirmed Ella's worst suspicions.

"The dog food was laced with rat poison," he said. "It's a good thing he hadn't eaten much and I was able to pump out his stomach in time. Has anyone in your household been trying to get rid of rodents lately?"

"No. My mother would never kill anything. She uses live traps and relocates any rodent that comes into the house. But in all fairness, we don't get very many. I think Two keeps them at bay."

"Then you think the poisoning was deliberate, maybe by a neighbor?"

"Something like that," Ella said. It wouldn't have been a neighbor. There wasn't anyone who lived that close except for Clifford, and her brother loved that dog.

"I'll let you know if I hear of any other poisoning incidents," the vet said. "I don't have a lot of experience with circumstances like these on the Rez, but usually they turn out to be more than an isolated incident. Somebody gets tired of barking dogs or there's a biting incident and they decide to shoot or poison the animals in the neighborhood. It goes on for a while until the individual is caught or the anger subsides. Or the other alternative is that it's a reaction to a problem dog who's coming into the neighbor's land and harassing their livestock."

"I doubt that either's the case here," Ella answered, not elaborating. The vet didn't need to know that it was probably linked to the break-in.

As she left the vet's office, Ella decided to make a stop by the hospital and pay Doctor Carolyn Roanhorse a visit. As the tribe's only forensic pathologist, Carolyn lived a lonely life, ostracized by most in the tribe. The People believed that someone who had physical contact with the dead couldn't help but be contaminated by the *chindi*, the evil in a man that remained earthbound after death.

Except for routine hospital work, Ella knew that this wasn't a particularly busy time for her friend. The tribe had enjoyed a time of peace since the incident last year with the terrorists.

Ella parked near the rear doors, then went directly to Carolyn's office down in the basement beside the morgue. Her large and outwardly intimidating friend was reading a trade journal and drinking some coffee.

"Hey, it looks like I caught you at a good time," Ella said.

"It's slow." Carolyn smiled. "During times like this I really wish I could help the doctors upstairs, but a lot of the patients don't feel comfortable with me around."

"What are you doing to keep busy?"

"Running lab tests for the staff, consulting with the doctors, and that sort of thing. I'm also catching up on my technical reading." She studied Ella for a long moment. "But this isn't a casual, friendly visit, is it?"

Ella shrugged. "Yes and no. I haven't been able to visit with you lately, and I wanted to drop by. But that's not the only reason."

"Trouble?" Carolyn sat up and leaned forward, resting her elbows on her desk. Ella noticed Carolyn's long hair was arranged into a bun as usual, but she had a silver barrette holding it together and was wearing lipstick and a subtle, flowery perfume. Usually Carolyn was indifferent to makeup.

"Someone poisoned Two, and picked a time when Clifford was unable to help out. My mom had to take the dog to a vet in order to save him. That same day we had a break-in, but nothing we know of was stolen except a diet cola and an apple or two. When things that don't add up start happening, I get worried."

"You think something bigger is brewing?"

"I feel . . . trouble in the air. I can't be more specific than that. But you know my hunches are seldom wrong. Has anything unusual been happening here at the hospital?"

Carolyn shook her head. "Not recently. Everything's pretty quiet. This time of year, people are busy getting ready for winter."

"If anything comes up—anything at all—let me know, will you?"

"Sure. I'll even ask around upstairs and see if anything new is going on."

"Thanks, Carolyn."

"How's Dawn and your mother?"

"Mom still won't let me hire anyone to come in and help, and that has me a little concerned. I'm afraid that Dawn will be too much for Mom, and that she may not admit it to me before disaster strikes."

Carolyn shook her head. "Rose would naturally be slow to admit she can't keep up with a toddler, but if she discovers that she needs help, she'll find a way to let you know."

"I still worry about her. Her legs have given her problems since the accident, and with cold weather coming on soon, the aches will get worse." Ella stood up. "But enough of that. I better get going."

"I've heard that Justine has been having problems at work getting along with people, especially you. Is there any truth to that rumor?"

"It's impossible to keep anything under wraps in this reservation," Ella said, and rolled her eyes. "To answer your question, yes, Justine and I have been having a few problems, but we'll work them out."

"Just remember that Justine's feeling more secure as a cop now that she's earned her own place in the department. She may begin to feel that she's in your shadow and needs to prove she's just as good as you are. I've seen that happen here with young residents and the teaching staff."

Ella shook her head. "No, that's not quite it. We had a misunderstanding. Normally we would have worked it out quickly, but I think Justine's having some personal problems and whatever's going on is really affecting her work. I might talk to my cousin Angela and try to find out what's going on. I'm certain she'd know, but whether or not she'll tell me is another matter. She's always been very protective of her daughters."

"Good luck." As her phone began to ring, Carolyn returned to work, and Ella waved silently, leaving the room.

Ella walked back out to her unit. Things looked peaceful around her, the air was fresh and clear, and the leaves were still on the trees. But there was an undercurrent of evil that was sending its spiderlike tendrils through everything around her. People were getting ugly and bad things were starting to happen. Wondering what was at the heart of it, and how long it would take for her to find answers, she headed back to her office.

———

Ella had just maneuvered into a parking space at the station when she got a call from dispatch, instructing her to switch to tactical frequency two for a message from FBI agent Blalock. She reached down and complied immediately.

"SI One now on TAC two. Go ahead, Fed One."

"This is Fed One. Ella, what's your 'twenty?'"

"Just arrived at the main station, Fed One. What's going on?"

"I'd like your backup before checking out a Rez house just east of Hogback. We're searching for a Navajo male bank robbery suspect. Your Sergeant Neskahi spotted a yellow sedan with the perp's license number and called us. He's got the vehicle under surveillance now at the white farmhouse, one mile east of where the old Turquoise Bar stood. The farmhouse is on the south side of the highway."

"Ten-four, Fed One. Has the suspect been observed?"

"Negative. Just the vehicle. No one has been seen in or near the farmhouse, either. We need to go search the premises. The suspect is of medium height and weight, Native American with very short hair, wearing a blue jacket and jeans."

"Ten-four. That description isn't very helpful. What's your 'twenty and what kind of backup do you have?"

"Agent Payestewa and I are in our vehicles a half mile west of the farmhouse. What's your ETA?" Blalock asked.

"Less than ten minutes if I hustle. I'll pass the farmhouse, then come back from the east. Once you see me go by, make your move."

"Sounds good, Clah. Neskahi will drive behind the house and cover the rear. We'll take the front and west sides. Be careful. The suspect indicated he was armed, though no weapon was seen during the robbery."

Blalock had good tactical training. In that respect the FBI Academy couldn't be beat. His plan seemed a reasonable alternative to waiting an hour or more for a SWAT team to assemble, and it was well thought out. If luck stayed on their side, it would be a smooth operation.

With her unmarked Jeep, Ella knew she wouldn't alarm anyone watching from the farmhouse, but she was careful not to stare when she drove past. Sergeant Neskahi's white police unit was hidden by some brush, and as he recognized her vehicle passing by, she saw him get on the move.

Ella waited for a civilian vehicle to pass her, then quickly turned around in a wide stretch of road and headed back toward the farmhouse.

Neskahi was already moving down the lane past the farmhouse when she pulled into the driveway. Ahead, Blalock's vehicle was coming to a halt almost at the front porch, and another she assumed was Agent Payestewa's moved up to the west side of the house, covering that side.

Ella left her Jeep, pulling out her own weapon about the same time as Blalock stepped up beside the front door. Out of the left corner of her eye, she could see Neskahi emerging from his own unit, shotgun ready.

Ella checked for signs of someone at the two windows on the east side of the house, noted both were curtained and closed, then ran to the northeast corner to cover Blalock.

"Open up! FBI," Blalock yelled, keeping one eye on the window to his right. Ella was watching the one to his left, and somewhere, out of sight, Payestewa was covering the west side.

"Woman by the front door!" The Hopi agent poked his head around the northwest corner. "She looks unarmed."

Blalock nodded, and stepped back as the door slowly opened, his pistol ready. "FBI agent, ma'am. Please step outside."

Ella watched as a thin, frightened-looking Navajo woman in her late fifties opened the screen door and stepped onto the porch. She was wearing a cotton dress with no belt at her waist, and high-topped shoes with white socks. "What's going on, Officers? Are you looking for the man from that car?" Her voice was shaking as she gestured toward the suspect vehicle underneath a nearby cottonwood tree.

"Yes. Is he here?" Blalock kept looking back and forth from the woman to the open door.

"No. He said the car wasn't running right and left it there. He ran off about a half hour ago, heading toward the Hogback Trading Post. He said he had a friend there who would drive over and fix it for him."

"Is there anyone else at home with you?" Ella asked, stepping closer, but still keeping an eye on the side of the house.

"No, I'm alone. That's why I wouldn't let the man in. He looked like he might be dangerous. Did he hurt somebody? Is that why you're looking for him?" the woman asked, brushing a lock of thinning black hair away from her face.

Blalock nodded. "You did the right thing by not letting him in. Was he carrying something, like a paper bag?" Blalock relaxed slightly, but still kept an eye on the door. Payestewa had moved close enough that he could hear the conversation too, and Ella could see Neskahi by the rear corner of the building.

"When he ran off, he stopped by the car to get a paper sack. How did you know?" the woman asked.

"That's what the perp had the teller put the money in," Blalock said, looking at Ella, who nodded.

"Would you allow us to search your house?" Ella asked. "I'm Investigator Clah with the Tribal Police. Sometimes a suspect you think has gone off is really hidden close by." Ella wanted to make sure the woman wasn't under duress, or a friend of the perp lying to get them to leave.

"Go ahead, Officers. But I'd like to go with you. I don't let anyone just wander around my home without me being there too."

Ella looked at Blalock, who nodded, knowing why she wanted to check out the residence. "We'll look together," Ella told the woman.

"You might want to take the sergeant and check out the Trading Post," Ella said to Blalock. "Maybe the perp switched cars."

"Good idea." Blalock waved Agent Payestewa over. "Lucas, check out the car, then look for footprints. Maybe he circled around or took off down by the river."

"I get the job because we Hopis are good trackers, right, boss?" Payestewa cracked.

"No, Lucas, it's because I'm in charge here, and if there's going to be a confrontation at the Trading Post, I've had more experience in a firefight. So has the sergeant."

"Well, I *am* a good tracker." Payestewa shrugged and walked toward the suspect's car, weapon out in the off chance he was hiding inside.

Blalock got Neskahi and they took off in a hurry in Blalock's vehicle. Ella watched until Payestewa waved that the car was clear, then she went inside with the Navajo woman to check out the house.

Five minutes later, Ella had verified that the woman wasn't hiding anyone inside, and that she'd never seen the suspect before. As she was giving Ella a description of the man, Ella realized that it fit Samuel Begaye down to the scar on the back of his wrist. Suddenly a call came though on Ella's handheld radio.

"He's long gone, Ella. One of the clerks at the Trading Post just discovered his pickup has been stolen. Neskahi is calling the Shiprock station, and they have officers checking the area now. I'll be back there in a few minutes, and we'll add what the woman knows to our information on the perp."

A half hour later, Ella was driving back toward Shiprock. Blalock and Payestewa were off pursuing the lead they had on the stolen vehicle, armed with the knowledge that the bank robber was probably Samuel Begaye, the escaped federal fugitive Harry Ute was after. Photos from a bank camera would verify that, and while they waited for that evidence to be turned over to them and processed, mug shots of Begaye were going to be shown to all the eyewitnesses. Harry Ute would be contacted, too, so they could better coordinate the manhunt.

Ella headed away from the scene knowing that Begaye's days as a fugitive were numbered.

NINE
——— ✖ ✖ ✖ ———

It was just after noon by the time she arrived at the station. Ella saw a dozen or so people gathered around the entrance, and she recognized a few of them from the disturbance at Window Rock. It was clear that Zah's relatives were lining up in moral support. But from the looks of it, the victim's family was also calling in the troops. Several Navajos were in the parking lot beside two pickups, and it looked like they had signs to wield.

Ella entered the building quickly after an officer stationed at the entrance unlocked the door for her. One way or another, she wanted to stay out of it this time unless it got out of hand. She had enough work to do today.

As Ella walked down the hall to her office, she saw a tall man in baggy black pants and polyester jacket leaning against the wall beside Justine's office door. As she got closer, Ella recognized Paul Natoni. The good-looking, oily-haired lowlife in his mid-twenties had a history of gang connections and misdemeanor jail time as a youth, though he'd never been convicted of anything, to her knowledge at least.

"Natoni, can I help you with something?"

"No, I'm just waiting for a friend."

"The jail's visiting rooms are on the other side of the building."

"You always assume the worst." He smiled patronizingly, folding his arms across his L.A. Raiders sports jacket. "For your information, I'm right where I should be."

"Oh, really? What are you waiting for, then?"

"I don't have to answer you. I'm not under arrest."

"Not yet," Ella answered. "But you're not supposed to be back here without an officer present."

"You're an officer, unless you just got fired."

"If you fail to answer my question, I'll have to ask you to leave the building."

"Threats?"   *WAITING FOR JUSTINE?*

"No, reality. I'll repeat. What are you doing here?"

"You're wasting your time. All you need to know is that I haven't broken any laws."

"Except loitering—unless you state your business here."

"Oh, come on! You've got to be kidding. Don't you have any real criminals to hassle today?"

"Either answer my question or leave the building right now."

"You can't kick me out." Natoni clenched his fists down by his sides and moved closer to her, squaring off like a pro wrestler in a staged confrontation.

Ella smiled slowly. "I started out in a rotten mood this morning, but you're brightening my day." In a lightning-flash move, she brought him to his knees with a painful pinch hold on the back of his hand. As he groaned, she twisted his arm behind his back, easing the pressure only slightly so he could stand. "Get up. You're leaving the building now."

As Ella hurried him down the hall, she wondered if he was somehow connected to their new prisoner, Zah. Slipping a man into the building to listen in on conversations and learn the layout would have been a good strategy.

As she reached the entrance, the officer on duty opened the door so they could pass through. Once Ella had forced Natoni outside, somebody in the group gathered on Zah's behalf recognized her as one of the officers who'd transferred him from Window Rock. Two women began hurling insults at her. She studied the faces casually, and slowly concluded that there was nothing to worry about yet, though it was clear that Zah's supporters blamed the police for his arrest.

Ella let go of Natoni's arm. "Go join your friends," she said, taking a step back away from him.

"You think I'm part of that crowd?" He shook his head. "These sheepherders mean nothing to me."

"So what were you doing inside the building?"

Natoni smiled. "I'm still not going to answer that."

"And I don't have time to play games."

Ella went back inside and strode down to the chief's office. His door was open as usual. As she knocked lightly on the door, the chief waved at her to come in.

She sat down on the chair across from his desk as he finished some paperwork. After a moment, he looked up. "Blalock has already briefed me by phone on the support you and Sergeant Neskahi gave him earlier. Good job. Now, what can I do for you, Shorty?"

"I wanted to warn you that many people in that crowd outside were involved in the disturbance at Window Rock when Officer Goodluck and I picked up Zah. So far they're playing it cool, but it may be a good idea to have some extra cops standing by just in case."

"Don't worry. I've been keeping an eye on things. You noticed we're already controlling access to the building? There are more people in the offices, out of sight, but ready if they're needed."

"By the way, I saw a small-time hustler named Paul Natoni hanging around the hall. He was one of the original Many Devils gang members several years ago. Any idea what he was doing in the building?"

"Maybe something to do with Zah?"

"I thought that too, but he denied it. On the other hand, he also refused to tell me what he was doing here."

"Natoni is bad news waiting to happen, Shorty. Run him out anytime he's not with another officer. I don't want him hanging around unless he's got specific business."

"I escorted him out this time," Ella said.

"Good. Let me know if you see him hanging around again."

"Will do."

Ella returned to her office. Today she had intended to look over all the arrest reports and files concerned with ongoing investigations. Maybe she could get a better feel for the trouble she sensed brewing.

After filing a quick report on the earlier assist at the farmhouse with Blalock, Ella went over every pending case in their area, but no matter how thorough her research, she simply couldn't find any signs of any conspiracy, or even of a link between cases that would hint at a greater problem.

It was midafternoon when Ella decided to take a break and walked to the vending machines down the hall. A moment later, after pulling the lever for a chocolate nougat bar, she heard quick footsteps coming toward her and turned around.

"I've been looking for you," Justine said coldly. "I heard that you ran off a friend of mine earlier today. Is that true?"

"That depends. Who's your friend?" Ella asked cautiously. She had a sinking feeling that it was Paul Natoni.

"The officer monitoring the door said that you forced Paul Natoni to leave. He was waiting for me in front of my office."

"The officer is right. I saw Natoni hanging around and I asked him what his business was here. He refused to give me an answer, so I escorted him outside."

"You had no right to do that." Justine's voice rose an octave. "He was waiting for me, and we were going out for a late lunch. I was the one who told him to wait by my office. Now you've managed to make me look like a fool."

"Keep your voice down, Justine," Ella growled, seeing three cops by the soft drink machine. "Paul was the fool. All he had to do was tell me the truth."

"You've crossed the line, Ella. You're my boss, but I have a right to a personal life."

"Which may be all you have if you keep falling apart like this on the job," Ella snapped.

"You can't fire me, Ella. That's not the way things work around here. So mind your own business."

Ella took a deep breath, struggling to keep her temper in check. "Listen to me very carefully, Justine, and this time, understand what I'm saying. Natoni is bad news. You and I both know that he's always around when there's trouble. That raises a lot of questions and none of them good."

"I know Paul has made a few mistakes, but what right do you have to smear his reputation?" Justine demanded. "He's my friend and, unlike you, a part of my personal life. So *back off*! I have a right to meet him for coffee, breakfast, or any other reason I can think of."

"Paul's attitude created the entire incident. Deal with it."

"I don't have to listen to you—not on something like this."

"Justine, you're becoming insubordinate, and that I can't tolerate. Either go to my office or get back to work. Your choice."

Justine spun around and stormed off, heading toward the rest room, cursing under her breath.

As Ella walked away, she heard Joseph Neskahi comment from the office he shared with two other sergeants. "What the hell's gotten into Justine? She flies off the handle all the time for no good reason these days."

"I think she's taking too many coffee breaks with Natoni," Sergeant Eddie Ben retorted. "It's either sleaze rubbing off, or way too much caffeine and sugar."

Ella spent the afternoon in departmental meetings with Big Ed and managed to avoid having to think about the problem for a while. The entire Tribal Police Department was being restructured, and everything, including patrol assignments, was being affected. Using the result of the latest stats, areas of concentrated population and greater criminal activity were being assigned more police officers. Since there were no additional officers, that meant shifting assignments and trying to take cops away from other, less populated areas with little crime.

By the time the last meeting was over, Ella felt ready to tackle any case—so long as it took her out of the station. As she returned to her own office to do paperwork, she saw that a note had been slipped under her door. She read it immediately.

It was a message from Justine asking Ella to meet her at Beautiful Mesa, a place not far from Ella's home, later that evening. She wanted a chance to talk to her privately so they could settle their problems. TRAP!

Ella breathed a sigh of relief. Maybe Justine would finally tell her what had been bothering her. Ella called Justine's office, but the message on voice mail informed her that she'd left for the day.

Ella checked her watch. It was almost time for her to leave as well. Grabbing her keys, she headed for the entrance. The groups of people involved in the Zah arrest had dispersed, at least for the most part, and the officer monitoring the door had obviously gone back to his regular duties.

Today, as she did every Wednesday, she'd go pick up Dawn and take her to visit her cousin Julian. While the kids played, Clifford would teach her about herbs and healing. She'd discovered an interest in herbs not long ago, and her brother had offered to teach her what he knew, which was considerable, supplementing what Ella could learn from Rose.

Ella was driving down the highway when a prickling sensation ran up her spine. She checked ahead on both sides of the highway, then looked in the rearview mirror. Sometimes cops developed radar for trouble, and that was the feeling she was getting now.

It wasn't dark yet, so she was able to study the cars behind her. Nothing seemed out of the ordinary. Braking quickly, she turned off the main highway and headed up a dirt track, constantly checking the area behind her. Any car joining her would raise a second cloud of dust into the air. Though she kept a careful watch on the track behind her, the only dust trail she could see was coming from her unit.

Still, the sensation persisted. Ella tried to ignore it, wondering if she was scaring herself more out of restlessness than any real threat.

Suddenly a huge flock of blackbirds rose from a field to her left, and Ella flinched, nearly swerving the Jeep to avoid the imagined threat. Chiding herself, she struggled to stay cool. Yet, no matter how she tried to reason it away, she could still feel a watcher's eyes on her.

She reached up, instinctively clasping the badger fetish at her neck. It felt hot. But of course, it would. It was warm in the car, and the sun had been shining directly on her since she'd turned west off the highway.

She took a deep breath, forcing her brain to rely on logic and push the irrationality of fear back. If someone were watching her from outside the vehicle, he would have selected high ground, but the hillsides around her were little more than contours in the terrain. Higher mesas were miles away.

She turned around and drove back toward the highway, then took another sudden, unexpected course to the north down an oil well service road. Again she failed to spot any vehicle following her, and in this section there was no place for anyone to hide, unless it was among the steady traffic running parallel down the main road a half mile to her right.

She thought of Begaye and the possibility that he'd decided to come after her now that he'd gotten enough money from the bank robbery to purchase suitable weapons. But Begaye had been an in-your-face fighter, and this cat-and-mouse game was just not his style.

Perhaps it was someone else who was part of the conspiracy she'd been warned about. But that was reaching. She had no idea what the supposed conspiracy was all about, or if it really existed at all. She'd certainly found no evidence of it so far.

Ella opted to remain vigilant, but to proceed as planned to her house. She'd accused Justine of being on edge, but clearly the problems at work were taking their toll on her, too.

Fifteen minutes later, Ella found Dawn in the living room playing quietly on the rug with all her stuffed animals. Rose was in the chair, asleep.

Ella saw her little girl look up and smile. "*Shimasání* sleepy."

Ella sat down on the floor and hugged her daughter. "You wore her out, didn't you, you stinker?"

Dawn laughed, and Rose woke up.

"I guess I must have dozed off," Rose said slowly.

"Mom, Dawn's an active kid, and she can wear anyone down. I sure wish you would let me hire someone—"

"No." Rose's tone was final. "That's not open for discussion, daughter. I am more than capable of looking after my granddaughter."

Ella said nothing, but made up her mind to talk to Clifford about it later.

"Will you be going over to your brother's hogan for your lesson on herbs?"

She nodded. "I'm running late already, but it couldn't be helped. Anything unusual happen around here today?"

Rose shook her head. "It's been quiet, and Two has been sleeping almost all day. I called Herman Cloud and he's going to replace the back door tomorrow, if it can't be fixed permanently."

"Sounds good. Just keep yourself safe, and listen to Two if he starts barking again. I'll be at my brother's for a few hours." She looked at Dawn. "Let's go play with your cousin."

"Cousin!" Dawn said happily.

Ella smiled. "She adores my brother's son, and he's so kind to her. He plays with her, and he never gets tired or impatient."

"I'm glad you take her over there to visit. Sometimes I wish my daughter-in-law would bring my grandson over to play more often, but I think she and your brother are having troubles."

"I've felt the tension between them too, and I'm afraid I may be part of the problem."

Rose shook her head. "No, the real reason is that your brother has too many patients. He doesn't know how to stop working."

Ella nodded. "I certainly understand that. I'm that way, too."

"It's more so with Clifford. You make time to be with your daughter, but he's always working, and that seldom leaves time for his wife or his son."

"But that's the way it tends to be in very traditional Navajo families anyway. Are you sure you're getting both sides of the story?" Ella asked, wondering if Loretta had come to complain.

Rose nodded. "My daughter-in-law hasn't said a word to me, but I have eyes and I see what's been happening. When a patient comes to your brother, he's there for them, and that's how it should be. But I think he should send some of them to another of the healers in the area."

Ella nodded. "Let me guess what this is leading to. You want me to talk to him?"

Rose smiled. "He might listen to you."

"He's going to think I'm butting in, and he would be right."

"It's for my grandson's sake that I ask, and for his parents' marriage."

"I know, but in all fairness, I understand how my brother feels. I have a job that often seems to take all my time. It's even more difficult for my brother. People go to him when they need a *hataalii* because they know he's the best. Turning them away goes against everything a *hataalii* is.''

"But he has to find a way to cut back. There are others who can step in and fill whatever void he leaves. He may have forgotten it, but he needs his wife and his son to be happy."

"Okay. I'll mention your concerns, but that's as far as I'll go. He's never meddled in my personal life, and I owe him the same courtesy."

"All right," Rose said at last. "Be careful when you drive over there. It isn't far, but it'll be night soon, and the desert has its own dangers."

TEN

✖ ✖ ✖

Ella strapped Dawn into her car seat, then started down the road to Clifford's home, which was farther from the highway than her mother's place. She had a feeling Loretta would welcome her visit as much as she would the plague. Her sister-in-law these days resented anyone and anything that took some of Clifford's precious time away from her and their son.

Her complaint was legitimate. Yet once or twice when Ella had suggested to Clifford that maybe they should cancel or at least scale back the lessons, her brother had been adamant about continuing. Ella suspected it had become a matter of wills, both of them determined to have their own way.

Ella pulled up to her brother's house a short time later. Loretta was outside, dressed in a traditional long skirt and velveteen blouse fastened at the waist with a woven belt. Her hair was in one long braid down her back. Loretta was playing catch with Julian, using a rubber ball. After she saw Ella's vehicle, her expression became one of barely disguised hostility.

The second Ella set her daughter down, Dawn ran toward Julian, a slender boy nearly four years old. He seemed just as happy to see her.

"When is this all going to end, Ella?" Loretta said bluntly, joining her. "I understand that you and my husband plan to give talks together on herbs and healing at the college." Loretta crossed her arms over her chest.

"We hope to begin next semester. It will be a way to show the tribe that we aren't having any trouble getting along. People are looking for a reason to distrust both of us. Surely you've heard the talk."

"I know what people suspect. When you pushed my husband off that roof last year, you saved his life. Yet before long, the rumor got started that you'd meant to hurt him instead, and that your family's legacy was catching up to you both. Now that you're spending more time together, they're convinced you'll corrupt him."

"You're his wife. You should know that's a vicious lie."

"Yes, I know the truth, but people delight in gossip. If you weren't so focused on protecting your own image, you'd stay away from here before this ruins his reputation."

"I refuse to allow these lies to cow me, and I think my brother feels the same as I do on this."

"He wants to show everyone that you haven't turned to evil— that he's not the only force for good left in the family. And you're allowing him to continue to do this—no matter what the cost to him—because you're afraid. You want to wear that badge proudly, and the more the gossip spreads, the worse it becomes for you."

"Sure, I love my job, but I'm not sacrificing my brother so I can make things easier on myself." Ella saw Loretta's expression and knew her words had fallen on deaf ears. Her sister-in-law was young, pretty, and almost as stubborn as her husband.

Clifford came out of the hogan finally, and seeing the children, picked up Dawn. Julian remained by his side, tugging at Clifford's pant leg. Then Clifford put Dawn down and picked up his son, ruffling his hair.

Loretta glanced at her, and Ella saw the anger on her face. "Why is it that his own family never comes first with him?" she asked quietly.

Clifford put his son back down, and as the two children moved off to play, he walked over to join them. "It's good to see you're finally here, sister," he said, a mild reproach in his voice.

"I ran into a bit of trouble earlier and got held up."

"Don't worry. He'll always make time for you and your daughter," Loretta said harshly. "Now all I have to do is explain that to a son who never sees his father."

Clifford's eyes narrowed in disapproval, but Loretta turned without looking at him and walked away toward the children.

"Come into the hogan and we'll begin," Clifford told Ella.

Ella looked at Dawn and Julian, wondering if she should leave her daughter in Loretta's care now.

"Don't worry. My wife is angry at me, not at them. She loves the children."

Ella watched Loretta sit down on the ground and begin a game of rolling the ball back and forth. Seeing how well the kids responded to her, Ella relaxed.

"Your wife does have a legitimate complaint, brother."

"This, I know. But for now, I can't slow down. There are a lot of older people getting sick now that the weather is turning colder. They worked too hard getting ready for winter, and have become worn down. I'm one of the few medicine men who still know most of the Sings and healing ways."

Ella followed her brother inside the hogan, sitting on the south side as was customary. Clifford was a good teacher. He placed the different herbs he'd collected on a blanket, making her identify each and explaining where on the reservation they could be found. Then they discussed how to make different infusions with the medicinal herbs. Instead of letting her write things down, Clifford kept quizzing her until she could repeat it back to him.

The hour passed quickly, and before Ella knew it, it was time for her to go. "I've got to get back to Mom. She was really looking tired today. Dawn is almost too much for her sometimes."

"And she still won't let you hire anyone?"

Ella shook her head. "I'll keep hammering at her, and hopefully I'll wear her down eventually." She paused, then continued. "By the way, there's something I want you to think about. I really appreciate these classes on herbs. It's an interest I'm eager to pursue. But I think we should rethink our plans to give lectures together to youth organizations and at the college."

"Does this have something to do with what my wife has been telling you?"

"This isn't about her, it's about you. You're running yourself ragged. You're trying to be all things to all people, and before you realize it, years will have gone by and you'll have missed your son's childhood. He's going to grow up not having the chance to know you very well. This may have been okay if your brother-in-law was around. The wife's brother plays a large role in a child's life. But since he's not, that puts a different slant on things. Your boy needs time to know you, his father, and you need to be there for him."

"I think this may be more of a reaction to what's missing in your family's life than what's wrong with mine," he said gently.

The blunt observation took her aback for a moment, but she considered it, then spoke. "No, that's not true. I really don't want Kevin to have a larger part in Dawn's life. He's not ready to be a full-time dad, and forcing it would be a mistake. I'd just hate to see you miss out on the best part of your son's life. They grow up fast, and one day you're going to look around and see that the boy is gone and it's too late to make up for lost time."

Ella walked outside with Clifford and picked up her daughter from where she was playing. After having Dawn say good-bye to her cousin and aunt, Ella carried her back to the car. Clifford watched as she placed her in the car seat. "Don't miss out on being a parent," she reiterated. "Nothing will ever mean more in the long run."

"I'll give what you've told me some serious thought."

As Ella slipped behind the driver's seat, Clifford leaned inside the open driver's-side window. "I've heard some rumors that there's serious trouble between you and our second cousin," he said, avoiding using Justine's name. "Is that true?"

She sighed. "It is."

"Did you also know that some of the traditionalists are saying that it's just another sign that you're turning to evil?"

She scowled. "I should have known they'd come up with something like that. Heck, face it, these days if I so much as sneeze, somebody will suggest it's an omen. Who told you, by the way, about my assistant and me? I know you don't like to use names because they have power, but I need to know."

"Jeremiah Manyfarms. You met him here, with our professor friend."

"Besides teaching at the college, what do you know about him?" Ella asked.

"I heard that he was a medic in the army, but now he's learning about traditional medicine. I treated him just the other day for a sudden headache," Clifford explained. "But getting back to the trouble between you and our cousin. Can you mend the relationship?"

"I don't know. Maybe. But she's acting really weird. I'm not sure about her anymore—and that's something I never thought I'd be saying about her."

"I've also heard that she's taken up with someone who won't do her any good. He used to be in a gang, and he's nothing but trouble. And that, by the way, didn't come from our friend's co-worker at the college."

"I know who you mean," she said, realizing her brother was referring to Paul Natoni. "But she won't listen to me on that."

"He's like a fat snake putting on a new skin. Did you know that he's one of the New Traditionalists?"

Ella cringed at the term. The New Traditionalists were a direct product of a tribe caught between two worlds, and either reflected the best of two cultures or the worst.

Clifford shook his head. "He's like many of the others in that group—opinionated and trying to force his beliefs down everyone's throats. He wears a headband to link himself to our heritage, and I understand that he's got Indian art all over his house. He's even trying to learn to speak our language."

"Are you telling me that he's no longer the rotten piece of garbage he used to be?"

"No, not at all. The changes are all on the outside, not in his heart. But then again, I have no love for the New Traditionalists. In my opinion, they're all show and no substance. They draw the line at leading the traditional life they claim to love when it means giving up their air conditioning and cable TV. They're part-time Navajos."

Ella laughed. "You're too harsh a critic."

Clifford shrugged. "I find the whole thing irritating. And knowing that their numbers are growing doesn't do much to endear them to me. They're gaining power and influence among The

People, and I think that's a dangerous trend. They've even got that half-Navajo, Branch, using his radio program to support the group. The New Traditionalists, you see, intend on using technology to promote the tribe's interest and culture."

"Any association with Branch is bound to result in a disaster. I know the man well enough to see he's got his own agenda."

"He sure gets people talking about his radio show, and I guess that makes his advertisers happy. Freedom of speech can be an impressive moneymaker even in misguided hands." Clifford shrugged.

"But we can't do anything about it except wait until the *Dineh* finally see the truth for themselves," Ella said, switching on the ignition.

"Tell Mom that I'll stop by and visit with her soon, sister."

"She'd like that, but she knows how busy you are, and won't really be expecting it."

"So I'll surprise her."

After Ella left Clifford's, she thought for a while about the New Traditionalists. If there was any truth to the conspiracy she'd been warned about, maybe that group was at the heart of it. Or maybe not. The more she thought about the alleged conspiracy, the more far-fetched it seemed. There was absolutely no evidence to support it. It had the earmarks of a hoax, or maybe it was just someone's idea of a good joke to play on her. She knew Joseph Neskahi, for one, would think it incredibly funny to drive her nuts looking for something that simply didn't exist.

Of course, if it was he, she'd have him directing traffic for a month.

Ella took Dawn inside her mother's house and put the sleepy child down to bed, reading her a story, as was their custom. Then she returned to the living room, where Rose was crocheting. "I've got to run one more errand, Mom. Can you check in on her, and maybe feed her some dinner if she wakes up, or are you still pretty tired?"

"No, I slept some more while you were gone, and I'm feeling better. I just haven't been resting well at night." She walked with her daughter to the door. "Where are you off to now? More police business?"

"Not really. I got a note from my second cousin asking me to meet her at Beautiful Mesa. I'm hoping that she'll finally tell me what's been bothering her, and we can settle our differences."

"She's a good woman. Give her a chance."

"She's always been my favorite cousin, Mom. But she's really been a pain in the neck lately."

"Be patient. I know she thinks the world of you, down inside. I'm certain that you two can work things out."

Ten minutes later, Ella was on the way down the highway. Turning off toward Beautiful Mesa, she drove over a small hill, then as she reached the cliffs of the mesa, saw a small fire burning. Expecting to find Justine there, she drove her Jeep off the path toward it.

The terrain was pretty solid, and a short time later, Ella stood by the abandoned campfire, composed of juniper branches. From the smell, it appeared someone had used gasoline to start the wood burning, and it was pretty hot, though in no danger of spreading unless the wind came up.

She looked around, but didn't see anyone in the area, so Ella brought the shovel from her car and quickly smothered the burning wood with sand. As she was about to return to her patrol unit, she heard footsteps and Justine walked up.

"What's going on?" Justine asked.

Ella filled her in. "Maybe someone passing through got cold and dragged some dead branches from a few junipers. I didn't see anyone around, and since the wind sometimes picks up after midnight and sparks could ignite the nearby brush, I thought I'd better put it out."

Ella walked with Justine back to where both their vehicles were parked, about fifty feet from the dirt road. "I'm glad we were able to meet like this. It's private out here and we'll cheat all the gossips." She paused, then added, "I've really hated the tension between us, Justine."

Justine nodded. "I'm sorry, Ella. I feel as if I've been wound up in knots. Every morning when I get to work I'm already so tense I just explode. I know that the chief was ordered to do away with Harry's position, but carrying his load of work and mine is really hard. And it's not fair. I can never catch up these days. When I make progress, the best I can say is that I'm less behind than I was. I hate that."

Ella nodded. "I wish we'd had this talk sooner, but rest assured I'll talk to Big Ed. We can't hire someone new, but I may be able to have someone else transferred over to our team, maybe even part-time. Sergeant Neskahi has always been available in a pinch for investigations, but to be honest, we're spread pretty thin all over the department. The sergeant just doesn't have the training Harry and you have for specialized forensic work, so I haven't got a clue as to who might be available to take some of the weight off you in the lab. But I apologize for my part in the misunderstanding with Big Ed on the robbery at the convenience store. I should have gotten to him first with a report."

"It probably wouldn't have mattered. Regardless of how it was explained, the fact remains that I was the one who screwed up. I'm going to do my best to try and get a full eight hours sleep and to keep a lid on my temper. I can't let things keep getting to me like they have."

"And I'll try to butt out of your personal life, too, Justine. I was over the line on that one. You were right. I apologize."

"Apology accepted," Justine said, then smiled. "I'm really glad I got your note, Ella. We needed this talk away from work, here on neutral ground and away from distractions."

Ella gave her a quick look. She hadn't sent Justine a note. Her cousin had sent one to her. Ella started to say something, but Justine continued, going on to something else. Intending to bring it up later, she didn't interrupt. Silently Ella wondered if one of the other officers had set this up, hoping things would work out somehow.

Justine stopped by Ella's car as she put the shovel in the back compartment. "Sometimes your life seems so organized and well planned in comparison to mine, Ella."

"Believe me, it's not. I just have more responsibilities these days that determine what I do and when, giving me a de facto schedule."

Justine mulled it over for a moment. "That makes sense."

"What about you?" Ella asked gently. "Now that you've lived the life for a while, do you regret having become a cop?"

Justine shook her head. "No, but it does carry a price, as you often said in the past. Sometimes it seems that work is at the center of everything I do and think."

A vehicle passed them on the road, slowing down briefly, then speeding up. Justine, like Ella, never took her eyes away from it, tensing for a moment, then relaxing after it went by.

"For a moment I thought it was Big Ed," Justine said. "He has a dark pickup like that."

"Yeah, I thought it was him, too, but if it had been the chief, he would have stopped. It was just someone curious about two women talking by the side of the road after dark."

"Yeah, well, now that you put it that way," Justine said.

"I'll see you tomorrow," Ella said, wondering if the person who'd set up the meeting by leaving the notes had come by to check and see if the plan had worked. Tomorrow, when they had a spare moment, she'd tell Justine what she suspected, and maybe together they could figure out who to thank.

"See you at the office bright and early. And, Ella?" She paused for a moment as if uncertain how to word what she wanted to say. "I'm glad things are back on track between us."

"So am I." Ella watched her drive away, then started her own vehicle. She was ill at ease out here all of a sudden. Checking the rearview mirror every few minutes, she drove around until she was certain no one was tailing her. At long last, telling herself that this time her instincts had to be wrong, she drove home.

ELEVEN

✕ ✕ ✕

Ella had been in her office for almost an hour when Joseph Neskahi knocked on the door.

"Hey, Ella. Do you know if Justine's coming in today? She's not in her office or the lab, and I haven't seen her around."

"As far as I know, she hasn't phoned in sick," Ella said. "Let me have a look, and check with the front desk."

The same uneasiness that had plagued her all night long began to gnaw at her again. She asked the duty officer, looked around the station, in Justine's office and the lab, and even checked the rest rooms, but there was no sign of her cousin.

Not seeing Justine's police vehicle in the parking lot, Ella returned to her office and called Justine's home. Angela answered the phone.

"I was just wondering if Justine's sick today," Ella said, making sure her voice remained calm and steady. She didn't want to alarm her cousin Angela.

"She's not with you?" Angela's voice tensed. "I know she came home yesterday, told us she'd received a note from you, and then went out to meet you later in the evening. As far as I know, she never came back. I thought she might have spent the night at your mom's place. What's going on?"

"She did meet me last night, but I never left a note for her. Actually, I received one that I thought was from her, and that's how we both ended up meeting at Beautiful Mesa. By any chance, did you see the note she got?''

"I think it's on her dresser. Wait, let me go check." Angela came back. "No, it's not here. She must have taken it with her. Is my daughter all right?" Fear tainted Angela's clear voice.

"I'm sure she is. Please don't worry. She probably went to see a friend after we talked, and spent the night," Ella said, thinking of Natoni.

She heard Angela's long sigh. "That may be. My daughter wouldn't necessarily check in with me. We just don't talk much lately. She's so tense all the time, I try not to ask her any questions that will make her angry, and she seldom volunteers anything. It hasn't been easy."

"I'll call you as soon as I find her," Ella said, sensing how worried her cousin was.

"Do that, please. All I know for sure is that she went to meet with you, hoping to work out that problem you two have been having at work."

Ella remembered the pickup that had driven by that reminded her of the chief's truck. For the first time she was forced to consider the possibility that whoever had sent the notes hadn't had good intentions at all. There was the chance they'd been set up somehow. Instinct told her that Justine's failure to show up was no coincidence. Something was wrong, and there was no time to lose.

Ella went out into the "pigpen," the office three of the sergeants shared, and found Joseph Neskahi. "Are you free right now?" she asked him.

"If you need me, I am," he replied.

"I'd like you to ride along with me," she said, then filled him in as they headed to her unit. "I can't find Justine. Apparently she didn't come home last night or call in sick this morning either. Nobody has heard from her since yesterday. I know she's been acting strange lately, but Justine's never been this irresponsible. I have a feeling something's happened to her."

Ella drove in silence, not ready to tell Joseph the details of her meeting with Justine last night. As she glanced over at him, she realized that the veteran officer knew there was more going on than she'd said, but hadn't breached her silence out of respect.

"We're going to Beautiful Mesa," she said at last, and filled him in on her meeting with Justine the night before.

"Do you have the note that Justine supposedly sent you?"

She nodded. "It looked like her handwriting. I would have noticed it otherwise."

"Maybe her vehicle broke down and she's having radio problems. Or perhaps she stayed with a friend, overslept, and is on her way to the station right now. She didn't call because she was hoping that no one would notice she was late."

"I don't buy it. That doesn't sound like Justine," Ella said.

"I hear what you're saying, but lately Justine hasn't been acting like Justine," Joseph pointed out.

Ella shook her head. "There's more going on."

"Your intuition?"

She knew what he was thinking. Her intuition, a part of the "gift" many attributed to her family's legacy, was legendary at the station. The inescapable fact was that her hunches usually paid off. "All I can tell you is that something's very wrong. I can just feel it."

They finally arrived at Beautiful Mesa, and she turned off the road at the same place she and Justine had been last night. The muscles in her stomach were so tense they ached. She left the unit wordlessly, and Joseph followed. Though he hadn't spoken, she could sense the same tension in him.

"Look over there," he said, breaking the silence.

Ella saw him purse his lips and cock his head to the side, pointing Navajo style. For a moment her breath froze in the back of her throat. The sergeant had found what appeared to be a shallow grave. The ground around the mound was disturbed, probably by a shovel, and was darker, filled with what looked like ash and burned plant debris.

"Was that here yesterday when you were around?"

"It was evening and I didn't notice. All I saw was a small campfire about thirty yards ahead. I'd just put out the burning branches by smothering them with dirt when Justine drove up. I could smell gasoline or some similar accelerant on the wood, probably used to start the fire."

"Let's go take a closer look at the place where the fire was, then we can check out the mound," Joseph said, walking ahead slowly.

She recognized his reluctance to go poking around a possible grave site. Despite being modernists, they'd been taught the same thing—stay away from the dead. And according to tradition, until four days had passed after the death, the *chindi*—the evil in a person that remained behind—would not have departed yet. They weren't even supposed to say the dead person's name during that time period, or touch something that belonged to the person. If you did, the *chindi* would come after you. You'd get sick for sure, and other terrible things would happen to you.

That belief had protected the *Dineh* from contagion and disease at times, but for a law enforcement officer, it only served to make an unpleasant duty even more difficult.

The burned juniper branches she'd smothered with shovel-loads of sand were easily uncovered. Neskahi poked around the branches gingerly with his boot, but it was pretty obvious what was there.

"I guess we need to check out that mound now. It could be an animal someone buried. It looks shallow," Joseph said as they walked back toward the disturbed ground, stopping ten feet away.

"Maybe." Ella's voice was taut as she tried to estimate the length of the mound, hoping it was too short to be a human body. Even the possibility that Justine could be lying beneath there terrified her.

Knowing that as the ranking officer, it fell to her to set the example, she took a few steps closer to the apparent grave and studied it closely, trying to remain objective. "We'll have to use our hands only. We don't want to disturb or lose any evidence. Keep an eye out for footprints or marks around the mound, too. We have to preserve the site in case it turns out to be a crime scene."

They looked around carefully, but there were no tracks other than their own within twenty feet of the site.

"Except for a few of what look like shovel or digging-tool scrapes, the tracks have been obliterated. Sand has been thrown over them, and a branch was used lightly, wiping out any marks on the sand," Neskahi pointed out, putting on one pair of latex gloves, then another pair over them. This prevented touching something that had touched the dead, and was accepted procedure by Navajo cops.

Ella did the same, extracting the gloves from her jacket pocket and putting them on as she spoke. "I suspect that whatever's there isn't someone's pet. This is something else, and whatever it is has been burned. Smell the gasoline still in the soil, along with all the ashes and burned debris?"

Even as she said the words, dread pried into her. She'd confronted death and loss before. Yet nothing, not even her father's murder, had prepared her for what this might be. She'd been here less than half a day ago, and her cousin had been with her. Now Justine was gone, and there was this one solitary grave. She needed to keep a cool head, but the iciness in her stomach and the prickling sensation all over her body fought against that resolve.

Joseph took a deep breath, holding his hands down at his sides as if they were already contaminated. "Maybe we should call in the coroner first."

She smiled hesitantly at him. "Dr. Roanhorse isn't about to dig, my friend, especially until we've confirmed that a body is here."

He nodded, then following her lead, crouched and began moving the sand aside with gloved hands.

She wondered if the sergeant would have an Enemy Way done, the Sing to remove contamination. She didn't really believe in that, but she felt dirty as she moved the sand, ashes, and dark debris particles aside, working to uncover what lay beneath. She would shower for a long time before she touched her daughter tonight.

Ella worked quickly, wanting to make up for Joseph's slow pace. Fear drove her. The possibility that she'd find Justine buried there filled her with dread so intense she could scarcely breathe. Then, slowly, the ground became warm enough to feel the heat through her double layer of gloves. It was obvious whatever was burned here had become very hot, and the residual heat was still present in the soil.

The debris began to look more like fragments of cloth. She wanted to stop, but somehow willed herself to continue, swallowing the bile at the back of her throat. A heartbeat later, she uncovered a charred piece of bone big enough to be part of an arm or leg. It was still smoking, and she had to drop it to avoid melting a hole in her gloves.

As she brushed the ash-laden dirt aside, the heated remnants of a shattered, badly burned human skull emerged. She wanted to vomit, but feeling Joseph's disgust and knowing he was watching her, she stood up slowly and took a deep breath.

"We have to stop now until the rest of the remains cool off. Whoever did this was almost successful in destroying the skeleton. The ME is going to have a hard time with this." Ella took off her first pair of gloves, put them in an evidence bag, sealed it, then took off the other pair.

"There's certainly no way to tell who that is," he said slowly, standing up and taking a step back.

What he really meant was that there was no way to tell if that was Justine.

"There was only that one fire when you were here last night?"

A shudder ripped through Ella. "Just the one you poked through over there. It had been left burning. I assumed that some- one had stopped to get warm and set fire to some fallen branches with a little gasoline."

"Justine saw it too?"

She nodded. But she had been the only one to see Justine, ex- cept for whoever was in that pickup. And as far as her cousin Angela knew, Justine had come here to meet her and never re- turned home. The possibility that she was being framed hit her suddenly.

She pushed back the thought. She had no evidence to indicate that it was Justine who lay buried in the fire pit before her. She was jumping to conclusions. Her cousin could show up at any mo- ment. Ella held on to that bit of logic and hope, knowing that to think anything else now would render her useless.

"I'll call Dr. Roanhorse," she said. "You call Big Ed and let him know we've found a body, and get Ralph Tache over here with the crime scene van."

"That will only make it you, me, and Tache working the scene. We're going to need some more help," Neskahi said.

She thought of Harry, but he was undercover, and no longer part of the department, though she might be able to get his help one way or the other. But if Samuel Begaye was behind this, she wanted Harry out there tracking the dirtbag. "There's FB-Eyes and Paycheck. They'll need to be part of this anyway."

"You want to call them or should I?"

"I'll take care of it." Ella grimly pulled out her cell phone.

Blalock and Payestewa arrived in the senior agent's vehicle a few hundred yards behind Dr. Carolyn Roanhorse's ME van and Ralph Tache in the crime scene vehicle. Ella waited for them by her own Jeep.

Carolyn reached her first, the ME's expression showing more emotion than usual. "You look like hell, Ella. Don't you think you should get out of here?" she asked quietly.

"I can't. I have to know if that's Justine."

"That type of ID is going to take some time. You know that."

"Yeah, I do," she admitted. "It's going to be hell waiting," she said. "But in the meantime, I have a job to do. I'm just finding it hard to stay focused. The possibility that it might be Justine's body over there scares the daylights out of me."

"I'll do the lab work as quickly as I can. But let me get started with the preliminary examination. I just hope we have enough of the remains to make a positive ID."

Carolyn slipped under the yellow crime scene tape Ella and the sergeant had erected and walked over to the grave. Neskahi and Tache followed, along with Ella. The partial skull was visible, along with the long bone that Ella had unearthed. "I hope you all don't think I'm going to dig up the rest of what's there. That's not my job." Carolyn stared at Joseph, who looked as pale as the sand-colored shirt Blalock was wearing.

Ella looked at the agents as they all put on their latex gloves. Payestewa was dressed up like a Hollywood version of an Indian-turned-cowboy. He was wearing a Stetson, a new pin-striped western-style suit, and shiny new boots.

Ella started to pick up the shovel, but Blalock beat her to it. "You shouldn't have to do this. Not this time, at least. We'll handle it." Blalock handed Payestewa the tool. "This is a job for younger men."

Payestewa scowled, but didn't argue. As he worked, Tache continued to take photos, recording everything. A short time later, a half dozen large fragments of bone and many smaller pieces had been uncovered from the fire pit that served as a grave. All of the soft tissue was destroyed, and most of the bones were charcoal. With only the upper portion of the skull and what Carolyn identified as a femur, there was scant evidence to work with, though the remains were human. From the size of the skull, Carolyn could only conclude that the skeleton belonged to a small woman or large child.

By now the bones were cool enough to touch, but the hideous smell—a combination of the sweet stench of burned tissue and gasoline—was revolting enough to make Joseph take off in a jog.

Carolyn studied the few pieces of bone intact enough to identify, setting them into a large plastic container once she'd looked them over. "It looks like the body was chopped up with an axe and a large knife, and maybe a saw. The pieces were then placed in a shallow pit and burned with gasoline or something similar. When the fire died down, the remains were probably stirred up and more fuel was added. This must have gone on for a few hours, but it wouldn't have been seen easily from the highway because of that ridge. The way I figure it, the fire must have burned very hot. That's the only way I can explain why so much of the skeleton is missing and why what's here is so charred."

"It had to have happened sometime after I left, about ten P.M.," Ella said, remembering. "Chopping up a body and then destroying it like this would have taken a lot of time. Of course, it's entirely possible that whoever did this had help." As she mentally reviewed the events, she had another disturbing thought. Perhaps the small fire she'd seen had all been part of a plan to lure her in and get her to leave her tracks at the crime scene.

"Identification will be tricky, maybe impossible," Carolyn warned. "The few fragments of teeth on the upper jaw may not do me any good, and the lower jaw is missing. We'll have to screen all the dirt around here and see what else we can find. Whoever cut up the body took special care to smash the teeth, probably against a rock. The teeth fragments that remain are unusable for dental records comparisons."

"What about DNA?" Ella asked, her voice so strained it sounded odd even in her own ears.

"These bones have been virtually destroyed. I doubt I'll be able to extract any DNA from their interior. I need fluids or some kind of tissue, and I doubt any still exists on or within the bones." Carolyn shook her head. "It's been vaporized."

"Maybe we can find something the victim was wearing, a ring or metal button, that will give us a clue," Ella said, looking at Neskahi, Tache, and the agents. "This all took place in the dark, so maybe the killer overlooked something."

Blalock nodded, and everyone at the scene except Carolyn began to search the ground on their hands and knees. Ella searched every square inch of the section that had been assigned to her, not overlooking a single blade of grass or pebble. Yet all the while she desperately hoped that someone else would make the discovery, if there was one to be made.

"I've got something," Neskahi said, pointing at something on the ground about six feet from the edge of the grave. "Doctor, you'd better get this yourself."

Carolyn walked over, squatted down next to an ant bed, then pulled a plastic bag out of her lab coat pocket. Ralph Tache walked over, carefully took a photograph, and stood again, pale as a ghost.

Carolyn picked something up with a pair of tweezers, brushed off the ants with her gloved hand, then put the small object into the bag. "I'll be able to identify the victim now. Count on it."

She looked at Ella, but didn't show her the bag. "It's a phalange, the end of a human finger, probably a Navajo's, that's been cut off at the last joint by a sharp knife or saw. It didn't make it into the fire." Carolyn walked back toward her van, muttering something about getting it on ice.

Ella felt everything spinning, but she managed to remain standing. Suddenly realizing that she was going to be sick, she took off running. Ella barely made it past the crime scene tape before emptying the contents of her stomach.

It took her several minutes before she felt controlled enough to return. Blalock was pale, and Payestewa was hunched over fifty yards away, his back to them. Those remaining were back on the ground, searching for more misplaced body parts. Blalock had lit up a cigar, and together with Tache was sifting through the soil, using a wire screen taken from the crime scene van. Carolyn was looking at something she'd placed in a large plastic refrigerator-type container.

Ella considered asking Blalock for a cigar, but suspected that one puff would make her vomit all over again. "Can you tell us anything about the cause of death from what you have?" she asked Carolyn in the strongest voice she could muster.

"The victim was shot right through the head, execution style. That part of the skull remains, so it was easy making the call. I can't do any toxicology reports, obviously, except on the fingertip, and that probably won't tell us much at all. So far the officers have managed to sift out a few traces of charred cloth and one relatively intact earring. I'll have the lab work done up on them."

"I saw the earring, but can't say for sure that I recognize it." Ella's voice was only a whisper. "Anything that looks like a badge?"

Carolyn shook her head. "Not yet, but they're still sifting through the surface dirt."

Ella turned away from the small artifacts that had once belonged to whoever died here last night. Unable to look at them one moment longer, she walked over to Joseph, who was still searching the ground in a widening spiral away from the grave.

"Badge?" she repeated unsteadily.

"No."

Ella turned and saw Agent Payestewa removing a metal detector from the tribal crime scene vehicle. They weren't going to miss anything, and that was another sign that good cops were at work here. She had to put her personal feelings aside, join them again, and do her part.

Ella returned to where Tache and Blalock were sifting through the dirt from around the grave, placing shovelfuls of sand onto the wire screen, slowly filtering the sand. Everything remaining on the screen was carefully examined, and anything not a rock or plant debris was collected, labeled, and placed in containers.

She had to start thinking of the deceased as merely "the victim," and of her and the others here as professionals just doing their jobs. It didn't serve anyone if she continued to assume the worst for Justine. Her cousin was probably somewhere else, safe and very much alive. Holding to that thought, she helped the others collect, label, and sort potential evidence.

Finally Ella walked over to where Carolyn was packing up her tape recorder and instruments.

While Payestewa circled farther away, checking for anything outside the crime scene tape that they might have overlooked, Ella joined Carolyn. "I've been thinking about this. I really don't believe the body belongs to my cousin. She left before I did and had no reason to come back here."

Yet even as she said it, she realized she was clinging to the Navajo belief that words had power and uttering them could make it so. It was entirely possible that the person who'd brought them together in the first place might have tricked Justine into returning. Or maybe she'd been kidnapped on the way home.

As if reading her thoughts, Carolyn shook her head. "You've got a personal stake in this and that's skewing your outlook. Let the case develop and the facts speak for themselves. Even your intuition is bound to fail you when you're scared. And you are. That's easy for me to see."

Hearing Blalock whistle shrilly, calling out to them from beyond the designated crime scene perimeter, she looked up and saw Payestewa running to meet him, as well as Neskahi.

"Now what?" Ella muttered, torn between fear and a heaviness of spirit that bordered on mental exhaustion.

She jogged up the slope that obstructed her view of the area beyond, then back down the opposite side to a large arroyo where the others had gathered. As she drew near, she saw a tribal unit inside the narrow wash, barely visible. A few tumbleweeds were on the top of the vehicle, as if someone had attempted to hide it from the air. Ella recognized it instantly from the code number. It was Justine's.

TWELVE

— ✖ ✖ ✖ —

Ella helped Payestewa and Blalock search the vehicle and dust for prints while Tache and Sergeant Neskahi examined the area around it. Everyone worked as quickly as they dared. There was no doubt now in anyone's mind that Justine was in trouble—just how serious was yet to be determined. All of them knew that Justine never would have abandoned her unit while it was still operational, leaving the shotgun in place and the keys in the ignition. Only one explanation made sense. Somehow, Justine had been lured out of her vehicle.

"There's a six-pack of cola in the back that hasn't been touched." Agent Payestewa noted. "And there are no signs of violence or a struggle I can find."

"Whoever she encountered passed up the shotgun and everything else inside," Ella said. "They deliberately hid the unit here, too, to delay discovery."

"There's an empty water bottle in the front with lipstick smears on it. I'll have the lab check against the brand Justine uses, but I'll need a sample for comparison." Blalock added.

Ella nodded mechanically. "I'll get it from her mother."

They continued to work the scene for three more hours. Ella, acutely aware of the passage of time, suspected that the news was probably all over Shiprock by now. A few cars had already driven by the original crime scene, and the presence of the FBI and the medical investigator's vehicle would send off an alarm.

As Ella continued to help the other officers search and collect evidence, her restlessness grew. Hair samples and fibers were gathered, labeled, and sealed, but throughout the process, Ella couldn't shake the feeling that they were missing something important.

The department sent a tow truck, and Justine's unit, though undamaged, was hauled away as evidence. An eternity later, the FBI agents and Ella and her team took a final look around.

"It's time to process everything we've collected and then start talking to her friends and relatives," Blalock said. "I don't need to tell everyone that we'll need to move fast on this."

Ella nodded and started to reply when she saw a familiar old four-wheel-drive SUV approaching from the highway. She took a deep, unsteady breath. This was the last thing she'd expected or needed.

Blalock looked up and signaled Payestewa. "Get rid of them if they stop."

"No, I'll take care of it. That's my cousin, Justine's mother, and it looks like one of her other daughters is with her."

A Chevy pulled up beside Ella's Jeep, and Angela Goodluck jumped out immediately, followed by Ruth, Justine's oldest sister. Seeing Ella, Angela and Ruth ran toward her. They were both pale and their eyes wide with fear.

"We heard the medical examiner was here and on the way passed my daughter's vehicle being towed. Tell me nothing's happened, that the rumors aren't true," Angela said, tears shimmering in her eyes.

"She's missing, and that's *all* we know," Ella said, hating herself for not being able to give them the answer they wanted. "You should both go home. As soon as there's any news, I'll call right away."

"Dr. Roanhorse was here, we heard," Ruth interjected. "Is my sister . . ."

"A body was found, but we have no reason to conclude it was your sister's," Ella said. "Don't jump to conclusions."

Angela gave Ella a look that seemed to go right through her. "Our family won't rest until my daughter's home or we have answers."

Ella shared their anguish, but now the load she carried seemed even more pronounced. She had to get to the bottom of this, and quickly. Either Justine had suddenly taken off, which seemed unlikely, been kidnapped, or been murdered and her body burned beyond recognition. The other possibility, that Justine herself was responsible for the charred body, was such a far-fetched notion that she wouldn't even consider it.

In either case, her priorities were clear. Justine had to be found, and the killer of the person they'd discovered in the shallow grave had to be tracked down and apprehended. Ella exhaled softly. There was no doubt in her mind that this would be the most emotional case she'd worked on since the death of her own father years ago.

As her handheld radio sputtered out her call sign, Ella answered, and Big Ed's booming voice came out clearly.

"What's happening out there, Shorty? Give me the highlights."

Ella did as he asked. "It looks pretty bad no matter how we interpret it," she added.

"Come to the station as soon as you finish. I want a full report."

Ella waited while more patrol officers arrived to assist in securing the area. As the officers joined them, Ella looked at her old friends.

Philip Cloud and Michael Cloud had been unlucky enough to draw the responsibility of guarding the crime scene tonight. She could see from their faces that they'd already heard all about the dismembered, burned body and would have preferred to put as much distance from here as they could.

"Any questions?" she asked, after briefing them.

"How long do you think it'll take to completely process this large an area?"

She knew what they meant. Finding officers who would step forward for this kind of duty was difficult. It was part of their job, but one no one here was really prepared for. Navajos considered nighttime at a place where someone had died an especially dangerous place to be.

"If you like, you can take four-hour shifts and spell each other," Ella said sympathetically. "Just don't let any civilians on the scene until Officer Tache, Blalock, or I say so. If the investigation here has to continue tomorrow, you guys will be free to leave once someone from the crime team returns in the morning."

Philip looked around. "This place already feels differently," he muttered. "Did you know that some officers are no longer calling it Beautiful Mesa? They're referring to it as Red Mesa now that a body's been dismembered and so much blood's been spilled here. I have a feeling that name will stick."

Ella suppressed a shudder. "Well, at least you know for sure that you won't have curious Navajos dropping by. Not many of our people would come near here now that death has contaminated this place."

Michael nodded slowly. "My brother and I will work out a schedule. The crime scene will be secured."

Leaving them, Ella caught up with Blalock and Payestewa by their cars. "Big Ed has called me in to make a report. Anything in particular you want me to tell him?"

"Just that I'm putting a rush on all the lab tests that we'll be sending through our Albuquerque lab. Without Justine, you have no one to process prints and that type of thing, is that right?" Blalock asked.

Ella nodded. "Carolyn can take care of some overlapping work when it falls under her area of expertise," Ella said, reminding them of the tip of a finger that had escaped destruction. "But other than that, we're not going to be able to do lab work. Hair and fiber samples will have to go to you too."

"Okay. The Bureau will handle it."

After saying good-bye, Ella drove directly to Shiprock. Each time fear whispered that her cousin was dead, she fought to push back the thought. She needed to hold on to hope now more than ever.

By the time she reached the station, Ella was eager and ready to get to work to find answers. Everything was connected to everything else. By finding the connections in the case, she could solve the crime and restore balance, her own and everyone else's. There were times, like now, when leaning on the old beliefs was the only way to find courage to face what needed to be done.

No one was around the station when she walked in except the staff behind the front desk. The officer on duty looked up, nodded, but didn't say a word. Maybe it was denial, but none of the cops

were ready to believe Justine was gone for good. They were clinging to hope as hard as she was. They wouldn't speak her name,
hoping to reserve the power it had just for her now that she was
in trouble.

Yet their motives weren't completely altruistic. There was fear
of the *chindi*, too. She wasn't kidding herself. Until they knew if
she was alive or dead, calling her name would be considered dangerous and not to be risked unless absolutely necessary.

Ella knocked on Big Ed's open door and walked inside as he
waved at her. His face was grim. "What I hear disturbs me, Shorty,
and I thought I'd heard it all. The crime on Red Mesa sounds particularly vicious."

She noted that he'd used "Red Mesa" naturally, without even
a second's hesitation. Nothing could have given her a clearer indication of how deeply this crime was affecting everyone. Justine
was a member of the force, and even the possibility that someone
had done something like that to one of their own had every member of the department on edge.

"We have no proof yet that it's my assistant's body," she said,
wanting to clarify that first, then proceeded to fill him in on the
details.

"You were the last person to see her," Big Ed said slowly. "Tell
me about your meeting."

Ella did, reluctantly admitting to herself for the first time that
she was a suspect herself.

"Whose idea was it to have that meeting?"

Ella shook her head. "I don't really know. We both got notes
we thought came from the other, but I didn't send her a note, and
from what she said, she didn't send me one either. Someone set us
up, Chief, but I didn't say anything to her about it because I
thought it was probably just a well-intentioned cop that we both
work with. It looks like there was a lot more to it than that."

"Who else knew about your plans to meet?" Big Ed said.

"I told my mother, but just her. Justine's mother knew, but I
don't know who else they might have talked to."

Big Ed nodded, but remained silent.

Ella didn't interrupt the silence and waited, used to lengthy
pauses. It was part of the rhythm of Navajo speech.

"If everything in her unit including her shotgun was left be-hind," Big Ed said, "and there were no signs of a struggle in her unit, then that means she pulled over willingly—for a friend, per-haps."

"Or a relative. It's a reasonable conclusion. But I wasn't there, so all I have to offer is speculation."

"Shorty, I know you had nothing to do with this, but I've got to tell you the truth. This might end up pointing in your direction. If the victim you found turns out to be your second cousin, and we all pray that won't happen, things are going to get really hot for you. Over the years you've made many enemies on the Rez, and I'm afraid they'll all come to the surface once word gets around that you two were having problems getting along. You've got to find out what happened, and you've got to move fast before the gossip begins.

"This case hits very close to home, and that's a strike against you in more ways than one," Big Ed continued. "People will be screaming that I take you off the case. And there's the chance that your intuition and logic won't be as reliable now."

"You can't take me off this case, and not just because doing so will feed the rumor mill about me being guilty of something. I quit the Bureau to come and work cases like these for The People. I'm the person most qualified to pursue this and you know it. If you hand this investigation over to someone else, you'll be using the second string. That's not fair to her or to me."

Big Ed nodded slowly. "Okay. For now, we'll keep things as they are. But as you work the case, there's a possibility I want you to look into. Our department has been responsible for foiling some big crimes since the Special Investigations unit was formed, and we haven't had to pay any big price—so far. If your assistant was the victim, then this may be only the first of several planned attacks on our police officers."

Ella remembered the instant message warning her about a con-spiracy. Without hesitation, she told Big Ed about her secret con-tact, leaving out the name "Coyote" in order to protect the person in case he or she was really undercover. "The problem is, I have no idea where the message came from or how valid it is. I tried to backtrack, but I reached nothing but dead ends and addresses that no longer exist. But the warning was clear. I was to trust no one."

"I'm glad you told me. But just in case this contact of yours is legit and working deep cover, we need to keep it to ourselves for now. If you're contacted again, talk to me right away. Maybe I can do some checking behind the scenes. There's one federal agency already working on our turf with someone undercover, but that's all I was told. I don't like it, mind you, but I was lucky to get that."

Ella nodded. The Marshals Service had notified Big Ed, undoubtedly. She wondered if Harry knew.

Ella returned to her office, more unsettled than ever. She wasn't sure which theory she preferred—that someone might be trying to frame her for Justine's disappearance, or that there was a conspiracy against police officers under way.

Knowing she needed to get started on the trail for the truth, Ella reached for the phone to dial Carolyn. The phone ran just as she touched the receiver.

Ella picked it up and immediately recognized Blalock's voice on the other end, though he didn't bother to identify himself.

"Ella, I have some very bad news. I had your department send me Justine's prints for comparison, and they're a match for the one Dr. Roanhorse lifted from the severed fingertip. That's Justine's body. I'm so sorry, I know how close you two were."

Ella's stomach sank. "But we can't be sure. It's just her fingertip," she argued, knowing how pitiful her protests were, but unable to let go of all hope. "What if it's a trick of some kind, and she's being held hostage somewhere?"

"There's more. One of the bone fragments we managed to find was from a severed finger, and the tip was missing, probably cut off by the same tool used to separate the fingertip. I know this is difficult for you, but reason it out. Why would somebody deliberately destroy a body so thoroughly, even smashing the teeth, unless they wanted to avoid positive proof of who they murdered? Killing a cop is a guarantee that the department will go after them full force."

"But we don't *know* anything for sure," Ella insisted, not wanting to even consider the possibility that Justine had been tortured before being killed.

"Does it really make sense to you that the perp killed one person and chopped off the finger of another just to mislead us? The fact is that he was planning on burning the body—and the evidence—then, in the dark, he missed burning the fingertip."

"Why bother chopping up the hands anyway, if he or they were going to burn up the entire body?" Ella wondered about the seeming inconsistency. "Any fire hot enough to destroy the femurs and the skull would have easily done away with the fingers."

"Whoever it was could have been full of rage and just lost control. It was, after all, an extremely violent crime. I've seen victims of stabbings and beatings where there were many post mortem blows inflicted. The killer or killers had worked themselves into a frenzy and just couldn't stop until they were too tired to continue. Psychological overkill, I guess. The profilers have a lot more to say about this than I do."

"I think all that chopping was deliberate rather than the act of a crazed, out-of-control killer, because the rest of the crime scene was so organized. The victim was shot first, and mercifully dead before the body was dismembered. That means that either the fingertip was dropped there for us to find and assume it was a slipup, or was accidental. Either way, it was a mistake, and if he made one mistake, he'll make more," Ella said. "We'll play it out before making any conclusions."

"Face facts, Ella. Officer Tache also found what turned out to be blood on some blades of grass close by where the body was burned. It's being tested now. Nearly all of the victim's body, even the skeleton, was turned to ashes in that fire pit."

"Let see what that evidence tells us then."

"Okay, but you should know that the ME doesn't think any of the other remains will be sufficient to refute her preliminary ID, though she really wanted to give us some hope that it wasn't Officer Goodluck who died."

Ella tried to keep her voice from cracking. "What else do we know from the vehicle?"

"The fingerprints we lifted from inside the car are hers, yours, and those of a prisoner transported recently named Zah."

"Even the ones right above the door on the roof, where someone talking to a driver would place his hand as he leaned against the car?" Ella managed.

"There were no clear prints on there, just smudges. The car was washed and waxed recently."

"Hair and fiber samples?"

Blalock sighed. "I called in a favor and had the Albuquerque lab check those for me right away, and most of the hair samples appear to be Justine's as well. They'll need samples of your hair, and also Zah's, the prisoner, to compare with those found that don't appear to belong to Justine."

"So there's no evidence that someone else got into the car or forced her out?"

"No," the FBI agent said, then continued. "But my guess is that she was approached by a friend, relative, or acquaintance she trusted. There was no call to dispatch, so she didn't pull anyone over or make a stop to investigate something she saw. The only theory that makes sense is that she was taken off-guard. But that's going to make your life difficult," Blalock warned.

"Do *you* think I had something to do with my cousin's death?" Ella knew she wasn't the only one who'd been having trouble getting along with Justine lately. To single her out was unfair.

"No, but my opinion doesn't count. It's the DA you have to worry about. For the record, I believe you've been set up. I think you better check your enemies and see who among them would have the know-how and be in a position to do this."

"I'll do that. Did you find out if the fragments of bone or skull can be checked for DNA or blood typing at all?"

"That's out of my league. You'll have to talk to the ME about that one."

"Okay. I'll handle it."

Ella took several deep breaths before dialing. Justine had been an integral part of her life, and to face the very real possibility that she was gone forever left her with an unbearable ache. It was a void that no one would be able to fill.

Ella stopped the thoughts cold. She was writing her cousin off, just like the others had already done, and it might be too soon for that.

Ella picked up the phone and dialed. The phone rang several times, and just before voice mail picked up, her friend answered.

"Do you have anything for me? Any hope that this is all a mistake?"

"I was just going to call you," Carolyn said in a weary voice. "I've just been postponing it because it's so hard. I loved Justine, too." Carolyn wasn't afraid of using a dead person's name. Her job required handling the dead, an even bigger taboo.

"So you've pretty much decided that the body is hers," Ella observed, her voice unsteady.

"Yeah. Believe me, I really wish I could find something to contradict the evidence we have. But it isn't going to happen. I heard from Blalock that the fingerprint matched. Now we also have a blood-type match from her medical records and from the sample recovered at the scene. It's the same as in the tissue samples we found—the finger joint."

Ella couldn't speak. All the hope she'd had seemed to drift away like a wisp of smoke.

"Are you okay?"

Ella tried to answer, but she couldn't manage it. She cleared her throat, more to let Carolyn know that she was there than for any other reason. She took several deep breaths, then, at last, spoke. "What about DNA in the bones?"

"No, we won't be doing that. The chances of finding any DNA we can work with is extremely slim, and the cost of doing such a test is way over our budget. The presence of the single digit that wasn't burned, and the blood match, is enough for us to make the determination that this is Justine's body. From that we can also make a few toxicological tests on her blood and muscle tissue. But those will take time, and may not tell us anything we don't already know. What I'm reasonably sure about at this point is that the cause of death is almost certainly that gunshot to the head."

The facts were inescapable, but instead of the crushing sorrow they should have evoked, Ella felt nothing. It was as if her heart had turned to ice, rendering her incapable of emotion. "Whoever did this was someone she trusted enough to let them get close. The person used that trust to kill her. I want him. Get me whatever you can, caliber of the bullet, tools used to dismember the body . . . anything," she said, her voice hard.

"You know I will. Is there anything else I can do for *you*?"

Ella hesitated, wondering if anyone or anything could help her deal with the grief. She thought of her father's murder, and how she'd found a way to cope. "Only one thing's going to help me now. I need to find whoever did this, and make sure he pays for what he's done. That's the only way any of us will be able to put this behind us."

"I agree. But do you think you'll be allowed to stay on this case, since you're personally involved? I thought the department discouraged things like that."

It was a legitimate question, but she couldn't help but wonder what else Carolyn had heard. "For now. Is that what your sources say too?"

"All I've heard is gossip from staff here at the hospital."

"What are they staying?" she pressed.

"That if Big Ed doesn't want to risk losing his job, he should place you on leave, and begin a full internal investigation."

"Thanks for the update. I have a feeling public opinion is going to weigh heavily against me now."

"If you need anything, even a friendly voice, I'm only a phone call away. Remember that."

"I will," Ella said, hanging up.

Hearing that Big Ed might already be under the gun had surprised her. The chief had given her no indication of that, but she should have known that her enemies wouldn't waste any time.

Ella looked around her office, her spirit heavy. She'd promised Angela she'd contact her as soon as they knew something, and that was a promise she had to keep. But she couldn't deliver the news over the phone. Justine's family deserved better than that.

Ella locked up her office door and walked out of the station. She'd go home first and get herself together. She wanted to break the news to Justine's family as gently as possible, but she had no idea how to even begin. Maybe her mother could come up with a suggestion that would help soften the blow to her cousins.

Ella drove home quickly and as she parked beside Rose's pickup, she saw her mother playing with Dawn outside in the back. Dawn was chasing a big yellow ball in her stiff-legged way and laughing.

"Hello, Mother," Ella said. "Hi, Short Stuff," she added, smiling at Dawn.

Seeing Ella, Dawn dropped the ball and ran over. Ella picked her up, giving a big hug and a kiss on the cheek. "I missed you!"

"*Shimasání* play ball!"

"You're going to wear out *Shimasání*!" Ella laughed as her daughter squirmed out of her hands and ran back to retrieve the ball.

"She reminds me of you at that age, daughter." Rose smiled. "You were always curious, always pushing yourself to try the things you can't quite do yet. She can nearly throw the ball now, or at least drop it in a particular direction, but every time she tries to kick it, she falls on her behind. Yet it never stops her. She continues to try."

"Stubbornness. It's a trait of our family."

Rose chuckled softly.

"Mom, we need to talk."

Rose looked up at her quickly. "It sounds very serious. Is it about your cousin?"

"It is."

"Then maybe it should wait until after your daughter's father comes and goes."

"Is he visiting today?"

"He called earlier. He's not busy right now and wondered if he could take your daughter to his home. He's bought some toys for her, I'm afraid."

"It's his right. She's his daughter, too."

"Yes, but I don't like the comparisons that leads to. Your daughter sees him as only a giver of gifts. He comes with little notice, takes her away for a few hours, then brings her back once he's bored. To her, he's becoming an everyday Santa Claus. That's not a good thing."

"What else can he do? Navajo men don't have traditional rights of custody. The state laws grant them, if the father demands it, but he'd be going against our customs and he would never do that. A move like that could turn some of the traditionalists against him. So being a part-time dad is the only option he's got."

"That's his choice. I have no problem with that. But I think he should visit her here, or when you're with him, not take her away to his house or elsewhere."

"Does it worry you?"

"I don't like it, that's all. I don't trust him to watch her as carefully as she needs. I don't think he's been around children very much."

"My daughter should have the chance to get to know her father and his family," Ella said.

"I don't think his family wants anything to do with her. They're of the Bitter Water Clan and are the ones appointed to watch our family and guard the tribe against the evil that's part of our legacy. None of them trust us. I doubt that your daughter will ever know what a *shínálí,* a paternal grandmother, is."

"Maybe that'll change as they get to know her."

"You don't really believe that."

"No, I guess not," Ella admitted. Hearing a car pulling up, she turned around and saw Kevin driving up in a sporty new foreign car.

"He's more Anglo than the Anglos sometimes," Rose muttered. "Look what he drives. A good Navajo is not supposed to call attention to himself, or invite comparisons that will make others feel inferior. Yet he does both with every breath he takes."

"He's not a bad man, Mom. He's just trying to project an image of success. In his own way, I believe he loves his daughter."

As Kevin climbed out of the low-slung vehicle, Dawn looked up and, dropping the ball, ran to him. *"Shizhé'é,"* she said in a loud, excited voice.

Ella looked at her mother in surprise. "You taught her the Navajo word for father?"

"I wanted to see if *he* knew it," she said, glancing at Kevin.

Ella tried not to laugh, but it was hard. Poor Kevin had a difficult enough time understanding his own daughter when she spoke English. Although Dawn's speech was perfectly clear to her and Rose, he often struggled to figure out what she was saying. Kid-speak took a specially trained ear, one he didn't seem to have developed.

"You're teaching her Navajo?" He looked at Ella, surprised.

"What's wrong with that?" Rose said. "I taught her that word," she added, still not giving him a clue as to the meaning.

"It's the word for father," Ella said, taking pity on him.

"I *thought* that was what she'd said," Kevin answered. "It just took me by surprise."

As Kevin held Dawn, Ella walked with him back to his car. "I need to talk to Mom, and then speak to my cousin Angela. It's important. Will you keep Dawn until I come by and pick her up?"

"No problem. But what's going on?"

Ella smiled at her daughter, and then looked back at Kevin and shook her head. "We'll talk later."

Shortly after Ella filled Dawn's diaper bag for him, Kevin drove off.

Ella turned her attention to Rose, who was sitting in the living room, waiting.

"Something bad has happened to your cousin, hasn't it?" Rose observed. "Tell me what it is."

Although she tried to break the news gently to her mother, it clearly left Rose devastated. Ella gave her mother some time to gather herself, then explained that she now had to go tell Justine's family.

"Let me go with you," Rose asked. "Maybe I can help. Your cousin will take this very hard. Like it is with me, her children are everything to her."

They left immediately and rode in silence for several minutes. "Mom, are you sure you're all right?" Ella asked quietly after looking over for the third time.

Rose nodded slowly. "I keep thinking how much like you your cousin was. Police work was everything to her, too. Now it's cost her and her family dearly. Do you finally understand why I worry so much about you?"

Ella had intended to tell her mother about the possibility that someone was trying to frame her for Justine's death, but changed her mind. Rose had enough on her mind now, and anything else except the tragedy of Justine's death seemed almost trivial by comparison.

Rose knew there was something else, though, and looked at her for several long moments. "But there's more to this than you're saying, isn't there?"

"Some may end up blaming me for her death," Ella admitted slowly.

"How could anyone believe something like that?" Pain and concern flashed in Rose's eyes.

Ella first considered evading her mother's question, but after a pause, decided to be honest and tell her the facts. Rose would never forgive her if she thought that Ella had tried to shield her from the truth.

Ella told her what had happened, then waited as her mother weighed what she'd just learned.

Rose nodded slowly, staring down at her clasped hands. "You're in for the fight of your life, daughter. Some of your friends, or the ones you thought were your friends, might desert you in this crisis. Be grateful that Dawn is still very young and not in school. She'll be spared what lies ahead."

"I've lost my cousin and a very dear friend, but I don't think anyone realizes just how much that loss means to me."

"Your sorrow is something your enemies will use to their advantage. If this was a frame, as you call it, it was planned carefully, and was meant to destroy you just as thoroughly as it did your cousin."

"I know," Ella whispered. "And that's why it scares me so much."

"Don't give in to fear, daughter. That's your biggest enemy. It'll prevent you from thinking clearly at a time when you'll need that skill the most. Use fear to help keep your senses sharp, but don't give it power over you. If you do, your enemies will win."

As they turned off the road leading to the Goodlucks' house, Rose exhaled softly. "I'm glad that your cousin's other daughters live near here. She'll need them now more than ever. Remember, too, that like your father, she's Christian. Hopefully that'll give her comfort as well."

As they pulled into the driveway, Angela came to the door of the house, almost as if she'd been waiting for them. Ella felt the weight her duty had cast upon her.

The second Angela saw the expression on Rose's face, she burst into tears. Rose turned to Ella. "Daughter, let me talk to her alone."

Without further word, the two older women walked down the driveway together.

Ruth, Justine's oldest sister, and Jayne, a year older than Justine, came out of the house and joined Ella.

"My sister is dead, isn't she?" Ruth said before Ella could even open her mouth.

Ella nodded, then told them what she knew, holding back the gruesome details of the crime.

Jayne took a step away from Ella. "Where were you when my sister was killed? I thought the two of you were supposed to work together. She depended on you!"

Ella felt every word as keenly as a knife to the gut. "I had no indication that there was a problem," she said, "and we weren't working on a case. We were just talking as cousins and friends when I saw her last."

"You two haven't been getting along lately. No wonder you didn't know Justine was in danger," Jayne shot back, ignoring the taboo against saying her name. "How could you let this happen?" Not giving Ella a chance to reply, she continued. "Why don't you just leave this house? You bring evil everywhere you go. I don't want you here."

Ruth tried to put a hand on her sister's arm, but Jayne recoiled. "No," she said, turning on her sister. "You're always being the good mother, trying to make peace here just like with your own children. But this is wrong. Ella's to blame." Jayne turned her back on them and ran to the SUV parked by the house.

"She shouldn't drive when she's hurt and angry." Ruth said quickly. "I'll go get her, but maybe you should leave for now."

Ella stared at Ruth walking away, too stunned to speak. She'd wanted to let them know how much she was going to miss Justine, and that she was hurting just like they were. But all the words were lodged in her throat.

Rose returned to join Ella as Angela and her daughters stood by the SUV talking. "We're not welcome here, daughter. It's time to leave. Your cousin is overwhelmed by grief and anger. She wants to blame someone, and is striking out at you and our family."

"Her daughters blame me, too," Ella said. "Mom, I'm sorry. I should have never brought you along. I didn't expect this."

"I'm glad I came. It'll help me get prepared for what lies ahead."

Ella nodded. There would be no peace for her or her family in this land between the sacred mountains until she found the truth. The *Dinetah,* always a very dangerous place, had suddenly become a land of betrayal.

THIRTEEN

——— ✖ ✖ ✖ ———

Ella returned home with her mother. With Dawn away with Kevin, the house seemed quiet and lonely all of a sudden. Ella suddenly understood why Dawn and her mother needed each other so much. For a woman like Rose, who had always had family within her home, this had become an empty nest despite Ella having returned to share the house. Rose had spent too much time alone here, listening to the silence. But with Dawn's birth, Rose had found a familiar and comforting purpose for herself again.

"This house seems too big and empty sometimes," Rose said, almost as if reading Ella's mind. "Someday I may have to accept that modern times make new demands on all of us. Families can't be as close as they once were." She shook her head sadly. "And they call it progress!"

"Your granddaughter will always be close to you, and I belong here too. Someday we'll also have a young woman from the tribe coming in to help with the chores." Ella looked at her mother and smiled. "And please don't tell me that you'll actually *mind* not doing so much laundry and cooking!"

Rose didn't answer.

Ella gave her mother a hug. "I'm going to go back to the office for a bit, then afterwards I'll stop, pick up my daughter, and come home. Will you be all right here?"

Rose nodded. "Two will keep me company." She scratched the

head of the furry mutt, who wagged his tail in response. "He's acting normal again, and it's a good thing."

"Are *you* all right?" Ella asked. Her mother seemed even more tired than usual. Then again, it had been a trying day for all of them.

"Your cousin's death has reminded me of how quickly I could lose you." Ella started to protest, but Rose held up one hand, stopping her. "I don't think I could stand a loss like that. When your father was killed, it took me a long time to accept his death and go on, but a woman never expects to bury her children."

"Mom, nothing is going to happen to me."

"Your cousin probably said the same thing to her mother."

"She had far less training and experience than I do. And she was always trying to prove herself. I'm past having to show how good I am at my job."

"Even so."

"I want to stay on the reservation, Mom, and I know that's what you want too. But being a cop is all I know. And it's the only career I can pursue here. In law enforcement the line between Anglo ways and our own is blurred enough to allow me to fit in."

"I wish you had never left the reservation in the first place. You've been torn in two ever since."

"And then where would I be today if I hadn't? I guess I could have been a clerk at a store, or a waitress at a restaurant, but I need more than that to be happy. You, of all people, know how hard I fought to find an identity at all. With a Christian preacher as a father and you following The Way, I learned I was most comfortable when walking the line between both worlds. Being a cop allowed me to give my life some meaning and still remain true to myself."

"And what has all your training gotten you? You're in a job where anything could happen to you at any time."

"But it's a job where I can make a difference. And one where I can earn enough money to be able to provide for us. We're not rich, but we don't lack anything either and we never will. And when I retire, I'll have a pension. I'll never have to depend on anyone to help me provide for my family."

Rose sighed, then sat down in her easy chair. "I know we've

had this conversation many times before, daughter, but I still worry about you."

"I know. You're my mom. That's your job," Ella teased.

Rose shook her head. "Go to the police station, if you must. Just bring my granddaughter back as soon as you can."

"You've got it."

Minutes later, as Ella headed down the highway, anger, then annoying tears, filled her eyes as she thought of Justine and everything that had happened. She would have to actively pursue whatever leads she had, and right now, only one seemed clear. Harry Ute was tracking a fugitive who had sworn to get his revenge on Justine and her, and recently he'd bankrolled himself, literally. She needed to talk to Harry about Samuel Begaye.

The problem, of course, was how to find Harry quickly. An undercover cop had to be careful every moment, and for Harry that meant he'd be hiding and blending with others, doing his best to disappear among the *Dineh*. Any attempt to find him could have disastrous results for his own operation.

As she weighed her options, Ella realized she had only one alternative open to her. When she reached the station, she called the Marshals Service and left a message for Harry to contact her as soon as he could. She did the same to the State Police Department, asking Rob Brown, the officer who was sharing his home with Harry, to contact her.

Ella sat back, unsure what else she could do to speed up the process. There didn't seem much, though she did leave a message with Blalock, who also knew Harry was in the area and might be contacted by him.

Next, Ella went to Justine's smaller office, in an alcove off the forensics lab, to try and find the note Justine believed Ella had written to her.

The moment she stepped into her cousin's office and saw the small pigs on a shelf above Justine's desk, the sadness Ella felt became almost unbearable. Each pig was different. There was a ceramic pig "cop," two cartoon characters in uniform, and a plain barnyard hog. There were four of them in total, one for each year Justine had been a police officer.

It was so hard to believe Justine was gone. Even the scent of her perfume lingered in the room, and there was a slight indentation in her desk chair where she'd spent so many hours on paperwork. The tears Ella felt running down her cheeks slowly became hot, and thoughts of revenge started her heart beating faster. Taking deep breaths, and wiping away the tears with a tissue, Ella slowly forced herself to focus back on reality.

She didn't want revenge. What she would work for was justice.

Ella couldn't bear to sit in Justine's chair, so she searched her late assistant's desk while standing. Within seconds she found the note atop a stack of unfinished reports. The signature was nearly identical to Ella's own, probably traced.

Ella brought the note back to her office and put it in the folder along with the one she'd received, labeling and dating the folder. Perhaps an FBI handwriting expert could prove that they were forgeries. If not, she was sure that the notes would eventually be used as evidence against her. As she mulled over her situation, Ella realized that even if they were proven to be forgeries, a good attorney could argue that she could have made the forgeries herself as easily as anyone else, even tracing her own signature to construct phony evidence.

Disgusted, Ella left the office and drove to Kevin's home. Dawn was asleep on his couch when she arrived.

Kevin held one finger over his lips. "She's been out for hours. I had hoped she wouldn't fall asleep so soon," he said, glancing over at the child, covered by a small quilt.

"Maybe you should try to schedule time with her earlier in the day, Kevin."

"It's hard for me to get away unless I have a last-minute cancellation or schedule change."

Ella nodded, distractedly.

"You look like you've been through hell and back. What's going on?" Kevin motioned for her to join him at the kitchen table.

Knowing he'd hear all about it by tomorrow morning at the very latest, she told him about her meeting with Justine and the subsequent events. "I still can't believe she's gone. It doesn't seem real, you know?"

"I received a note from her recently. You can have it for handwriting comparison, if you think it'll help."

"Are you sure it was from my second cousin, and not a for-gery?"

"It was real," Kevin assured. "She followed it up with a phone call. She was worried about the problems her aunt Lena was having with the Hopis over water."

"Did you meet with her?"

"No, I only spoke to her on the phone. We'd scheduled a meeting for later this week." Kevin paused, then continued. "Is it possible that she made some bad enemies stemming from that Hopi-Navajo dispute her aunt had?"

"I can't see how. That took place way over in Arizona, and seemed like a local problem," Ella said. "There was a prisoner transfer from Window Rock that same day, too, but neither she nor I was the focus of that."

"Okay. It was just a thought. If there's anything I can do to help, just let me know." Kevin touched her gently on the arm.

"Actually, there is. As an attorney for the tribe, you have your own contacts in the legal system, and you also have access to tribal investigators. Can you find out if any criminals we've put away have made threats against either her or me recently, or if there are any rumors that may shed light on what's happened?"

"Okay. I'll get on it first thing tomorrow."

Ella looked at Dawn, who was sleeping so comfortably, she almost hated to move her.

"I know you don't really want to disturb her now, but we don't have a choice. I have to be in court early tomorrow. That means waking up in time to rush out the door and race to my office. I won't have time to take care of the baby in the morning."

Ella nodded. "I couldn't leave her here tonight anyway. Mom would kill me. She really misses Dawn when she's not around." Yet, despite that, Kevin's admission still bothered her. Sometimes she got the feeling that fatherhood was only okay with him when it was convenient.

Dawn fussed a little when Ella picked her up and put her in the car seat, but before long, she drifted off to sleep again. By the time Ella pulled up in front of her mother's house, Rose was sitting on the darkened porch in her rocking chair, Two beside her.

A minute later Ella lifted Dawn out of the car and handed her to her grandmother, who was waiting with open arms.

"*Hatsói*, my daughter's child," she whispered as Dawn began to fuss again. "Sleep now." The little girl settled quickly in her arms.

After Dawn was safely in her own bed, tonight without the need for a bedtime story, Ella said good night to her mother and went to her room. Although she suspected that Rose wanted to talk, she just wasn't up to it. The details of Justine's death were bearing down on her, and it was hard to think of anything else, even for a moment.

In hopes that her Internet contact "Coyote" had sent her a message, she checked her E-mail, then remained logged on to the Internet provider where she'd received the previous instant message. After about fifteen minutes she received E-mail, but it was just spam asking her if she'd like to become rich working at home. She deleted the message, its contents obvious from the subject line.

Knowing that she had to remain on-line to receive an instant message, Ella cruised the basic services of her provider, checking local weather and reading the news updates on national and international events. Local news was still only available from radio, newspapers, and a local cable TV station that ran a teletypelike service.

Tired of seeing the same old information repeated endlessly, she decided to call it a night. She was about to log off when she heard the electronic tone signaling an instant message. A brief message flashed on the screen in the little white box.

> Your partner's death may only be part of a larger picture.
> I'm trying to uncover the truth. Watch your back.
>
> Coyote

The instant message stayed on her screen, but the sender was gone before she could reply. Irritated because she hadn't been able to ask him some questions, she printed out the message, switched off the computer, and crawled into bed.

Although she wanted to sleep, slumber eluded her. Her mind raced with thoughts of Justine, the crime scene, and a thousand other details.

Trying to relax, Ella let her thoughts shift to Dawn. Her little girl meant everything to her. It was really a shame she'd never have the kind of dad Ella would have wanted for her. And from what she could see, Kevin's family wasn't interested in Dawn either, at least not enough to play an active part in her life. Wondering if she should be relieved or sad, she drifted off to an uneasy sleep.

Ella woke up the following morning ready to tackle the murder investigation once more. There was a lot for her to do, and there was no time to waste. One day had already passed, and with each additional hour the chances of catching the killer or killers grew more distant. Dressing quickly, she said good-bye to her mother and Dawn and went to work early.

By nine, she'd questioned every officer and civilian staff member who'd been in the building the day Justine and she had received the notes that had lured them to what was rapidly becoming known as Red Mesa.

It seemed a lot of people had come and gone that day. Although the officers could recall who they'd personally seen there, no one had noticed anything that could help her identify who'd delivered the notes. The only thing she was certain about was that the person responsible for those notes couldn't have been Begaye. The last place he would have gone to was a police station. Too many of the officers would have known him, even if he'd been in disguise.

But that left her with no other real suspects, unless Begaye had recruited one of his relatives for the job. But that seemed unlikely. Begaye wasn't a team player. Not willing to overlook any possibility, however, Ella checked the names she'd collected from the officers against the information she had on the fugitive's relatives and known associates. There were no leads there.

Ella then made a list of prisoners and suspects who had been brought to the station, and decided to check and determine who was related to those individuals. Unfortunately, the only prisoner on hand, besides a few in the drunk tank who had already been released, was Zah. But he hadn't been allowed any visitors except for his attorney because of the earlier incident at Window Rock.

Ella had just sat down, going over the lists one more time, when Big Ed showed up at her door. "Ella, you probably already know about this, but just in case you don't, there's going to be a memorial service for your cousin at one this afternoon, over at St. John's Chapel. The Christian side of her family will have the remains interred privately, but they want this service done right away. They notified the department and asked that the officers all be informed so those who don't find it offensive can attend."

"I'd really like to be there, but I wasn't invited, and I'm not sure how her family will feel about that." She told the chief how Angela and her daughters had reacted when they learned of Justine's death.

Big Ed seemed to consider the matter for an eternity. "Okay, it's probably a good idea for you to lay low then, maybe sit in the back. But I think you should still attend. You've done nothing wrong, and you shouldn't let innuendo and rumor wear away at your reputation or the reputation of this department."

Ella nodded once. Though she wanted to attend, she wondered if Big Ed was wrong to pressure her into going. Harsh words and bad feelings would have no place at that service, out of respect for Justine if for no one else.

Ella spent the next few hours filling out reports on her most recent activities. It seemed like an incredible waste of time now with everything she was facing, and so much left to be done on Justine's murder investigation. But there was no escaping the bureaucracy.

Later, in the parking lot, as she was unlocking her car door to leave for the church, Ella heard her call sign come over her hand-held radio.

"We have a situation," the dispatcher said. "Gladys Zah, the wife of the prisoner you transported, is at the Desert Moon Motel. She's been threatening to kill her two children and then commit suicide. Management called us when she refused to let housekeeping inside her room and threatened to shoot whoever bothered her. They saw a rifle."

The Desert Moon was a rough place known for attracting trouble because of its cheap rates and reputation for illegal alcohol.

"How old are the kids?" Ella asked in a taut voice.

"There's a five-month-old girl and a four-year-old boy."

Ella knew that the kids' presence pretty much ruled out tear gas. It would be mostly negotiation. "I'm on my way to my partner's memorial service. Is there someone else you can send?" Ella turned around in the parking lot, looking for other police units. There were none at all except for the car assigned to the watch officer.

"Not on this. And you should know that Gladys Zah asked for you specifically. She claims you destroyed her family when you arrested her husband, and said she wants you to see the harm you've done."

Frustration and anger made her body shake. It was truly amazing how quickly people blamed the arresting officers when their relatives broke the law. "I'll take the call. Send backup if you can find any, even if you have to get the county sheriff."

"I'm trying to get hold of Sergeant Neskahi. He's on his way in from Teece Nos Pos," the dispatcher said.

"Ten-four."

Ella switched on her flashers, then sped down the highway toward the motel.

FOURTEEN

—— ✖ ✖ ✖ ——

Trying to stay focused, Ella reached Neskahi on the radio. After verifying that he would arrive at approximately the same time she would, she called dispatch and asked the woman to tell Big Ed she might have to miss the memorial service for Justine.

Then Ella mentally began to review hostage procedures. In these situations what was needed most was clear thinking and a lot of luck. The obvious danger to the children terrified her.

She arrived at the scene within twenty minutes, and saw Neskahi waiting outside one of the motel rooms, standing behind his patrol vehicle. People were milling about the doorway of the main entrance, watching curiously.

Ella approached cautiously, noting someone peering through the curtain of the motel room window in front of the sergeant's vehicle. "What's the situation?" she asked.

"I tried to open negotiations, but Mrs. Zah demanded to speak to you. Her speech is slurred, so I suspect she's been drinking. I wouldn't trust her not to try and shoot you, and maybe her children, too. The motel manager said that when he went to talk to her he saw that she's got a hunting rifle, a Winchester lever action. That'll penetrate everything but the real heavy SWAT vests."

Joseph offered to let her use the speaker system on his car radio, but she decided just to shout. It might be less frightening to the woman and her children if she didn't magnify her voice. "This is Special Investigator Ella Clah, ma'am. Why don't you set the rifle down and come out now. We can talk."

"No, you come in here," Gladys shouted back.

"If you come out unarmed and stand by the door where we can see you, I'll approach."

"You'll just arrest me, just like you did my husband. You won't listen or even try to understand."

"I can help you, ma'am. I know this is a difficult time for you, but think of your children and their safety. I'll make sure they have someone to take care of them while you get the help you need. There are counselors and lawyers that will listen to you too," Ella said, trying her best to reason with her.

"You lie. That's all the Tribal Police has ever done," Gladys yelled.

"We don't want anyone to get hurt, including you. Your children need their mother. Why don't you at least send the kids out and show us you're thinking of their safety?"

"No. They stay with me." Mrs. Zah said something to one of the children that Ella couldn't hear.

"If you want me to cooperate with you, you have to meet me halfway on this," Ella insisted. "Send the kids out and the sergeant can watch them."

"Will you talk to me then?"

"If your son and daughter come out safely, I'll come and talk to you. But you'll have to do exactly as I say."

"Like what?"

"I'll leave my weapon with the sergeant, but you have to place your rifle on the ground outside the door before I walk any closer. I won't talk until we're both unarmed."

"You're not serious, are you?" Neskahi whispered.

"I'll have my backup, but if I can get her to surrender her rifle, the biggest problem will be solved."

"We don't know if she's got just the one rifle."

"It's risky, I'm not denying it. But we can't fire off tear gas, or try to take her out, without the risk of hurting the kids. Do you have a better plan?"

Neskahi said nothing for several long moments. "No," he said finally. "But leave your radio on so I can hear what she's saying to you. If you spot another gun, say something about the chief. If she has a different kind of weapon, mention my name. I'll at least know what you're up against. Okay?"

"Fair enough." Ella turned and shouted toward the window again. "So what's it going to be, Mrs. Zah?"

"I can't send the baby out. She's sick. But you can see my boy."

"Both kids, or I'm not coming any closer. I have to know they're both safe."

"No. Robert can't carry Kellie, and she's really sick."

"Then we should get Kellie to a doctor. The PHS clinic near the river has a good staff. But we need to speed things up if your baby needs help. Send Robert out now. You can keep Kellie in your arms, but you'll still have to set the rifle on the ground when you get to the door. Deal?"

"All right."

"You're thinking that there's no way she can fire a rifle as long as she's holding the little girl?" Neskahi whispered.

Ella nodded, speaking quietly. "That's exactly what I'm counting on. If the baby's as sick as she said, frustration may have been what sent her over the edge. Although medical help is free, a lot of our people are still afraid of hospitals because people die there. Many think the place is filled with the *chindi*. What I have to do somehow is get her attention focused back on her baby instead of on her personal situation."

Gladys appeared with the infant just moments after the little boy walked timidly out the door. After the woman set the rifle down on the ground, Ella placed her pistol on the hood of Neskahi's car, then walked up slowly, her hands out, showing she was unarmed.

Neskahi watched from behind the car, then as soon as the little boy was close, went out to get him. Moving quickly, he picked him up and hustled him inside the squad car.

Ella stepped closer, nodding and smiling at Mrs. Zah, but watching her carefully for signs that she had a knife or other concealed weapon.

As Ella stood before her, she glanced down at the baby in the woman's arms. The moment she saw the infant's face clearly, her heart froze. She'd seen this before. Fetal alcohol syndrome was high among native people. The infant's head seemed much too small in proportion to the rest of her body. Her eyes were small as well, and the mid portion of her face was flattened. Her expression seemed vacant somehow, indicating poor brain development. Ella could tell that the baby was also badly malnourished.

The incidence of child mortality was high in New Mexico's rural areas, more so than in the rest of country, but it was especially bad on the Navajo Nation.

"I had a Sing done for her, but she kept getting worse."

"Has Kellie been to the clinic or to the hospital?"

"Yes, but they wanted to keep her for tests and treatment. They wanted me to leave my little girl with them, but there was no way I could do that. My husband had been helping me before he got arrested, giving her pollen and water to drink and some herbs, but you took him to jail. I was all alone then. My family lives too far away, and my husband's clan isn't much help."

Ella tried to control her fear. The child needed medical help right away. She was barely moving. "You know why your husband was arrested. But your child has done nothing to deserve what's happening to her and she needs more help than you can give her. You've got to trust the clinic doctors because they're her only chance now."

"The *hataalii* said she's sick because we don't live in harmony. That wine and whiskey have put our lives out of balance, so sickness has come. The clinic can't do anything to help us or my child. We don't walk in beauty."

"It's true that you'll have to get your own life back in balance. Getting alcohol out of your lives takes a lot of hard work. But there are clinics and programs that can help you. That will all take time, but right now you need to accept the help the doctors can give your child. Your baby is counting on you. Don't take away her only chance. She doesn't deserve to die."

Gladys broke down into tears. "Please save my daughter. I just can't help her anymore."

"Come with us, then. We'll take Kellie to the hospital, and talk about getting help for your family while the doctors see her. You can have another Sing done for her there. Our hospital allows that."

"I haven't got any more money for a Sing. I can't even buy food for my children."

"No *hataalii* will turn you down on that basis. You know that."

Gladys looked down at the infant. "Do you think Anglo medicine can help her?"

Ella hesitated, unwilling to lie to her now. "I don't know, but we owe it to Kellie to give them a chance."

Ella knew that the child's future wasn't good. Many of their people, in an attempt to avoid death, would leave the infirm at the hospital, then go back to their lives. She had no doubt that this was why Mrs. Zah had been so afraid to leave her daughter at the hospital. It had been tantamount to accepting that her daughter would die. "You can stay with her for as long as you like at the hospital, too. No one will run you out."

Gladys looked at her child, then back up at Ella. "She's so small . . ."

Ella bit back the response she wanted to shout—that it wouldn't have happened if she hadn't been drinking all through her pregnancy—but instead, she took her to the Jeep, leaving Neskahi to deal with the weapon.

"What will happen to my son?"

"The sergeant will take him to a safe place. The tribe has people who will look after him while you're in the hospital with the baby. He'll be just fine, and safe." And probably better off, Ella thought grimly. At least he'd get some balanced meals, and he'd be away from the danger an alcoholic mother always posed.

Ella drove the woman and her child to the hospital and remained with her throughout the process of admission. Mrs. Zah stayed with the baby as the emergency room doctor examined the child. The nurse spoke Navajo, and that helped Gladys relax.

Hearing her call sign on the radio, Ella picked it up, wondering if this would be another delay. At this rate she'd never make it to the memorial service.

"The motel has decided not to press charges," dispatch said. "So it's up to you whether you want to bring her in or not."

"She's needed here more," Ella said, then ended the transmission.

Gladys looked back at Ella, who gave her a nod as the staff members led her to the hospital's nursery. She could see that Mrs. Zah was more comfortable now with the decision she'd made to bring the baby here.

Ella exhaled softly and started down the hall to the elevators, but before she could step inside, she heard her name being called.

Turning her head, she saw Carolyn Roanhorse. "I didn't want Gladys Zah to see me and become frightened, but I overheard the conversation the doctor had with the nurse in the ER and thought you'd want to know. The baby is badly dehydrated and obviously undernourished. She's got an ear infection and a lot of other problems, but she should make it."

Ella nodded. "But she's mentally impaired from the alcohol, isn't she?"

"Yes, but it's too soon to know to what extent. She may yet be able to lead an almost normal life."

"I get so tired of dealing with alcohol-related disasters," Ella said, recalling the drunken driver who had nearly claimed her mother's life.

"And you don't see half of what I do," Carolyn replied.

Ella glanced up at the clock on the wall and cursed. "I've got to go. I wanted to attend my cousin's memorial service, but now I'm afraid I've probably missed the entire thing."

"No, it's still under way. They were having a Mass. But—" She clamped her mouth shut. "No, never mind."

"Go on. What were you going to say?"

"You may be in for a rough welcome. I understand that some of the family blames you, at least partially, for Justine's death, so stay on your guard."

"Thanks for the warning, but I have to go. Big Ed wants me there, though I think it might be better for the family if I just didn't show up."

"You're not guilty of anything, so don't let anyone push you into acting as if you are. I know you're thinking of their feelings, and that's commendable, but not wise. It's bound to be misconstrued and used against you."

"How come you're not there?"

"I wouldn't be shunned in a church service like that since

mostly modernists are part of the congregation, but there's no denying that I make people uncomfortable—even Navajos who admit they don't know squat about our ways. I sent flowers, and suggested in the note that went with it that maybe I should avoid attending the memorial service. I figured I'd go if the family called and told me to come anyway, but no one did."

"They still know you were a good friend to her," Ella said.

Ella left the hospital and drove directly to the memorial service. By the time she found a parking place and walked up to the main entrance, people had just started coming out of the church.

Ella saw Justine's family in a group, meeting visitors. She remained in the background, but as Angela turned to speak to someone, their eyes met. The pain in Angela's eyes tore a hole through her. Angela now existed in another reality—one of only loss, regret, and naked sorrow. No one's words could reach her now. She was past listening, past seeing the things around her, and past caring about anything except the pain in her heart.

As Ruth and Jayne turned and saw Ella, Ruth immediately went to her mother's side and started to lead her away. But Jayne strode to where Ella stood and faced her squarely.

"You wanted us to believe that you were our sister's friend, but you couldn't even show up on time at her service," Jayne said, sorrow and anger in her every word.

"I was sent on an emergency call. I apologize. It couldn't be helped."

"Or maybe it was just a guilty conscience. I don't know if you did anything to cause her death, or just weren't around in time to help her. Either way, you've got my sister's blood on your hands."

Ella felt everyone staring at her. She was being singled out in front of her friends and relatives, and there was nothing she could say to defend herself that wouldn't just make things worse.

Paul Natoni came up then, and never looking at Ella, led Jayne away by the arm. Ella was surprised to see Natoni there at all, but as she looked around the small gathering, she realized that very few of Justine's other friends had come. Of course, that wasn't surprising. Because of the belief that saying the name of the dead within four days of the person's death could call forth their *chindi*, a memorial service could be dangerous.

The only place more hazardous in the minds of the traditionalists was Red Mesa, because that was where Justine was presumably killed, and where her *chindi* most likely remained.

Ella stood at the edge of the crowd, watching her cousins receive condolences from members of the community. Big Ed was in the group and gave Ella an encouraging nod, but made no attempt to join her. Then she saw Harry Ute. He spoke to several people, then came up to Ella.

Standing away from the crowd, yet still watching everyone, Harry spoke in a soft, low voice. "The story is that I was on assignment in Albuquerque and flew in for the service."

"Got it."

"I also received your message. What's up?"

"Could Samuel Begaye be the one who did this?" she asked, her voice a bare whisper.

"I don't know for sure. I had an unconfirmed report of Begaye over near Crownpoint that night, and that probably puts him too far away to be directly connected to the murder."

"But you said it was unconfirmed."

"I haven't had a chance to follow it up and verify the source. But either way, it doesn't remove him from the suspect list entirely. It's possible he's working in tandem with someone else. To stay at large, he's needed help. But your cousin's murder looks well planned, and that MO is all wrong for Begaye. He doesn't seem to worry about the mess or anyone identifying the body. He's not a premeditated type of killer. Begaye kills when drunk and provoked, and then it's sloppy."

She nodded. "Yeah. You're right. But if you find anything that links Begaye to this crime, let me know right away. I'm under the gun on this one."

Harry nodded. "So I've heard, and I wish I could give you a hand with the investigation. But unless I find a connection, I can't help. My priority is finding Begaye. I can't get involved in your case unless the trail leads to my fugitive."

"I know." Ella was disappointed, but she hadn't really expected anything different.

"There's one thing I want you to understand. If I find even the remotest possibility that there's a connection, you'll be the first to know. If the man I was sent here to find killed our friend, I want him—probably even more than you do."

"Be careful about making it personal, Harry," she warned. "Believe me, it just gives you one more complication to worry about. Mentally, I'm already there. I knew she was experiencing some problems and I should have seen this coming."

"When something like this happens, everyone wants to take the blame. But the only person responsible is the one, or maybe the ones, who killed her."

She nodded. "I hear you, but it's really hard not to second-guess everything."

"Stick to the case. In fact, immerse yourself in it. That's my advice."

"That's exactly what I intend to do. I'm going to check out every enemy my cousin ever made. Begaye will go on that list, so our cases may intersect at some point."

Harry nodded. "Just let me know if they do."

"Also keep your eyes and ears open for any other kind of trouble on the reservation," Ella asked.

"Like what?"

"I'm not exactly sure. But there's a chance that the Tribal Police Department may have been targeted by a person or a group out there, and we've just seen the first casualty. We have nothing substantial to base that on. It's just a theory. But I'd like you to stay alert to the possibility."

"All right." He moved off, disappearing into a small group of mourners with an ease only Harry possessed.

Ella saw Abigail Yellowhair taking a puff from her asthma inhaler. Abigail's eyes met hers for a split second before the late senator's wife looked away, nervously. Ella guessed that she was the last person Mrs. Yellowhair wanted to be seen with today.

By the time Ella left the church grounds, she felt drained of all energy and emotion. It had been difficult for her when she'd first returned to the reservation more than four years ago. She'd been an outsider and been treated as such, but she expected things to be even worse for her now. She was going to be treated like a pariah until she could prove she hadn't turned to evil.

Ella went home, hoping to have a very late lunch, unwind, then get back to work, but when she pulled up in the driveway she saw her brother's pickup.

Bracing herself for more tension between her and her sister-in-law, Loretta, who was probably inside, Ella stepped out of the Jeep.

Clifford, who'd apparently seen her drive up, came outside. "I didn't expect you to be coming home this early," he said.

"I just left the memorial service and wanted time to myself, away from the station."

He nodded slowly. "I wondered if you'd go to the Mass."

"I didn't have a choice. Big Ed practically made it an order. But I missed the service itself. I had to take an emergency call. Of course, that made things even worse for me with our cousin's family."

"Are things as bad for you as I've heard?"

"What have you heard?"

"That some of our relatives are holding you responsible for the death, and that our cousin is starting to believe it too."

"Yes, all that's true."

"That's the bad news. But there's even more trouble to come. I'm certain that many traditionalists will see these events as proof that you've turned to evil and now are a danger to the tribe."

She nodded. "The traditionalists will be the first, but sooner or later, a lot of others will see what's happened in the same light. Public opinion will condemn me based on circumstantial evidence alone."

Loretta came out looking for Clifford, saw Ella, and refusing to even acknowledge her presence, went back inside.

"Forgive her. She doesn't mean to be that way."

"Yes, she does."

Clifford smiled wryly. "You're probably right, but she's never known you or understood you like I do."

"Few do."

"That's part of what worries me the most. I understand what it's like when everything goes wrong and friends turn against you. I was on the run once, alone, and wondering if the truth would ever bear me out. It was the most difficult time of my life," he said, referring to the time when he'd been the prime suspect in their father's murder.

"I'll get through it like you did," Ella said.

"No, not like I did. I had my beliefs to sustain me. You still don't have something like that to hold on to. You walk the line between the Navajo and Anglo worlds, but neither one will welcome you now. I'll counter all the lies and the rumors I hear about you, but because we're brother and sister, the good I can do you will be limited."

Ella understood what he meant. Many would distrust him, too, thinking she'd corrupted him. It was suddenly very clear to her that she might have to face things completely on her own, and that was something she'd rarely done since becoming a cop. Even her fellow officers might begin to doubt her if the evidence against her continued to mount. One way or another, she'd have to uncover the truth quickly, or her entire life would come apart at the seams.

FIFTEEN
——— ✖ ✖ ✖ ———

In a pensive mood, Ella ate a sandwich on the old picnic table while Dawn played outside in the sandbox beside her, stacking blocks of wood as high as she could, then laughing when the precariously stacked columns fell down. Dawn had already eaten, but came back every few minutes for a bite of Ella's sandwich. It was one way Ella had spoiled her already.

Ella had sensed that Clifford and Loretta had wanted to be alone with Rose, and that had suited her perfectly. The only company she really wanted right now was that of her daughter. Ella got down beside her in the sandbox and made her own stack of wood blocks, but soon Dawn was tired of stacking blocks and began to play with her dinosaur, making furrows in the sand with the stuffed creature's legs and long tail.

When Dawn nearly fell asleep sitting in the sand, Ella picked her up, brushed the sand gently off her daughter, and took the little girl back inside.

"Mom, I've got to go back to work," Ella said. Clifford and his wife were seated on the sofa, and Rose in her favorite chair. "Dawn's sleepy, so she might be ready for an early nap today."

"I've learned not to count on things like that," Rose said, laughing as she reached out for Dawn, who stumbled toward her.

"Before you go, sister, I need to speak to you," Clifford said unexpectedly.

Ella saw the venomous glare Loretta gave her, and decided that the reason her brother and his wife had wanted to be alone with Rose was that they'd had a family meeting of sorts. It didn't take a genius to guess the topic of discussion, either.

Curious, she tried to read her mother's expression, but Rose's attention was focused on Dawn. The only thing she could read on Loretta's face was strong disapproval, but that didn't tell her anything new.

Ella picked up her weapon from the top shelf of the bookcase where she'd left it before going out with Dawn. As she fastened the pancake holster to her belt, Clifford came into the kitchen.

"I want to help you find this killer," he said.

"What did you have in mind?"

"As I thought about the events, one possibility came to me. I don't like it, but I need to make sure we're not going up against our old enemies again."

"We're not," she said, knowing he meant skinwalkers. "The signs are wrong. This is more brutal and direct in its own way. I just need to get some solid evidence or a witness who's credible before I'll know exactly what happened. I think the killer or killers are enemies our cousin and I have made through the course of our work."

"Maybe I can still help. You know that I wouldn't volunteer to do this lightly, but why don't you take me to where the crime took place? I may be able to see or sense something you and the others may have missed. I know how observant you are, but we just don't look at things from the same perspective. That could be an asset to you now."

Ella considered it. She knew what a sacrifice this was for Clifford, but he was right. His insight would be invaluable. She looked for physical evidence, but he looked for the *hózhq*, harmony in the relationship all things had to each other. That was why he could often quickly spot things that didn't belong. An animal or even an insect that shouldn't be there could have far-reaching consequences. This was an idea that forensic pathologists were just beginning to discover when they took into account seemingly unrelated things like the gestation of certain insects on dead flesh.

"A particularly bad death occurred there—so bad that some have renamed the place Red Mesa. Are you sure you're up to going?" Ella asked, knowing that his beliefs would make a place like that totally abhorrent to him.

"Our relative was murdered, and you might start losing some of your allies, sister. You need me now and I'm going to help you in whatever way I can."

As they went outside, Ella saw Loretta glancing out the window, and the expression on her face stunned her. She knew Clifford would have already told his wife what he'd intended to do, and she'd expected Loretta to have been spitting mad. Yet it wasn't anger that she glimpsed in her sister-in-law's expression, it was fear.

Ella drove her brother to the site of the fire and filled him in on the details of the crime as they walked to the exact spot. He looked paler than usual, but still very much in control of himself. Considering that to Clifford the threat the *chindi* posed to the living was solid, incontrovertible fact, she had to admire his courage.

Clifford took his time studying the place where the body had been found and the surrounding terrain. Finally he looked up and shook his head slowly. "All I can tell you is that this isn't the work of the evil ones. It has none of their trademarks. From what you've told me, this wasn't a ritual killing. It was just a brutal, calculated crime by cold-blooded killers. Judging from the time it must have taken, there were two of them, maybe more."

"I was warned by an informant that there's a conspiracy on the Navajo Nation. The problem is that I don't know what kind of conspiracy. There's a chance the crime against our cousin was just the first of many to come."

Ella saw him wince and wanted to kick herself for not thinking before speaking. As a *hataalii*, her brother truly believed that words had power and that just voicing it could make it come true. "I'm sorry. Police work and your beliefs don't mix easily."

Clifford nodded. "You could be an even better cop if you learned to trust the power of our ways more, and blend them with all the training you've received."

Hearing a vehicle approaching, Ella glanced up and saw Carolyn and Dr. Michael Lavery, the chief pathologist from the university's medical school, pull up beside her Jeep in a new-looking SUV. Ella had met Michael Lavery before when they'd worked on the death of Senator Yellowhair's daughter. The physician was a tall, slender Anglo with sharp gray eyes and short blonde hair, which encircled an expanding, well-tanned bald patch in the center of his scalp.

Seeing Clifford, Carolyn gave him a startled look. "Forgive me, but you're the last person I expected to see here," Carolyn said to Ella's brother, avoiding the use of his name out of respect.

"I thought I could be of some use to my sister in searching for evidence, but it doesn't seem so."

"That's not true," Ella said. "You've helped me eliminate some theories and open the door to new ones."

Carolyn introduced Michael to Clifford, and Ella was grateful when Michael didn't immediately hold out his hand to shake Clifford's. Navajos normally disliked touching strangers, but the last person a *hataalii* would want to touch was a pathologist.

"What brings you here?" Ella asked.

"Both of us wanted to go over the area again in case we missed something," Carolyn said. "I don't expect to find anything new, but it's worth a try."

"I appreciate you both coming here to help. I know that you're in the middle of moving, and that's always a hassle."

"You'll have to see our new house in Waterflow. Michael likes to garden now that he's retired, and he's already planning a huge rose garden." Carolyn paused. "By the way, we'd planned to go on vacation together in a few days, but with everything that's happened, I'm going to cancel."

"No, don't do that," Ella said. "You haven't had time off in years. You deserve a break from work."

"Oh, please," Carolyn said, smiling. "I'm getting this advice from a certified workaholic? When's the last time you took time off?" Carolyn asked.

"I took maternity leave not so long ago," Ella answered. "And these days, rather than take two weeks once a year, I find it easier to take a day here and a day there. But we're getting off the subject. You really have to go on vacation. You've been giving your work everything for too long. You have to recharge your batteries."

"You need balance and harmony, Doctor," Clifford said. "When things are out of balance, sickness comes. It's inevitable."

"Medical science is just starting to come around to that thinking, too," Michael agreed. "And what they say is true, honey, you seldom take time off. You've earned a few weeks to call your own."

Carolyn had a frustrated look. "But right now—"

"Is as good a time as any," Ella replied.

Carolyn sighed, then reached into her purse and extracted a small notebook. She wrote quickly and then tore off the sheet and handed it to Ella. "That's where I'll be. If you need me, or if there's anything I can do, call. I can be back here in a matter of hours."

As they walked away, Ella saw Lavery reach for her hand. She smiled, glad that love had found her dear friend. Carolyn had so few friends on the Navajo Nation, she needed someone like Lavery in her life, a man she had much in common with.

"They make a good pair," Clifford said quietly. "They'll be good for each other if they'll give themselves the time to let their relationship deepen naturally. But for people who are used to being in control of every facet of their private lives, it won't be easy."

Ella nodded slowly. "She cares about him a lot. That'll help." Ella glanced back at Clifford. "Thanks for treating her like a friend. I know that's especially hard for you."

"I don't like what she does for a living, sister, and I don't enjoy being around her. That's the truth. But I also recognize that she's doing what she feels is a service for the tribe. She's a good person, and her motives are equally good. That deserves respect."

As they walked back to the unit, Ella heard her call sign on the handheld radio. She answered and dispatch informed her that Big Ed wanted to see her when she came back to the station.

Ella drove Clifford back to Rose's house first. "It won't be easy for you now," she said. "Loretta's going to be afraid to be around you since you've been at that place of death."

"I know. I won't get near her or my son until later today. I need to perform some rites first."

"Would you prefer I drop you off at your medicine hogan?"

He shook his head. "Let her see me and gain the assurance that I'm all right. I'll walk home then without going into our mother's house. My wife will know where I'm headed, and her mind will be more at ease that way."

Ella looked at her brother for a moment before focusing on the road. No matter how many arguments they had, she knew that her brother loved his wife and his son deeply. In his heart, they would always come first.

She couldn't help but wonder if anyone would ever love her that much, and if she was really capable of giving that kind of love in return. She loved Dawn with all her heart, and her daughter was the center of her life, but it was different between a mother and child. The relationship between two adults was always much more complex and, in her experience, never one that was on such an instinctual level. She'd heard of soul mates, of course, but if there was such a thing, she'd never experienced it.

Ella dropped Clifford off, waved to her mother, ignored Loretta, then headed straight to the station. She had a feeling that what lay ahead for her with the chief was not good.

She wasn't wrong. Fifteen minutes later when she walked inside the chief's office, his somber expression confirmed her suspicions.

"Sit down, Shorty." Directness had always been Big Ed's strength. "We have a problem with procedures that we need to work out. In the past few years we've had some major policy changes coming down from the tribe, and from federal guidelines that I never really expected to have to deal with. I'd have fought harder if I'd realized the implications," he added, almost under his breath. "The bottom line is that when one of our officers is the victim of a homicide, we are required to have someone outside the immediate chain of command—in this situation meaning the FBI— look into it."

"Does that mean you're taking me off my assistant's case?" She'd expected this sooner or later. In almost every police or sheriff's department, a cop was not allowed to lead an investigation where he or she was personally involved. Still, it didn't make accepting the news any easier.

"I don't like handing departmental matters completely over to outsiders, Shorty, so I'm assigning Sergeant Neskahi to work as our liaison, and with Blalock directly. The sergeant's never been assigned to the SI team permanently, so I can get away with it. I would do the job personally, but many believe that I won't be objective. I'm too protective of everyone under my command."

She nodded slowly. "Joseph is a good officer. But without Harry Ute on the team anymore, that makes us dangerously short of investigators," Ella said. "Neskahi may have to work some long, long hours."

She immediately thought of, but didn't mention, Sergeant Manuelito, who'd presented such a thorn in her side on previous investigations. Manuelito was a seasoned officer, but he possessed not only a closed mind, but also a chip on his shoulder where she was concerned. He was the only officer in the entire department she actually considered an enemy.

"No one here really wanted the job, Shorty. We all know that the circumstantial evidence right now makes you a suspect. But I had a long conversation with the sergeant. I convinced him that it's not only a matter of duty, but if he's involved, you'll at least be given the benefit of the doubt and not railroaded by anyone eager to close a messy case. Agent Blalock has turned out better than we all expected, but unfortunately, the Bureau tends to choke on all their rules, you know?"

She nodded. "I'm glad you assigned Joseph to this. He'll bend over backwards to be fair. But that means we'll also be shorthanded on other cases."

"You know I would have replaced Harry long before now if I hadn't been forced to keep his position vacant because of funding cuts. Everyone in your team has been working overtime a lot. I'm aware of that. I was hoping that when the president and Tribal Council settle on funding for the next year, we would be given more support. I was promised as much by several councilmen and the tribal president, but that still leaves us with a problem the rest of this fiscal year."

"So while Neskahi is on loan, you want me to take up the slack around here?"

Big Ed nodded. "I know that you're going to continue to look into what happened, Shorty. I don't really expect anything else. But officially, you're off that case, and taking care of all the other pending investigations. Clear?"

"Perfectly." At least she hadn't been put on administrative leave. Ella knew that in a large department she might have been transferred to another section and given a desk job.

Almost as if reading her mind, he added, "You're lucky we're so shorthanded right now. Otherwise I would have been pressured to keep you at the station or take you off duty until everything was settled."

A knock sounded at the chief's door, and hearing it, Ella turned her head. FBI agents Blalock and Payestewa stood there. Payestewa gave Ella an uneasy look, but Blalock greeted her with his customary nod.

Big Ed waved them into his office. "Come in, fellows. I'm glad you were able to stop by so quickly."

The chief briefed the Bureau agents on the reassignments, then added, "Our Special Investigations people are at your disposal except for Ella. She'll be handling other cases. You'll of course need to get a copy of all her reports pertaining to Officer Goodluck's homicide, but other than that, Ella's officially off the case."

"Count on us to give you a fair shake, Ella," Blalock said. "I know what's going on, and I don't like it any more than you do."

"Let's get down to work," Big Ed said, then looked at Ella. "I believe you have other things to attend to now, Special Investigator."

Ella stood and left the office, closing the door behind her. Everything she had worked so hard to achieve was beginning to slip away. As she started down the hall to her office, Sergeant Manuelito came out of one of the squad rooms and stood in her way.

"I just want you to know that I'm volunteering to help out in the Officer Goodluck investigation," he said. "I've got the credentials, and this is my chance to prove my skills as a major crimes investigator." He paused, then added, "With you as head of the unit, I knew I'd never get an even break, but it looks like lots of things will be changing for the better."

Not rising to the bait, Ella walked past him slowly, taking advantage of her height to force him to look up to her. He'd always had a problem with her and the way she got things done. To him, going by the book was everything.

His attitude only served to remind her of the road ahead. Her enemies would rise against her, united in one purpose—that of destroying her. At the same time, the few friends she had would find their loyalties tested to the limit. And after it was all over, no matter how it turned out, nothing would ever be the same again.

SIXTEEN

————— ✖ ✖ ✖ —————

Ella reported to work at the usual time the next day and spent the entire shift catching up on paperwork despite her desire to join the search for Justine's killer. It was nearly evening when the desk sergeant came in with three thick file folders. "I just finished updating each of these with a short summary. Big Ed said you'd be handling these cases now."

Ella took the files and scanned them, deciding which case had the greatest priority. The one ending up on top was the Thomas Zah case, the prisoner she and Justine had arrested and later on transferred back to Shiprock from Window Rock. He'd been taken to Window Rock initially because that was where the crime had occurred, but fearing that he wouldn't get a fair trial there, his lawyer had arranged to have him moved back to Shiprock. His wife had been responsible for the hostage crisis earlier.

Ella studied the latest incident in the murder case, as described in a report made by a patrolman working the Twin Lakes area, east of Window Rock and on the New Mexico side of the Rez. The case was pretty straightforward, involving drinking and the brutal killing of an in-law in front of several witnesses.

Family feuds weren't very common on the Rez, but when they did occur they were usually between members of different clans. This was natural, because marriages were traditionally outside the clan. These feuds could become very nasty, and go on for years. Ella had observed that although many of her people were quite easygoing, a perceived offense or slight between in-laws could generate hard feelings that often resulted in property damage, theft of livestock, or even violence.

Now Jimmy Begaye, one of the sons of the murdered man, was threatening to even the score and go after Thomas Zah's relatives. Jimmy's wife, Allison, worried that her husband would try and make good on his threat, had reported him missing. Jimmy had apparently left home, taking his hunting bow and knife with him.

Ella checked out the APBs and learned that a vehicle matching the description of Jimmy's truck had been reported passing by the home of one of Zah's cousins who lived near the police station. Though a patrolman had failed to find the vehicle, he'd warned the Zah family to spend the night with friends, advice they'd promptly taken. It was believed that Jimmy was still in the area.

Ella checked her weapon, deciding to work the neighborhood near the home of Zah's cousin. From the looks of it, Begaye was staking out the house and would strike there.

As she got ready to leave, she found herself missing Justine. Grief engulfed her, weighing down her spirit. Justine would have gone with her on a call like this, lending her support, and they would have watched each other's backs. Justine would have probably cracked a joke about having to duck Indian arrows.

Brushing aside the wave of sorrow that threatened to destroy her concentration, Ella adjusted her bullet-resistant vest, put on her jacket, then walked to her Jeep. She knew that a distracted cop was one in constant danger, and she owed Dawn more than that. Her daughter depended on her, as did Rose, and Ella knew that as long as she kept that firmly in mind, she'd never fail to come home from work.

It was dusk by the time she approached the wood-frame house at the end of a quiet dirt track. She was still about a hundred yards away when she saw a man who fit Jimmy Begaye's description coming out of the Zah house. She couldn't be sure, but it appeared Begaye was hiding something beneath his coat.

Ella could see him heading toward his vehicle, parked at the side of the house. Zah's relatives had left already, so Ella figured that Begaye must have broken in and trashed the place or perhaps set some kind of trap. Ella made a call to dispatch, asking that someone check out the house while she moved in on Begaye.

Ella felt her skin prickle, and the badger fetish beneath her blouse against her skin felt warm. Instead of getting into his truck, which she'd expected, Jimmy passed it by and walked around to the backyard. Reaching a barbed-wire fence, Jimmy stopped, pulled a carbine or small rifle from beneath his full-length coat, then set the weapon down on the other side. A moment later, he slipped through the fence, stepping on the bottom strand and slipping under the top wire.

Once on the other side, he calmly picked up the rifle and slipped it back inside his coat, then headed into a small apple orchard. If he continued that direction, he'd end up at the police station, about a quarter of a mile away. It didn't take Ella long to guess his plan. Unable to find Zah's relatives at home, Jimmy had decided to make a move on Thomas Zah himself. Somewhere along the way, perhaps even at the Zah home, he'd traded his bow and arrows for a firearm.

Ella called dispatch again, then warned the desk sergeant of a possible attack. She stayed on Jimmy's tail, keeping some distance between her and the man, looking for a way to gain the upper hand. Begaye stopped often and looked around, waiting and watching, but she was careful not to move when he was stationary.

Soon they reached a small, dry arroyo which ran past the police station, now visible ahead. Jimmy jumped down into the arroyo, and she lost sight of him for a moment. Knowing that he probably wouldn't hear her—the wind was blowing in her direction—she called in and reported Begaye's position and direction of travel.

Dispatch, according to orders, patched her through to Big Ed. "What's going on, Shorty?"

Ella filled him in quickly. "I don't know what he's up to, but it looks like trouble."

"We'll be ready. Watch yourself."

Ella quickly followed the suspect down into the arroyo, but as she reached the bottom, it was as if he'd vanished into thin air. She stopped, listening carefully, but all she could hear were cars in the distance. She peered ahead carefully, but there were no signs of movement anywhere. She waited, guessing he was also doing the same thing. If he'd seen her, then he'd be laying out a trap. She felt the danger as keenly as she could the chill in the air.

She remained still, scarcely breathing, listening for sounds of his approach. Finally she heard footsteps moving away from her. Ella followed again, matching the pace he'd set.

Soon she was certain that the station was his destination. Ella knew that some of Zah's relatives had made it a practice to hang out by the rear doors of the station, waiting for a chance to visit Thomas. Although she was sure that by now Big Ed and the other officers had relocated them somewhere safe inside the building, she still worried that trouble would escalate fast if she let him continue with his plan to reach the station. There were too many civilians coming and going there these days.

At the field behind the station, Begaye scrambled out of the arroyo, weapon in hand, but behind his back.

Ella followed suit, but now she was at her most vulnerable. There wasn't any cover outside the arroyo. Her only ally was the darkness outside the cones of the parking lot lights.

As a semi roared past the station on the highway, Ella took advantage of the noise. Running as fast as she could, she tackled Jimmy from behind, knocking him to the asphalt of the parking lot about twenty-five yards from the station. His rifle flew out of his hands and landed several feet away.

Ella didn't have to wrestle with the man long before help arrived. Within seconds, half a dozen officers swarmed over Begaye and he was handcuffed and taken inside.

As Ella followed the suspect in, Big Ed met her at the booking desk. "I sent an officer to check the Zah house. It was broken into, but otherwise nothing else seems to be wrong. Good job, Shorty," he said.

"Thanks."

Sergeant Manuelito was there, and as Big Ed moved off, he caught her eye. "I thought Jimmy's wife wanted you to keep him from getting into trouble, not have him arrested for assault with a deadly weapon. Looks like you've made yourself a few more enemies tonight, Clah."

He moved off before she could answer, but it didn't matter anyway, she wouldn't have responded. Ella knew that Manuelito was already regarded as an arrogant ass by most of the other officers. His opinion carried little weight on the force.

Right now she had other worries. She needed to catch a ride back to her unit, then return back to the station for at least another hour of paperwork.

Ella left her office shortly after 8:00 P.M. This latest incident had left her exhausted, but she wanted to make one more stop before going home.

Ella drove to the home Justine had shared with her mother and sisters. It was a matter of obligation and duty to family, regardless of how badly they'd treated her. By now they would have heard that she wasn't on the case anymore, and she had to let them know that she wouldn't forget or turn her back on her responsibility to Justine. She'd uncover the truth and see the perps apprehended, even if the department suspended her.

Ella parked and started up the sidewalk toward the front porch when Angela turned on the porch light and came to the door. Ella could see it on her face—that almost desperate need to hear that it had all been a mistake and Justine was fine, and would be home soon. But she had no comforting news to offer her yet.

Ella stopped as she reached the front step. "I'm so sorry for what you've been going through, cousin."

Before Angela could answer, Jayne brushed past her mother and stepped onto the porch. "You should be. You're at the heart of this, Ella."

Angela shot her daughter a hard look. "That's enough." She turned her attention back to Ella. "Why have you come? I know it isn't to give us good news. That's not possible anymore."

By then, Ruth had come outside to stand beside her mother and sister. "I heard what happened at that motel, and why you were late to the service," Ruth said. "My friend is one of the dispatchers. You saved the lives of a mother and her two children."

"She's trying to make up for the one she took. But it doesn't work that way," Jayne shot out.

"That's beneath you," Ella said, glaring at Jayne. "You're convicting me on nothing more than vicious gossip, even though you know very well that I loved my cousin, and I would have done anything to protect her."

"All I know is that my sister and you were arguing constantly lately. Maybe you were afraid that she was going to be a better cop than you ever could be."

"Nothing would have made me more proud," Ella said honestly, then looked at Angela. "I came to tell you that I've been taken off the case for two reasons. First because we were in the same unit together, and secondly because I'm a relative. But I won't give up looking for answers. No matter what happens, I *will* find out what happened, and why."

"Oh, how noble of you!" Jayne said, rolling her eyes.

"Be quiet," Ruth said. "Ella didn't have to come by at all. She knew she'd be subjected to your abuse. She's doing this out of respect, which is a lot more than you're showing at the moment."

Jayne glared at Ruth but said nothing more.

"Thank you," Angela said coldly. "But until you do have answers, I don't want to see you again. Every time I look at you, all I see is the police officer who led my daughter into a trap, then left her alone to die."

Ella felt the stinging truth in her words. Regretting the fact that she'd come in the first place, Ella turned and headed back to her vehicle.

She was on the way home when she heard the short burst of a siren behind her. As she looked in her rearview mirror, she recognized the outline of Blalock's sedan. She pulled over to the side and waited as Blalock and Payestewa approached together from the same side. Ella realized with some irony that had they come to arrest her, the two would have come in different directions, backing each other up, and spotlighted her car to blind her. At least it hadn't gone that far yet.

"How you holding up?" Blalock asked.

"As well as can be expected. But I've got to tell you, someone is working real hard to nail me. The heat keeps building."

"I realize that someone is setting you up, Ella, but I'm not sure how much help I'll be able to give you. Evidence is all I can go by, not gut feelings," Blalock added.

"I know that. But thanks for the psychological support."

"By the way, the note that you found in Justine's office and the one you received have gone to our handwriting experts at the crime lab in Washington. They look like forgeries to me, too, but we'll have to wait for them to verify it. Although they're backlogged, I succeeded in bumping it up the list because Justine was a police officer. But don't expect a response any time soon."

"I appreciate what you're doing, but those notes won't prove I didn't play a part in her death. I'm sure you know that as well as I do. Whoever's doing this to me has played it smart all the way down the line." She started to say more, then hesitated.

"Go on. Don't hold out on me now, Ella. I'm one of the few people you need to trust completely," the senior agent said.

"You already know Samuel Begaye, the fugitive Harry Ute is after, is in the area," Ella said.

"And that bank job he pulled made him over three thousand dollars richer. That could fund him for a while," Payestewa added.

"I know you're already after him for pulling that bank job," Ella continued, "but keep in mind that he's got a big grudge against my cousin and me. We're the ones who sent him to prison."

"If you're right about him, he might be the key to everything that's been happening around here," Blalock said.

"To be honest, it doesn't fit the profile of the fugitive—not as I remember him," Ella said. "But it's definitely something worth looking into."

"Maybe prison changed him," Payestewa suggested. "He may have learned a lot from some of the masters he did time with."

"I suspect that Begaye is part of the picture somehow, but I have a feeling that someone else orchestrated this frame." Ella decided not to tell them about the instant messages she'd received warning her of a conspiracy. Big Ed knew and he'd look into it himself.

"One more thing," Blalock said. "You've already stated in your report that you were at the scene the night of the crime, and the tire prints at the crime scene have confirmed that fact. Your footprints were there, too, as we knew they would be, and have been identified as well. The weird thing is that most of the footprints that belonged to you had been brushed away as if someone had tried to obliterate them."

"Nice touch," she said, shaking her head. "He's making it look like I tried to cover up, but just didn't think of everything. This person's really out to pin my hide to the wall."

"The soil on your shovel also matched that of the area, including the soot from the fire," Payestewa added.

"Again, just as predicted. I was there, and I used the shovel to put out the fire. I admitted that."

"I know. Now, here's something new that may be good news. Several hundred yards from where the body was found, in the opposite direction of where Justine's car was dumped, we found another set of tire marks. We haven't identified them yet. They may have come from departmental vehicles or from that dark pickup you mentioned in your first report. We also found other footprints we haven't been able to account for yet," Blalock said.

Blalock shifted restlessly, then cleared his throat. "But this isn't the reason I stopped you." He reached into his jacket pocket and brought out a document. "I have a warrant to search your home for Justine's weapon, badge, and for tools which may have been used in the crime."

Ella suppressed the shudder that traveled up her spine. He meant an axe, knife, or any other sharp implements that could have been used to dismember Justine's body. She took the paper from his hands. "Give me a minute or two to break this to my mother first, okay?"

"Sure. I thought you might want to do that. That's the reason I flagged you down," Blalock said.

Ella stared at the warrant. "I realize that you're looking for whatever was used to dismember the body, but that could have been any combination of blades or cutting tools. Do you intend to confiscate every kitchen knife we have?" Ella said, unable to keep the anger out of her voice.

Noting it, Blalock gave her a long look. "You're a cop, Ella. I'm just doing my job and cutting you as much slack as I can. A search for the murder weapon is pretty much standard. We'll do the same at the places Begaye has been staying in once we or Harry Ute catch up to him." He paused, then added, "Do you mind if I give you a piece of advice?"

"Go on."

"Despite the pressure to solve this case as quickly as possible, I've got to investigate the case by the book, especially because we've worked together so much in the past. If I don't, somebody is going to call the investigation a whitewash. You have an advantage I don't. You know you're not guilty, so you won't have to waste time touching all the bases, like me. This is the time for you to call in favors and get me some evidence I can really use. Go after whoever did this every spare minute you have. Get me what I need to clear your name. Once that's done, you'll have more access to this case, and the truth is that I need your help as much as you need mine."

Ella nodded. "I'll get what you need. Count on it."

"Good. For now, let's get this search warrant executed."

Ella drove ahead of them, leading the way to the house. She was worried about her mother. Rose didn't like strangers in her home, let alone looking through everything they owned.

When they arrived, Blalock followed her to the front door, keeping an eye on Two, who was sitting on the porch, alert. "In staying by the book, you know I can't let you go inside and talk to your mom unless I'm present. You can whisper, I won't eavesdrop, but I can't give you or her access to the house now that you both know we have a warrant."

"Understood." Instead of going into the house, she called her mother out onto the porch. "They have to search the house, Mom. Where's my daughter?"

"Taking her nap," Rose answered. "I'll bring her outside. The men moving around the house and going through things may scare her."

Blalock stood by the door and looked at Ella as Rose opened the door to go back inside.

"Go with her, if you need," Ella said.

Blalock followed Rose noiselessly, and even though she never said a word, Ella could sense her mother's disapproval. Two followed Blalock, not making a sound either.

To Blalock's credit, neither he nor Agent Payestewa left things strewn about as she'd seen many officers do during the course of their work. But he and the Hopi agent were both methodical and thorough. Though their house was small, it took them close to two hours to go through everything to their satisfaction.

Blalock finally came back outside where Rose was sitting, protected by Two and holding Dawn, who was wrapped in a blanket, fast asleep. The senior agent looked at the small storage shed across the way, pulled a flashlight from his jacket pocket, and handed it to his subordinate.

The Hopi agent looked at the light, smiled, then handed it back, producing a brand-new, even larger flashlight from his coat pocket.

"What do you know? Mine is bigger than yours," Payestewa deadpanned.

Blalock groaned. "We're going to have to go in there too, Mrs. Destea," Blalock said, gesturing toward the shed.

"Nothing's in there except some gardening tools and a box of organic insecticide," Rose said.

Payestewa made a thorough search of the shack and the surrounding area, Blalock at his heels. Two followed, watching the strangers carefully.

Stopping in front of an old stump, Payestewa looked at the scarred wood carefully. "You have an axe, right?"

Blalock looked at Ella, who nodded. "Mom or I usually leave it wedged into the stump. Maybe somebody borrowed it." Ella's throat tightened as she saw her mother looking into the shed.

Rose saw she was being watched. "It should be around here somewhere. Everyone I know around here has their own tools for gathering firewood. Why would anyone run off with it?"

While Payestewa took one last look around the front yard, Blalock joined Ella, a worried frown on his face. "I wish we could find that axe."

"You and me both. If it turns up somewhere, I'll let you know." Ella shook her head slowly. "I don't like the coincidences we're starting to find, Dwayne."

"Neither do I. But you still might find it somewhere else, maybe where you last went to gather firewood."

"You're probably right," Ella conceded. Though she knew it was probably hopeless, they checked in her and her mother's vehicles, but the axe wasn't there either.

By the time Blalock left, even Dawn seemed uncharacteristically quiet. Two went back over the ground the men had checked, sniff-

ing every inch of their paths. The tension in the air was impossible
to miss.

While Dawn, wide-awake now, played with her stuffed animals, Rose sat down wearily on the couch, adjusting a cushion that
had been replaced backward.

"Things are worse for you now that they know the axe is missing, aren't they?"

"Yes, but it's not your fault, Mom. Maybe we'll remember
where it is and everything will be fine." Seeing Rose nod, but with
her expression no more optimistic, Ella continued. "Someone is out
to get me, and the problem is that I don't have a clue who that
could be."

"When your brother was learning to be a Singer, he often got
frustrated because he couldn't remember things exactly right and
he was always making mistakes. What he learned—the hard way—
was that the only way to get things right is to start at the beginning
and make your progress one step at a time."

Ella considered her mother's words, then at last nodded.
"You're right. I'm going in too many directions at once and getting
nowhere. I have to rethink everything from the moment I first noticed that things were starting to change between Justine and me."

"It'll be hard. You're scared. I can feel it. Your intuition won't
help you either, not at a time when everything in your life is out
of balance and without order."

Ella stood at the window. The house was quiet now, but she
could still feel Blalock's presence in the trace scent of cigars that
always lingered on his clothes.

A while later, after putting Dawn to bed, Ella went back to her
office, though it was getting late. Here she could focus solely on
the investigation and try to lay out a clear plan. She could use the
break-in of her home as a starting point, or the missing axe, or
Two's poisoning, or, lastly, Justine's private life.

After weighing all the options, she decided to start with the
latter. She'd begin by talking to Natoni about Justine, though it
would have to be an unofficial visit since she was no longer on the
case. With that in mind, she checked her watch, then stood and
headed out of the building. Now would be a good time to catch
him at home.

Ella got his address from the phone book, then drove to an area where several old trailer homes were clustered. Discarded washing machines and derelict cars littered the area. Each trailer space was defined more by the trash around it than the pieced-together chicken wire that usually held a family's thin, feather-impaired hens and a wooden crate or two that served as their shelter. The glare of her headlights only served to highlight the ugliness of the place, though she suspected that in daylight it probably looked even worse.

Disgust and anger filled her as she looked around. She knew that hopelessness and poverty reigned here. When The People's spirit was broken, they stopped caring. The worst part was that children grew up in areas like these never knowing that they deserved something better.

She'd never liked Natoni, but she knew where he'd come from, and why he was still here. Poverty wasn't inevitable, but for some, it was a lifetime excuse to strike out at those who'd worked harder or made smarter choices.

Ella knocked loudly on the front door, trying to be heard over the television set. She thought she heard a woman's voice, but she couldn't be sure. It might have only been the TV.

A few minutes later Natoni finally came to the door. His shirt was open and he held a can of beer in one hand.

He looked at Ella in surprise, brushing his oily hair away from his eyes. "You're the last person I expected to see. Now that everyone's convinced you're guilty of the crime, the police chief should have had enough sense to take away your badge."

Ella wanted to smash his nose, but using all the willpower she had, remained perfectly still. She even managed a smile.

"I have a few questions for you."

"About Justine? You *are* off the case, right?"

"Not quite," she answered, refusing to acknowledge what he was saying. Not waiting for an invitation, she brushed past him and climbed up the steps.

Natoni laughed. "Come into my humble home, won't you? Just don't expect me to offer you a beer."

"What was happening to my cousin? There was something wrong with her the last few weeks of her life. If you were around her as much as she said, you should have noticed it, too."

"Oh, please. What's next, bad Karma, or a lesson about the perils of not walking in beauty and living in a state of disharmony? Justine was just being Justine. You just couldn't accept that she was different from you. Face it, Ella. You didn't want an assistant—you wanted a clone."

Natoni was baiting her, and there was no way she would let him get to her. "Save the sarcasm. I just want to know what part you played in my cousin's troubles."

"*I* was the one who tried to help her. From what Justine told me, you were hell-bent on undermining her career and her life. You wanted to make sure she didn't advance too quickly and steal your thunder in the department. You obviously have an ego problem," Natoni sneered.

"She knew me better than that. This sounds more like something you were trying to drill into her head." Ella leaned back on the sofa, feigning ease. The scent of something familiar came from the worn fabric. "Look, I have no other commitments tonight. If you want to entertain me with your witticisms for the rest of the evening, that's fine by me."

Suddenly his expression changed. "You're not staying long."

"Why? What's so important? Expecting company?"

"I have a life to lead, and you're not going to become part of it." Natoni crushed the empty beer can with his hand, then tossed it into a wastebasket.

"I don't know about that. Actually, I'm just starting to feel at home." Ella put her feet up on the narrow coffee table.

"Look, all I know is that Justine said she was tired of being number two to you, always your gopher and backup. She wanted more responsibility, and not just in the lab. But as long as you were the head of the team, she knew she'd never get a chance for promotion. You never treated her right."

Ella stood and began to walk around the small room, decorated with prints by Navajo artists she recognized and a small rug probably from a local weaver. As she reached the hallway, she heard the sound of someone moving on the other side of the thin veneer door. It was open a crack, but as she tried to peer in, Natoni stepped in her path.

Ella turned away, wondering if it had been a trick of her senses. She could have sworn she'd caught a whiff of Justine's perfume. Maybe it was just something that had lingered in the air from her last visit.

She started to step around him, but Natoni blocked her way again, pulling the door shut.

"You're leaving, Investigator Clah. You have no right to be here, and let's face it, if I complain, you'll be in a mess of trouble."

Ella knew he'd won this battle, but the war was far from over. "If I find out that you had anything to do with what happened to my cousin, my one goal in life will be to ruin yours. Do you understand what I'm saying?"

"Your threats mean nothing to me. Now, get out or I'll call the *real* police."

As he reached for the phone on the wall, a current of air brought a gentle violet scent toward her. There was no doubt in her mind now that it was the same perfume Justine always used.

Of course, Justine wasn't the only woman who wore that scent, but it wasn't available locally. It had been her cousin's one luxury, and she even carried a small vial of it in her purse. Stores in Albuquerque carried the perfume, but none around here. She knew, because she'd tried to find it for her one Christmas. What if Justine was somehow still alive?

As she stepped to the door, Ella heard footsteps coming from the hallway. She looked straight at Natoni, then decided to check for herself. Natoni crossed the room in a flash, blocking her way.

"Who I entertain in my home is none of your business," he snapped.

Ella knew she could have forced him to his knees with one well-placed kick. Unfortunately, she'd forfeit her job for a stunt like that, unless whoever was behind that door solved the case for her right then.

It wasn't worth it without more to go on. Suspension without pay pending a hearing was the last thing she needed now. She didn't have enough savings in the bank to take care of her mother's and daughter's needs.

Reluctantly she left the trailer, never once looking back at Natoni. Seeing a smug, self-satisfied look on his face would have been more temptation than she could bear, and she was certain she would have tried, and succeeded, in wiping it off.

Ella stood by her unit, trying to decide if she should just sit there until someone had to come out, or drive off and stake out the trailer from a distance. Knowing Natoni was watching her, Ella got into her unit, then drove out of the area. Once she was a hundred yards past the last trailer, she went off the road and parked behind some junipers. In the darkness no one would be able to see the unit among the low trees. But this wasn't all she planned to do.

She considered her next step very carefully. On nothing more than the scent of a particular perfume and the sound of movement, she was going to risk her career by going back to peek in Natoni's windows. If he or a neighbor caught her, or the woman with him complained, she'd be explaining herself to the police—and eventually to Big Ed, who would not be very understanding at all.

Yet her visit to Natoni's trailer had uncovered a new, exciting possibility. What if Natoni was keeping Justine prisoner, perhaps drugged, while the police were being led around in circles? The body they'd found could have been somebody else's, and the fingerprint comparison faked somehow by switching records at the station.

Although deep down she suspected it was only wishful thinking, she knew she had to go check things out more closely or she'd never have another moment's rest.

Ella jogged back to Natoni's trailer, staying in the shadows. The willingness to take a risk was what had always made her a good cop, and this was no time to shy away from that.

The trek back took Ella nearly a half hour, because she proceeded slowly and carefully, not wanting to set off an alarm by frightening a chicken or other animal. Fortunately, she hadn't seen or heard any dogs. By the time she reached Natoni's trailer, the lights inside were off. Ella could see a figure walking around inside, but just the one. It looked like Natoni and he seemed to be alone. As she brought her ear close to the window, she overheard him on the phone.

"I'm telling you she's trouble." Natoni paused. "No, there's nothing for her to find here—not anymore. I've taken care of everything."

Ella knew that her instincts had been right. Someone else had been in the trailer earlier. But that person was no longer there, perhaps having left out the back door. Either that or she was still inside, asleep or drugged.

But it was all conjecture. Ella still had nothing to offer Blalock. Fear gnawed at her. She'd have to do better. If she didn't, she'd soon learn all about the dismal fate of a cop in prison.

SEVENTEEN

———✖ ✖ ✖———

Ella arrived at her office an hour early, resigned to the grisly task of tracking down Justine's killer. Her excitement over the possibility of her cousin still being alive had disappeared with the morning and a reexamination of the physical evidence.

She had to face the truth head-on, and expend her energy on finding Justine's killer. It had been absurd to muster any hope at all based upon the lingering scent of a perfume, which proved nothing.

Today she wanted to access several databases, but without any interruptions. With a chocolate-covered doughnut and some black coffee beside her, she studied the police records of everyone Justine and she had investigated this past year. From what she could see, Justine had made enemies, but no more or less than any other cop.

The phone interrupted her analysis, and grumbling, Ella picked it up on the third ring.

It was Carolyn Roanhorse. "I'm calling to let you know I'm going on vacation as of today, Ella. The medical examiner's officer in Albuquerque will take care of any autopsies that are needed as the result of a crime. They handle the rest of the state anyway. I've also managed to get a forensic pathologist to take my place if needed in a crisis. He's works for the Public Health Services and is based in Colorado, but he'll fly down if it becomes necessary."

"Go and have a great time. Forget all about work for a while. Believe me, if I could, I would."

"You can't. You're not wired that way. And neither am I. I'll be away from my office, but my mind will be here."

Ella thought for a moment about what had been bothering her, then decided to go ahead and bring it out one last time. "Carolyn, I need to ask you something. Are you still very certain that the body we found was Justine's?" Immediately she realized that she'd slipped up and said the name out loud for the first time since she'd heard it was Justine who'd died, but Carolyn was beyond allowing that to upset her.

There was a long silence. "Why does this sound like a trick question?"

"Just answer me."

"Based on the evidence, yes, I believe that was Justine. The print taken from the fingertip we recovered matched those we have on file for her. Fingerprints are, essentially, one hundred percent reliable. The bones dug up were no help, and the tooth fragments were just too incomplete to do any comparisons with dental records. The same with the portion of the skull we recovered."

Carolyn thought a moment, then continued. "Anyone arrested for killing Justine wouldn't get any forensic help from me, that's for sure. The physical evidence, probably all that a prosecutor really needs, is there." There was another pause. "But let me guess. You've found something that appears to contradict that?"

"Maybe." She told Carolyn what had happened at Paul Natoni's trailer the night before.

"That perfume isn't common, but it isn't unique either," Carolyn said slowly. "It could have been stolen from her and is now being used by another woman. But if Justine is somehow really alive, what you're talking about is an elaborate conspiracy that would need a lot of convincing evidence to mislead the police."

"I know. It would involve chopping off Justine's finger and using somebody else's body. It's a stretch, and maybe I'm just wishful-thinking here, but if it happened to be true, that would mean Justine could be somebody's prisoner right now."

"If someone is keeping Justine alive somewhere, there has to be a reason. And maybe it's not just to frame you, Ella. Anyone disturbed enough to do something like this could be out to hurt a lot of people."

"That's a given. But what could they hope to achieve?"

"I don't know." She paused, then added, "Want me to cancel my vacation?"

"Don't you dare. You're only going to be gone for two weeks."

"One week," she corrected. "That's the most I can manage with a minimum of guilt."

"You're hopeless."

"Look who's talking," Carolyn replied.

As Ella hung up, she felt the ripple of fear that had become her constant companion. She didn't like fighting battles like these. Since the day she'd given birth to Dawn, her whole outlook had changed. The exhilaration and the thrill of the chase were always tempered by what she stood to lose if she got careless, and by her responsibility to her daughter. Being maternal had disadvantages to a cop, including the uncomfortable bullet-resistant vest she now wore beneath her blouse.

Ella continued looking through the arrest records and old files, searching for an enemy cunning and motivated enough to generate a scheme like this. Fortunately, the most dangerous people she could think of were already dead or locked away. But that left her without viable suspects. After another hour, she still had nothing, not even a possible owner of the dark-colored pickup that had passed by that evening. All the neighbors had been ruled out. She was forced to return to the facts. Justine was dead, and a killer was out there to be found.

Hearing someone at the door, Ella looked up. It was Big Ed. He glanced at the half-eaten doughnut on her desk with envy.

"Have you got anything more for me on Jimmy Begaye's attack on the station?"

"I'm going to try and track down exactly where Begaye got the rifle he was carrying. All he owned was a hunting bow, supposedly. What we have against him so far is the break-in at the house of Zah's relative, which I was a witness to, and his stealthy approach to the station. It's pretty open and shut."

"Good. Then explain that to his wife. She's here and wants to talk to you."

Ella took a deep breath. "Okay. I'll bring her back here."

"Afterwards, come to my office. There's another rumor I want to talk to you about."

"Rumor?"

"Later," Big Ed said. "You have to talk to Allison Begaye now."

Ella walked down the hall to the lobby area. She'd expected Allison to be Navajo, but the woman who met her in traditional skirt and turquoise jewelry was a petite blonde with ice blue eyes and a somber expression.

"I need to talk to you, but in private," she said.

"My office is a good place, then," Ella said, leading her down the hall.

Once in Ella's office, Allison sat down. "Could we close the door?"

Ella studied her expression. She felt no immediate threat from the woman, so she complied. "What can I do for you?"

"First, I want you to know that I'm very disappointed in this police department. I told you what my husband was going to do so you could stop him. I was hoping you would talk to him before it escalated instead of waiting until he got ready to attack this station before doing something about it."

"Actually, the way things played out, I didn't have any other choice. No one could even locate him until I found him leaving the Zah home, armed with a rifle, and heading for the station. His course was set. He might have been killed by an officer if he'd tried to come inside the station with that rifle."

Ella continued. "But he's alive, and was charged with resisting arrest and assault with a deadly weapon. An additional charge of breaking and entering the Zah house near the station will probably be added to that as well, but a murder charge would have been far worse. Do you know if he had a specific target in mind?"

"I don't think he ever thought it through. He knew Thomas Zah's relatives were here, hanging about, but I don't believe he would have really shot anyone. Jimmy isn't like the others in his family."

Ella nodded, but didn't say anything. "Did you know he stole a rifle?"

She nodded. "I believe that it belongs to Thomas Zah. I heard that Samuel contacted Jimmy and told him where to find it. Samuel was a friend of Zah's uncle, and that's the house Jimmy went to. Jimmy and Samuel figured that it would add something to the revenge if Jimmy used Thomas' own gun against one of his clan." She paused. "But at most, Jimmy would have wounded someone, not killed them."

Now Ella knew that Samuel Begaye was taking an active part in the events happening around him. Despite Blalock's and Harry Ute's efforts, the Begaye brothers had been in contact. If revenge was so important to Samuel that he'd risk meeting his brother, it was entirely possible that he was behind what had happened to Justine, too.

"Samuel Begaye has sworn revenge on me and my cousin."

Allison's eyes grew large. "If you think either of them is behind what happened to that woman police officer, you're way off base. I know my husband and his brother. They can be cruel, but that type of gruesome murder is way beyond them."

Ella had heard the denial in the testimony of the loved ones of criminals too many times to take their character references seriously. Games were being played on all sides now.

"I just want you to know one thing," Allison said. "By having put Samuel and Jimmy in jail, you've made a very big mistake. You could have turned my husband's clan into your friends by helping Jimmy. And they never forget a friend. But that isn't what happened, is it?"

"And they never forget an enemy? Is that what you're really trying to tell me here?"

Allison shrugged. "Let's just say that they've got long memories."

"I'm supposed to consider this a threat?"

Allison shook her head. "No, I just came to tell you that what you did was wrong—in every imaginable way. You know how the Navajo people believe that everything in life is connected?" Seeing Ella nod, she continued. "Well, what you did—or didn't do—will catch up to you. You'll pay your own price before the balance is restored and all of us find harmony."

Ella regarded her thoughtfully, recalling that Allison had avoided using Justine's name. "You've learned much about the ways of the *Dineh*."

"I live here in the *Dinetah*. When I followed my husband to his home, I promised myself that I'd be more than just another outsider. I will never really belong here or be fully accepted, I know that now, but I can at least be aware of the customs and the way of thinking of those around me."

She stood up with dignity and, not giving Ella a chance to say anything else, walked out.

Ella stared pensively across the room for a moment. Like Allison, she knew what it was like not to belong. Outside the four sacred mountains, she'd been a stranger who'd had to prove herself every step of the way. Then, when she'd returned to the Rez, she'd had to earn her place among the tribe again.

It was worse, however, for those who were not part of the *Dineh* at all, yet still tried to live among the tribe. Her heart went out to Allison. She hadn't chosen an easy life.

Ella verified the information about the stolen rifle, though it wasn't an easy task. Until recently, except for handguns, firearms weren't officially regulated in New Mexico. Thousands of firearms owned by families had been passed down from generation to generation, or bought, sold, and traded among the citizens with no paperwork or records at all. The best she was able to do was confirm the theft through hearsay. Zah's wife, who was still staying at the hospital with her child, verified it for her.

Ella switched off the computer, then walked to Big Ed's office. She felt restless and frustrated working on cases that weren't nearly as important to her as what had happened to Justine. And if there was even the slightest chance that Justine was still alive, she had to give the case top priority if she was to have a chance at finding her cousin again.

Knocking on Big Ed's open door, she walked inside and accepted his invitation to sit down.

"Shorty, I heard a very disturbing story early this morning. My aunt Dezbah was visiting at the trailer court north of here last evening. She said she saw you paying a visit to Paul Natoni."

"I stopped by there for a short time after my shift. I know he and my cousin were close, and I wondered how he was handling the loss."

"So it had nothing to do with police work?" the chief said slowly.

"I would have gone while on duty if it was related to any of the cases I've been assigned."

Big Ed's eagle-sharp gaze rested on her. "You're walking a fine line, Shorty. My aunt also told me that she could have sworn Natoni had a Peeping Tom not long after you left."

Had the blasted woman spent all her time looking out the window? Ella said nothing.

"Of course, I'm sure that if you'd found out anything that would have helped any police investigators, you would have shared it with this department."

Ella hesitated.

"Look, Shorty, we all know you wouldn't harm your cousin and that the circumstantial evidence against you requires that you do all you can to clear your name. But no charges have been filed against you, nor are they likely to be unless something really damning turns up. So don't start holding back on me. I *am* on your side and you know it."

"Chief, what I have is speculation mingled with a lot of hope. Nothing you can use."

"But you found out something, didn't you?" Not waiting for an answer, he continued. "Remember that I'm in a position to follow up on things like this, you're not. I can make sure that this department uses all its resources and that the FBI does the same. Don't try to handle this on your own."

Ella took a deep breath and then answered him, telling Big Ed about the scent of Justine's perfume, Natoni's discomfort, someone else's presence in the trailer, and the theory that she couldn't quite put out of her mind that maybe Justine's fingertip had been left near someone else's body to make them believe she was dead.

"That's quite a stretch, and I have a hard time buying in to it. But we should still keep an eye on Paul Natoni as a suspect in whatever happened. My aunt goes over to that trailer court quite often. Her daughter is living there temporarily. I'll ask her to keep her eyes open for anything unusual. She has a lot of experience being a busybody. Even if Natoni catches her hanging around, he probably won't think anything of it. In fact, he's probably used to it by now," he added with a chuckle. "Having a large family like mine can be an asset sometimes," he said, reaching for the ringing phone.

As the chief answered the call, Ella stood and let herself out of the office. The chief's words had given her an idea.

Ella returned to her office. The one thing she hadn't done was investigate Justine's family. It hadn't really occurred to her to do that until now. It seemed wrong, somehow, like an unforgivable breach of privacy, but she didn't have any other options. She'd still uncovered nothing that would explain why Justine had been so on edge lately. Maybe it had been the result of family problems.

Justine was the youngest of seven kids, but out of her entire family, only three remained on the reservation. There was Justine, Ruth, who was married and had two kids, and Jayne, who was the middle child, and a free spirit from everything Ella had ever heard. Almost every time they'd met, Jayne was just starting a new job or had a new man in her life. Jayne had a wild streak a mile long, and had always seemed a bit jealous of her younger sister Justine, the prettiest of the daughters.

Ella started the background checks by accessing credit reports. Ruth owed some money, but nothing substantial except a home mortgage, which was currently paid up. Her husband was an electrician at the power plant and made a decent income, and Ruth herself worked in one of the elementary school cafeterias.

Jayne was a different story. She'd maxed out several credit cards, and had recently been fired from her last job at the Totah Cafe where she'd been working as a waitress.

Ella left the station and drove directly to the cafe. Justine and she had routinely stopped there for coffee, or for iced tea during the summer, and shared a jumbo order of French fries. Memories crowded her mind as she went inside the clean but otherwise typical roadside eatery.

She started toward their usual table, but stopped halfway. She wouldn't sit there again.

Ella chose a stool at the counter, and before long Mary Lou Bitsillie, the new manager of the cafe, came over. Ella had known Mary Lou practically all her life.

Mary Lou poured Ella a cup of coffee. "How are you holding up? I know this is a terrible time for you, but I want you to know that I'm very sorry about what happened to your cousin, and that I'm still your friend. If you need anything, just let me know. I don't believe any of this crap I've been hearing. I know you too well."

"Thanks," Ella said, glad to hear friendly words for a change. "There is something you can do. I need to ask you a few questions about a former employee, but it's really important that you don't tell anyone."

"You've got it. Ella, I still remember how you spent the better part of a semester helping me cope with the fact that my mom was dying. No one wanted to talk about death, and almost everyone started avoiding me because I was so depressed. But you never did and I've never forgotten that."

"I remember. No one meant to be cruel, but everyone believes, to one extent or the other, that words have power and even talking about death could call it to you."

Mary Lou nodded solemnly. "But you were there for me anyway, and that's what counts. If you ever need any help, I'm here. Now, tell me who it is you need information on."

"Jayne Goodluck, my second cousin."

She sucked in her breath. "That could be a powder keg for you, Ella. Not many people like her, but she's sure got a lot of sympathy lately." Mary Lou looked around, then continued. "Good thing this is my slow time of the day," she said. "What you ask will take more than a quick answer."

"I'm listening."

"I fired Jayne, though it wasn't something I did easily. I like her family, and I know that Jayne was trying to get herself together. But she kept missing work and not calling in, or showing up late after I'd found someone to take her shift. A few times, Ruth came in to work in her place. I think those were probably times when Jayne was fighting a hangover."

"She drinks too much?"

"Yeah, and she gambles constantly. She owes everyone money, including Justine. I heard she'd even bailed Jayne out of jail more than once." Mary Lou looked around. "Does it bother you if I say her name out loud?" she added.

Ella shook her head, not wanting to inhibit her friend at the moment. "Any idea where Jayne goes to gamble? We don't have any casinos on the reservation, and the closest legal places are half-way across the state, except for scratchers and the lotteries."

"I think she goes to a small back-room operation in the Farmington area. She likes to play poker and throw the dice, but loses more than she wins. She got in over her head recently, but she kept gambling, believing each time that her luck was going to change. Then, when all the money suddenly disappeared from the cash register at the end of her shift one day, that was the last straw."

"Did you report it to the police?"

"Sorta. I called Justine. She told me to total up the amount taken based upon the receipts, and I did. It was evening, and since I hadn't made a deposit earlier that day, it came out to several hundred dollars. Justine came by a few hours later with a check and paid it in full."

"But you still fired Jayne?"

"I had to. I couldn't trust her, not after that. I think she'd tapped in to it before, since she always came up short. But at least I didn't have her arrested."

"Good point," Ella said. "And I don't blame you for firing her."

"I heard later, from Ruth, that Justine also gave Jayne a cash loan to square her debts. But Jayne blew the money on scratchers and lottery tickets." Mary Lou paused. "You know, when I first heard the rumor that Justine had disappeared, I thought that maybe Jayne had flipped out."

"Have you seen her get violent?"

"I was at the Chapter House one night when she started throwing punches at Justine outside in the parking lot. Jayne had been drinking that night, and Justine had tried to get her to quiet down because she was embarrassing herself. I remember that night clearly because everyone was in a bad mood. There was a meeting going on about the power lines that were going to be built through our land."

"So other people saw this too?"

"Yeah. At first they pretended not to notice that Jayne had come to the meeting a little drunk, but she kept cussing and interrupting the utility company speaker. Justine escorted her out and then we all heard a commotion. There are windows facing the parking lot, so we all saw what was going on."

Ella considered it. This was certainly one reason for Justine to have been on edge. Jayne's actions would have made it difficult for Justine to get any sensitive jobs within the department that required political approval along the way. Being protective of her sister and of her own career would have torn Justine in two. Maybe having to remain on her guard around Ella had put Justine on edge.

"If I were you," Mary Lou said, I'd seriously consider Jayne as a suspect. Mind you, I don't think she would have killed Justine on purpose, but her temper, particularly when she's been drinking, is really something. She loses control of herself."

Ella left the Totah Cafe feeling even more unsettled than before. She needed to make some sense out of the crazy picture that was emerging.

Ella drove back to the station and walked to Tache's office, which connected to Justine's small forensics lab from another hall. Ralph sat alone, going through photographs and reports from the crime scene.

"Ralph, I need a favor," she said, taking a seat in the generic plastic and steel chair across from his desk. He wasn't a traditionalist, and she knew she could talk to him about Justine without making him any more uneasy that he already was.

Tache looked up. "Name it, Ella."

"I need some information. You've got access to the most recent reports on Justine's case, but I can only access what's already been transcribed into the computer system."

"What do you want to know?"

"Where was Jayne Goodluck at the time the body was being destroyed?"

"Being a relative, I suppose you already know about the frequent arguments she had with Justine?"

"Yeah."

"FB-Eyes, Agent Blalock, questioned her yesterday, and I understand she was furious when she was asked to account for her time. She accused Blalock of trying to make her a suspect to take the blame away from you," Ralph said.

"That must have endeared her to him." Ella smiled.

"She didn't help her cause when she picked up an ashtray and nearly threw it at him. Blalock made sure that detail went into his report," Tache replied, looking through the updated paperwork that had been sent to all investigating officers. "Here it is. She said she was over at the Daily Double tavern in Farmington at the time. She's working there as a waitress now."

"Thanks."

"Ella, if you go talk to her or her employers, you didn't get this information from me, okay? Blalock didn't want any leaks."

"No problem."

Ella was in her unit, heading east toward Farmington, when she saw a tribal vehicle behind her flashing his lights.

Ella pulled over, and noticed Sergeant Neskahi getting out of his unit. A moment later they stood by the side of the road.

"What's up?" Ella asked.

"I have a bit of news for you." Neskahi had a deep voice, and when he spoke, it made him seem older than he really was. The sergeant was built like a wrestler, and his physical strength had come in handy on more than one felony arrest in the past.

"Come up with a new development in the case, Joseph?"

"No, nothing so earth-shattering. Just a sign of the way the wind's blowing, at least the political hot air, anyway. Have you heard Yellowhair's new ads on the radio?"

Ella remembered that Abigail had used her in print and radio ads, pointing to Ella as a great police officer and role model for young Navajos. "Let me guess, my name's been dropped?"

"Yeah, and it's pretty obvious. Everyone knew it was there before, and now that section has been replaced with something about putting a stop to crime on the Rez."

"I'm not at all surprised," Ella said with a shrug. "She'll probably end up calling for my resignation by next week."

"Yeah, well, I went over to the Yellowhair home a little earlier today. Mrs. Yellowhair's hosting a political party and wants to hire a handful of off-duty cops to provide security and take care of gate crashers."

Ella looked at Joseph, who seemed to be preoccupied. Neskahi wouldn't have pulled her over just to give her a status report on someone's party, or talk politics. She knew him pretty well, and those issues didn't rate high in his list of priorities.

"While I was there, offering my services, Abigail Yellowhair had me step into her office. She asked me privately about you—how you were holding up under the gossip and suspicion."

"And you told her I was fine, I hope."

"Yeah, but I kept it vague, and told her if she wanted to know how you were, she should ask you. She took my advice and asked me to bring you a message. Mrs. Yellowhair wants to meet with you unofficially, at your convenience. She said she'd be at home all day today, and if you could drop by, she'd be grateful. She specifically asked that you don't call her on the phone, but come in person instead."

"Interesting. Did she give you any idea what it was all about?"

"No, not really. But I don't think she's your enemy. On the other hand, she doesn't appear to be your friend either. She wouldn't have taken your name out of her ads if she was."

"Abigail Yellowhair has her own agenda. That's very clear to me."

"Then be careful. There's something not quite right about that woman. She's a real mixture of contradictions. She's supposed to have traditionalist leanings, yet she's going after her husband's job in politics. She also offers to shake hands, and looks you straight in the eye, like an Anglo or a preacher." Joseph paused. "It's like she's trying to be all things to all people, and I can't bring myself to trust anyone who is that changeable."

Ella nodded. She'd felt that way, too. "I appreciate you delivering me the message, and thanks for the warning. I'll go see what she wants," Ella said, then went back to her vehicle.

She'd intended on paying her cousin Jayne a visit next, but now thought she should go see Abigail Yellowhair first. The way the woman had gone about setting up the meeting was making Ella undeniably curious.

Ella reversed direction and headed back to the reservation. She arrived at the Yellowhair residence, a fancy Spanish-style home not far from Big Ed Atcitty's, thirty minutes later. The only vehicle there was a sedan she knew Abigail drove. The late senator's BMW, one of his prized possessions, so she'd always heard, had been sold shortly after his death. It was commonly believed that the man's *chindi* could contaminate the things he loved, so his car had been sold to an Anglo family off the reservation.

Abigail's new car was a nondescript light blue Ford. It was a simple, durable car that matched Abigail's no-nonsense style well.

Apparently having heard Ella's vehicle coming up the long graveled drive, Abigail came out to meet her. Ella parked beside the sidewalk and got out of the Jeep warily. She had nothing against Abigail Yellowhair, but this nearly clandestine meeting was making her skin crawl.

"I understand you wanted to see me, Mrs. Yellowhair," Ella said, not knowing if saying her name aloud would bother the woman.

Abigail waved her inside. "Call me Abigail, Ella. I've been meaning to talk to you, but my situation is, well, delicate. I wanted to pick a time when there weren't others around to overhear or to spread gossip later on."

Unsure of what to say, Ella opted to remain silent and took a seat.

Abigail sat on the soft leather sofa opposite Ella's chair. "I've heard what some people are saying about you. I was wondering how you were holding up under all those thinly veiled accusations."

"I can take the heat, if that's what you're asking, but I also intend to find out who's behind the murder, no matter what that may do to my career. I loved my cousin, and no one is going to kill her and get away with it."

Abigail smiled. "That's what I hoped you'd say. You caught the person who murdered my husband, and that case was very complex and sensitive, not only to the tribe, but to the entire country. I have no doubt that you can find the truth now as well."

"Was there another reason why you wanted to see me?" Ella asked.

"You and your cousin helped me out during a very difficult time in my life, and I won't forget your hard work. I can't support you publicly right now. I still have an election coming up next year, and advisers in my party say I shouldn't take a public position on your situation. But I still have a considerable amount of influence here on the Rez without the politics. I wanted you to know I'm on your side, and I'll work on your behalf behind the scenes whenever the question comes up. If things really get bad, all you have to do is let me know, and I'll do whatever I can."

Mrs. Yellowhair stood up. "In the long run, I think you'll see I can do more good for you if I stay behind the lines. I'll exert much greater influence over events that way."

Not to mention that she wouldn't get dirty by association with all the innuendo and accusations facing Ella. It was a good politician's ploy. She'd look good no matter what happened to Ella. But Ella had never figured Abigail for a game player. Maybe Abigail had learned far more from her double-dealing husband than anyone realized.

Abigail smiled. "I know what you're thinking—that I used to be much more direct than this. That now I'm playing a game. And you're right, I am. I'm a fast learner. You see, I believe I can accomplish what my husband never could. I can pull the different factions here together. That will make our tribe stronger and better able to face the future. But for me to get the chance to do that, I'm going to have to learn to outplay the boys and use their own rules to get what I want."

Ella thought about Abigail's words as she got back to her tribal unit. In a way, they weren't so different from each other. They were both women who had learned to do whatever it took to accomplish the good they set out to do.

Ella headed away from the Yellowhairs' home, dust trailing behind her vehicle. She had work to do, and like Abigail, she intended to do whatever it took to win.

EIGHTEEN

———— ✘ ✘ ✘ ————

Ella parked outside the Daily Double tavern, a faded-looking cinder-block building on the eastern outskirts of Farmington. The self-proclaimed sports bar did a reasonable amount of business, judging from the dozen or so pickups and cars that nearly filled the small parking lot.

Ella went into the dimly lit establishment, and stood by the entrance until her eyes adjusted to the darkness. There were at least thirty customers, and only two tables unoccupied. Most were eating lunch while watching a baseball game on the large-screen TV.

Jayne was nowhere in sight, and Ella began to wonder if she'd be showing up for work at all today. Jayne was a modernist, like her sister Justine, but might still be keeping a four-day mourning period out of respect, or at least for appearances' sake.

Ella checked with the waitress who hurried to bring her coffee, a young Anglo girl whose name tag said "Annie."

"When does Jayne Goodluck start her shift, or is she coming in today?" Ella saw the girl tense up when she saw the pistol under her unbuttoned jacket.

"Are you a cop? Do you have some identification?"

"Yes, but this isn't an official call." Ella flashed her badge to satisfy the employee. "I was a friend of her sister's." Ella had hoped that proving she was an officer would make the girl relax, but she still looked guarded and uneasy.

"If you don't know when she's supposed to be at work, maybe you can ask the manager for me?" Ella added.

Annie glanced over at a door with a sign that said "Employees Only," then shook her head. "Don't need to. Jayne called this morning and said she was coming in for work. As a matter of fact, she should have been here about two hours ago. I'm not sure if the manager noticed, or if I managed to cover up for her. But please don't bring it up now if he comes out of his office."

"Then you're a friend of Jayne's?"

Annie nodded. "And she really needs this job right now."

"She owes a lot of people, doesn't she?" Ella observed, using a technique that often worked well for her. When you pretended to know more than you actually did, people tended to open up a lot easier. "I bet you've had some really nasty-looking guys coming by, looking for her."

"Oh, you bet. And our manager, Mr. Serna, hates that. Jayne almost lost her job last time it happened."

Ella was thinking that perhaps Jayne didn't deserve Annie's loyalty, when another thought occurred to her. "When did Jayne start working here?"

"Let's see. For a while she came by once a week, just to ask Serna to hire her, and prove she was really interested in the job. Serna had learned she'd been fired from her last job and didn't want to take a chance. But after a month of that, he hired her. That was around three weeks ago. And today she's late."

"Was Jayne here last Wednesday?"

Annie hesitated. "That was the day her sister was killed, wasn't it?"

Ella nodded. "Did she work that night?"

"I . . ."

"She asked you to cover for her, didn't she?" Ella observed. "I wouldn't do it, Annie. This is a murder investigation, and no real friend would ask you to lie to the police. You could end up in jail yourself."

"I thought you said this wasn't official."

"On this matter, it is."

Annie started to leave, but Ella grabbed her arm gently. "Annie, you could face charges if you're caught in a lie. Is that what you want?"

Annie shook her head slowly. "Look, Jayne helped me out when I needed a place to stay and had no other place to go. My dad . . . well, he drinks too much and things can get rough at home. I owe her."

"So you covered for her today. That's one thing. But to give her a false alibi in a murder case—well, that's something else, and you could end up facing a truckload of trouble."

Annie nodded. "Jayne knew people would ask, and she begged me to help. But I wasn't lying—just stretching the truth. She *had* been here. All I was supposed to do was fudge a bit on the time."

"When was it that she actually asked you to do this favor for her?"

"The evening after the murder. I'd read about Justine in the paper, so I wasn't expecting to see Jayne here at work. But she stopped by during my shift. She said that all kinds of people were mad at her, and if she revealed where she'd been the night of her sister's murder and what she'd been doing, everything would come apart for her."

Ella weighed what Annie was telling her. A new possibility was emerging. Even if Jayne hadn't committed the crime, it was possible someone associated with her had, either by mistake, in retaliation, or as a warning. It all hinged on how much trouble Jayne was actually facing.

"Jayne never told me where she'd been that night and I didn't ask," Annie continued. "My guess is that she was off gambling somewhere and didn't want anyone to know."

"Do you have any idea where she goes to gamble?"

"No, not really. There's the race track, but I don't think she goes there very often. She told me before that she prefers places that are less public and that'll give her credit if she runs out of money."

"Thanks, Annie."

"Look, don't tell her that I said anything to you, okay? Jayne has really been a friend to me and I'd like to keep it that way. I know she has a problem with gambling, and borrowing money, but she's a good person. She just has big dreams and puts too much hope on getting lucky and making a bundle of money."

"I'll keep your name out of it. Don't give it another thought," Ella said.

As she walked back out to the parking lot, Ella tried to think of a way to get a fix on her cousin Jayne. She was turning out to be more of a puzzle than Ella had ever dreamed.

Maybe Jayne had been responsible for most of the pressure Justine had been under. She was almost certainly responsible for part of it. Somehow, Ella had to find out exactly how much trouble Jayne was in. Maybe Jayne's tactic of blaming Ella had been an attempt to hide her own involvement in what had happened to Justine.

Ella drove back to the reservation. She had to tell Blalock what she'd learned. He had the resources to follow up on something like this that was taking place outside reservation borders. He also had jurisdiction, which she did not.

Ella stopped at a gas station in Shiprock to fill up the tank. As she went inside to pay the clerk, she saw her cousin Ruth back by the dairy case picking out a gallon of milk.

Seeing Ella, Ruth came up to her. "I want you to know that I don't believe that what happened to my sister was your fault in any way."

"Thanks, that means a lot to me. I really enjoyed working with her. We were very close until about a week ago when her whole attitude seemed to go downhill in a hurry."

"I can't understand why my sister was having so much trouble with you—and everyone else—recently. We all saw how she'd started to change." Ruth's voice was uneven.

"I tried to talk to her about that more than once, but I didn't have any luck getting a straight answer. Now I'm thinking at least part of it had to do with Jayne." Ella kept her voice low so that only Ruth could hear.

Ruth's eyes widened. "How much do you know?"

"She does have quite a problem with gambling," Ella said, not answering directly.

Ruth sighed. "We've all been trying to help her, Mom included, but Jayne's got a mind of her own. She's addicted to gambling, though she can't see it. To her, the only problem is that she's had a streak of bad luck."

"It's often that way with compulsive gamblers."

"I'm just glad that the Rez doesn't have a casino like most of the pueblos along the Rio Grande. I don't think Jayne could handle that."

"Do you have any idea how much she's in debt?"

"Jayne's lost her car, all her jewelry, and even hocked some of Mom's, which she had no right to touch. And she had a problem with my sister because—" Ruth stopped, then turned away. "No, I'm not going to say any more. I know where this is leading, and you're wrong. Jayne couldn't have hurt her own sister, for money or any other reason."

"Can you say the same about the people Jayne owed money to?"

Ruth stared wide-eyed at Ella. "I can't help you, I'm sorry."

"Can't or won't?" Ella pressed.

"I would if I could, but I just don't know the people Jayne hangs around with. We live in separate worlds."

"Even one name . . ."

"There was one man Jayne knows who came to the house once. Mom threw him out. But I don't remember his name."

"Was he Navajo?"

"He was Indian, but not Navajo. Maybe Pueblo, but I don't know. He had a Spanish name, let me think. Oh, yeah. It was Bobby Lujan. I remember because it seemed like a real friendly name. But the guy sure was creepy."

"Why did your mom kick him out?"

"She turned around to use the phone, and he began to wander around the house, snooping. Mom found him in my sister's room and she was furious."

"Did you ever see him again?"

"No. When Jayne came home, Mom told her what he'd been doing. Jayne said not to worry. She promised that the guy would never come by again. She must have talked to him, because he never returned."

Ruth paid for her purchase, then walked with Ella to the door. "You know, I've been wondering if what happened to Justine"—

Ruth whispered the name, knowing four days still hadn't passed since Justine's death—"wasn't a case of mistaken identity. Maybe someone was after Jayne and grabbed my other sister instead. The two of them looked a lot alike."

"I suppose they did," Ella said slowly. Both wore their hair in the same style and both were petite and nearly the same age. Then there was the family resemblance. "But the fact is that Justine was driving her patrol vehicle that night." Ella said her cousin's name softly, as Ruth had.

"But it's unmarked, like yours, and in the dark resembles my mom's SUV."

Ella nodded thoughtfully. "Good point."

"Do you want me to talk to Jayne? I know she said some really nasty things to you, but I don't think she meant them all. You don't know her like I do. She's just scared. She's in a huge mess with these people because of her gambling debts, and I think that deep down she's terrified that somehow this led to Justine's murder."

"I hope for all our sakes that isn't the case, because that means the danger isn't over yet. Jayne could become the next target."

"I don't think any of us can help Jayne. She won't allow it. But it's Mom I worry about most. I know she's a strong woman. That's how she made it after Dad left. But my brothers and sisters are everything to her, and it's hard enough for her to accept that Justine's gone forever. If on top of that she found out that one of her other daughters had a hand in her death . . ." Ruth shook her head. "That's just too awful to think about. And if something happened to Jayne as well, I don't think Mom would ever recover."

"Do you have any idea where Jayne is right now?" Ella asked.

Ruth glanced at her watch. "None of us can afford to take any more time off from work, especially Jayne. She should be at the Daily Double, over in Farmington. She usually works a lunch-to-dinner shift. But if she's not there, check the Bull's Eye, out on the Bloomfield highway. According to Jayne, they have a small-stakes crap game in the back. But I don't know how you'll get in if they don't know you. I tried to find her there once, and couldn't get past the bartender. He looked at me as if I were crazy and swore there wasn't anything in the back except cases of booze. But Jayne had the family's SUV and it was parked outside."

"Thanks. I'll let you know if I find out anything new."

Ella returned to her vehicle. Talking about Justine in the past tense seemed wrong, and having to whisper her name to avoid danger from her *chindi* was even worse. Maybe part of her was just trying to deny reality, but she couldn't quite accept the fact that Justine was truly dead.

Ella pushed her doubts aside and focused. She was a cop. She needed to concentrate on finding a trail of evidence. That was the only way she'd ever settle the matter once and for all.

She drove back to Farmington, then continued east toward Bloomfield, easily locating the Bull's Eye bar. With some luck she'd find Bobby Lujan there, or come across Jayne. Maybe the element of surprise would give her an advantage and help her get some useful information from her cousin or her male friend.

Ella went inside the rowdy country western bar, which was serving an after-work crowd of local cowboys, construction workers, and oil field roughnecks. Finding a stool at one end of the bar, she ordered a draft beer. She rarely drank, and wouldn't even be tempted to take more than a sip tonight, but it would give her a good cover as she watched people come and go.

Time passed. Every once in a while she'd see someone who was obviously not an employee come out of a door marked "Employees Only." It was clear that some kind of activity was going on back there.

As Ella saw a tall cowboy heading for the doors, she tried to follow, pretending to be with him, but the bartender intercepted her.

"No one goes back there, except employees."

"Aw, come on, give me a break. There's a game going on, and I have a little extra cash burning a hole in my pocket."

"You don't work here, and I don't know you either. The only entertainment around here is at the bar. You want another beer?"

"Come on, I'm just looking for a little action," Ella continued, determined to gain access. "What do you say?"

For a moment or two she thought she was about to talk herself into the game, but suddenly the door opened and a Navajo man she recognized came out. She'd arrested Herbert Nez on several occasions, mostly for illegal alcohol sales on the Rez.

The moment he saw her, anger flashed in his eyes. "What are you doing here, cop! Who sent you, my wife?"

The bartender glared at her. "Unless you can prove that you have jurisdiction here, I don't have to waste my time talking to you."

"You want me to bring in the county sheriff?"

"Do it. But use the phone outside. I'm sure they'll be around in what, ten minutes? But don't plan on catching anyone doing anything illegal, and expect a lawsuit from my boss's lawyer. He knows how to deal with police harassment."

"Oh, I don't have to leave the room. I have a cell phone, and a good eye for faces coming out this door in the meantime."

"Knock yourself out. But you'll also need a search warrant or some kind of reasonable cause before I allow you or anyone else to look around. How long do you think that'll take?"

Ella knew that she'd never be able to get any cops here in time to stop an illegal gambling operation, but that hadn't been her objective anyway. As the door opened and a surprised cowboy stopped in the entrance, she glanced inside. She caught a glimpse of an open back door, and a woman who looked like Jayne ducking outside.

Intent on intercepting her, Ella turned on her heels and ran to the front entrance to the bar, colliding with a man and woman coming in at the same time. By the time she and they had untangled and apologized and Ella reached the parking lot, Jayne's SUV was gone.

Cursing her luck, Ella returned to her vehicle and drove back to the reservation. It was shortly after seven when Ella arrived in Shiprock. She needed to meet with Blalock and fill him in on what she'd learned. Picking up her cell phone, she punched out his number. He answered on the first ring.

"I have some information you may find useful," she said.

"Stop. Don't give it to me over the air. I still don't trust these wireless things. Let's meet and exchange information face-to-face," Blalock said.

Ella arranged to join him for a working dinner at the Totah Cafe, and twenty minutes later she sat across the table from him in a corner booth.

Mary Lou brought them two chalupa platters, cup-shaped tor-tillas filled with beans, salsa, and cheese, garnished with guaca-mole. As they ate, Ella filled him in on what she'd learned about Jayne and her activities. "That's all I know," she said at last.

"You've gotten further than I have, but that's not surprising," Blalock said, finishing the last of his dinner. "I've worked this area for years, but the Four Corners is still your turf."

"I wish I could find all the answers before things really get ugly. My cousin is gone, my life may be irreversibly changed, and now this fight is taking all of my time. I have a little girl who I've barely gotten to see since this happened."

"There are always times like this for a cop—no matter where you work, whether you're federal or local."

"I know. It's lousy pay, even lousier hours, and yet it's the work I love. That's the irony of all this, you know. I've given my career everything, and whoever's behind this trouble has not only taken someone I love, he's now trying to take away my job, my reputation, and everything else that defines me as well."

Hearing a familiar voice over the cafe's radio, Ella groaned. "George Branch. He's all I need to complete a crappy day."

One of the employees turned the volume up, and Ella suddenly heard a reference to law enforcement. Branch was on a tirade, ac-cusing the tribal police of protecting their own by not kicking "a criminal cop" off the force and bringing the officer to justice. To make things worse, he was accusing the tribal government of wide-spread corruption, mentioning kickbacks and bribes to outsider big businesses such as power companies, mining operations, and man-ufacturing concerns.

Ella listened for as long as she could, then stood up, tossing several bills on the table. She could feel everyone's eyes on her as she headed to the door.

Mary Lou hurried over to her. "I'm sorry about that, Ella. I was out in the back when one of the waitresses turned the radio on. Our customers like to argue about him. By the time I heard what he was talking about, it was already too late."

"Don't worry about it. It's just one of the many things I'll have to deal with until my cousin's killer is arrested. Unfortunately, the Constitution protects idiots like him."

Ella was halfway to her vehicle when Blalock caught up to her. "Can you have one of your people follow Branch and see who he meets and where he goes when he's away from work? I think we better check this guy out and see what's on his agenda. I'd just love to find out he's got his hand in something dirty so I can come down on him like a ton of bricks."

"I'll pass your request along to Big Ed," Ella replied.

Ella parted company with Blalock and drove directly to the station. There were no new cases waiting on her desk. With a sigh of relief, she delivered Blalock's request to Big Ed.

"The heat's coming down on this department, Shorty, and I'll have to juggle schedules to find any officers to check up on Branch. As for you, I want you to stay low profile. Take time off if you want. But whatever you do, don't make waves right now."

"What's going on?"

"The usual—politics. When Abigail Yellowhair had all the references to you pulled from her ads, one of the tribal councilmen was overheard saying that it was because she had the inside track on the investigation and knew of evidence that would prove you were involved in our officer's death."

"That's a lie. She was just playing it safe, trying to distance herself from any scandal or controversy. She wants to be elected."

"I know that and you know that, but you've made quite a few enemies over the years. For instance, bringing down the terrorists who'd set up their base of operations here made you an international hero, but also resulted in the Tribal Council and some of their appointees looking really bad. Publicly they applauded your investigation, but privately they've always wanted revenge for making them look corrupt and gullible."

"I know, but there's nothing I can do about that now. Even after I find the truth about my cousin, they'll still be lying in wait for me, and biding their time, like hawks circling above a rabbit hole." She stood up. "I'm going home. For once, I'd like to see my daughter while she's still awake enough to know who is giving her a good-night kiss."

Ella arrived just as Rose had finished bathing Dawn, and Ella helped her into her pajamas. As the freshly scrubbed little girl ran into the living room to play, Ella joined her on the floor, each making her own stack with the colored pieces of plastic. Every once in a while Dawn would take one of the blocks off of Ella's stack and put in on top of her own.

"*Shimá*, play," Dawn said, laughing as she took another of Ella's blocks.

Ella handed Dawn the blocks, asking her each time what color it was. Dawn already knew her basic colors, but Ella loved to reinforce the lesson. She watched her daughter, entranced as Dawn struggled to arrange the blocks. It was easy to see a piece of herself mirrored in her daughter's curiosity and her attention to whatever she was doing. It filled her with a sense of awe as she thought of the continuity of family and the future Dawn represented. Right now Dawn was completely absorbed in her stacking game. Her attention span was never long, natural for a child her age, but her concentration was complete. Ella was already planning on buying more blocks, this time with letters or animal images on them.

Dawn seemed much smarter than any of the other children Ella had seen, including Julian at this age. But maybe that was just the proud mom in her. To her, her daughter seemed like a miracle in motion.

As Dawn tired of the game, she stood and, with her bowlegged-looking gait, ran to where she'd left the rag doll Rose had made for her.

"*Shimasání* make present," she said, and showed the doll to Ella.

"It's very pretty! Did you say thank you?"

Dawn shook her head. "Navajos say *ahéhee'*."

Ella laughed. "Mom, that's cool. She's going to know Navajo before she reaches three, at this rate!"

"I raised you the same way. Maybe with her, it'll stick. Sometimes I wonder how much you actually remember. You spent too many years trying to forget who you were."

Ella steered clear of the old argument, not wanting to remind her of the scarcity of Navajo-speaking agents to converse with those years she was part of the Bureau. Besides, her mother was right about how much of the language Ella retained. She understood Navajo a lot better than she spoke it.

Dawn finally walked to the TV set and pointed. "Watch TV."

"No," Rose said.

"Mom, she's got the cartoon video I bought for her. That would take her up to bedtime."

"I don't like to have her watch TV at night. She'll end up sleepy and cranky because she won't go to bed when she gets tired. A little in the morning, but that's all."

Ella bit back the curt retort that often seemed foremost in her mind. Dawn was her kid, and she should have the final say-so in how she was raised. But that kind of autonomy was impossible while they all lived here with Rose. Besides, she knew her mom was probably right. The cartoon would probably just get Dawn excited at the wrong time, and she'd get restless and cranky later on.

Ella looked at her daughter, who was now pulling a toy horse around the room. The wooden toy had been something she'd inherited from Julian. When the toy snagged on the back of a chair, Dawn pulled on the string, fell down on her bottom when the toy remained snagged, then let out an ear-piercing shriek.

"*T'adoo*. Stop that," Rose said, adding the English translation immediately. "There's no need for that."

Rose leaned over to untangle the string, but then groaned, slipping down on one knee.

Ella stood up and rushed to her mother's side. "Mom, are you okay?"

Rose pushed her away. "I'm fine. It's just age talking. My joints don't work as well as yours do some days."

She made it a point to untangle the string before Ella could, gritting her teeth the entire time.

"You could take some aspirins for the soreness and inflammation. Remember that the doctor said that you could do that whenever you needed."

"He gave me pills for my pain before, and all I could do was sleep. Now he gives me more pills," Rose said, shaking her head. "With him, all the answers to all the questions come in a pill."

"Mom, after your accident, you needed the rest. But an aspirin is nothing, unless you take too many. I take them at work for a headache or minor ache, and I wouldn't be able to do that if there was a problem with side effects."

"Give them time. They'll find some."

Ella sighed. She wouldn't change Rose's mind on this either. She knew that, so why was she wasting her time trying? She just hated to see her mother making things even more difficult for herself.

"I have some herbs and an ointment your brother fixed for me. I'll use those tonight after your daughter is asleep."

"I'll stay up with her, Mom. You can go ahead and go to bed now if you want."

"And if you get an emergency call and have to go back to work? Better I should stay awake."

"If that happens, then I'll wake you up, I promise." Ella looked at Dawn, who was now curled up on the sofa, clutching her rag doll. "She's getting tired anyway."

"No!" Dawn said loudly.

"Okay, you're not," Ella said. She remembered the stories of how difficult it had been to put her to bed when she was Dawn's age.

Ella looked back at her mother, noting that her face looked drawn. Taking care of Dawn could sap anyone's energy some days. She had to find a way to get Rose to accept help. But she would pick the time, and this wasn't it.

Ella led her mother down the hall. "Mom, I don't get a lot of time alone with her when things are busy at work, so let me enjoy her tonight. You'll be doing this for me, not just yourself."

"Normally I would disagree, but it's true that you need time alone with your daughter. She misses you when you're away."

Ella shook her head. "No, she sees you as her other *shimá*."

"I'm her *shimasání*, and she knows the difference. I can fill in for you, but I can't be her mother."

"Navajo kids know many mothers, not just one. I'm glad she has you."

"Even when we don't agree?" Rose asked, sitting on the edge of the bed and slipping off her shoes.

"You're teaching her Navajo, and about The Way already. She knows who and what she is, even at her young age. If I'd lived alone with her anywhere else, she would have been a lot poorer for it."

Rose nodded thoughtfully. "I see that you've given the idea of living away from the Rez some consideration."

Ella knew enough not to lie. "With pressure on government agencies to hire minorities, I thought of applying for some other job in law enforcement. Maybe a desk job somewhere, which would mean regular hours. But even if I could talk you into coming with me, my daughter would grow up outside the sacred mountains—feeling different from others but not really understanding why that's a good thing and not a bad one. It's not an acceptable trade-off."

"I wouldn't leave my home."

"Yeah, I figured you'd put up a fight, but sometimes I win."

"Not on that," Rose said flatly.

Ella walked to the door. "If you need me, just call."

By the time she reached the living room, Dawn was sitting up, looking at her through sleepy eyes.

"*Shimá,* pick up," she said, holding out her tiny arms.

Ella held her daughter, wishing she could be around to do this more often.

"*Shimasání* sick?"

"She just needs to rest," Ella answered, rocking her. As her little girl settled quietly against her, Ella felt a sense of peace, then a twinge of sadness thinking about all the special times she'd missed with her child already. She hadn't been able to nurse her own daughter for more than a few weeks. Her job had made it practically impossible. Dawn had been brought up with formulas and modern diapers, yet the copper-skinned baby who gazed up at her was all Navajo, and very much a part of a world that always seemed to hover between the old and the new.

"*Shimá* tired too?"

"A bit," Ella said, holding her daughter close.

"*Shimá* go to bed."

"Will Dawn go to bed, too?"

She nodded slowly.

Ella took Dawn to her room and tucked her beneath the covers, then began telling her a favorite bedtime story, about the Hero twins and Coyote. Noticing that Dawn couldn't keep her eyes open,

Ella cut the story short tonight and gave her daughter a kiss on the cheek.

"*Ayóó ninshné,*" Dawn said sleepily.

"I love you, too," Ella said, and gave her daughter another kiss on the forehead.

By the time she reached the door, Dawn's breathing was even. She'd fallen fast asleep. Ella put the gate up so her daughter wouldn't wander out into the hall in the middle of the night. Dawn's door would remain open.

Ella returned to her own room and switched on her computer to check E-mail. She then waited on-line for a possible instant message, but none came. After a while she switched the computer off and got ready for bed. As she kicked off her shoes, her cell phone rang. Ella picked it up on the first ring.

"This is Blalock," he said, as if she might have trouble recognizing his voice. "You'll want to be in on this. Officer Tache just made an officer-in-trouble call. He's come under fire north of the river just west of the reservation border."

"I'm on my way." As Ella pulled on her boots, Rose came to the door.

"You have to go out?"

She nodded, and looked at her mother, wondering if she'd somehow known there would be trouble tonight. Her mother sometimes knew things before they happened.

"I had a feeling." Rose shrugged, answering Ella's unspoken question.

Ella reached for her badger fetish and placed it inside her shirt but outside the now ever-present vest.

"Be very careful tonight, daughter. Things are never quite what they seem."

"Do you know something, Mom? I don't care if it's a feeling that you had, or if you heard a rumor. Please don't keep anything back right now."

"I'm not. I just know that someone out there wants to destroy this family."

Ella checked her pistols, both the one in the holster and the backup in her boot. She would stay sharp out there tonight. Her survival skills were too well honed to allow her to be otherwise.

"I'll be back," she promised, then rushed out the door.

NINETEEN

Ella arrived at the site near Hogback a few minutes behind Blalock and Payestewa. Joseph Neskahi was already there, having responded ahead of all of them.

Guns drawn, the three late arrivals found Ralph Tache and Neskahi behind the sergeant's tribal unit. Neskahi was carrying a riot gun. Ella saw Tache's car ahead, illuminated by Neskahi's spotlight. At least two tires were flat, but no perp was visible, nor any other vehicles.

"What's going on?" she asked Tache

"I followed Branch down this dirt road to a sweat lodge by the river. He met with two other Indians, neither of them Navajo. Although they were constantly coming out, checking to make sure they hadn't been followed, I still managed to get a couple of photographs with my telephoto lens. Then, when they got ready to leave, I decided to tail one of the two I didn't know. He headed toward the old road and I stayed with him. I spotted Arizona plates on his car, but I couldn't get the number with the dust he was raising."

"And the others?" Ella asked.

"Branch headed off toward the highway, followed by the second man, and that was the last I saw of them. But everything fell apart when the man I was tailing made a circle and spotted me. He came up from behind my unit and opened fire. He took out my two back tires with two shots, even though I was dodging and trying to blind him with my spotlight. Lucky he wasn't shooting at me. That guy hit whatever he aimed at."

"Which direction was he traveling the last time you saw him?"

"He drove farther up this track, which leads to the ditch road that parallels the river. But I don't think he could have gone far. I hit one of his rear tires after three shots—just to return the favor."

"We'll split up and cover more ground that way," Blalock said. "I'll go east because that leads off the Rez."

"Good idea. Did you all know that George Branch lives just a few miles from here?" Ella asked.

"Go over to his house then, Ella, and check things out," Blalock said. "If they're compadres, the one in trouble might head there."

"I'll go west," Neskahi said, and Blalock nodded at the same time Ella did.

"Accompany Clah to Branch's," Blalock ordered Payestewa. Blalock then looked at Ella and added, "We want to make sure your involvement and jurisdiction isn't questioned further down the line."

Ella didn't like it, but Blalock was right and this was no time to quibble.

Ella led the way in her unit, sticking to a farm road that paralleled the main highway. It would serve as a shortcut and allow them to approach Branch's house from the south. The route was bumpy, and as she looked behind her at Payestewa's shiny new sedan, Ella wondered if she'd made a mistake. But the sedan managed to keep up, the road smoothed out a little, and in a matter of minutes, they drove past a small, neglected apple orchard and arrived at Branch's home.

Payestewa walked over to meet her. "Let me ask the questions, since we're off the Rez now," he suggested.

"Fine. Just let me warn you that George Branch has an extensive gun collection, probably a good home security system, and doesn't like federal law enforcement—especially the FBI," Ella said, remembering a previous visit here.

"I'm insured," Payestewa said cheerfully, but his eyes were alert. He also had his pistol in his hand, down by his side.

"Stop right there." A voice from inside the house rang out. "I'm armed."

"Right on schedule," the Hopi agent mumbled. "FBI, Mr. Branch."

The front door opened and a porch light went on. "Why the hell didn't you say so sooner? It's dark, and you're trespassing. I could have blown your head off."

"You always this cautious?" Payestewa asked, holstering his weapon.

"I have to be. A radio program like mine is bound to make a man enemies among those conspiring to take away our freedom. I also have an extensive gun collection that any thief would love, as your companion no doubt has already informed you." The heavy-set half-Navajo man waved them inside the house.

"What's going on?" the talk-radio host pressed, looking closely at Ella's waist, trying to spot her weapon. "I can't believe that they're still allowing you to run around and play cop."

Ella remained silent, knowing Branch was baiting her. He was hoping she'd react, and give him even more material for his show. She kept her expression neutral and listened, glancing around the room and into the kitchen and hall, searching for some sign that he was hiding someone there.

"Where were you tonight?" Payestewa asked. "The last three hours will do."

"Why the interest?"

"Just answer the question, Mr. Branch," Payestewa said, his voice uncharacteristically hard.

"I drove to Kirtland to buy a six-pack of beer a bit earlier."

"Where? Which establishment and when, exactly?" Payestewa pressed, walking into the kitchen and switching on the light. "Did you put it in the refrigerator?"

"I never got the beer. I'd intended to go to the package store at the Palomino Lounge, but halfway there I realized I didn't have my wallet. I ended up having to come back. Then as I was getting ready to leave again, I heard you two coming in from the orchard road. Your lights weren't on, and it's pretty damn dark out there. I figured it might have been some of the kids from Kirtland that have been raising hell around here. A few have been breaking into houses, and I would imagine stealing from me would be a feather in their cap."

"Kids don't listen to your show. There's no music," Ella said. "And they wouldn't try to break in, because they know they'd get shot."

"Okay, I'm getting tired of this. Let's cut to the chase. Where did you think I was? I have a feeling you've got me mixed up with someone else."

Ella shook his head. "I don't think so and I advise you to stop playing games. We have evidence that can place you someplace else tonight."

"Yeah? Then produce it."

"Why don't we just take you in for threatening two law enforcement officers and get the ball rolling that way?" Payestewa suggested.

"Whoa. I explained that. Besides, we both know you'll never make that stick. You didn't identify yourselves clearly until I asked you to leave. All you're both doing right now is giving me material for tomorrow's show."

"I wouldn't go off half-cocked, or you might find yourself trying to do a remote broadcast from the county jail," Ella said. "It isn't a bluff. We're processing evidence now that will prove you weren't where you said. If we can also link you to a crime that was committed—"

"Wait a second. What crime?"

"Assault with a deadly weapon on a police officer," the Hopi agent joined in.

"Who got shot? By whom?"

"You'll know more when we make things public. For now, just try to process the information we've given you," Payestewa said. "I'm sure that a man in your position realizes that lying to a federal officer conducting a criminal investigation is a very bad idea. It can bring a wagonload of trouble down on you."

"I'll keep it in mind," Branch said, neither confirming or denying his words.

Getting a call on his cell phone, Payestewa stepped into the kitchen for a moment.

"Spill it, Clah. What's going on?" Branch whispered.

"A lot of things, and none of them good for you if you're connected to any of them."

"What's this, a threat?"

"No, consider it a guarantee." Ella saw Payestewa cock his head and motion for them to leave.

"I'll be seeing you again, I expect," Ella said, then hurried out, stopping beside Payestewa's car. "What's up?"

"Blalock found some shells from a .45, but no sign of the third man or a vehicle."

"I don't think anyone's inside Branch's house unless they came on foot, and I doubt there was time for that," Ella said.

"Well, there's no other car around here except Branch's SUV. And there's no garage or outbuildings big enough to house one. The orchard's got nothing but trees, and I didn't spot a vehicle in any of the surrounding fields."

"Then let's get back and help the others search. The third car has got to be around somewhere," Ella said.

"He may have already changed the tire, or just driven it on the rim until he was out of the area, depending on how desperate he was. It wouldn't be hard to hide a vehicle down by the river."

Ella started to get inside her unit, but stopped when he spoke again.

"By the way, Ella, you shouldn't have engaged in conversation with him. You practically told him we had solid evidence and were ready to arrest him."

"No, I didn't. I was just applying a little bit of pressure, hoping to persuade him to talk."

"Just don't do that again. If this is linked to Officer Goodluck's death, it's a Bureau case, and we'll dictate the way things go down."

As he returned to his sedan and drove off, Ella's temper spewed to the surface. The little strutting peacock! The officer fired upon was part of the SI team and this was her turf. She knew how to deal with a jerk like Branch better than the agent did.

As she mentally reviewed the hard-nosed way he'd handled questioning Branch, she suddenly realized something. Up to now, Payestewa had seemed almost too laid-back to be a federal agent, but in there, he'd shown his true colors. Paycheck, as the others called him, had disappeared. There had been a hard edge to Payestewa as he worked the case that she'd never seen before. One thing was clear. There was more to this guy than met the eye, and it was obvious he'd been hiding behind a carefully developed smoke screen.

Ella drove back to where Blalock had suggested they meet, then joined the others in an all-out effort to locate the third vehicle. Eventually Sergeant Neskahi was able to spot where the old sedan had been hidden. The disturbed ground indicated that the driver had driven on the rim for a short distance, gone down below the ditch levee out of sight, then had run back and wiped out the vehicle tracks as well as he could.

"He must have changed the tire down here," Neskahi pointed out. "The darkness hid him well. He drove out once he saw I'd passed by."

As they walked back up to the road where their own vehicles were parked, Ella looked at Tache. "How soon can you develop the photos you took of Branch and the other two?"

"A few hours, but I'll have to mix up fresh chemicals first and it's late and I'm tired. We'd all be better off if I waited to do that in the morning. I may have to really play with the exposure and the development time to get a good image. I guessed at the exposure because I had to use the telephoto lens."

Ella glanced at Blalock, who nodded. "Okay. Morning will do," she said.

"Call me as soon as you have some prints ready," Blalock said.

"Done," Tache said.

As Tache moved off, Payestewa looked around and then expelled his breath in a hiss. "Look, we didn't find anything, and there are no guarantees that Tache's photo will be worth anything to the investigation unless we can ID one or both of the other players. Let me try to get a court order to tap Branch's phone."

"On what grounds?" Blalock asked. "That one of us saw him meeting with two men? Remember that Tache's story stipulates that the third man shot at him *after* Branch left."

"It's a matter of presenting it to the right judge," Payestewa said, looking at Ella.

Ella had a feeling she knew what he was up to, but she remained quiet. If her guess was right, Payestewa had looked into Justine's background very carefully. In fact, a man like him probably hadn't stopped there. Instinct told her that he'd probably researched all their backgrounds equally as thoroughly.

"No judge is going to give you a warrant to tap Branch's phone based on what we have, no matter how charming you think you are," Blalock said. "We need Tache's photos. Then we can take *that* to a judge."

"By then our window of opportunity may be gone."

"Not at all. We'll just have to get a record of all incoming calls made to Branch's home and to the radio station where he works and follow them up."

"We can circumvent all this waiting if we approach a judge who's as motivated as we are to see justice done. Then, if the shooter contacts Branch, we can make our move right away."

"Which judge do you have in mind?" Blalock said. "It sounds like you know a perfect candidate for the job," Blalock said.

"I do. Judge Goodluck."

"When did you find out about my cousin's grandfather?" Ella asked.

"A few hours after I was told I'd be working this case. I believe in doing my homework," Payestewa answered.

"Have you met this judge?" Blalock asked Ella.

She nodded. "He's helped us in the past. He adores ... adored ... my cousin. But my coming along when you make your request won't help. Her family doesn't trust me at the moment."

"I'll take care of it then," Payestewa said.

"Do you know where he lives?" Ella asked.

The Hopi agent nodded. "I have his address. I'll handle this, then get back to both of you." He looked at Neskahi, then at Blalock. "Do you think we should have someone stake out Branch's place and see if anyone shows up?"

"We'll have to take a pass on that for now," Blalock said. "From the looks of it, the moon's going to be behind the clouds for hours. That means visibility is going to be poor, and the night scope is back in Shiprock, locked up in my office."

"I'm not used to having all that government technology," Sergeant Neskahi reminded them. "I'll find a good hiding place to keep watch up close."

"One-man surveillance? I don't know ..." Blalock said slowly.

"Joseph can call in at regular intervals on my cell phone. If we don't hear, we come running," Ella suggested, handing Neskahi the phone. "I can also check with the sheriff's department and see who has this patrol area tonight. I can request that the officer stay relatively close by unless he has to answer a call."

Blalock shook his head. "No. I'll call the sheriff's and let them know it's my operation." He looked at Neskahi. "Call in every hour."

"Okay, but who do I call?" Neskahi looked at Ella first, then at Blalock.

Ella said nothing. With Dawn sleeping, she was hoping that Blalock would take it himself, but she didn't want to beg off if she was needed.

Blalock looked at Ella, then shook his head. "It'll have to be me, folks, for the same reason as before."

"No problem," Ella answered.

As they headed back to their vehicles, Ella felt the knot in her stomach. She was in a situation where she wasn't supposed to be trusted. Blalock had cut her some slack, but he was still bound by protocols.

Even during her years on the outside, she'd always felt a sense of belonging by identifying herself as part of a law enforcement team. But now her fellow officers were being forced to treat her like a suspect. She tried to push back her own sense of betrayal knowing that they were only doing their jobs. Yet logic did little to silence the outrage that pounded through her with every beat of her heart.

TWENTY

✖ ✖ ✖

They met in Tache's darkroom the next morning. The prints were drying on a makeshift line. The photos had been taken through an infrared viewer, and were more detailed than any of them expected. But the only person they could identify was Branch. The other two men never turned face-on to the camera, or even presented a good profile.

"I'll run this by Judge Goodluck, along with a copy of Officer Tache's report of the shooting. He cut us a break by giving us a court order when we asked for it, so this should help convince him that he made the right decision," Payestewa said.

Ella watched him carefully. When it came to business, Payestewa also knew how to play politics. The more she dealt with him, the more convinced she became that they'd all underestimated the young Hopi agent. They'd taken him at face value, and with Payestewa, that was a very small part of the true picture.

"I got the list of telephone numbers we wanted from the phone company this morning," Blalock said. "The only calls Branch gets at home are from the radio station, some relatives in the area, and three of his known associates, including the station manager and the producer of his radio program." He looked at Payestewa. "I want you to check all those people out."

Ella said nothing, guessing that Blalock approved of Payestewa's attention to detail when doing background checks.

Payestewa looked at a notebook he'd produced from his jacket pocket. "The calls Branch gets at the station include a lot of kooks and reactionaries his show seems to bring out from beneath the woodwork. The few we managed to identify as Indians living in the area don't match those in the photos, judging by height and overall shape. Their vehicles also don't match the descriptions of the ones that Tache spotted. One Navajo, a professor at the Shiprock branch college named Jeremiah Manyfarms, called him on the air at least three times and tried to pressure Branch to contribute funds to a youth program that's being run here on the reservation. Manyfarms appears legit, though. Doesn't even have a traffic citation since moving here from California."

"I've met Manyfarms. He's working with Wilson Joe on those youth programs, and has approached my brother concerning visits for his group with a medicine man. And Neskahi called me before he finally went home this morning, confirming what you probably already know. No one came to pay Branch a visit last night," Ella said. "I told him to catch up on his sleep before coming in. I also checked the nearby gas stations to see if anyone came in to purchase a tire, but I didn't have any luck."

"This guy knew enough to keep his cool and elude us. I don't think he's careless or stupid. My guess is that he's either going to lay low or has already left the area," Payestewa said.

Blalock looked at Ella. "If any of us turn up something useful, I'll let you know. But from this point on, we have to keep your involvement to a minimum. This is getting to be high profile, and Big Ed wants to see you actively working on something other than this case. I spoke to him last night. Some of the politicians are putting an incredible amount of pressure on him. They want him to take your badge and gun until Justine's case is resolved."

"All right. Consider me out of this then," she said.

Ella left the two FBI agents and Ralph Tache and walked back to her office. The station's day shift was just getting started, so she'd have to make it a point to avoid Blalock and the others. It didn't take much to get people talking, and from the sounds of it, things were difficult enough for the chief already.

Ella looked at her caseload, which had diminished to practically nothing with the arrest of Jimmy Begaye. Making a spur-of-the-moment decision, she decided to visit Jeremiah Manyfarms. Maybe he'd had some contact with Branch other than on the phone, and could suggest some other avenue of investigation for them. It wasn't her case, but she could help herself a lot if she could find something that would effectively muzzle Branch for a while.

First Ella called up Wilson Joe, who she knew worked with Jeremiah sponsoring the teen groups that met on campus after school.

"He's here today," Wilson verified. "Right now I think the professor is trying to get the basketball coach to donate some of his time to practice with the kids."

"Professor Manyfarms is really dedicated, isn't he?"

"It seems like it," Wilson replied coldly.

Ella smiled. Wilson was just being himself, jumping to conclusions and seeing her interest as a personal one. She should have let him stew, but she didn't have the heart.

"I want to talk to him because I think he may be able to help with a case I'm working on."

"I heard that you've been taken off your cousin's case. Is that true?"

"Yes, but I'm still keeping tabs on it."

"From your tone, I gather things aren't going well?"

"It's a difficult investigation," she answered, knowing that she hadn't given away anything. All it meant was that Wilson's imagination was on overdrive.

"Watch out for Jeremiah Manyfarms, Ella. I'm telling you this as a friend. He isn't all he seems to be."

"Can you be more specific?"

Wilson paused for a few moments. "He's trying too hard. This youth program is a terrific idea, but he's constantly pushing both the kids and the sponsors. It's become almost an obsession for him."

"So he feels strongly about keeping kids out of gangs. What's wrong with that?"

"Nothing—it's the way he goes about it. He's too controlling. Everything has to be done his way, according to his plans and his schedule. His attitude is all wrong for a Navajo. One person shouldn't presume to make all decisions for a group."

"You know he's been away for years living in California.

Things are a lot different there. It sometimes takes time to get back into the groove here on the Rez."

"You're not identifying with him because you spent time away too, are you? You two are nothing alike, believe me," Wilson said.

Ella smiled, glad that he couldn't see her reaction. It would have only ticked him off.

"I've got to run, Ella. I've got a class in a few minutes."

After saying good-bye, Ella hung up. The trip to campus would help her relax. It was hard to dwell on her problems on such a clear New Mexico day.

By the time she arrived, she was eager to get started. Ella knew the Shiprock campus pretty well, and drove around to the visitors' parking area. From there she walked to the gym, but as she approached, she saw Jeremiah enter the portable building adjacent to it. Ella followed him inside a few moments later. As she stepped through the open doorway, she saw Jeremiah writing on a portable chalkboard.

"Whoa, is this supposed to be school after school?" she teased.

"Hey, Ella, how's it going?" Jeremiah smiled, then turned back to his drawing of the outline of a basketball court. "This is going to help the boys visualize every player's responsibilities on the court. They'll need that skill to run the offense and defense—I hope."

Ella sat down on one of the chairs. "You certainly offer diverse activities in your program. You're still planning on taking them to my brother's medicine hogan?"

"I certainly am, if we can come up with a schedule. I want to expose these young people to as many different things as I can. Some of them have short attention spans, and I don't want to give them a chance to get bored."

"Basketball will hold their interest for sure. Everyone loves the games here. When the high school plays our big rival, Kirtland Central, half the town goes to see the game. If the college was large enough to have a team, everyone would be in seventh heaven."

"The college has PE in the gym and intramural games, but that's about it. We don't have the budget to make the trips. Plus, we're too small a school to give anyone else any real competition."

He regarded her thoughtfully. "But that's not why you're here."

"No, I came by to ask you a few questions about George Branch."

Manyfarms scowled. "That crank? He's not my favorite person. Around here I hear you either love or hate him, and I'm in the latter category. He's making a lot of money, I'm told, and he has a lot of listeners. Yet, despite all that, he refuses to raise a finger to help our teen programs. He could have helped us throw one really kickass fund-raiser with some public service announcements on his program, but he says his listeners are more concerned with the big issues in the community. The bottom line is that he won't do a thing. Well, he made a twenty-dollar contribution once, then asked for a receipt."

"How well do you know him?"

"Not well at all. I've never even met him in person. I tried, mind you. I went to the radio station two or three times, but although I made sure I didn't catch him on the air, he was always too busy to see me. Finally I called his show, but he brushed me off. I wanted to tell his audience about our youth program so we could reach people who didn't know about us, but he never gave me a chance."

"I appreciate the information. Thanks."

"Is he in some kind of legal trouble?"

"Not really. He's just a pain and I like to keep track of what my enemies are doing."

Jeremiah nodded. "I heard him allude to you the other day. He sure didn't pull many punches."

"He likes to push freedom of speech as close to a lawsuit as he can." Ella started back out the door, then stopped. "What kind of car do you drive?"

"Why do you ask? Am I about to get a ticket?"

"Nah. I'm just looking at that nice blue sedan over there. It's a Beemer, isn't it?"

He met her by the door. "Sure is. I saw a lot of them in California. Unfortunately, that car isn't mine. I drive that old Chevy truck over there, the red one." He looked back at the car she'd pointed out. "I don't know who owns that, but it sure isn't someone who lives on the Rez full-time. No one I know around here has that kind of money."

"Some do, but they usually don't flaunt it."

A moment later, Ella saw Abigail Yellowhair leave the adjacent building and make her way to the car. "How about that," she muttered. Ella recalled the generic-looking Ford sedan she'd seen parked at the Yellowhair house only a few days ago. Had Abigail kept her husband's car after all so she could use whichever car fit the image she was trying to project at the time?

He made a disgusted sound. "Wouldn't it figure it would belong to a politician? Maybe Branch's shots about corruption weren't totally off the mark."

Ella nodded, her thoughts racing. Maybe this was part of the conspiracy her informant had mentioned. If Branch created unrest, new politicians like Abigail Yellowhair would find it easier to get elected. She discarded the thought even as it formed. Abigail Yellowhair and George Branch working together? That was just plain crazy.

Ella stopped by her home, and as she walked in, saw Rose twining yarn into a ball. Her mother's face was drawn and she looked as if she'd been crying.

"Mom, what's happened?" She looked around quickly and saw Dawn on the sofa taking a nap.

Rose placed a finger over her lips and motioned Ella into the kitchen.

"Let me fix you some lunch," Rose said, pulling things out of the refrigerator.

"Mom, talk to me." She would have taken the casserole dish from her mother, but knew it would be a mistake. Whenever her mother was really upset, she would search for something to do with her hands. It was almost therapeutic.

Ella sat down at the kitchen table while Rose heated up leftover mutton stew. "Mother, something must have happened. Tell me what it was," she asked again.

"It's my daughter-in-law. I hadn't seen my grandson in a while.

The last two times I went by, she wasn't home, so I called and tried to find a time when she could come here with him or I could go visit." Rose's voice grew softer. "She started making a million excuses. I couldn't believe it. She doesn't want me to see my own grandchild."

"Have you told my brother?" Ella asked. Once Clifford knew, he'd put a stop to it fast.

"He's not home today. But the two of them are having problems, daughter. I think my daughter-in-law's family is putting pressure on her to stay away from us. I went to the store earlier and I overheard some gossip. They're saying that our family legacy is true and that it's caught up to us. They believe you've turned to evil, and that if I'm protecting you, I must be part of the problem, too."

Ella felt her mother's pain as keenly as she did her own. Trying to remain calm, she took a deep, steadying breath.

"Listen, Mom, people are going to talk. Gossip is a favorite pastime here, next to basketball," she added, trying to make her mom smile but failing.

"I just don't know what to do. If I tell your brother that his wife believes the rumors, that she won't let me see my grandson because she's afraid of what you or I will do to him, it'll hurt him deeply. Even worse, it'll create more problems in his marriage, and that's the last thing I want to do."

"Let me talk to him. What his wife is doing is wrong and it has to be set right," Ella insisted.

"No. Let me see if there's another way to handle this first. I have to find out if his wife is truly frightened or just trying to punish us. You know she already thinks that we take too much of your brother's time."

"I have a better idea. Let *me* have a talk with her," Ella suggested.

"You don't really want to just talk to her. You want to back her up against the wall like you do with your suspects," Rose said, and this time she smiled.

"Tempting, isn't it?" Ella said wistfully.

Rose chuckled. "Daughter, your way of confronting this issue is going to stir up even more trouble. I'll handle this."

"I don't want to see you hurt, Mom, but with everything that's happening . . ."

Dawn tottered into the kitchen just then. "Pick up," she said, holding her hands up to Ella.

Ella lifted her up. "Hey, sweetheart."

"*Shimasání* crying," she said, reaching out to her grandmother. "*T'adoo.*"

Ella laughed. "That's right, Grandma, stop that! I guess that's one Navajo word she hears a lot!"

Rose laughed, and Ella realized how much her daughter and her mother needed each other. At the moment, it was hard to tell who was really taking care of whom. Dawn had given Rose a new lease on life.

Ella ate a quick lunch with her mother and daughter, then set out again, assured that Rose was feeling better. She was tempted to drive over to Loretta's and give her a piece of her mind, but knew she shouldn't, particularly after her mother had specifically asked her not to.

Hearing her cell phone ring, Ella picked it up. It was Blalock.

"I just wanted to let you know that Branch is gunning for all of us now. The jerk is looking for trouble, *but he's mine,*" FB-Eyes growled. "Is that clear? When he calls the local FBI corrupt on the air, then it falls on my side of the court, and it's up to me to return the ball."

"I assume he said this on the new morning segment of his show?" Ella asked.

"Yeah. He's got the radio station to split his program so that he gets morning and evening drive-time traffic. That way he'll increase his listening audience."

"What do you plan to do?"

"Well, he's being escorted down to your police station, for starters. He barely got to sign off on his program. Since he's made my life more miserable than it was, I'm now going to dedicate myself to returning that favor."

Ella laughed. "Tread carefully, old friend."

"Yeah. Payestewa is a lawyer, so we're going to threaten him with personal libel and drown him in legalese. It won't go anywhere, but I guarantee we'll get his attention and make the station think twice about permitting his personal attacks. One more thing. It would be best for you not to come down to the police station right now. You have two reporters waiting. They're from the local and the morning Albuquerque papers."

"Thanks for the tip. I'll steer clear for a while."

As Ella put the phone down, she tried to come up with a plan of action. This morning's incident with her mother had made it very clear that she couldn't just sit by and wait for Blalock to find answers. Justine's death was ripping her family apart, and she simply couldn't stay waiting on the sidelines, going in for an occasional play. With Harry Ute and the FBI already after Samuel Begaye, and Branch distracting Blalock, she decided to concentrate on Jayne. Ella called Ruth and learned that her cousin would be getting off work at the Daily Double in another forty minutes.

Ella set out for the bar on the east side of Farmington, ready to get some answers. As she pulled into the cafe's parking lot, Ella saw Jayne walking west away from the cafe along the south side of the highway.

Ella parked quickly and started to follow her on foot. Hoping not to get spotted, Ella hung well back. There was one business right after the other in this area, many of them construction companies or trucking firms, and it was easy to follow Jayne because the vehicles in each of the parking lots gave her cover.

When Jayne stopped at a gas station to speak to two men, obviously friends of hers, Ella watched her carefully. It was remarkable how much Jayne resembled Justine. They not only looked alike physically, they also moved with the same quick strides short, energetic people often used.

Five minutes later, Jayne left the gas station and continued down the street. The bar she gambled at was just past the next corner, and Ella figured that was probably where she was heading.

Ella saw her turn down an alley between two old brick buildings, now used for storage, that had their windows painted over. The minute Ella followed Jayne into the shadows, she knew she'd walked into a trap.

Hearing footsteps behind her, she turned her head. The men Jayne had met at the gas station were now blocking her way back out. Ella faced them squarely. "You're about to make a very big mistake. I'm a cop."

"One who is the only real suspect in my sister's death," Jayne said from behind Ella. "And who is *way* out of her jurisdiction."

"And one who is armed," Ella said, putting her hand down on the butt of her pistol. "Don't be asking for trouble."

The men backed up a step, but Jayne picked up a piece of lumber from an old pallet and threw it at Ella.

Unable to dodge effectively in the narrow space between the buildings, Ella was forced to block the chunk of wood, and it bounced painfully off her right forearm.

Before she knew it, the men were upon her. Ella ducked under a fist, went down, then kicked her attacker's legs out from under him. Rolling, she drew her pistol and aimed it at the pair. "Back off."

The two men glanced at each other, stepped back out of the alley, and split up, disappearing in opposite directions.

Jayne stood in front of Ella, unable to pass by and blocked at the other end by a six-foot fence. "Looks like you've trapped me here."

"Stay where you are, Jayne. We have to talk," Ella said, scrambling back to her feet.

Jayne put her back against one of the buildings, trying to inch past Ella. "No way. I'm not talking to you. I'm getting out of here and there's nothing you can do to stop me. If you shoot me or beat me up, there's no way you'll stay out of jail, not with the charges you're already facing."

"There *are* no charges against me," Ella reminded her, holstering her weapon.

"Oh, but the evidence is there, and you've got enemies who are ready to make sure the police don't sweep everything under the rug."

"You're really eager to put the blame on me, aren't you? I wonder if it's because you're worried that your sister's death is linked to you and your gambling problems."

"I don't have to listen to this," Jayne said, inching farther out of the alley. "You're the one who's at fault. My sister is dead because of you, not me," Jayne said, choking back a sob.

Before Ella could say another word, Jayne brushed past her and ran out of the alley. Ella didn't go after her. It seemed pointless now. Instead, she walked back quickly to her unit.

She was unlocking the door when her cell phone rang. Ella recognized her brother's voice instantly.

"What's wrong?" she asked, knowing he never called when she was working unless it was important.

"I need to talk to you. Can you come to the hogan?"

"I'll be there in forty-five minutes."

"Come sooner if you can," he said.

Knowing that her brother moved on what was called Indian Time, and that he never rushed, only made his urgent request more compelling.

Putting the tribal unit in gear, she flipped on her emergency lights and pulled out onto the highway.

TWENTY-ONE

— ✶ ✶ ✶ —

Ella was just braking to a stop outside Clifford's medicine hogan when he stepped out from behind the wool blanket that served as a door and waved at her. Ella had expected to see Julian playing and Loretta someplace nearby, but neither was around.

As she climbed out of the Jeep and looked for his family, Clifford shook his head. "Later. Right now we have to get going. We should take my truck, though, not your police vehicle."

"What have you got?"

"I've located a person who has seen Samuel Begaye recently—Old Shadow Man."

She knew the man. His name was Daniel Benally. "He's got to be close to one hundred now. He's not still living alone in that hogan out past Big Gap, is he?"

"Yes, he is. I went to do a prayer for him, and from what I could see, he's in real good shape. His family has tried to get him to move into Shiprock, to tribal housing on the east side, but he won't have it."

"So how did he meet the fugitive?"

"Apparently he showed up out of the blue, armed with a rifle, and demanded food and water. Shadow Man gave him what he could, and the fugitive stayed for quite a few hours just talking before he shoved off. That's why I thought you might want to speak to the old man yourself."

"Thanks. But if he's still the staunch traditionalist that he used to be, I may not get much out of him. He might disapprove of me on principle."

"That's why I'm offering to go along. I'll try to smooth things for you."

Ella suddenly had a feeling that there was another reason Clifford was trying so hard to help her. "Is there something about this case that's troubling you?"

Clifford didn't answer right away. "Words have power. To speak of something evil is to call it to you. Wait and see what happens when you go back to the station."

A chill touched her soul. Something bad was going to happen. Yet Ella knew she had to put it all out of her mind for now. Finding Samuel Begaye could give her a lead, and she had to focus on getting the most information from old Daniel Benally.

"Don't interrupt him, even if you think he's fallen asleep. He'll be testing you, sister. It's his way."

"I'll remember."

It took twenty minutes of driving, the last ten on a dirt track that must have disappeared each rainy season. After several especially bone-jarring bumps, she glanced at her brother. "Now I know why you always took so long to buy your trucks. They have to be practically indestructible."

He laughed. "At least here you can see which way to go. Some of these old-timers make it a point to build their hogans as far as they can from highways and modernists."

When they finally reached their destination, Ella was ready to climb out of the truck and stretch. She started to open the door, but Clifford stopped her.

"Wait. Let me get out instead. He may be a little jumpy since Begaye paid him a visit, but he knows me, and once he sees me, he should invite us both in."

It didn't take long for Daniel Benally to come to the entrance of his hogan. He'd replaced the traditional wool blanket with a handmade door of pine planks, probably because of the lack of protection out here from winter winds.

Ella studied the man. She'd met him when she was a teenager

and he'd seemed ancient then, but strangely enough, in the last twenty years he hadn't changed at all. He stood upright and, shielding his eyes from the sun with his hand, he waved at them.

Clifford glanced at Ella. "Remember. No names. And women sit on the south side."

Ella followed her brother.

"*Yáat'ééh*, Uncle," Clifford greeted, saying hello.

Benally nodded to him, then looked at Ella with open suspicion. "So you are the *hataalii*'s sister," he said after a moment.

"Yes, Uncle," she said, using the word as her brother had, to denote respect, not actual kinship.

They went inside and sat down on the ground on sheepskin blankets, Ella being careful to stay on the southern side of the center.

"I know why you've come," Benally said. "You want to turn over one of the *Dineh* to the *bilagáanas*, the white people."

"It's not that simple, Uncle," Ella said. "The man who came to you here went to prison because he took the life of another Navajo. I want to make sure that he doesn't have the chance to hurt anyone else again. Yet, as things stand, it's possible that he may have already done so. We're looking for the killer of a young Navajo woman, our second cousin."

"We used to deal with things like this among ourselves," Benally grunted.

"The new laws give us a chance to keep things in order. We need to restore the *hózhq*, the harmony and balance that brings us peace, when a situation like this comes up. Policemen are there to do that so our people can tend to their own lives." Ella spoke slowly, hoping she wouldn't stick her foot in her mouth. She needed this man's help.

He nodded thoughtfully.

She continued, carefully. "Uncle, I need your help. Can you tell me what direction the man who came here went after he left, and how he was traveling?"

Benally waited before answering, and Ella was grateful she'd been warned about showing impatience. She sat quietly nearly four minutes before the man spoke again. "He had an old truck, and he drove off to the northwest. He was scared, even with a rifle. I could see it in his eyes. He had the look of a mustang cut off from the herd, and forced to run from danger."

"What did he talk about when he was here?"

This time Benally didn't test her, instead answering immediately. "He said people had misjudged him. He said he was innocent and had only killed in self-defense. But the police had taken him away, and the judge put him in jail. He said he had expected to serve his time, but then his father was murdered. He came back to find justice for his family."

"Did he mention how he was going to do that?"

"He said he would make sure that the guilty were punished. But after he was finished, he wouldn't go back to prison. He said he would live on his own out here until they gave up looking for him." He paused. "But I don't think he'll succeed. He was soft— like the modernists who grow up watching television and sitting under the air conditioner."

"Is there any place around here where he could find shelter and water?"

"I'll tell you what I told him when he asked me the same thing. Shelter, yes. There are hogans scattered about. Water is more difficult. It takes a bumpy drive to Big Gap Lake or one of the springs in the foothills."

"Did he ask you to draw him a map to those hogans you mentioned?"

"I made one on the sand with a stick. But I don't think he'll find his way very easily. He comes from over by Gallup. I think he'll do what the *bilagáanas* from the university do when they come to learn about the old ways. They stay around until it gets uncomfortable for them, then they go back to the city."

"If he returns, be careful. He's a very dangerous man."

"He won't come back. He was disappointed because there was nothing to steal, and his rifle was better than mine." He paused, then continued. "But you should be wary of him. That man feels a lot of hatred for you."

"Did he speak of our cousin?"

"He only spoke of you."

"Thank you, Uncle," she said.

As they left the hogan, Ella looked around at the sparse vegetation and low, undulating terrain falling away toward the distant river valley to the east. On the west side, the desert extended up to the foothills of the sacred mountains, which were still dry, but less so. "If Begaye is still out here, he's going to find few people, and even fewer allies."

"That's only going to make him more dangerous," Clifford said.

Ella shook her head slowly. "The crazy thing is that although I know he hates me and would enjoy seeing me in a world of hurt, I honestly don't think he's directly involved in what happened to our cousin. I want to find him mostly because I'm hoping he's learned something about what's going on. The people he associates with—the criminal element—probably know far more than we do right now."

"Let's search the area together then. We'll see things the other one doesn't. You depend on your training, I depend on the land itself."

They spent the rest of the day searching the dusty tracks leading to one-family hogans and water-carved canyons. Some of the hogans were abandoned, the former inhabitants having left to seek a more hospitable location, perhaps. Everywhere they went, the history of hardship the tribe had endured was written in every makeshift building, in the carcasses of animals that had perished from the lack of water, and in the stark, barren land that extended everywhere until meeting a source of water.

Only twice did they come across another human being, and both times it was men riding horseback and herding sheep and goats in search of grass.

It was after dark by the time they returned to Clifford's home. Loretta was waiting on the porch, and when she saw the pickup, she strode out angrily.

Hands on her hips, she stared at her husband, then at Ella as they climbed down out of the truck. "When will you two wake up and realize the harm you're doing to yourselves and your family?"

Ella stared at her. "What on earth are you talking about?"

"The more time you spend together, the more talk it generates. Someone who came by here before dark said you were looking inside abandoned hogans."

"They weren't ones where a death had occurred," Clifford said, a touch of anger tainting his voice. "I know the difference. What else have you heard?"

"That your sister is trying to corrupt you." Loretta wiped a tear from her face. "I won't live like this, being shamed and having my son and me turned away because people have been told to avoid us."

"The gossip will go away once the truth becomes known," Clifford said, his voice steady and sure. "And our son is too young to know what's going on."

"He knows that his friends aren't allowed to visit us and that he's not welcome at their homes."

Clifford looked at Ella. "My wife and I need to talk. Let me know if there's anything more I can do to help you."

"Thanks for everything."

"If you truly love your brother, stay away from him before you ruin all of us," Loretta said quietly.

As Ella got into her Jeep, she felt mentally exhausted. If her enemy's goal was to put unremitting pressure on her, it was working. She had never felt so alone in her entire life.

Ella drove directly home, and as she pulled into the driveway, she saw Kevin's vehicle by the house. Surprised, she parked and went inside.

Her daughter's father was in the living room, playing with Dawn and her blocks. Rose sat on her chair, crocheting and keeping a close eye on them. She didn't trust Kevin, and made no attempt to hide it.

As soon as Dawn saw Ella in the doorway, she held up her hands. "Pick up!"

Ella laughed and lifted Dawn up, then swung her around in a circle. Dawn squealed and laughed, enjoying the game. Kevin watched them, a serious look on his face. As soon as Ella put Dawn back on the floor, he cocked his head toward the kitchen. "I need to talk to you, Ella. It'll only take a moment."

"What's up?" Ella asked, leading the way. The last thing she wanted to face tonight was another complication, but she had no choice now that Dawn's father was here.

"I've been approached by some influential people who want me to run for Tribal Council," Kevin confided once they were alone in the kitchen.

Ella studied his expression, trying to figure out why he needed to tell her this now, and why he was so serious. Everything she knew about Kevin told her that he had to be delighted with the prospect. "This is something you've wanted for a long time. Why are you acting so glum?"

"Everything I do, everything I say, from this moment on will be scrutinized. Politics is a rough game," he said slowly. "You are a part of my life, and the rumors going around about you . . ." He let the sentence hang.

"Hey, I'm not thrilled about what's being said either. Nobody likes to hear lies and gossip about themselves. But I don't see what you expect me to do about it."

"My name's on Dawn's birth certificate. Although we haven't made that information public, that'll probably come to light as people in the press check on my background."

"Kevin, what is it you want from me? I can't do anything about the birth certificate now. If you're worried about what people are going to think, don't attract attention by coming to see either of us. Put as much distance between us as you want. Dawn and I will be fine. Then, once everything calms down, come back and see your daughter if you still want to."

"I want to play a role in my daughter's life, but I won't be able to do that unless you keep your name out of the headlines and the local gossip. You're a magnet for trouble, Ella. It's only been four days since Justine's murder, and already you're right in the middle of it all. Every time you make another move, you just seem to generate more talk and negative publicity for yourself. Can't you just lay low, take some time off, and let the FBI and the Tribal Police handle Justine's case?"

"You're not worried about negative publicity for me, though. You're just worried about yourself."

"In this particular case, yes. I can do a lot of good for this tribe, but I need to get elected first."

She shrugged. "So go for it. You don't have to worry about keeping bad company. Our tribe sees the kids as the mother's responsibility. You don't have to be associated with us at all."

"But that's just it. I want to be around Dawn and you. I'm just trying to get you to help me out a little bit here."

"Kevin, my neck's on the line. I can't quit doing my job because you're worried about your career. I've got to keep investigating and stirring up the waters until the garbage floats to the surface and the truth is there for everyone to see. If you really want to demonstrate what it takes to be a good leader, then accept your situation and handle it."

"You're backing me up against a wall, Ella."

"Everything in your life can't be just about you. Deal with it." She went back to the living room and opened the front door. "Say good night to your daughter, then let me get some rest. I've had a long day."

Kevin gave his daughter a hug, then started toward the door. As he passed by Ella, he paused. "I've already heard about your day, Ella. Sometimes you can be your own worst enemy."

Ella fought the urge to kick him in the shins, or higher. He'd said that on purpose, hoping to force her hand in front of Rose. As Kevin drove off and Ella turned, she saw the questions in her mother's eyes.

"Later," Ella said. "Let me put Dawn to bed first."

Ella played with her daughter on the floor with her stuffed toys and blocks until Dawn began to get bored, then bathed her. By that time Dawn could barely keep her eyes open. She settled down for the night much easier than Ella had expected, and went right to sleep before Ella finished reading the story about the lambs.

When Ella returned to the living room, Rose's eyes were bright with questions. Ella wanted to protect her, but it was impossible to keep the news of what was happening from her mother. If she didn't tell her, Rose would just hear it from someone else.

Ella opted for complete honesty. "My brother and I are trying to find this man, hoping he'll give me a lead to who killed our cousin, but people are out for blood. I've got enemies in very high places, and they're doing everything they can to get people stirred

up. Somebody is watching everything I do, and using each opportunity to spread more lies about me."

"This kind of talk will die, eventually, but your sister-in-law is
right, to a point. It can do your brother a great deal of harm. His
patients have to believe he's beyond reproach. Something like this
could ruin him for good."

"Mom, my cousin's killer could walk free, and I could end up
going to prison for a crime I didn't commit if any more of this
contrived evidence shows up. I'm facing some serious stuff here,
too. There's much more at stake than my brother's reputation."

"I never said otherwise. But your brother's patients depend on
him. When they're sick, they need to trust your brother's knowledge and willingness to help them. He's in the same position that
the *bilagáana* doctors at the hospital are in. His reputation is everything."

Ella nodded, understanding. At least she was still collecting a
paycheck. But Clifford's livelihood could be compromised by the
company he kept. Without his patients, he wouldn't be able to provide for his family, and that had to weigh heavily on his mind as
well as Loretta's.

"Mom, I'm too tired to think. I'm going to bed." Ella went to
her room. As she undressed, she switched on the computer, hoping
that another instant message would come in from her informant.
But as she finished getting ready for bed, none had come on-screen.

Figuring that it was the perfect ending to an entirely crappy
day, she crawled beneath the covers. As she drifted off to sleep,
she was finally at peace.

Ella left for work even before Dawn was awake the next morning.
She wanted to search the databases, but knew it was better for her
to do that when others weren't around to check on what she was
doing, especially because she was trying to track down Justine's
killer before the trail was stone-cold.

Sitting at her desk, Ella started by trying to find out all she
could about Bobby Lujan through department and FBI databases.
Ruth had told her a little bit about him, naming him as one of the

people Jayne had been hanging around with recently, but Ella needed more. The search revealed that Lujan's only local arrest had been a drunken-driving charge, but that was very common on the Rez. She accessed the databases of the county and neighboring police departments, and even the national database through the Feds, but found nothing except two minor disorderly conduct charges.

Ella picked up the phone and called Blalock. A gravelly voice answered the call, and Ella realized that she'd probably woken FB-Eyes up.

"Good morning, Dwayne. I know it's early, but I needed to talk to you about someone." She told him about Bobby Lujan and her interest in him, especially in regards to Jayne and illegal gambling. "I've got nothing on Lujan, but it's possible he knows something pertinent to this investigation."

"You're thinking that he may have wanted to use Justine as leverage to collect a gambling debt and things got out of hand?"

"Yes. Jayne could be right in the middle of what happened to her sister."

"I'll look into it. And, Ella, don't get caught working on this case. You hear me?"

"Perfectly."

Ella then left a priority call for Harry Ute through the Marshals Service, telling him what she'd learned about Samuel Begaye from Daniel Benally. As she placed the phone down, she could hear the first of the morning-shift people coming into the station.

Ella decided to leave. Maintaining a low profile now was a matter of necessity. She was walking out the side door when Joseph Neskahi stopped her on the steps.

"Ella, I'm really sorry to hear that your brother's having a difficult time right now."

"What do you mean?" she asked, a touch of fear creeping beneath her skin.

"My uncle, who's a friend of Loretta's family, came by to visit me last night. He mentioned that Loretta had taken Julian and moved back in with her mother. Then, earlier this morning, I ran into your brother at the Trading Post. He sure looked like a man who hasn't slept very much lately."

Ella felt her heart sink. "He's so used to playing things close to his chest, he didn't tell Mom and me." Ella rubbed the back of her neck, shaking her head at how things seemed to be unraveling around her.

"Maybe it's a good a thing I told you, then. You should also be aware that there's some nasty gossip about you going around. It's just garbage about your family legacy and you turning to evil, and hints that you had something to do with Justine's death. I've made it a point to come down heavily on anyone I hear talking about it."

"I used to think that no one ever paid attention to that stuff except the old ones, but now I just don't know," Ella said.

"Well, the ones in our generation interpret 'turning to evil' as you going psycho. They don't really buy the rest of the story. And the younger adults think you're just another cop who's flipped out under the pressure."

"The gossip won't stop until the truth comes out." Ella exhaled softly. "I just wish I knew who hates me and hated Justine enough to do this to us."

Ella thanked the sergeant and walked over to her unit. Moments later, she was on her way to the college. Wilson not only taught the college students, but he was spending a lot of time working with younger groups. Kids talked freely, the younger ones even more so than the older ones. Maybe he or Jeremiah had heard something that she would find useful.

Ella used the drive time to unwind, focusing on traffic and the warm, pleasant morning. By the time she reached the campus, she felt more in control. There was nothing like a plan to keep her mind focused on business. It was also the best way she'd found to keep her fear at bay.

Ella walked quickly to Wilson's office and found him just closing the door, about to leave.

"I see I've come at a bad time. You must have a class now," she said.

"No, actually I have to meet Jeremiah out by one of the portable buildings. He's setting up an activity. We're starting early because the middle-school kids have the afternoon off. Their teachers are having meetings today. Why don't you walk with me?"

"Okay. That'll give us a chance to talk."

"Did you plan on staying for your brother's and Herman Cloud's lecture on the traditional way of life?"

That was the second reference to her brother that had taken her by surprise. But then again, none of it should have. Her brother and she led separate lives, and rarely compared schedules. "I've been so caught up in the things that have been happening lately, I didn't even know he was coming."

"He probably didn't say anything because he didn't think of it."

"I suspect it's a little more complicated than that." She told him about Loretta taking Julian and going to stay with her mother.

Wilson stared at her in amazement. "And he still showed up today? Your brother never ceases to amaze me."

Ella nodded. "He tries to be strong—for everyone's sake—but sometimes Clifford forgets he doesn't have to be a superhero."

"Maybe you should talk to him. I know he's already on campus somewhere. He's probably in the auditorium reviewing some notes. You can catch up to me later at the portable building or the gym."

"When's he scheduled to give his talk?"

Wilson checked his watch. "In ten minutes or so."

Ella shook her head. "I better let him finish his talk first. I'll stick with you for now."

When they reached the portable building, they discovered the door was propped open. The strong smell of solvent drifted from the entrance. Inside were five high schoolers, scrubbing two of the walls.

"What happened?" Ella asked, looking at the graffiti spray painted on the metal and hard vinyl surfaces.

"Someone broke in last night and wrecked our place," Fred Billey said. "They came in through one of the vents next to the heater."

The young teen looked like one of the gang members Ella had dealt with before, but she couldn't be sure until she saw a tattoo on his hand.

The boy saw where she was looking. "Yeah, I was in the Many Devils once. So were these other guys. But after all the trouble and shootings, we quit that way of life. Not officially. We'd be their enemies if we did that. We just don't hang out with them anymore." He looked at Wilson Joe. "Professor, we've got some more solvent and paper towels in the truck. Want to give me a hand while these guys keep scrubbing? We're trying to get it all off before it sets up hard."

"No problem."

Jeremiah Manyfarms came out of a storage closet with a mop and bucket with a wringer just after Wilson left. "They're really good kids," he said. "They've been working their butts off all morning, and have cleaned two of the walls already."

"Have you had this kind of trouble here before? Did any of the other buildings get hit too?"

"No, this room was the target, probably to make a point. But don't worry. This is actually a good sign. The gangs are seeing that they're losing this battle and they're worried. That's why they attacked us. Trust me, I know how they think."

"I wouldn't make any assumptions if I were you. The behavior of the few boys you've met and have brought over to your side doesn't tell you much about what the rest are doing or thinking. This is a tricky issue. As an officer, I've battled this for quite a while."

"I know. But I've also worked with kids for a long time." He paused, then continued in a low voice. "I moved to California several years ago. Back then I was so heavily involved with Indian rights, I stopped paying much attention to my family. That was when my teenaged boys joined a gang. Then, two years ago, we came home to the Rez to visit relatives. My youngest boy was wearing gang colors, and looked at a local gang kid the wrong way, I guess. That got him shot and killed."

Jeremiah was gripping the mop handle so hard his knuckles were white. "That's when I realized what was happening to the kids—my own as well as the other children here on our land. Indian rights was suddenly a lot less important to me. I knew that to stand up for Indian rights, our kids have to know that they're Indian, and today, half of them haven't got a clue what it means to be Navajo. To them, it's skin color and living on the Rez—if that. Since they don't know who and what they are, they're lost between two worlds. Our kids then reach out to the Anglo world for identity and end up destroying themselves."

"They watch television shows and see the Anglo world—one that really doesn't exist—and want to experience that life. The media, especially movies and TV, are powerful models," Ella said.

"And there are those, like you, who bring the Anglo world in, meshing our way and theirs, and blur things even more for everyone."

"But we need that blend. That's the key to our own survival," Ella said.

"Maybe, but before you can blend, you have to know what you have to gain and what you stand to lose. Our kids don't know enough to make the right choices. They're just plain lost. They desperately want to belong, not understanding that they already do. They're part of a tribe that has lived through horrors few can ever imagine, and endured to this day. Our strength as a people is something they can be proud of, but they have to be taught to take pride in who they are."

Jeremiah started mopping some of the dissolved paint that had made it to the floor. "Some people think I harp on family involvement too much. But we need to have strong families. Moms and dads are too busy working to pay attention to what's happening at home, and that's where we have to start. We have to get the parents involved. Tonight we're having the kids bring their families to watch them practice, then we're going to have a cookout."

Wilson came back into the room carrying a cardboard box containing cleaning supplies. "Ella, I just saw Herman Cloud and your brother leaving the auditorium. They've finished their lecture. I must have gotten the wrong time for their presentation."

Ella excused herself and went outside to find her brother.

TWENTY-TWO

✖ ✖ ✖

Clifford was surrounded by young men and women. At least here, among students who were constantly exposed to new ideas, unsubstantiated lies and the threat of the legacy didn't carry much weight.

Ella saw Clifford leave Herman Cloud to answer the students' questions and come toward her.

"It's good to see you here," Ella said. "You must have been a hit," she added, gesturing to the small crowd around Herman.

Clifford shook his head and spoke softly. "Don't kid yourself. They wanted more than knowledge about our ways. Some of them had heard about the *hataalii* who is known to have special powers, and they wanted to take a look for themselves. A lot of the knowledge they gain at this college tells them to rely only on what they observe, yet in their hearts, they know that the world is comprised of far more than what can be measured and touched. I think they were hoping to see a little magic and a miracle or two, or at least have me read their minds."

"I wish I knew how to put a stop to the gossip about me and our family."

"It'll die down eventually."

Ella could see the sadness in Clifford's eyes. His personal life was even worse than hers at the moment, and that was saying something. At least her daughter would be home when she quit work today.

When Herman called out to him, Clifford excused himself and went to join him. As Clifford walked away, Ella felt the chill of despair envelop her. She had to find Justine's killer soon, because the biggest danger she faced wasn't an empty home. It was being placed in a cell until her daughter had children of her own.

When the crowd of students around Clifford dwindled, Ella walked back to where her brother was standing.

"He really loves this," Clifford said, gesturing to Herman Cloud, who was still speaking to two young men. Herman was a longtime friend of their family. His shoulder-length hair was all white, but he stood tall, like a warrior. "I think he's been lonely since his wife died. With Philip and Michael working and busy with their own families, he spends too much time alone. I suggested that he take part in this lecture series about living a Navajo life in the new millennium because I felt he needed to get involved in something. At first he turned me down, but now he's always ready and waiting for me to pick him up whenever we give talks."

Ella knew her brother had purposely avoided mentioning Loretta and Julian, but she could see that Neskahi had been right. Clifford hadn't slept much. He looked weary and sad, the kind of emotional burden that settled over a person like a lengthy shadow.

"I heard about your wife," she said quietly.

Clifford nodded slowly. "I expected that you would." He looked at Ella. "You know that I'll have to go and bring her back, or if she won't come, then stay with her. I can't let my son go without his father's protection, especially now."

Herman Cloud came up and joined them before Ella could ask what her brother meant. "It's good to see you," he said. "Now that your brother will be gone for a while, I was hoping that you would come by and join me once in a while when I'm scheduled to speak."

"If I can, I'd be very happy to."

"It's been working out so well. Your brother speaks to them about being a *hataalii* and I speak to them about living day to day like a traditionalist. Of course, now that your brother has received those threats, he'll have to protect his wife and son."

"What? You've received threats? From whom?" Ella frowned at Clifford.

"I'll be leaving now, nephew." Herman walked away quickly before Ella could question him.

"I need to know what's happened," Ella said.

"I went for a walk late last night, trying to get tired enough to sleep, and two Navajo men ambushed me near my hogan when I returned. I knew someone was there, but I thought it might have been my wife, so I walked right into it. They had their faces covered. I took a few punches, but nothing serious. Then they told me to stop protecting my 'killer' sister, or I'd share in the punishment that was in store for you. They left me tied to the bumper of my truck, and by the time I got free, they were gone."

"Why didn't you call me after it happened?"

"What could you have done?"

"Look for a vehicle, search the area, watch the highway. Something!"

"I had no description of any vehicle to give you, I only heard it leaving in the dark. And you know how few neighbors we have. They could have gone in any direction. There wasn't much you could have done."

"Well, by not calling me right away, you certainly made a fact out of that statement."

Clifford looked at his sister sadly. "You still don't know when to fight and when to hang back. You better learn quickly, sister. More trouble is on the horizon."

As Clifford went to retrieve some items he'd brought to the lecture, Ella walked away toward her vehicle. She knew that she could no longer count on her brother's help. He would go to protect Loretta and his son, which was as it should be, but she had to continue the battle.

Her most important ally had now been taken from her. Ella wasn't sure how much more she could endure before she finally lost heart.

Ella arrived at her patrol unit, and as she slipped behind the wheel, her cell phone rang. It was Harry Ute.

"I got your message. And I got a brand-new lead just a few minutes ago. I'd like you along as my cover officer. Can you swing it?"

"You bet."

"I've got a tip that Samuel Begaye is going to meet his wife at the West Farmington Mall at noon. I'd like to be in place before they arrive."

"I'll be there. Where shall we meet?"

"Go to the coffee shop just across the street on the east side. We'll meet there. And wear sunglasses and a cap or something. Try to be shorter, too," he joked.

"What about you? Will you be wearing a disguise?"

"Yeah, but don't worry. You'll still know me."

Ella stopped by the house, and after picking up her daughter and saying hello, she went into the bedroom to change. First she took off her boots and removed her backup holster rig from her right leg. That went into her closet, but she placed the derringer inside her jacket pocket. Running shoes took an inch off her height, but masking her taller-than-average stature was something she could do only with limited success. Ella brushed her long, black hair so it cascaded around her shoulders, then put on a tan cowboy hat. With her dark glasses on, she looked like another person.

Rose came in and looked at her daughter. "You look beautiful and not at all like a cop. Is that what you were aiming for?"

"Yep, but the problem is that close up I still look like me. I may be able to fool someone who doesn't know me very well, though. I guess I'll just have to try it out and see."

When Dawn went back to the living room to get her doll, Rose gave Ella a worried look. "Another team operation? Things are getting too dangerous right now for you to trust anyone, maybe even the people you usually work with."

Ella sighed. "Yes, I know, but I have to be able to trust somebody, or I'm already lost."

Rose nodded. "Your brother is going to join his wife, in spite of the fact that she's staying with her mother. He called me earlier today. I never thought things would go this far."

Ella knew that Rose had taken the news that Clifford had to leave, perhaps for a long time, very hard. She'd always been close to her son, and she adored Julian.

"This will have an end, Mom. He'll be back." Ella said good-bye to her daughter and mother, then left to meet Harry in Farmington.

Ella arrived at her destination forty minutes later and parked in the rear parking area. As she started to go inside, a man in a brown jacket approached her. She took a defensive stance, her hand in her pocket atop the derringer, wondering if he was about to try to rob her or attempt a carjacking.

It took her a second, but she quickly relaxed. With the mustache and baseball cap, Harry looked more Hispanic than he did Navajo. "Wow. You've learned a trick or two in the Marshals Service, I see."

He smiled. "You look great, Ella," he said, giving her a once-over. "Where have you been all my life?"

It was so uncharacteristic for Harry that Ella didn't exactly know what to say. "Hey, beneath the police person there's a lady. Did you doubt it?"

"No, but I never thought about it much until now."

"Gee, thanks," Ella said.

He grinned. "Okay, ready to get to work? Let's take my sedan. Your tribal unit is a dead giveaway to anyone who's seen you in it."

"At least it's not marked. I should also tell you that I won't be able to stay out of contact for long. I didn't tell dispatch or the chief because I'm assuming you still want to stay undercover."

"You bet. Thanks. Until I've got Samuel Begaye in handcuffs, I doubt my status will change."

"I'm really hoping that Begaye might know something about Justine's killer. It's a slim hope, but it's all I've got," Ella said.

"That's why I called you. With luck, I'll have this slippery sucker in custody before dinnertime."

After reaching the mall, they matched frequencies on their handheld radios, then split up. Ella took the north side of the mall, and Harry the south. If Begaye was here, they'd see him soon as they moved from opposite ends.

Ella had just reached one of the shoe stores when she saw Begaye and his wife, Jean, standing near a side entrance. She called Harry on her handheld, ducking into the store as she did, then moved forward cautiously.

Before she could get close, she felt a gun pressed to the small of her back. "Don't turn around, just walk out with me. And keep your eyes straight ahead." She didn't recognize the man's voice, but it could have been a Navajo.

Ella saw the anger on Begaye's face as she walked past him and was forced outside. She'd lost one suspect, but right now she had another perp to worry about. Maybe, if she could turn the tables on her captor, she'd still be able to find Begaye before he left the area.

Suddenly the man behind her pushed her forward hard, right into the path of a shopper's van. Ella rolled quickly out of the way, escaping the squealing tires only by inches. She scrambled to her feet instantly, but by then the van driver had stopped, and people were gathering around her. Ella looked around, but had no idea who might have been her would-be killer. No faces looked familiar in the crowd.

By the time she broke away from the confusion and made it back inside the small shopping mall, both Harry and Begaye were gone. Ella tried to raise him on the radio, but got no response. Either he'd switched off the unit or the signal was blocked.

Worried about him, she searched the entire area, including the parking lot, but there was no sign of either man, and Harry's vehicle was gone. Ella knew that Harry could be in trouble, but she wasn't sure how to help without blowing his cover. She decided to wait it out, and if Harry didn't contact her very soon, she'd phone in a situation report to the Marshals Service.

Ella was driving back to Shiprock when she noticed a beat-up sedan about a quarter mile behind her. It paced itself well, neither advancing or gaining on her despite other cars passing or being passed. Curious, she kept checking on it, wondering if the driver was tailing her or simply on the same road moving at the same pace.

Finally she turned off onto the old highway, which led through the farming communities just north of the river. Finding a large cottonwood tree just around a curve, she pulled off quickly and used the tree as cover.

The sedan continued down the narrow road, seemingly uninterested in her disappearance. Yet as it passed by, she caught a glimpse of the person inside. It was Jean Begaye, Samuel's wife. She remembered the woman well, because Jean had attacked Justine and her when they'd arrested her husband.

Flashers and sirens on, Ella pulled her over. As she called dispatch, she also wrote down the vehicle tag number and identity of the occupant on her notepad.

Raw hatred shone in Mrs. Begaye's eyes as she got out of the car and placed her keys on the top as Ella ordered. "What? Was I going too fast?" she snapped. "Are we even on the reservation here?"

Ella saw the flicker in her eyes. Jean was goading her, daring her to prove that she'd just come back from meeting her husband.

Ella would have preferred having a cover officer, which was procedure when making a possible felony stop, but decided to do the next best thing.

"Move away from the car now," Ella ordered, then handcuffed Jean to a speed-limit sign before frisking her for weapons. Next, Ella checked the interior of the car, satisfied that Jean couldn't run away or attack. The inside of the car was empty, except for a purse on the seat and a shopping bag from a mall clothing store. The purse didn't contain a weapon, Ella noted without having to remove any of the contents.

Grabbing the car keys from the roof of the car, she opened the trunk carefully, crouching down low and to one side. She'd heard of a cop being shot from the inside once. The trunk was empty except for a worn, flat-looking spare, bumper jack, and a set of jumper cables.

Jean laughed at Ella's caution. "You think I was hiding my husband in there?"

"What makes you think I'm after your husband?" Ella shot back.

"So you're after *me* now?" She laughed. "Tell me, what law have I broken?"

"Aiding and abetting an escaped federal fugitive."

"Really? And what are you going to use for proof?"

"I saw you with him at the Farmington Mall. Don't try to deny it."

"Of course I'll deny it. That means you'll have to prove it, and that'll be tough for you. The way things are going for you lately, your word isn't worth much now, and it'll be worth nothing at all once the cops prove you killed your cousin.''

''Don't count on it,'' she said, uncuffing Jean from the sign, then cuffing both the woman's hands behind her back and leading her to the tribal unit. ''I bet one of the stores at the mall has you two on a security tape. With that in mind, I'm taking you into custody.''

Ella recited Jean her rights, retrieved the woman's purse, and locked up the vehicle. She then headed back toward the station with her prisoner. It was possible that Jean Begaye knew something that could help her find Harry, and maybe even Justine's killer. But until she had more leverage, getting any information from her was going to be next to impossible.

''You're going to be facing a murder charge soon yourself,'' Jean goaded. ''Then you'll have a firsthand look at what my husband has had to go through in jail. But it'll be worse for you. You're going to have a lot of enemies in prison, don't you think?''

''Your husband is guilty of murder. You know it as well as I do. Half the bar saw him, and was willing to testify.''

''There were circumstances you never took time to find out about, things the others didn't know about either. My husband was fighting for his life. It was self-defense.''

''He started the fight, and he killed a man over a spilled bottle of beer. How much of that was self-defense?''

''I hope they hang you.''

''They only do that in Utah, around here. I hope you won't be disappointed, but there hasn't been an execution in New Mexico for decades.''

After that exchange, they rode in silence. Ella considered her options. She would have Neskahi question Mrs. Begaye. He'd have better luck with her. She'd also ask him to follow up on the videotapes from the Farmington mall. He was the perfect choice since he already knew about Samuel Begaye being in the area, having been the one who spotted the bank-robbery vehicle Begaye was believed to have used in the job.

As she pulled into the station and brought Mrs. Begaye inside, the somber faces of the officers at the front desk and booking area told her there was something new going on. It didn't take intuition to know that she could expect more trouble.

After she finished processing Mrs. Begaye, Ella went to find Neskahi and found him in the squad area known as the pigpen, filled with desks and chairs but no private offices or partitions. He was at a desk talking to Agent Payestewa.

As she approached, Payestewa excused himself quickly, giving her a curt nod as he left the room. Ella gave Neskahi a puzzled look. "What's going on with Paycheck?"

"The Feds are running in circles around here. Paycheck is of no help here except to keep us warm by breathing down our necks. At least Blalock has learned how to work with the department." He shook his head. "Never mind. That's not why you're here. What do you need?"

She told him about Jean Begaye, and his expression perked up. "I'll interview her. If she has any pertinent information, I'll get it."

"Thanks."

As he walked away, Sergeant Manuelito approached her. "You're only damaging Neskahi's career by having him help you. When you go down, your reputation will stain his."

"Thanks for your professional objectivity on this case," Ella snapped.

He scowled at her. "I've heard that you've been taking the law into your own hands for years. I don't know why I'm wasting my time talking to you now."

"Why are you so happy that one of your fellow officers may be dead and another is facing trumped-up charges?" Ella asked. "What did I ever do to you except perform my job?"

"I'm not happy about Goodluck's murder, but it was your influence here that kept me from getting the promotions I deserved. I should have made lieutenant by now, or even had your job."

"I had nothing to do with that. My guess is Big Ed also knows that your arrogance and your blind adherence to procedures prevent you from being more than a mediocre cop. Like now," she added pointedly.

"Good police work is done by the book. You like to make up your own rules as you go, and that's what's going to take you down. You'll destroy yourself, Clah, and I'm just going to stand by and watch."

As Manuelito walked away, Ella realized how much resentment he harbored. No amount of logic would get through to him now. He was her enemy, pure and simple. With luck, she wouldn't be put in any situation where she had to depend on him.

Seeing her walking back toward her office, Big Ed stopped her in the hall. "We have to talk, Shorty. Can you come to my office?"

Ella followed him, knowing, deep down, that he was about to deliver even more bad news.

"Have a seat," he said, as he went to his desk.

Ella took a chair and waited. Big Ed said nothing for several moments. Ella realized that he was having a difficult time getting started, and that was not a good sign.

"You're an important part of this department, and I want you to know that I intend to continue monitoring this investigation until your name is cleared. But in the meantime . . . well, things have to follow their own course."

"I don't understand. What are you saying?"

He exhaled softly. "We've received an anonymous tip that you've got evidence hidden in your office."

"What? That's crazy! Whoever made that statement obviously planted something in there. That's the only thing that makes sense."

"I know, and that's what I believe, too. But this isn't something that the police department can ignore. We've got the Tribal Council watching our every move."

"So what's going to happen? Have you already made a search?"

"Because it's on our premises, and it's part of internal affairs, you know we don't need a warrant. So Blalock is in there now, and they're turning it inside out. Now, think hard, Shorty. Is there *anything* they'll find that's going to create a problem?"

Ella shook her head. "Of course not—except for what someone may have planted in there. That's not a reach either, especially since the call came out of nowhere. I haven't locked my office for years."

Big Ed was about to say something when Blalock came in. He looked at Ella and attempted a half smile. The gesture was so untypical that it made Ella's skin grow clammy. Something was very, very wrong.

"Do you remember the one earring we found at the crime scene?" Blalock asked her and Big Ed.

Ella nodded, and saw Big Ed do the same.

"We found its partner. It was in your office, Ella. It was fashioned into a pendant and placed inside a hollowed-out book."

"Take prints from that book. You won't find mine on it, at least in the hollowed-out part."

"If this is as good a frame as I think, it may be your book and your prints will be on it somewhere. Don't jump the gun."

"I want to see what you've found."

They went down the hall together, and as they went into her office, she held her breath. Every drawer had been upended into a big pile on her desktop, and even the cushion on her chair had been checked.

"Show it to her," Blalock said curtly, nodding to Payestewa.

The Hopi agent picked up a suspense novel with a gloved hand, then opened it.

Ella saw the hollowed-out interior and the pendant inside. "The book's not mine. Fingerprint it. Then when you don't find my prints, start asking yourselves why I would put that in my office and still wipe my prints off it."

"Some killers like to keep trophies," Blalock said. "That's a well-known fact."

"I'm a cop. I wouldn't be stupid enough to put that in my office. And how would anyone be able to tell you that it was in there unless they'd placed it themselves? Can you track down the person who made the call?"

"We tried," Big Ed said. "It came from a pay phone and there were too many prints on it to get anything we could use."

Ella stared at the faces around her. "You *know* I had nothing to do with this. A defense lawyer would raise all kinds of reasonable doubt about a trick like this."

Big Ed nodded. "But I'm still going to have to place you on administrative leave, and take your weapon and your badge. Leave your unit parked when you get home, and I know I don't have to tell you this, but don't travel out of the area."

"My home and family are here. I won't be far." Ella removed her service pistol from its holster, unloaded it, then handed the handgun and her badge to the chief. She wanted to demand that they *do* something and help her fight this, but she knew she'd never manage it without her voice cracking.

Holding her head up, Ella strode out of the room. Anger made her hands shake. As she had when her father was killed, she would still investigate what had happened regardless of the consequences. Someone was out to get her, and now that she was no longer officially a cop, she didn't need to follow any police procedures. It was time to find the truth, no matter what she had to do to get it.

Ella slipped into her vehicle, and as she started the motor, Neskahi came out, waving to her before she could pull out of the parking place. For a moment, hope filled her. "Did Mrs. Begaye tell you something useful?"

"Not exactly, but she said that before this was over, the department itself would be in chaos. She told me that once The People lost confidence in us, then we'd all feel the anger of those we'd sold out."

"Huh? Is that political or revolutionary talk, or just BS?"

"Yeah, exactly. I have no idea what she was talking about either, but she was serious. I get the feeling that the entire police department is ultimately going to be the target of this frame, not just you."

"Yeah, but I'm at the top of their list." She thought of her cousin and how they would have worked the case together. They had different approaches to things, but that had always made them a strong team.

"I'm going home, Joseph," she said, shaking her head. "I've just been suspended. You'll find out why from Blalock."

"I'll stay on it, Ella, and get those tapes to look at from the mall. You've got friends here. We're not going to let anyone take you down. No way."

Hearing him say it made her feel a little better. Friends were scarce when careers were on the line. "But watch yourself. If you're seen as my friend, then you could end up under the shadow that covers me now."

"Cops take care of their own. We'll handle this."

As Ella drove home, she thought of Neskahi's words. She knew that Blalock and Big Ed would give her every possible break, but what they needed was physical evidence, and the only thing that had come to the surface so far was what her enemy had planted for them to find.

There was only one way out for her now. She'd have to dig deeper. The key was still Justine. It had all started with her, beginning with the unraveling of their friendship because of her cousin's sudden change in attitude.

When she drove up to her home, Ella saw that both Dawn and Rose were gone. Her mother had probably taken her along to one of her weaving classes. Dawn would play with the other toddlers and usually came back tired and sleepy, after having had a wonderful day.

Ella, relieved at the chance to be alone and not have to explain her suspension, went and checked her computer. There were no messages. Leaning back, she tried to think back to the very beginning. She was missing something. She felt it in her bones.

As she sat before the computer, her gaze unfocused, a small tone told her an instant message had just appeared on-screen. It was her informant, Coyote. The message was curt, as usual.

As she read the message, her skin turned cold.

> You and the police are only one of many targets. The terrorist activity on the Rez last year marked the beginning of a plan designed to create chaos on the Navajo Nation. What I don't know is what the ultimate goal of the conspiracy is, though it's tied somehow to political power.

She typed a response, asking questions, but by the time she hit the send key, Coyote had signed off. Cursing her luck, she turned off the computer and stared at the blank screen, lost in thought again.

Ella knew she should tell Blalock, but she couldn't bring herself to talk to him or anyone at the PD right now. Too restless to remain idle, she stood up and paced. The only person who would talk to her freely about Justine now was Wilson. He'd known Justine almost as well as she had. It was time for them to sit down like the old friends they were, and try to puzzle this out together.

TWENTY-THREE
———— ✖ ✖ ✖ ————

It was past five by the time she arrived at the college, and Wilson was alone in his office, grading papers.

Seeing her standing in the doorway, he smiled and stood. "Two visits in one day? To what do I owe this honor?"

"I need a friend," she said, coming in and closing the door behind her. Sitting down on the other side of his desk, she explained what had happened, and about her suspension.

"Ella, I'm really sorry! Chief Atcitty shouldn't have done that to you. He knows you would never have harmed Justine."

"He didn't have a choice, not with all the circumstantial evidence mounting up against me. The law can be very inflexible, and it's even tougher on cops. We don't have the same rights a civilian has," she said in a weary voice. "Whoever is behind all this is doing one bang-up job of ruining me."

"Then we'll have to return the favor. Where do you want to start?" Wilson poured her a cup of coffee from a small pot, then topped off his own cup.

Ella smiled. Wilson was one friend she could count on, no matter what happened. "I've been thinking about how everything started. Justine began acting really peculiar, always on edge, which was not like her. And it wasn't just with me. She was having some serious family problems, and that, I suspect, affected her a lot more than anyone realized."

"You mean Jayne and her gambling?"

"Yeah. I didn't realize you knew."

"We have an older student here, Bobby Lujan, who's bad news everywhere he goes. I saw Jayne talking with him several times, and I checked around. Apparently she owes Bobby quite a bit of money."

"The guy has no criminal record, at least not yet. I checked him out. What I didn't know was that he was a student here."

"He's been attending off and on for several years. Lujan's apparently well off. I know he likes to gamble, but I hear that he always seems to come out ahead. He's particularly good at cards, especially poker."

"Did you ever talk to Jayne about him?"

"I tried, but I think at the time she was in love with him. When I asked her if he was really the sort she wanted to hang around with, she defended him vehemently."

"Did you ever tell Justine?"

"Yeah, we discussed it over coffee a week before she died. She thanked me for my concern, then basically told me to mind my own business. She said that she could take care of her sister without any help."

"That doesn't sound like the Justine we knew. She wasn't on medication, because she hadn't had any prescriptions filled for months, and Justine wasn't the type to get into drugs. She loved her work with the police department and she was very protective of her career. She saw it like I do—something that gave her a purpose and made her feel good about getting up in the morning."

"So what does that leave us with?" Wilson said, his voice thoughtful. "Had she had a physical recently?"

"Yeah, we all do on the anniversary of our employment with the department. It's mandatory."

"I was thinking of something like a brain tumor, but maybe what we're dealing with is harder to pinpoint. Have you considered the possibility that the skinwalkers are at the root of this? They've certainly caused enough problems. I can tell you that they've got knowledge of herbs that will scramble someone's thinking big time. Remember what they did to me? They drugged me, and I never even knew it." He stood up and began to pace. "It could be them, all right. The more I think about it, the more it makes sense."

"No, Wilson, calm down." Ella knew Wilson had a tendency to go off half-cocked, but it was to be expected considering what those people had put him through not long ago. To this day, he tended to blame everything he couldn't explain on the skinwalkers. "But you've made a good point. Justine may have been drugged by someone close to her. A friend, or maybe a relative."

"You don't think Jayne would do something like that, do you?"

Ella considered it. "No. It doesn't fit her personality. I don't think she has the knowledge, either, though she did have the opportunity, seeing her sister regularly."

"Then who else was Justine close to? It would have to be someone she spent a lot of time with, and someone she trusted."

"Paul Natoni," Ella said. "Justine was seeing him on a regular basis, and I think she was getting serious about him. They met for breakfast a lot, more than one person told me." She remembered the experience she'd had at Paul Natoni's trailer.

"Go on. Don't hold out on me now. We're on the same side here, okay?"

Ella nodded. There were precious few people who still believed in her like Wilson did, and he deserved more from her than this. She told him everything that had happened, as well as detecting the scent of Justine's perfume.

"Do you think Justine could really still be alive?"

"Logic tells me no, but in here," she said, pointing to her heart, "I don't think I've ever really accepted her death. I don't know if that's just wishful thinking or not. Carolyn thinks she's dead, and I've never seen her make a mistake on forensic matters."

"Even if Dr. Roanhorse is right, you've still got to check out Natoni," Wilson said. "You owe it to Justine."

Ella remembered Coyote's warnings about a conspiracy. Maybe another mistake she'd made all along was in searching for one suspect. Maybe in this case, her enemy acted as one, but was in reality many people. Such a conspiracy would provide alibis for a lot of people, each involved in one step of the plan.

"Justine knew your associate Jeremiah Manyfarms, too, didn't she?" Ella recalled.

Wilson nodded slowly. "Justine liked him. In fact, she considered him a friend. I thought she should have been more careful around him, but I don't think there was anything going on sexually. I think all she wanted was someone older to talk to."

"What do you really know about Professor Manyfarms, the man?"

"Not much. He doesn't talk about himself or his family. But I get the feeling that he's the type who needs a cause to identify with. Before it was Indian rights. Now it's gangs. Do you know what I mean?"

She nodded. "But his current involvement with the youth programs is understandable. The loss of his youngest son because of the gang thing must have devastated him. The other day he told me what had happened."

Wilson nodded slowly. "I remember reading about the incident in the local paper at the time. It must have torn his heart out. We expect to bury our parents, never our kids." He paused. "But I don't see him as the type to drug someone. He's too confident, and would rather try to charm or intimidate them. And even if he was the one drugging her, it certainly couldn't have been on a regular basis."

Ella nodded, but didn't tell him about the conspiracy she'd been warned about. She wasn't sure of the source, and if Coyote really was an undercover cop, he deserved to have his secrets guarded.

"How will you check up on Natoni? You can't access the police computer files anymore, can you?" he asked.

"No, and if I tried, I'd get caught. I'm going to have to go low-tech. I'll tail him and maybe do the PI thing. As a cop, I had to follow a lot of rules. But now that I'm on my own time, I can afford to be more . . . shall we say, flexible?"

He chuckled softly. "Be careful, Ella. Don't give anyone else a reason to come gunning for you. You've got enough enemies already."

"Ain't that the truth." She walked to the door. "If you hear anything that might help, call me right away."

"Count on it. And, Ella?" She turned her head and he continued. "You'll get out of this. You're very resourceful, and more importantly, you never give up. Sooner or later your enemies will realize that you can't defeat an opponent who won't stay down."

Ella laughed. "What a sweet-talker."

"I wouldn't waste my breath trying to flatter you. You have BS radar."

She laughed. "Thanks—I think."

Ella crossed the campus and went to her personal vehicle, a four-year-old white pickup she usually drove only on weekends and when off work. She was soon heading south toward home. For once, she wanted to be there on a weekday when Dawn ate dinner. Little moments with her family seemed even more important now that there was a good chance she could end up in jail, at least for a while.

She thought about what she'd do if she ever found out she was about to be arrested. Would she go on the run, knowing that in order to clear her name, she'd need to remain free? No matter what, her first priority would have to be doing what was best for her daughter as well as herself. Dawn would have enough on her shoulders with the weight of the family legacy. She didn't need the added shame of having her mother in prison, convicted of murder.

She turned on the radio, refusing to dwell on it any longer. A newscaster on the same AM station was playing excerpts from Branch's radio show. Apparently the gadfly was continuing his attacks on the integrity of the police department, calling for the immediate firing of most of the current officers, including Big Ed Atcitty, though he was careful not to mention any names. Branch had also suggested that the tribal president and most of the Council resign. Although he never mentioned Ella by name, he also hammered on the crimes committed by one "well-known police officer" and the efforts of the "entire department" to protect her.

Ella felt the full sting of the accusations, though they were based on lies and planted evidence. But there was nothing she could do. She continued to listen, unwilling to turn it off. No matter how difficult it was for her to hear, she had to know what her enemies were saying in order to learn their motives. This could perhaps lead to discovering their identities.

This local commentator was less obnoxious than Branch, but he shared one important viewpoint with her nemesis. On the le-

galized-gambling issue, the current hot topic on the Rez, they were
of one mind. By all reports, almost all of the other New Mexico
tribes were experiencing prosperity because of their newly opened
casinos. Some Navajos supporting legalized gambling believed that
opening a casino on the Rez would help bring many Navajos out
of poverty. It would also allow the tribe to fund programs that
would benefit The People without relying on federal subsidies that
came with strings attached.

In the past, every time the issue of legalized gambling on the
Navajo Rez had come up, it had been voted down, but now pro-
ponents were unifying and amassing their strength. The commentator read off the names of prominent leaders and influential
Navajos who supported a specialized referendum to legalize gambling. It didn't come as a surprise to her to hear Kevin's name on
that list.

It hadn't occurred to her before, but she suddenly understood
why he'd been so determined to distance himself from the scandal
surrounding her. His public stand on gambling already entailed a
risk. Now that he was running for office, Kevin had to make sure
he came across as above reproach. He had to lend credibility to the
progambling stand his most influential supporters were probably
taking.

Ella wondered if this was part of the conspiracy Coyote had
warned her about. Although she had no reason to trust this informant, she had a strong feeling he was legit.

If the conspiracy required creating chaos and unrest on the reservation as a tool to winning political power, she had no doubt that
George Branch was heavily involved. Certainly, when propaganda
came to mind, his was the loudest voice in the area.

Yet it was also possible that he was being used by someone
who understood that Branch's primary motivation was his job—he
needed ratings. It wouldn't be hard to manipulate an egotist like
Branch by feeding him information meant to undermine others in
power.

It was dusk when Ella glanced in her rearview mirror and saw
another, tan or yellow pickup behind her. The vehicle stayed with
her and closed the distance slowly. She wasn't in the tribal unit, so
if she'd picked up a tail, it would have to be someone who knew

her personal vehicle. She slowed down, trying to get a closer look, and then realized it was Blalock driving either his own or a rented pickup.

She pulled over and a moment later met him by the side of the road.

"I was just about to call you on your cell phone," he said. "I didn't want to alarm you."

"It's okay. What's up?"

"I just wanted you to know that everything will take a backseat to this investigation. You'll be reinstated in the department before you know it."

"I certainly hope so, but I'm not going to kid myself either. My chances at the moment stink."

"True." He hesitated. "Listen, I wanted you to know that I checked out Bobby Lujan. This was his last known address," Blalock said, handing her a slip of paper, "and the number below is his license plate and make and model truck."

She smiled. "Thanks."

"For what? This never happened." He looked her straight in the eyes. "Look, Ella, it's just Payestewa and me working this case, plus two of your department officers who are assigned to us part-time. Things are complicated, and we're stretched to the limit, so if you should choose to look into this and find out something useful, pass it along. I'm all ears."

"Deal. By the way, Dwayne, do you recall if Paul Natoni had an alibi for the night of the murder?" Ella asked.

"The guy who was dating Justine?" Seeing her nod, he continued. "I'd have to check my notes, but I think he was at Professor Jeremiah Manyfarms' house watching a basketball game. He was one of the first on my list," Blalock answered.

"Thanks."

"No problem."

After Blalock drove off, Ella looked at Lujan's address. It was in a new residential section between her home and Shiprock. She decided to stop by there first before going home.

Ella turned onto a newly paved street and drove past several individual homes and duplexes. Finally she reached three small apartment buildings, each with four units side by side. She parked in a space beside the third building, walked to the door marked C-3, and knocked loudly. There was no response or sound from the other side of the door.

Hearing a vehicle pulling up, Ella turned and saw a truck parking beside hers.

"Are you looking for Bobby?" a young Navajo woman asked. She climbed out of the sedan, grabbed a bag of groceries, and walked toward C-2.

"Yes, I am. Do you know where I can find him?"

She shook her head. "He moved out a few days ago and didn't leave a forwarding address. I know because the manager asked me if I could tell where he'd gone. Apparently he didn't pay last month's rent."

"Were you a friend of Bobby's?"

"Not really. I'm just his neighbor. The last time I saw him it was late at night and he was loading up all his things into his Suburban. I remember thinking it was an odd time to move. I'd just come off my shift at the Quick Stop, so I know it was after midnight."

"You said he had a Suburban? I thought he had a Dodge truck."

"When he moved in here he did, but about a month ago he came home in that huge SUV. He told me he'd just borrowed it, but if he did, it must have been a long-term loan because he's been driving it ever since."

"Thanks."

The woman looked at her for a long time. "You're that officer who's under investigation, aren't you?"

Ella nodded. She'd avoided mentioning her own name or asking for one, hoping to avoid this. The truth was that she had no legal jurisdiction here anymore, and she'd hoped to keep her visit low profile.

"You really helped a cousin of mine once, Ernest Redhouse. He was in the North Siders. He might have gotten killed if you hadn't stopped the gangs from mixing it up. For what it's worth, I'm on your side on this. I think you care too much about being a cop to kill your own cousin like that."

"Thank you," she said. "I'm not guilty, and I *will* prove it.

Hearing that there are people like you who still believe in me really helps keep me going.''

It was dark by the time she was back on the highway heading home. This section of Highway 666 was nearly deserted this time of night and void of streetlights except for a stretch near Gallup. It was like entering an inky black hole that swallowed up even the headlights of her car.

Ella thought of Dawn. She'd wanted to have dinner with her tonight, but by now she'd be lucky to see her still awake. Ella felt the unrelenting tension and pressure that had become her constant companions these days. Yet for her family's sake, she'd have to work really hard to look calm and project confidence around Rose. There was no way she wanted her mother any more worried than she already was, or Dawn frightened by something she'd never be able to understand.

Deep in thought, Ella spotted the car coming up behind her a few seconds too late. It had approached with the lights turned off, and she was nearly blinded by the sudden headlights on high beams. As it swung out rapidly to pass her, she knew she was in trouble.

Ella reached for her pistol, then realized it wasn't there. All she had now was the backup derringer in her boot. She pressed down on the accelerator and dialed the police emergency number on her cell phone.

She was waiting for a connection when the driver of the car pulled up beside her. Switching from gas pedal to brakes, Ella suddenly cut speed and leaned back into the seat, dropping the phone so she could put both hands on the wheel. The next sounds she heard were the loud thumps of four bullets passing through the cab. As the side window was penetrated, glass exploded into her face, stinging her cheek but missing her eyes.

Ella felt heat slash across her left thigh like someone had dropped a burning cigarette on her leg, but the leg continued to function, so she assumed it was just a graze.

Heart racing, she braked hard, swerving to the right onto the shoulder and trying to keep the pickup from rolling as she hit soft ground.

As she focused on controlling her truck, Ella heard the squeal of tires telling her the shooter was also braking, trying to slow enough to turn and continue the pursuit. Headlights flashed into her rearview mirror, but by then Ella was heading parallel to the highway across a relatively level stretch of desert.

The driver, seeing her pulling away, fired two more shots, but they whined overhead, missing the truck completely. Ella spotted a set of wheel ruts running nearly parallel to hers, and swung the pickup onto them, hoping for an easier path. The lights in her mirror dimmed as Ella pressed down on the accelerator. The track she was on led down into a shallow, sandy wash, and she was certain that the sedan couldn't follow her very far there.

She turned off her lights and came to a stop a few hundred yards down the arroyo, hoping to get a glimpse of the car and maybe get a make or color, but the driver didn't follow her into the wash. Instead, he turned and headed back to the highway.

Ella knew her truck's engine was far from the souped-up package in the tribal unit, but acting on instinct alone, she turned her truck around and went after him, leaving her own headlights off. He arrived at the highway, and as he turned onto the good road, she closed to within fifty yards and flipped on her headlights. For just a split second, she caught a glimpse of the driver's face as he was looking in her direction. She couldn't swear to it, but he looked like Samuel Begaye.

Anger and frustration ripped through her. If he *was* involved, she wanted to haul his sorry butt to jail. She was racing down the highway after him when she suddenly realized that she was heading straight into danger without anything to back her up except a two-shot .22 derringer and a pocketknife. She couldn't request cover officers be dispatched to her location, or even force him to pull over on her own. All she could do was get herself killed.

Ella grasped the steering wheel so hard that her hands hurt, but she gave up the chase as he increased his own speed in order to escape. He hadn't known she was outgunned, obviously, which had turned out to be a lucky break for her.

Ella found the cell phone on the floorboard and called Blalock. Help had never arrived because she'd never completed the call to the department. After describing the vehicle, tag number, and Begaye's direction of travel, she turned the matter over to him. Handing police business over to someone else was one of the hardest things she'd ever done.

She knew then that she'd have to find a new way to work around her limited resources. Her enemies had succeeded in making things more difficult for her, so she'd have to learn to improvise so she could get the job done.

Ella arrived home edgy and tired, but grateful that her bullet-ridden truck still worked. Her mood suddenly worsened when she saw Kevin's car parked near the side of the house. She went inside, wondering if her already miserable day was about to get worse.

It didn't take long to find out. Kevin's expression was decidedly somber as he turned Dawn over to Rose. "What happened to your leg, Ella?"

She looked down at the bloody tear in her slacks. The wound was about two inches long, but not more than a good scratch, fortunately. "Would you believe I bumped up against a nail?"

"Better wash it off, then." Kevin shrugged, accepting her suggestion without question.

Ella kissed her daughter good night and promised to come read her a story in a few minutes.

"This is going to take more than a few minutes," Kevin said. "Now that you're finally home, we have to have a serious talk."

She didn't like his tone. "Then you'll have to wait. Dawn will expect me. Let me take care of her first, wash off this scratch, then I'll deal with whatever's bothering you."

She saw his eyes narrow, but other than that, there was no response. Rose just smiled at both of them and went into her sewing room.

By the time Ella returned to the living room, thirty minutes had passed and Kevin was pretending to read this morning's newspaper. One look at his face and she knew she'd made him angry.

She smiled at him calmly and cocked her head toward the kitchen. "Let's go in there. I need something to snack on. All I've had for hours is a cup of coffee. Do you want a diet cola or something?"

"No, thank you," he replied stiffly.

Ella took a can of soda from the refrigerator, grabbed a handful of homemade oatmeal cookies from the cookie jar, then sat across the kitchen table from him. "All right. You've got my full attention. What's the problem?"

"I heard that this has been a really bad day for you," he said slowly. "I understand that you were asked to turn in your badge."

He waited, but Ella said nothing, instead eating a cookie hungrily, then washing it down with swallows of soda. There was nothing for her to say. His sources were impeccable.

"That's why I came over. Now that you're no longer a cop, you're more at the mercy of your enemies than ever."

"Where did you get that idea? I turned in my badge, not my brain."

He shook his head. "Same old Ella."

"What did you expect? I'm not going to curl up into a ball and die. I've had to work with less resources before. I can handle this without a crime team or partner."

"Yes, I suppose you can. But what about Dawn?"

"She has no idea what's going on. She's just a baby."

"Exactly. She's just a baby. While you go investigate things on your own—and don't bother to deny that you'll be doing just that—she'll be here, an easy target for any of the people you've ticked off over the years. Or worse. Maybe she'll be the target of the person who's working so hard to put you away for good."

"You're jumping to conclusions. We have no reason to believe that whoever is after me will strike at anyone else in my family. And if they try something here, the police department will come into the picture. Big Ed will do whatever it takes to keep Mom and Dawn safe."

"I'm amazed that you have so much confidence in the same people that have hung you out to dry."

"I don't see it that way," she said in clipped tones.

"Are you willing to gamble our daughter's life on your opinion?"

"And I suppose this is what you've been leading up to. What do you have in mind?"

"I'd like to send Dawn to live with my sister Mary Ann. She's a teacher in Scottsdale. Her husband is Anglo and they're well off, living in a very safe neighborhood. Dawn will be protected and have everything she needs."

"Except her mother and her grandmother," Ella snapped. "My daughter stays here with my mother and with me. She'll be well looked after."

"You're not thinking straight."

Ella regarded him coolly. "And of course, your eagerness to send Dawn away has nothing to do with the pressure people who want you to run for office are putting on you to sever the connection between us. Since the heart of that connection is Dawn, our daughter, sending her away could remove a potential problem standing in the way of getting you elected. Out of sight is out of mind. Very convenient, I admit, but I'm not buying in to this. Dawn stays home."

She had never seen him this angry before. He stood up so quickly, the chair nearly toppled over.

"I can't believe you said that to me."

"The thought never occurred to you, or at least to your powerful friends?" she asked, nonplussed.

"Even if it has, that wasn't why I came here and suggested it to you."

"So it did occur to them," Ella observed.

"Think carefully, Ella. This isn't about politics. This is about Dawn and keeping her out of harm's way. Can you guarantee her safety here?"

"I can't guarantee her safety anywhere, but if I really believed that she was in danger, I wouldn't send her anyplace that's so easily traced, such as to a relative of yours. But we have no reason to believe that anyone is interested in Dawn."

"So you're just going to wait and take that chance?"

"It's not a matter of taking a chance. It's a matter of my judgment, based upon the facts. But let me warn you, Kevin. If you or your friends are talking about this subject with other people, you could be giving my enemies some ideas that they're better off not having."

"Nice. So if anything happens, it'll be my fault now."

She stood up and began walking him to the door. "Kevin, I'm

tired. The point I'm making is that your self-serving friends are making a problem where there isn't one, and if they continue with this, things could get worse, not better."

Kevin strode past her wordlessly, closing the door a bit louder than usual. A moment later she heard him speed away in his pickup, spewing gravel halfway up the drive.

"He's not worried about Dawn. He's worried about himself," Rose said from where she was standing in the doorway to the kitchen. "It's a good thing, too, that you pointed out the harm his friends could do. He'll discourage any talk about Dawn being sent away now if he really cares about his daughter."

"Yeah, but I probably should have handled it differently. His name is on the birth certificate as the father. Kevin's never disagreed with me about custody, but he could if he wanted to."

"You mean if he thought it would serve him. But it won't, and he knows it."

Ella rubbed her eyes, then sighed. "It's been an awful day."

"I heard what he said. Is it true? You've been suspended?"

Ella nodded. "I guess now I get to see how a private investigator works. They have fewer rules, you know. I may get to like the freedom from having to follow the nitpicking police procedures."

Rose shook her head. "No, you like the structure the rules provide. You'll be back on the force before long."

"You sound very certain, Mom."

"I am. I've learned to accept many things about you and the path you've chosen in life."

After Rose went to bed, Ella fixed herself a sandwich using leftovers, then went to her room and turned on the computer. Coyote was nowhere to be seen tonight. She answered a few E-mails that had accumulated from friends on-line, then crawled into bed.

Two began barking furiously just as soon as she'd closed her eyes. Ella reached for the service pistol she normally kept on the nightstand, then remembered she didn't have it anymore. Not wasting time, she hurried to her closet and reached for the upper shelf, bringing down her father's old hunting rifle. It had been in the family for years and it hadn't been checked any time recently, but she knew it would work. What's more, her aim was deadly with it.

Ella loaded the rifle and, as she went out into the hall, met Rose. "Stay here with Dawn. I'll go see what's going on."

Ella grabbed a flashlight from the drawer as she walked through the kitchen. Keeping it off and using the darkness to hide her, she stepped outside.

The full moon bathed everything in a muted light. Two was watching an area just beyond the garden. As she started to move forward, Two positioned himself in front of her, his hackles raised. The low sound coming from his throat was a deadly challenge to whatever was out there.

Ella moved carefully, still not using the flashlight. Hearing a strange rustle through the brush, she stopped and raised the rifle to her shoulder. "Come out where I can see you. I'm armed."

There was a pause, then she heard a familiar voice. "Don't shoot. I'm not your enemy."

Herman Cloud stepped past a small juniper and appeared in the open.

"You're the last person I expected to see here," Ella said. "What on earth are you doing?"

"My nephews told me what happened to you at the police department. They'll be keeping a watch on your place unofficially, but right now they're both patrolling areas well away from here. That's why I came over to watch over you and your family while you slept."

Ella fought the impulse to hug him. Philip and Michael Cloud were two of the best cops in the department, and Herman, their uncle, had been a solid ally. Although in his seventies, he stood tall and proud, wearing a red headband. His black eyes were fierce with determination.

"You're going to freeze out here. Come in and have something warm to drink."

He shook his head. "My place is out here for now. I stood beside you once when your enemies were all around you, and I'll do the same again. But don't worry. I'm not alone out here." He whistled, making a long, mournful sound. Someone answered, imitating his call.

"What made you think we would need protection here at home?" Ella felt her skin prickle as it often did when danger was near.

"I have friends where your lawyer friend works. They want your daughter out of the way. Because of that, we don't trust them."

"We?"

"It's better that you don't know any names other than mine. But rest easy. You have many friends."

Ella felt the power and confidence behind his words. He was a man on a mission. She could no more dissuade him from this duty than she could change Mount Rushmore.

"Thank you, old friend," she said quietly.

As she walked back inside the house, she felt her spirits lift. She now knew that the battle was no longer hers alone.

TWENTY-FOUR

✖ ✖ ✖

Ella woke long after the sun had risen. Not used to sleeping late, she looked at the clock radio and realized she'd never set it the night before. Not that she needed to do that now. Still, it surprised her that such a long, ingrained habit could be broken so easily.

Dressing quickly, she went outside with a cup of warm coffee in hand, searching for Herman. He'd need this by now, though she suspected he and whoever had been with him had brought their own provisions.

After several minutes of searching, she realized he'd gone home. His watch must have concluded at dawn.

Rose came outside. "Why on earth are you standing out here?"

"I thought I'd give our old friend a cup of coffee."

"Daughter, he's been gone for hours! We had a talk, then he left."

"I guess I must have really slept like a log. I didn't hear any of that." Ella yawned.

"You looked exhausted when you came home. I figured you'd need your sleep even more because we all got up in the middle of the night, so I turned off the alarm on your clock radio."

"Mom, you shouldn't have done that!"

"Why? You don't have to report to work, do you?"

"No, but I still have a lot to do on my own."

Rose glanced at the position of the sun. "It's almost time for

Dawn and me to get going. We'll be attending a weavers' workshop at the Chapter House today. It'll be an all-day event. Why don't you come and take your mind off things for a while?"

"Some other time, Mom. I've got some leads I want to follow up today on my cousin's case. It's been six days now since it happened, and unless I catch whoever's responsible soon, I may never get another chance."

Ella helped get Dawn breakfast and ready for her day. Her daughter was so used to Rose's morning routines that Ella felt almost superfluous. For a brief moment she found herself wishing that those little routines had been ones that she and Dawn had always shared. But there was no sense in dwelling on what could never be. At least Dawn had a grandmother who adored her.

Ella walked her mother and daughter to the truck, then went back inside the house. The stillness seemed unbearable. Ella showered and dressed, mentally trying to organize her day and come up with a schedule. She was so used to reporting her whereabouts and having the bulk of her assignments set out for her that it felt strange to do things this way.

She'd just sat down to have breakfast when the phone rang.

"Ella, it's Ruth."

Getting a call from her cousin at home surprised her. Justine's oldest sister had given her the lead about Jayne and her connection to gambling, but Ella hadn't expected any more after that.

"What's going on?" Ella asked.

"I heard Bobby Lujan and Jayne arguing last night outside by his truck. He's really starting to scare me. When my sister finally came in, she had a huge bruise on her cheek."

"Did you hear what the argument was about?"

"Some, but I didn't hear it all. All I know for sure is that he was threatening her, saying that if she told anyone else, he'd cut her into little pieces."

"Told anyone what?"

"That's the part I didn't hear. I asked Jayne when she came in, but she wouldn't talk to Mom or to me. She just went and locked herself in the bathroom."

"What about this morning?"

"I didn't have a chance to talk to her. I had to get my kids to school, and then take Mom by the hospital. Her doctor is going to give her something to help her sleep."

"How is she holding up?"

"Not well, Ella, not well at all. I know you're in deep trouble, and that you've been suspended, but the price Mom's paying is just as high, even if it's for a different reason."

"Does she still think I hurt Justine?" Ella regretted her words instantly. She shouldn't have asked Ruth to speak for her mother.

"I don't think she believes you killed her. Most of the time she's just angry with you because she thinks you should have caught the killer by now," Ruth said.

"I'm working very hard to do just that. My own life depends on it."

"I know. Will you make sure Jayne is okay? Maybe you can talk to Bobby," Ruth said.

"Where is he? The address I had for him is no longer valid."

"I don't know, but I'll try to find out."

"Is your sister home right now?"

"Yeah, but she'll be taking off soon. She's got a new job in Farmington."

"Do you know where?" Ella asked. Jayne's job-hopping would make finding her just that much harder unless Ruth could help.

"She told me she quit her job at the Daily Double and is now a cocktail waitress at a bar called The Fancy. She's supposed to be there just before noon."

Not wanting Jayne to recognize her right off, Ella left her hair loose and wore a western-cut blouse, denim skirt, and blue-tinted glasses. This wasn't an outfit people would associate with her. She then cleaned out the glass from the broken window in her truck. The passenger-side glass had been spared, but two bullet holes in the driver's-side door and four on the passenger side would be objects of discussion sooner or later when her mom noticed them.

After a forty-minute drive, she located the bar beside the highway between Farmington and Aztec near a large, private stable. Parking in the gravel parking lot, Ella went inside The Fancy and sat down at a table in a dark corner of the room. From this spot she could watch the door and the bar at the same time.

She deliberately opted to be there when Jayne arrived rather than tailing her. Today she wanted to keep an eye on Jayne for a while before making any move. Jayne, she knew from experience, would bolt like a jackrabbit at the first sign of trouble.

It was still early for lunch, and only a few unemployed or retired patrons were in the outer room. From the noise she picked up from her location beside an interior wall, she suspected there was gambling going on in the next room, but she wouldn't push it for now.

Time passed slowly. Ella ordered coffee from a young-looking waitress, preferring to sip that rather than alcohol, which could slow her down or dull her reactions at just the wrong time. No one spoke to her and no one asked any questions, though most of the men looked her over at least once, probably assessing their chances. To discourage their approach, she was careful not to lead anyone on by making eye contact.

Two hours passed, and the lunch crowd had come and gone, but there was still no sign of Jayne. Ella put a few bills on the table and was ready to leave when she saw Jayne walk in with a tall man she guessed to be Bobby Lujan. Whoever he was, the rough-looking character was holding on to her arm in a death grip.

"Don't give me any more crap," he growled loud enough for Ella to hear.

As the man forced Jayne to sit at an empty table close to the bar, Ella moved her chair back so she was in the shadows. Safe from being identified, Ella watched the two openly.

She could see the fear in Jayne's face plainly, but suspected that if she came out into the open and offered to help her cousin, Jayne would side against her and nothing would be accomplished.

"I can't do it, Bobby," Jayne whispered loudly.

"How else are you going to square your debt? Unless you pay Manny Rodriguez, he's going to come looking for you. And get one thing straight. I'm not bailing you out again unless you come through for me."

"What you're asking me to do . . . I can't. That man is disgusting. He hurts people. I heard talk."

"He likes to get a little rough, but he just loves being with Indian women. He won't really hurt you, and in a few hours you'll have a couple of hundred dollars—more if you stay with him all night. With the cash you'll be making, you'll be able to square your debts. Or at least most of them. You'll still owe me, but we can work something out—unless you want me to go straight to the police and tell them everything I know."

"I'm sorry, I just can't do this, no matter what it costs. Just let me go." She stood up, but Bobby grabbed her shoulders and jerked her against his chest. Grasping her hand, he twisted it backwards until she cried out.

"You and I need to have a private talk."

Ella watched them head to the door, and noticed other patrons doing the same, trying to decide if they should risk a fight by stepping in. Domestic disputes were the most volatile of situations, and cops hated them more than almost any other call. But Ella was afraid not to interfere. Jayne couldn't handle Bobby alone, and she couldn't let them leave without putting her cousin in even more danger.

Ella followed as Bobby hauled her outside. Jayne tried to bolt out on the sidewalk, but he caught her before she'd gone more than a few feet.

"We're going to my place now." He started pulling her toward a shiny, low-slung luxury car.

"No, Bobby, don't. I can get the money some other way."

Ella, still unnoticed by the preoccupied couple, stepped out from behind the Dumpster and kicked Bobby in the back of the knees.

"Damn!" he yelled as his leg gave out. Recovering his balance quickly, he let go of Jayne and swung his fist around.

Ella stepped back and grabbed his extended arm, using Bobby's own momentum to twist his arm behind his back and shove him face-first into the side of the car. "That's enough." Ella looked over at Jayne, who was about to bolt again. "Don't run. He'll just find you again, Jayne."

"Count on it," Bobby growled.

"I'm the best chance you've got, Jayne," Ella added.

"An ex-cop?" he scoffed. "You'll be in jail yourself before long."

Ignoring the lowlife, she held Jayne's gaze. "Think, cousin. How many options do you have left?"

Bobby looked up and called out to a guy coming out of the bar. "Jerry, give me a hand."

It was the bartender, a man the size and shape of a vending machine, and Ella knew that it was about to get very rough. She tried to turn Lujan around so he would be the one to face the bartender, but a beefy hand grasped her shoulder like a vise.

Ella expected Jayne to bolt. After all, it was something she did well. Instead, Jayne kicked Jerry right in the groin. The bartender, who clearly hadn't expected the move, groaned and doubled over, releasing Ella and clutching something even more important to him.

Bobby tried to slip past Ella and grab Jayne, but Ella slammed him across the bridge of his nose with the side of her hand. He staggered back, moaning as blood flowed from his nostrils.

Just then the wail of a siren sounded in the distance. "Cops!" Jayne yelled. "I've got to get out of here!" She turned and ran toward the alley behind the bar.

Ella took off after her and caught up within a hundred feet.

"I don't have a car! I came with Bobby. Where's yours?"

"Follow me!" Ella answered.

Ella led the way around the back of the bar onto the other side, where her pickup was parked. She didn't have to look back to know Jayne was right behind her.

When they reached Ella's truck, they scrambled inside. "I need to get back on the Rez. I have no jurisdiction here," Ella said.

"You have no jurisdiction anywhere. You're suspended," Jayne yelled as Ella started the truck and backed out of the parking slot.

"Yeah. I forgot."

Jayne said nothing for a while as Ella headed back to the Rez.

"It's really hard for you, isn't it?" Jayne said at last. "I mean not knowing what's going to happen next, after being a cop all these years."

"Yeah, it is."

"Why did you help me back there with Bobby? You're not an official cop anymore, and you could have been in a lot more trouble than me."

"I had to follow you. I'm trying to find out more about Bobby," Ella said, leaving Ruth's name out of it. "But when I realized that you were in serious trouble, that Bobby meant business, I couldn't risk letting you handle it on your own."

Taking her eyes off the road for a moment, Ella glanced over at her cousin. "Your family has been very good to me for many years. I owe Justine more than to let something happen to her sister when I could have put a stop to it. You don't honestly think that I would turn my back on you, Jayne, do you? Or, for that matter, that I had anything to do with Justine's death?"

"No, I know you didn't kill her," she said quietly. "You two weren't just partners, you were friends, too. But why are you focusing on me? Do you still think I had something to do with Justine's death?"

"No, not directly, but I think it's possible that the people you hang around with might have decided to use Justine as leverage against you in some way. My guess is that they tried to kidnap her, but Justine fought back, and in the struggle, they ended up killing her."

"You're right to think Justine would have fought hard. She didn't take any bull from anyone. But you're off base about your suspects. Bobby would have avoided Justine because she was a cop. Bobby's a gambler, but he likes more favorable odds than that."

"Maybe someone he answers to had a different opinion," Ella said.

Jayne considered it. "Every once in a while, Bobby tries to force me to do what he calls a 'favor' for one of his buddies. Its always something illegal and often it's just plain dangerous. I think Bobby gets pressured into that, but I don't know by whom, unless it's Manny Rodriguez."

"The state police and more than one local PD have been after Manny Rodriguez for years, but they've never managed to keep him in jail for more than an overnight stay. He's got a lot of money, and that buys him top-of-the-line lawyers."

"Hasn't anyone ever pressed charges?" Jayne asked.

"A few have. But it's always been thrown out of court. He probably manages to buy their eventual silence—one way or another."

Jayne hesitated. "I owe you one, Ella, so I'm going to give it to you straight this time. Bobby found out that the night Justine was killed, I was at the Palomino Lounge, alone. They have slot machines in the back room and I go there a lot. But if the cops raid the place or go in there asking questions, the manager will know I was the one who snitched and I'll be in even more trouble than I am now. The owner has an enemies list, and real bad things happen to those people."

"I'm not after illegal gambling operations. I just want Justine's killer. By the way, where was Bobby that night?"

"He said he was at a pueblo casino near Albuquerque. He won big that night at one of the slot machines, so there'll be plenty of people who'll remember him. In fact, I think the casino takes photos of their big winners, so there's probably a snapshot of him on the board there."

Ella got the name of the casino. She'd have Blalock check out Bobby's alibi later.

"Why aren't you investigating Justine's friends, like Paul Natoni? The guy practically drips slime, but Justine always got really angry whenever I pointed that out. In my book, he's worse than Bobby. Bobby's no prize, but at least he doesn't put on an act. Paul's a con man. He has great packaging, and he loves making promises, but it's all a show. Deep down he's a heavy-duty creep."

"I agree with you about Natoni. I disliked him from the very beginning."

"He really bad-mouthed you to Justine every time he could, telling her you were just using her to advance your own career, and stuff like that. If you're looking for enemies who may have framed you, I'd start with him." She paused, then added, "Does he have an alibi for the time my sister was killed?"

Ella nodded. "He was with Jeremiah Manyfarms."

Jayne laughed derisively. "So he's got no alibi."

"No, I just told you—"

"Paul is Jeremiah's adopted son. Didn't you know that? Paul elected to keep his own name, but Jeremiah adopted him legally when Paul was just fourteen."

Ella stared at Jayne. "When did you find this out?"

"Justine told me. She was a friend of Manyfarms, too."

Ella said nothing. The news had taken her by surprise. Suddenly there was a new twist to the conspiracy theory. She'd suspected that Justine was being drugged, and that more than one person could have been responsible for what happened. Maybe Natoni and Manyfarms had worked together on this.

"Ella, what happened to your truck? These look like bullet holes. That's something that happened a long time ago, right?" Jayne pointed to the holes in the passenger door.

Ella shook her head. "Somebody wants me dead," Ella said. "I just happened to be faster, or luckier, than Justine was this time."

"When did this all happen? Do the police know about it?" Jayne's voice rose an octave.

"Just the other night. The FBI's working on it already." She explained briefly what happened, not mentioning who she suspected, Samuel Begaye. The less said, the better, until she could put the pieces together.

"I'm surprised you've even left the house after that." Jayne slumped down in her seat, then, noticing the holes on Ella's side too, she sat up again and scrunched back into the cushion.

After a while, Jayne spoke again. "Listen, I just happen to know where there's a key to Paul's trailer. Wanna take a look around inside?"

"I sure do, but I'll have to do it alone. I'm not a cop anymore, and I obviously can't get any kind of warrant. If I get caught, it's going to be a clear case of breaking and entering."

"We'll go together. You'll need a lookout."

"Jayne, it's not a good idea for you to get involved. I thought you wanted to stay out of jail."

"I'll furnish the key only if I get to go with you. I hate that man and the way he was using Justine, poisoning her mind. If he's got anything to do with what happened to my sister, I want a piece of him, too."

"The only thing you're likely to get is a ticket to jail. I don't want that on my conscience," Ella argued.

"You have my terms. What's it going to be?" Jayne folded her arms across her chest and stared at her.

Ella sighed, then nodded slowly. "All right." It may not have been wise, but she just couldn't pass this up. What she desperately needed now was evidence, and proof of her own innocence so she could be reinstated. There were other avenues of investigation that a free agent could pursue, but she missed being able to tap into records to verify a fact or having a team of investigators working with her.

"Where's the key, Jayne?"

"Drop me by my mom's house. The cops never saw it because Justine didn't keep the key in her room. I think she just didn't want Mom to find it. I know where it is because I saw her hiding it once and asked about it. She told me Paul had given it to her in case of an emergency."

"Where did she hide the key?"

"Justine put it inside the cactus planter in the living room by the front window. Personally, I think Paul had hoped she'd come by and spend the night with him, but I don't think she ever did. She liked Paul, but I don't think she was ready to make any kind of commitment."

Ella parked by the Goodluck home and waited as Jayne ran inside. She came back out within seconds, key in hand, and they got under way.

"I don't want to park right in front of his mobile home, so we have to approach from the back," Ella said. "But I warn you. It's broad daylight, so it'll be risky."

"It's probably less dangerous now than in the evening. The elderly lady who lives next door to Paul likes to spy on him, but she watches cartoons in the afternoon. You can hear the television blaring all the way down the trailer court. I was there once with Bobby, and Paul really complained about her."

"I really wish you'd reconsider, Jayne. If we get caught, it's going to be a disaster, and I can't guarantee that we won't be seen. For all I know, Paul could be there, whether or not his pickup is outside."

"Then park down the road. If his pickup is not there and it looks like nobody's home, I'll walk up to the front door and ring the bell. If no one answers, I'll use the key and go inside. Then I'll go to the back window and wave if it's safe for you to come and join me."

Ella considered it. It wasn't a bad plan. Jayne would attract a lot less attention than she would. "Okay."

Ella parked by the turnoff where the mailboxes were, but close enough to see the trailer. As Jayne strolled down the road to Natoni's trailer, Ella couldn't help but compare her to Justine. The two not only resembled each other, they acted a lot alike, too. Justine had been a gambler in her own way, enjoying taking risks. Unfortunately, Jayne had channeled that same energy into less productive avenues. Still, if Jayne could have gotten her act together, she might have made a decent cop.

Five minutes later, Ella saw Jayne wave from the back window. She approached carefully, staying out of sight by making sure another trailer always screened her from the old woman's home. Several minutes later, she was inside.

"Do you smell it?" Jayne asked, her voice hushed. "I noticed it as soon as I walked in."

Ella nodded. "Justine's perfume. I want to check out the bedroom."

With Jayne at her heels, she went down the narrow hall to the back. The bed was unmade and there were traces of duct tape still attached to the bedposts. Faint, discolored stains marked the pale yellow sheets on one side. Ella's heart almost stopped when she realized the implications.

"That could be blood someone tried to wash out," Ella said, thinking out loud, her voice sounding strange, even to herself.

Jayne shuddered. "Either he's into some really disturbed games, or he held someone here against their will."

"Search for anything that belonged to Justine—something she wouldn't have just left here, like her badge, or maybe something she did leave behind hoping we'd find it."

Jayne froze and stared at her. "You don't think my sister could still be alive?"

"What we've seen here certainly raises the possibility. But I can't prove anything unless we find more evidence to support it."

"Your intuition . . ."

"I don't know if that applies here. It's true that my hunches usually play out right, but I'm personally involved, and that alters my perspective."

Jayne crouched by the bed and retrieved something small from the floor.

"What have you got there?" Ella asked.

She held out her palm. "It's a piece of rose quartz that's obviously part of a pendant. See the loop where the chain would go through?" she asked, pointing it out. "Justine had one just like this. It was her lucky charm."

Ella studied the half-inch crystal, her heart pounding. "I remember seeing her wear this. She always had it with her, just like I always wear my badger fetish."

"Doesn't this prove that she was here the day she was killed?"

"It proves that she was here, but not when, and that's the kind of proof we need."

"I'm going to keep it," Jayne said, slipping it into her pocket.

"All right." Ella knew that positively identifying it as Justine's crystal was unlikely anyway.

Jayne looked at her somberly. "You've probably heard this kind of talk before, but this time it's for real. Starting today, I'm going to get my life turned around. And the first thing I'm going to do is help you find out what happened to my sister."

"No. This is as involved as you should get. Until I figure out exactly who and what I'm fighting, you're one of the last people I want involved." Ella saw the anger flash in Jane's eyes. "It's not a matter of trust, cousin. I just don't think your mother would be able to handle losing two of her daughters."

Jayne exhaled softly, then nodded. "You're probably right."

After checking the medicine cabinet for anything that might have been used to drug Justine, and finding nothing, they decided to leave, separately.

Ella was first. She slipped out through a side window that was shaded by two piñon pines, then hurried back to the truck. A few minutes later Jayne joined her after locking up the trailer again.

"Where shall I drop you?" Ella asked.

"Back home."

"You're not in the clear with Bobby Lujan. You realize that, don't you?"

"Somehow I'm going to get the money I owe him and Manny. Mom will help me, particularly if I assure her I'm going to quit gambling and get help from Gambler's Anonymous. I'll also have to tell her what they've been trying to force me to do. Then I'll go meet Bobby at the Totah Cafe and square things. It's real public there. If he doesn't leave me alone after that, I'll file a complaint against him. It's time I took charge of my own life."

As Ella watched her cousin enter her home, she wondered if Jayne's resolve would really hold. It wouldn't be easy for her. No addiction was easy to shake.

As she got under way, Ella dialed Blalock's number and, after filling him in on what she'd learned about Bobby Lujan, asked him to check up on the man's alibi. What she needed now was a third person who could verify that Paul and Jeremiah had really been together that night and at Manyfarms' place.

Ella dialed Wilson Joe. "I need a favor," she said, suspecting that by the time this case was finished, she'd owe half the reservation something.

"What can I do for you?"

"I'm uncovering all kinds of interesting information about Paul Natoni and Jeremiah Manyfarms. Did you know those two are related?"

"You're kidding. Where did you hear that?"

"Jayne Goodluck told me that Justine had mentioned it to her. Manyfarms is Natoni's alibi, so I need to check that out and verify that they were where they said. Natoni told Blalock that he and Manyfarms watched the basketball game that night."

"I watched the same game. Let me ask Jeremiah about it, and Paul, too, if I can find him. Then I'll let you know if they actually saw the game or not. I'm off at three today. Meet me at my home in another hour. How's that?"

"You got it."

Ella returned home, hoping to spend some time with Dawn, but her mother and Dawn were still away. The silence in the house seemed oppressive. Ella went to her computer, but there was no new mail and no messages from Coyote.

Finally, too restless to stay at home, especially now that she had at least one reason to hope Justine could still be alive, Ella drove out to Wilson's place. She took the long way, and arrived twenty-five minutes later. He used to live farther away, but now his home was a tribal-built house near the college. She waited in her truck for him to arrive, and it didn't take long.

Ella met him at the door ten minutes later. From his expression, she could tell that he'd found out something important.

Wilson led the way to the kitchen, pulled two soft-drink cans from the refrigerator, and handed her one. "I spoke to Jeremiah in his office, and I worked the conversation into a discussion of the game. I described a play that never happened, and he went along with it. He never saw the game. All he talked about was the kind of season one of the key players was having, not the game itself."

"Interesting."

"It gets better. I was about to leave when Paul Natoni showed up at the door. Jeremiah never bothered introducing us. All he said is that he'd been waiting all day for this guy to show up and he had to excuse himself.

"I tried to talk to Paul, but he cut me off and went inside Jeremiah's office, closing the door behind him. I decided to stick around for a bit, and that's when I heard them arguing."

"About what?"

"Jeremiah said that he was being careless, but that's all I heard before I had to leave. For all I know, it was in reference to furniture."

"Huh?"

"I checked around. Natoni now has a job at a rental and used furniture store."

"I'd love to go and lean on both of them, but if I do, the department will have me up on interfering with an ongoing investigation. I've got to use the back door whenever possible on this case." She met Wilson's gaze. "I can't tell you how much I hate that."

He smiled. "I can imagine. Remember what it was like when we were trying to clear your brother? You hated having to walk the fence. If anyone was born to be a cop, it's you."

She nodded slowly. "Yeah, I guess you're right. But who knows? Given enough time, I may decide I like the freedom of freelance better."

"Yeah, I can see that happening," he said sarcastically.

Ella was about to respond when her cell phone rang. She flipped it open with one hand and identified herself.

"This is Tache," a hurried voice said at the other end. "Paycheck received another of those 'anonymous' tips. He was told to go past the turnoff to Red Mesa and check behind the next billboard south of there. The person said that they'd find everything they needed to convict you."

"What? When did this happen?"

"Less than five minutes ago. A search team is being organized and I'm calling from the van. I'm already on the way."

"Thanks for letting me know." Ella disconnected the call.

"What's wrong, Ella?" Wilson put his hand on her shoulder gently. "You look almost sick."

"I just might be. I've known all along that someone's out to frame me. But now it looks like they may have come up with a way to get me arrested."

TWENTY-FIVE

——— ✖ ✖ ✖ ———

Ella was crouched behind an outcropping of rock overlooking the area where the police search team was working. With the sun at her back, and at that distance, she was nearly invisible.

From what she could see through her powerful binoculars, and guessing on the rest, the clothing in the plastic trash bag they'd unearthed belonged to Justine. She swallowed back the bitter taste that lined the back of her throat. Whoever had buried those things had selected the halfway point between where the burned body had been found and Rose's house.

Her cell phone ran and she jumped. It was Blalock. "I think it's you over there," he said, moving away from the others. "I thought you'd like to know that we've found an old butcher knife, Justine's badge, her wallet, and all her clothing, including her underwear and boots. There are hair samples stuck to the clothing where it's bloody. Most of it is Justine's, I think. At least it's the right color and length, but some of it . . ."

"Some of it what?" she pressed impatiently.

"Well, if I had to lay odds, I'd say they'll turn out to be yours. They're thick, black, and longer than Justine's."

"In that case, I think they were probably taken from Justine's car. I rode in there for hours the day before she disappeared."

"We've also found an axe here," Blalock added.

Ella felt the blood drain from her face. "We're missing ours."

"Exactly what I was thinking. If your prints are on it . . ."

"Of course they'll be on the handle. I chop wood for Mom all the time."

"It's got blood on it. So does the knife, but your mother didn't report one of those missing."

"No, she didn't," Ella agreed. "But my mom usually keeps the old knives as spares even after she's bought new ones. If this one belonged to her, she wouldn't have necessarily noticed it was missing. It was probably taken the afternoon someone broke into the house."

Blalock didn't answer. He didn't have to. They both knew that until this evidence could be refuted, it would point directly to Ella. The frame had been skillfully planned and executed from the very beginning. There was no doubt she was fighting for her life. The murder of a police officer would mean prison with no chance of parole.

"Whoever processes the axe won't find my *bloody* prints on it, or on the knife either. That's going to be a fact in my favor. There's no way whoever did this could have managed that. But I've still got to find them," Ella said.

"Some of the other evidence could go your way, too, if you have a good lawyer."

"I may not be able to get the best anymore. They don't come cheap. But do one thing for me. Check the source of the anonymous tip that led you to this stash. My guess is that the caller was either the killer or someone he hired. One more thing. I'm beginning to suspect that Justine was being drugged with a personality-altering herb or drug that induced paranoia in her. I think that was why she was overreacting to things with her family and at work. Find out who had access to Justine's food when she was away from home. And look at the connection between Manyfarms and Natoni," Ella said, letting him know what she'd learned.

"They have a shaky alibi," she added, "and that puts their association in a very bad light."

"I'll get every angle I can on those two characters. I also checked out this Bobby Lujan character. He was where you said. He didn't exactly win big, though. He was actually caught cheating, so everyone remembers him that night quite well. He was thrown out after spending a long time in their security office."

"I know there's a lot against me right now, but at least I've got some good informants. Sooner or later, I'll come up with something that can clear me."

Ella thought about mentioning the slim possibility that Justine was still alive and captive somewhere, and decided she had nothing to lose, and Justine had everything to gain, if she could be found—alive. She explained about Natoni's trailer, leaving out Jayne's involvement. It was a risk, knowing that her own entry into the trailer would taint any evidence.

Blalock didn't say anything for a moment, then finally responded. "That would explain the fingertip, I suppose, and suggests that it was left there for us to find, and wasn't just an oversight in the dark. I'll keep an open mind to the possibility, but in the meantime, I've got a job to do, in spite of the obvious frame job being done on you." He paused, then added, "Expect me to show up at your home within two hours or so."

Ella suddenly understood she was being told that her arrest was imminent. As soon as the hair was processed, a photo of the axe and the kitchen knife would be brought for Rose to identify, probably along with a warrant for Ella's arrest. But whether he actually believed Justine could still be alive, Blalock knew she was innocent, and had just given her a break. He was giving her the chance to go into hiding, and continue to investigate to clear herself, which, of course, was exactly what she'd be doing.

Ella found herself shaking as she tried to put the cell phone back into her pocket. She was afraid for her daughter as much as for herself. If she went down, her daughter would grow up being shunned by others and seen as the daughter of evil. Rose wouldn't be able to take care of Dawn forever, and after that, Dawn would have no one who would love her and give her a good home. Clifford wouldn't be able to take her into his family—not as long as he was married to Loretta.

She had to fight—and win—not only for her own sake, but for her daughter's. She hadn't brought Dawn into this world to live out her life in shame, or like a castoff with Kevin's family in Arizona.

Ella ran to her truck and drove home quickly, knowing that the lead time Blalock had given her was only approximate. She couldn't let herself be arrested. If she did, neither she nor Dawn would have a chance except through sheer luck. No one would fight harder for her or her daughter than she would.

Ella rushed in the front door, kissed her daughter, who was playing with both her wooden and plastic blocks together, then motioned for her mother to meet her in the bedroom.

Ella filled Rose in quickly as she packed a tape recorder, flashlight with extra batteries, and a change of clothes. Finally she slipped into loose-fitting jeans and a Red Chief's baseball cap. Tucking her hair inside it, she fitted the cap low over her face. "I've got to leave now. They're coming after me," she said, explaining the rest while she checked her computer one last time. "I'll call you when I can, and tell you I'm Francis. That'll mean that I want you to check my computer. I've left it on, so all you have to do is touch this key here on top that looks like a small rocket. It'll get you on-line." She scribbled the log-off directions onto a notepad.

"I don't know . . ."

"Just touch the right keys. It'll do the rest. And don't tell a soul. Not even your most trusted friend."

Rose nodded, and as Ella studied her mother's expression, she was surprised to see how calm Rose looked.

"Mom, will you be all right?"

Rose nodded. "I felt that this day would come. I've been planning ahead, more so, it seems, than you have."

"What do you mean?"

"You can't drive my truck, or your own. You'll be spotted in no time."

"I can't rent one either, Mom. I've got no choice."

"Go by the home of our night guardian," she said, referring to Herman Cloud. "Leave your truck with him. He'll hide it, and in the meantime, you can use his old one. It was recently rebuilt, and though it uses a lot of gas, it's got one of those fast engines."

"He didn't do that just for me?"

Rose smiled. "No. He fixed up the truck for himself, saying he was going to be a teenager one more time before he died. He wants you to take it now. No one will track you with it, and he assures me that no one will catch you either unless they have a helicopter or set up a roadblock ahead of you."

Ella gave Rose a hug. "Take care of Dawn for me, Mom, and tell her I love her every night when you read her a story. Her favorite one is about the lambs, remember. I'll try to end this soon."

Rose held her daughter. "You're frightened, and you have reason to be, but don't stop fighting. The truth will eventually come out. A lie can only exist if no one is around to expose it for what it is."

"I'll do my best and I won't give up, Mom, but I won't be able to come back home until it's over, and I don't know how long that'll be. They'll be watching you and this place constantly."

"I'll take care of things here. Don't worry about us. We have friends watching the house at night, remember? Just worry about yourself and what you have to do. And be safe."

Holding Dawn tightly for one last good-bye was gut-wrenching for Ella. She knew that the chances of her getting killed, maybe even by a fellow police officer, were higher than they'd ever been. As she hugged her daughter, knowing it could be for the very last time, Ella's heart nearly broke, but somehow she managed not to cry in front of her. Still, Dawn was unusually quiet, and looked at her very seriously as Ella sat her down.

"'Bye, Momma," Dawn said just once, and grabbed hold of Rose's skirt, hiding her face except for one eye. The last thing Ella saw as she left the room was her daughter's tiny hand out, waving good-bye slowly as she clung to Rose's skirt.

A short time later, armed with her derringer and her father's old hunting rifle and some ammo, she was back on the road. Now that she was alone, tears streamed down her face. Ella wiped them off with her hand and forced herself to focus on what she had to do next.

Ella switched off her cell phone. It could be used only for extreme emergencies now. Although neither the reservation police nor the local FBI had the tracking equipment capable of pinpointing a cell phone caller's location, it could be brought in, depending on outside pressure, and she wouldn't take any chances.

Ella drove directly to Herman Cloud. By the time she arrived at his home, he was outside, waiting, having heard her drive up.

Ella started to tell him why she'd come, but he shook his head. She realized that the less he knew, the less he'd have to answer for later if the police found out she'd been there. Herman led the way to a corrugated metal loafing shed out in the back beside the corrals. Underneath was an old seventies-model Chevy pickup, the finish faded to a pale green by the sun. "I got some training in the army, and used to be a mechanic before they started adding all those electronic gizmos to everything with wheels. For years I worked at that old filling station that used to be by the port of entry. We'd fix up anything then, just to see how much speed we could get out of an engine. This may look like Grampa's old truck, but she's got a rebuilt four-hundred-fifty-four-cubic-inch engine, four-barrel carburetor, and a few other extras that can make her haul like no one's business. And it's got a police scanner." He smiled. "I didn't want a ticket when I took her out to see what she could do."

Ella laughed, realizing that there was still a lot she had to learn about the people she'd grown up around. There was so much a child never paid attention to in her environment. Would it be the same for Dawn?

The thought brought her predicament back to focus, and she grew serious again. "Are you sure you want to do this? You could be arrested for helping me. It's serious stuff."

"A man has to decide whether his loyalty lies in the rules other men have drawn up, or in his own sense of right. I've made my decision."

"I haven't been arrested for anything, so technically you didn't help a fugitive. But if I get caught, I'll say I took your truck without permission. All you have to do is agree, and explain that it's your second vehicle and that you weren't aware that it was gone because you haven't been working on it lately."

"You won't get caught. And don't worry about anything here. Your truck will be safely hidden where no one will ever find it until you return. I can put a few bales of hay around it, throw a tarp over the whole thing, and it's an instant stack of alfalfa."

"You're a good friend," she said, impulsively giving him a hug. "Thank you."

"Hurry and get done with this unpleasantness. We need to bring some harmony back to this part of the Rez."

As Ella drove off, she tried to get her thoughts in order. She had no idea where she was going, or even which direction to turn when she got to the highway.

Ella considered her options. The only suspects who seemed to have the planning skills and connections to pull off the crime were Manyfarms and Natoni, but Blalock would be taking care of them using routine methods of investigation. What she wanted—what she needed—was something more definite. She had to find a clear motive and establish opportunity. That was the only way to verify or disprove Manyfarms' and Natoni's link to Justine's murder—or her captivity, if such a thing could be true. Whatever the case, Ella had to move quickly.

She glanced at her watch. Thursdays was Wilson's busiest teaching day, but the university computer would give her access to police data banks via the Internet, providing no one had changed her user codes.

Ella considered it. Even if they traced her access location, they'd only find the terminal she used at the university. It was worth the risk, as long as she didn't remain on-line very long.

Turning on the police scanner, she listened to routine calls as she headed for the university. Once the arrest warrant was issued and Blalock didn't find her or her truck at home, she would officially be labeled a fugitive and there would be no safe place for her anywhere.

Careful not to risk a traffic stop, Ella kept her speed within the limit, but the drive only served to make her even more tense. Finally, as she approached the college, she heard dispatch announce that there had been an arrest warrant issued for her, adding the usual caution about confronting a well-trained and probably armed suspect. She'd expected the news, but somehow, hearing it on the scanner made it sound even worse. Her stomach tightened into a knot. It wouldn't be long before the news was on the local radio stations as well.

One thing was certain. She had to stay away from Wilson. Someone would be watching him as well as Rose. But in Rose's case, that would only serve to protect her and Dawn, and that was a blessing in disguise.

Ella parked in the student parking lot. Making sure her long hair was completely tucked inside the Red Chief's baseball cap she was wearing, she climbed out of the truck and went toward Wilson Joe's office. He'd be teaching right now, and if someone was watching Wilson, he'd be in class or right outside the lecture hall door.

Hating what she was about to do, she stepped inside her friend's office and shut the door. She knew that Wilson kept his computer access codes on a tiny sheet of paper taped to the bottom of his desk drawer. Copying what she needed, she quickly left the room. Although Wilson had a computer in his office, it didn't have Internet access.

To get to the computer lab, she'd have to go past the main lecture hall, and since that was where Wilson was teaching, it entailed some risk. Hopefully no one would recognize her.

Ella walked quickly, and as she passed a large trash can, she saw someone's discarded backpack, which had a broken strap. Slipping it over one shoulder, hoping it would enhance her image as one of the students, she hurried through the large building, keeping her head down.

As she passed a corridor that led to the inside entrance of the lecture hall, she caught a brief glimpse of the last man she wanted to see. Sergeant Manuelito was just inside the hallway, lying in wait for her. Somehow it figured that he'd be the one watching Wilson. He didn't miss a trick.

She'd only had a brief glimpse, and he'd been looking in the other direction, so she had no reason to suspect trouble. Yet his presence was still unsettling. She hurried to the computer lab and sat down behind one of the terminals closest to the open door leading to the next classroom. Hopefully it would give her a quick way to make an exit, if it came to that.

Ella used Wilson's code to access the Internet through the college's mainframe. Once in that network, she began to enter her own user code, necessary to get her into the police system. But she stopped abruptly before typing in the last digit. If they'd played it smart, they would have set things up so that the moment she logged on, a trace would begin.

Ordinarily it would have taken some time for them to send an officer, but not now, with Sergeant Manuelito already on campus. One call on his handheld radio and he could be there in a few minutes.

Frustrated, she looked at the keyboard. There had to be another way. She smiled slowly, coming up with the answer. Wherever Justine was now, she would have appreciated this. Using her cousin's code, she logged on. They wouldn't have deleted the code of an officer they thought was dead until the end of the month, which was days away.

As she logged on, she saw the mail icon with a file attached. It said, "Activate Coyote."

Smiling to herself, she looked around. Nobody was in sight. Her informant had been a lot more clever than she'd ever anticipated. He was obviously in the loop with law enforcement, at least enough to know her current predicament. He must have even seen Justine's file, to know her access code, too. Yet, despite the obstacles, he'd found a way to communicate with her by guessing her next move.

Ella clicked on the "Coyote" file and read the contents.

> Hello, Ella. I thought you'd eventually stop by here. Enter
> your FBI badge number within the next twenty seconds,
> then hit the return key to access information that
> hopefully will help you. If the wrong number is entered,
> or if no number is keyed in, this program will shut down
> and be deleted.

Ella carefully typed in the numbers and hit the return key, and the prompt told her she was accessing an Internet address. A file appeared with FBI letterhead, headings, and format. It was a series of classified reports that were not available to other agencies on the activities of Professor Jeremiah Manyfarms. From what Ella could see, and what she remembered from her days in the FBI, the file looked legit.

Ella read the information carefully. The FBI had obviously kept a close eye on Manyfarms for quite some time. He'd been involved in Indian activism with several tribes in California and other western states as well. The FBI also believed he was forming espionage-style "cells," which were defined as autonomous groups that would act independently of each other. The goals of these cells had not been determined. Unsubstantiated reports claimed, however, that a select number of these cells had banded together to try and gain political control of several tribal governments by whatever means necessary. If true, it would represent a threat to the legitimate governments of the targeted Indian tribes.

Ella then glanced at Manyfarms' personal history. In addition to the teen he'd lost to gang violence, Manyfarms had twin nineteen-year-old sons and was still married to the mother of his children. The files listed a long history of suspected spousal abuse and the fact that currently Manyfarms was estranged from his wife.

Ella copied Susana Manyfarms' address onto a sheet of form-feed paper. The woman lived in Gallup, which was several hours away by the back roads through Burnham, White Rock, and Crownpoint. She didn't dare travel the main route.

Ella would go visit her next. With luck, Susana wouldn't have heard about the warrant for her arrest, and might give her information she could use.

She was entering commands, trying to figure out how to print the information on the screen, when she heard footsteps behind her.

"I thought I'd find you here," Manuelito growled. "I saw you on the sidewalk outside, and waited for you to make your way into the lecture hall. When you didn't show, I went looking."

Ella reached out quickly to turn off the computer. Trying to stop her, Manuelito dove, but he was too late. As the screen flickered off, she kicked out, knocking him back a few steps.

Manuelito reached for his weapon then, but she pushed the chair back hard, slamming it into his midsection. Manuelito fell backwards onto the floor.

Ella didn't wait to see how fast he could draw his firearm while flat on his back. She exited the way she'd come in, ran halfway down the corridor, and pulled the fire alarm.

In ten seconds the hallway was filled to capacity with students leaving all the classrooms. Ella was already outside by then, and as she glanced back, Manuelito was nowhere in sight.

She didn't slow down rounding the corner, and the extra adrenaline pumping through her system helped her now. In a matter of minutes, she was in the truck, speeding away from campus, going east. She checked the rearview mirror often, searching for patrol cars, knowing that she'd have to do her best to avoid them. She was willing to break rules, but she would never jeopardize the life of a citizen or another officer.

As soon as she reached the turnoff near Hogback and headed south, she breathed easier. Patrol units were few and far between out here, and anyone who'd seen her heading east toward Farmington when she'd left the college would be unlikely to suspect she'd be turning south instead. Once she arrived in Gallup, the danger to her would diminish. It was unlikely that she'd be running into people she knew so far from Shiprock.

The trip seemed endless. She kept the scanner on and monitored all the calls, which faded once she got far enough from Shiprock. Manuelito had reported in, but so far they were looking for her own truck, and she had a feeling Herman Cloud had already hidden it well.

With plenty of time to think along the slow, dusty roads, Ella tried to figure out the best way to approach Susana Manyfarms. She was reluctant to use her name, and she had no badge. Finally she settled on the only approach. She still had the college ID in her wallet from when she'd started helping Wilson with his youth program. She'd use that and claim to be with the college, doing a routine background check on Susana's husband, who hadn't been a professor in Shiprock for long.

The circuitous route, after getting lost two times, took nearly five hours, and by the time she arrived at the small stucco home in Gallup, she was more than ready to get to work. The tape from her small pocket-sized recorder couldn't be used as evidence, but by recording the interview, and playing it back later, she might be able to discover a clue she'd missed.

Ella knocked, and a middle-aged Navajo woman came to the door. Although in jeans, she was wearing thick foundation makeup and the darkest shade of red lipstick Ella had ever seen. Susana obviously believed in makeup—lots of it.

Ella introduced herself as planned, then went inside. As she studied the woman's face, she suddenly understood why Susana wore so much makeup. Despite the layers of foundation and powder, bruises and a slight swelling peered through in more than one place. Her cheek was dark and the edge of her mouth slightly swollen.

"Are you all right?" Ella asked softly.

"The makeup doesn't really hide the marks, does it?"

"No," Ella replied gently. "But maybe in a day or two..."

Susana nodded. "Yeah, maybe then." She sat back, then winced as she tried to find a comfortable position. "If you've come here asking me to extol my husband's virtues, forget it. With luck, our divorce will be final soon."

"He's applied for access into all our science labs and computer rooms, and that requires a little extra background check. Everything you tell me will be completely confidential."

"Jeremiah is a self-centered rat who takes from everyone and gives nothing but false promises in return. He's always managed to present a nice face to the public. He's not so kind with mine."

"I can't imagine what it must be like for you," Ella said honestly. "Why do you let him near you if he's going to do this?"

"He comes to see the twins regularly, and when they're here, nothing happens. But when they're not, he doesn't put on his act. Sometimes he loses control and his temper goes wild. He still blames me for everything that happened with our youngest son."

"I know he was killed."

Pain flashed over her features. "Carlton needed the influence of a strong father, but Jeremiah was out there claiming to be taking care of Indians everywhere. Unfortunately, he didn't take time for his own son. I tried to warn him that I was having problems with Carlton. I couldn't get our son to even talk to me. I begged Jeremiah for his help, but he would always tell me that the children were my responsibility. His was making a living and supporting us. Now, of course, he blames everyone but himself for what happened. Whenever we're alone, the issue of Carl always comes up and he takes it out on me."

"Who else does he blame? The gangs?"

"Well, yes, of course, but he mainly blames the Navajo Police in Shiprock. He says they stirred up trouble between the gangs, and Carlton was caught in the middle. Carl was barely fourteen when he was shot." She paused. "Jeremiah believes that the reason our marriage fell apart is because I couldn't deal with our son's death. But it's not me. It's him. He won't let me forget. Look at my face and you'll see I'm telling the truth," she said.

"What happened this time? Was it a fight about the divorce?"

She nodded. "He didn't want to sign the papers. He said I was making a big mistake, that we had to square things with the past first. He promised me that soon everyone responsible for Carl's death would be brought to justice, and that it was my duty to see it through with him. But I know him too well. All that means is that he wants me around so he'll have someone to beat on if things don't go the way he wants."

"Why haven't you gotten a restraining order?"

"I have, but it's just a piece of paper. He always violates it, and unless the cops catch him, it's just his word against mine."

"I understand you two adopted Paul Natoni several years ago. That just doesn't seem in character with the man you've described."

"That happened well before my son's death. At the time I went along with it, willingly. Jeremiah was a close friend of Paul Natoni's parents. When they died, we legally adopted Paul. He lived with us for about four years. By the time Jeremiah began his involvement with Indian rights, Paul was already eighteen and out on his own, hustling for money in bars and pool halls, or playing cards in back rooms." She shook her head. "It's a wonder Paul hasn't ended up dead or in jail."

"Are Jeremiah and Paul close?" Ella asked.

"Yes, more so these days than when Paul was young. There's a ruthlessness about Paul that I think Jeremiah wishes he would have had when he was that young. When Paul wants something, he goes after it without worrying about the consequences, and he doesn't stop until he gets it."

"How does Paul get along with the twins?"

"There's some rivalry between them, but nothing serious."

Ella's gaze fell on a family photograph on the coffee table. The twins were young men now, dressed in graduation gowns at what was obviously a graduation party. "Those are your boys? They've graduated from high school, I can see."

She nodded. "They've been running around a lot since then, and I'm very worried about them. They left last week for California to visit with their cousins, but they never showed up. I called and their aunt hasn't even seen them. When I called Jeremiah, worried about what had happened to them, he told me to let them be, that they were men and needed their freedom. But I don't understand why they lied to me. That's just not like them, and I have a feeling their father is behind this somehow."

Ella studied the photo. The boys were tall and slender for Navajos and appeared to be about her own height and weight. As she remembered the shooting fiasco at the convenience store that had started the trouble between Justine and her, an idea formed in her mind. Maybe Justine and she had both been right. If twins, dressed in clothing like hers, had pulled off that robbery, the discrepancies in Justine's story and her own could be easily explained. It would have definitely been one way of stirring up trouble between her and Justine. Had luck been with the boys, they might have even managed to get Justine and her to shoot each other.

Ella stood up. "I better be going now."

"I've told you the way things are. I hope that you don't see my husband as anything but what he is—a man who has many faces. But please don't tell him that the information you got came from me. His anger . . . scares me, and the police here can't protect me from him."

"Don't worry. A man like your husband believes that he can get away with anything, but that's usually his downfall. It'll catch up to him sooner or later."

Ella went out to the truck, and was pulling out into the street when she caught a glimpse of a Tribal Police unit coming toward her from the end of the block. It didn't take a genius to figure out Manuelito had somehow guessed where she was going and decided to come here, though it was out of his jurisdiction.

As the police vehicle narrowed the gap between them, Ella pushed down on the accelerator and headed for the open highway, hoping the Gallup police weren't in the area to give him backup.

TWENTY-SIX

———— ✖ ✖ ✖ ————

The tribal unit tried gamely to stay in pursuit, but the Chevy truck's big 454-cubic-inch engine was everything Herman had said it was, and once she reached the open highway, she was able to pull away from the officer almost as if he were standing still. When she was past the well-lighted section of Highway 666 north of Gallup, she was able to lose sight of her pursuer. At the first opportunity, she slowed quickly and drove off the highway down a dirt road and into an arroyo.

Night had descended, and in the dark, no one would be able to see her there except up close. As she waited for Manuelito to pass by her location, she recorded her latest findings and suspicions on the small tape recorder she'd brought along in her jacket pocket. Without a witness or partner, this might be all she had to contribute to the investigation if something happened to her.

Ella kept the police-band scanner on, and heard the frustration in Manuelito's voice as he called in, asking for an officer farther north to set up a roadblock to intercept her.

Either the sergeant had managed to catch a glimpse of Many-farms' name on the computer screen back at the college, or the printer had been merely taking its time warming up, and delayed printing out the file until after she'd left. Even with the computer turned off, enough data could have passed to the printer for Manuelito to get the drift of what she'd been checking. And with the circuitous route she'd taken to Gallup, Manuelito would have had plenty of time to locate Jeremiah on campus, or guessed where she was headed and driven to Gallup to stake out Mrs. Manyfarms' house.

Ella smiled, knowing that she'd eluded Manuelito again. But now she had to tell Blalock what she'd learned. She looked at her cell phone. She'd make a quick call—too short to trace even if they'd managed by some miracle to get the technology and put it in place.

Ella phoned in, and Blalock answered on the first ring.

"How the hell did you get access to an FBI file like that?" Blalock asked when she'd finished.

"That's something I can't tell you. But check it out with your sources. I think you'll find the file is legit, and it still should be secure, unless Sergeant Manuelito was able to get a partial printout."

"At least he's a cop. Ella, where are you, and when are—"

Ella hung up without letting Blalock finish his sentence or saying good-bye, and headed south, back in the direction she'd come. She wasn't far from Loretta's mother's house now, which was south of Coyote Canyon. She decided to stake the place out. Knowing her brother, he'd never stay at his mother-in-law's home. Avoidance between a mother-in-law and a son-in-law was a centuries-old cultural rule and not one that Clifford would be likely to break.

She picked a vantage point on the west side, atop a small hill, and using binoculars, scouted the canyon below, making sure no police cars were around, watching for her to show up. There was a camping tent a few hundred yards from Loretta's mother's home.

The tent was old army surplus, a sturdy canvas model Clifford had purchased many years ago in Farmington. Ella approached slowly and cautiously from a small arroyo running northwest. Sure they'd turn her in to the police, Ella was determined to avoid being spotted by Loretta or her mother.

As she drew near to the camp, she saw her brother sitting near a campfire alone, looking in her direction.

"Come out, sister," he said. "I'm alone and my wife is at her mother's."

"How did you know?"

He smiled. "You still have the footsteps of an elephant."

"I do not," she growled. "You must have seen me coming down the hill earlier, or heard the truck."

He smiled. "Come and warm yourself, just don't face the house in front of the fire in case someone looks this direction. There's no chance my wife will come over to visit right now. She's with our son, and still has no desire to speak to me. She heard on the radio that the police are searching for you in connection to our cousin's murder."

"I'm in serious trouble at the moment, that's true. But I could be close to finding the truth."

"Good. Our mother and your daughter need you back at your home."

Ella told him briefly why she was on the run, and what she'd put together about Natoni and Manyfarms, then waited for his reaction.

Clifford's expression was troubled. "I should have suspected that college professor long before now."

"What makes you say that?"

"Do you remember when Mom had to take Two to the vet?"

"Sure. You were gone, visiting a patient."

He nodded. "Yes, it was Jeremiah Manyfarms. I can see now why he called me, though he didn't seem ill at all. Without me, or Two, or you around, it was easy for his accomplice to break into our mother's home, steal the kitchen knife, axe, and hair samples, probably from your own hairbrush or pillow, and have what he needed to frame you."

Ella smiled knowing he was using the name of his enemy to strip him of its power and undermine him. "If Jeremiah was with you, that means that his stepson or the twins poisoned Two and did the actual legwork for him."

"It was carefully planned," Clifford acknowledged.

"I also believe his twin sons played a part in the incident that created such trouble between Justine and me," she said, filling him in on what she now suspected about the shooting at the convenience store.

"Did you know that Jeremiah Manyfarms is skilled at repairing radios and electronic equipment? He has a small business on the side. I saw his workshop when I went to his home," Clifford announced. "That could explain why you and our cousin couldn't use your radios to communicate."

"Maybe FB-Eyes can locate the twins, but I have a feeling Jeremiah has ordered them to stay in hiding."

"If they're on the reservation, I may be able to find them for you. If I do, I'll send the information to FB-Eyes."

Ella stood up. "I better get going."

"Where will you go? Do you have supplies?"

"Some. I can get more."

"You'll be taking a chance if you go into a store. They may all have your photos on their cash registers by now." He waved her to the canned food and fresh water bottles in the back of his truck. "Take some of mine. I'll have no problem getting more."

"Are you sure?"

"Of course. Take the tent, too, if you want."

She shook her head. "No, I won't need it. The place I'm going to has a good solid roof."

"I won't ask where, but you may have to change hiding places before this is over. Take all the supplies you need," he said, helping her load water and some food into the tent storage bag so she could carry them back to her truck. "Just remember to stay away from the places that'll bring you more trouble than safety, like abandoned hogans. Those with a hole punched in the side pose a danger even if you can't see it."

"I know. If a death has occurred there, then there's danger of contamination by the *chindi*," she said, completing his thought. "Don't worry. I've got enough enemies already. I'm not looking for any more."

"And if you need me, send word any way you can. I'll do my best to help you."

Ella motioned toward the house. "Have you been able to talk with your wife yet?"

Clifford shook his head. "We used to understand each other very well. Now it's like we disagree on everything. I'm not sure what happened. Or, more importantly, how to fix it. But I'm not giving up."

"Take care of yourself," Ella whispered as she turned to head back to her truck.

"You, too."

It was late and she was tired, but the safe house was one of several that Blalock had once told her about, and this one would serve her well tonight.

Exhaustion undermined her as she struggled to remember the directions of the one she had in mind. It was south of Captain Tom Wash, east of the community of Newcomb, and near an old coal mine.

The last stretch was the worst, and she got out several times to look for vehicle tracks. Blalock didn't have enough men at his disposal to stake out every hiding place she might know about, but she had to be careful anyway. After a three-mile drive up one of the roughest roads she'd ever seen, she finally reached the safe house located in an old mining camp. The stone house must have originally belonged to a superintendent of the mine. It was the only one still standing. The lack of recent tire tracks or footprints suggested that no one had been around for quite some time, or come in from another direction, and no vehicles or lights were visible anywhere.

Parking around back, close to the house so the pickup couldn't be seen by someone approaching, she walked around front. Remembering Blalock's directions, she used a key she found under the first stone of the flagstone walk leading to the front porch and went inside.

It wasn't fancy, just four walls and a roof, but it would do. She searched the entire house using her flashlight, and in the kitchen closet found an oil lamp and a metal can of fuel for it.

Bringing out the lamp, she set it on the bare kitchen table so it would be close by, if needed. Next she brought in her sleeping bag, rifle, and a bottle of water from the truck, and placed them in the kitchen, closest to the back door and the truck outside.

Taking one last precaution, she went from room to room, standing in the darkness, listening. Finally satisfied that she was alone, she crawled into the sleeping bag and drifted off to sleep.

A commotion right outside jolted her awake sometime later. Ella grabbed the rifle from where it rested beside her, and crouched by the kitchen window. In the soft glow of the moon, she could see Harry Ute standing over a man who lay prone on the ground, not moving.

Ella watched, uncertain whether to trust Harry now.

"I know you're there, Ella, but don't come out. I was closing in on Samuel Begaye, and spotted him while he was watching the turnoff toward your brother's mother-in-law's house. He must have learned that Clifford was there, and was hoping you'd show up. I waited, and followed him when he followed you. If yours hadn't been the only vehicle leaving the area, you might have fooled both of us in that unfamiliar pickup. He hit his head when I took him down and he's out cold now, but once I get him to Shiprock, he'll be questioned extensively at the station. Unless I miss my guess, he'll be dying to tell everyone where you're at, so you better get a move on. It's not safe for you here anymore."

"I'll clear out," Ella said, now standing in the shadows.

"I'm sorry. I wish I could help you more. You're not on my fugitives list, so if I'm asked, I never actually saw you."

"And you didn't," she said, watching Harry as he carried his unconscious prisoner over his shoulder and dropped him in the backseat of his sedan.

As soon as she could see his taillights, Ella gathered up her things, locked the house, replaced the key, then left.

More than anything, she would have liked to present during Begaye's questioning. It was possible that he knew something about Justine's murder, or at the very least, that he might slip up and comment about nearly killing Ella in the drive-by that night when she was in her own truck. He would know who'd come up behind her in the Farmington Mall, too, or at least have a description. But there was no sense in dwelling on a missed opportunity. It was something that was as out of her reach as her badge was now.

Ella drove northeast through Burnham, and ended up several miles south of Morgan Lake. There was a lot of ground cover here beside the hogback and it would be safe for her to camp out, though she wouldn't risk building a fire.

All she really needed now was a few hours of uninterrupted

sleep, and for that, this was the ideal place. She was absolutely certain no one had followed her. The unimproved roads behind her had long stretches of open ground around them, and anyone following without headlights would have lost her. Now, between two small hills, she'd take her rest in the bed of the pickup.

Ella woke up before sunrise, her back stiff from the metal surface beneath her sleeping bag. She opened her eyes slowly, and for a moment, panic set in until she remembered where she was. She had to head back to Shiprock now. The only chance she had to find out if Justine was still alive, and if not, at least clear her name, lay with Manyfarms and Natoni.

Ella went back through Shiprock, reversing the route she'd taken yesterday, west of Waterflow across the small bridge, then along side roads north of Highway 64. It was risky, but she didn't think Manuelito would consider her foolhardy enough to come back here. Using her binoculars, she watched from the top of the mesa opposite the college, trying to find Manyfarms and searching for any Tribal Police units on stakeout. She found neither, but it was still quite early.

Not having Jeremiah's address and not wanting to risk contacting Wilson now, Ella went to Paul Natoni's trailer park, then maneuvered around to an arroyo opposite the main entrance, parking the truck below ground level, out of sight from the road. Selecting a vantage point that was somewhat risky, but close in, and out of view of Natoni's nosy neighbor, she lay down prone behind a clump of brush, settling in for a long wait. An unfamiliar-looking car was parked beside the trailer, but Natoni's vehicle was gone.

Ella had been there for about a half hour when a woman wearing a nurse's uniform came out of the trailer and got into the car. It was still relatively early, barely six-thirty in the morning. The woman, from a distance, was the same height and body type as Justine, but even with binoculars, she couldn't ID her. Unwilling to let it go, Ella ran back to her truck, intending to tail her.

With only one road leading from the trailer park, Ella was able to catch up enough to follow her to the hospital.

Ella pulled in and parked a few spaces behind the woman. She waited until the nurse got out of her car, then moved to intercept her. A moment later Ella cut her off, staring at her in surprise. "What the hell?"

TWENTY-SEVEN

————— ✖ ✖ ✖ —————

It was Justine's traditionalist aunt Lena, though it was obvious now that she'd been an imposter. Her hospital ID gave an entirely different name.

The woman's eyes widened. "You!"

"Yeah, it's me. But who are *you*?" Ella grasped her forearm and held her there. "You aren't anyone's aunt Lena, and you're no more a traditionalist than I'm an Anglo. It should have occurred to me that you didn't live out at that hogan. Your hands are too soft and smooth to have ever chopped wood. And look at those rings. They're the same ones you wore that day."

"My name's Lupe Dearman and that's all I'm going to say. Not without a lawyer." She stared defiantly at Ella.

"You're better off talking to me now than to the police once they catch on to you. They may be a week old by now, but some of your prints will be around the real Lena's farm, if that's what it really was. They're probably all over the hogan."

Lupe nodded. "So what? You can't prove that I was the one who impersonated her. It would just be your word against mine. And right now your word probably isn't worth much."

"I'll volunteer to take a lie detector test. Do you think you can pass one too? Think hard, because you're looking at charges of being an accessory to murder."

The woman's face grew pale. "I haven't killed anyone. I played the part of Lena Clani while the woman was away visiting relatives or something."

"And what were you doing staying with Paul Natoni? I followed you from his trailer."

"He's my boyfriend, not that it's any of your business."

"Just how long has this been going on?"

She smiled. "For months. Paul was just faking an interest in Justine. He was going to humiliate her and ruin her reputation with the police department. I was going to sneak in and take some photos of them in bed, then he'd spread them around. He wanted to strike back at the police department because of what happened to his stepbrother Carlton."

"So where is the real Lena?"

"I have no idea. Jeremiah told Paul that she was away visiting relatives. She probably never even knew we were there. We left it just the way we found it."

"Then what about Justine? Did you help Paul kill her? And cut her up into pieces?"

"*Me?* Are you crazy? No way. Paul wanted to ruin her reputation, but that's all. You were the one that killed her, not us."

"Just how well do you know Jeremiah, Paul's stepfather?"

"Paul and he are close, so I've seen him a bunch of times."

"Has he ever asked you to do anything for him?"

Lupe shrugged. "Nothing like what Paul and I were doing to trash Justine's reputation, if that's what you mean. All I ever did was loan him some outdated, surplus medical supplies and tools."

"What kind of supplies and tools?"

"A surgical saw, scalpels, painkillers, and bandages."

Ella felt a shudder touch her spine. "Why would he need all that?"

"Jeremiah told me that he needed to amputate the leg of a calf that had been caught in a trap. It had gotten infected. He'd received training on trauma and first aid in the military, so he knew what to do."

Ella considered it for a moment. Those tools could have been used to cut up Justine's body after she was killed, but then why the bandages? Did they torture her first? "Did you provide him with any other drugs? And think hard on this," she added.

She hesitated, then continued. "I gave him some phenmetrazine hydrochloride. It's a diet aid used as an appetite suppressant. It has some bad side effects, making a person edgy and paranoid if they get an overdose, but I warned him about that."

"Did he tell you what he wanted it for?"

"No, but I didn't ask. I trust him."

Ella knew now why Natoni had met so often with Justine for breakfast. Jeremiah had passed the drug along to Paul, who'd probably given Justine a dose of the drug each morning in her food. By the time she got to work, she was ready for a confrontation. The question was, what else had their plans entailed?

"What did they have planned for Justine?" Ella added. She needed to learn all she could, and quickly. Other cars were pulling into the parking lot now for the day shift, and several of the staff would recognize her.

"Nothing, except what I've already told you. All I did was pretend to be her shrewish aunt. Paul told me what I needed to know ahead of time. He didn't get the chance to seduce her because she turned up dead. But you know more about that than I do. You're the suspect, not me."

"You're not out of this yet, Lupe. You'll have to account for your time the night of the murder, and I hope you have a solid alibi."

"Paul will back me up on this. We were together all that night."

"Wrong answer. And you can forget about Paul saving your behind. Right now he's probably running for his life. Every cop in the four-state area is already on the lookout for him. Think about it. The drugs, the saw and surgical tools, Justine's paranoid behavior. That was all part of their plan. Don't you realize what kind of revenge they were really after, and how they went about trying to frame me for their crime? They were using you too, just to get the tools they needed. Put the facts together and you'll know who really killed my cousin."

Lupe stood there a moment, tears forming in her eyes as she finally realized what Ella was saying. "They'll never catch Paul for any of this. He's too smart."

"Lupe, if you really care about him, you'll tell me where to look. Once I tell the police what you've said, he and Jeremiah will go to the top of their list. The first time he shows his face anywhere, he's liable to get shot."

"You're in the same boat. You're still a murder suspect until you or the police can prove it was him or Jeremiah. And I'm not saying anything to anyone."

"Too late. I've already gotten the testimony the police will need." She pulled a tape recorder out of her pocket. "This is going straight to the FBI," Ella said, switching it off. The small tape was nearly all used. "You're guilty of conspiracy in at least one murder, maybe more, if we can't find Aunt Lena."

Lupe's jaw dropped, and she turned pale. "Oh no, you can't do that to me. I'm not really part of any of this. I was just playacting to trick Justine, nothing more."

"I doubt a judge will buy that. The best advice I can give you is to turn yourself in. Get an attorney and cut a deal. You've helped us with information, and that's worth something. Sign a statement and testify in court, and you'll get a break. Now tell me where Paul is hiding, before he or Jeremiah have the chance to hurt someone else. I'll try to take him alive, but I can't promise how other officers will approach a cop killer."

"Promise me that you won't let anyone hurt him, or hurt him yourself. I've read about you in the past, with those terrorists and before that. I don't trust you. You've got the killer instinct."

The words stung. Ella knew better than anyone else how many criminals she'd been forced to kill in the line of duty. Those memories would always haunt her dreams, and she didn't want to add to her nightmares any more than Lupe did. "I'll do everything in my power to see to it that he's not harmed."

Ella memorized the directions Lupe gave her to a hogan in the mountains west of Shiprock. It was on land assigned to Jeremiah's mother by the tribe. The hogan, Lupe explained, had been modernized. It even had electricity and had been equipped with remote video cameras and a monitor that maintained surveillance on the main path. Jeremiah was one of the New Traditionalists, Lupe reminded her, and he used technology to protect himself and his family.

Ella knew that any place that well guarded meant trouble, and before she went out there she'd have to make sure Lupe couldn't get to a phone and warn Paul and Jeremiah. Ella grabbed Lupe's arm and, before she could react, handcuffed her to the door handle of her car.

Then Ella locked Lupe's car with the keys inside, and searched Lupe's pockets to rule out her having a cell phone.

Apologizing but ignoring Lupe's protests, Ella drove out of the parking lot, using her cell phone to place a call to the station. She left a short message for Big Ed on voice mail, telling him where a material witness was handcuffed to a car, and needed to be watched in case she changed her mind and tried to warn Justine's killer that Ella was coming after him. She gave the woman's name and the exact location, then hung up.

Big Ed would want to know where she was going, but she needed to make sure she got there first. The easiest way to accomplish both was to see to it that the tape with Lupe's statement found its way to Blalock or Big Ed, but mailing it would take too long.

By the time she'd finished the thought, Ella realized that she was also headed in the direction of Wilson Joe's home. Deciding to take a chance, she drove over there. The backyard of his home was open to the desert, and offered plenty of cover. With luck, he'd still be at home. If she could get him to drop the tape off, then she'd handle the rest.

Ella took the back roads south again, and parked near a dry arroyo. After looking around the entire area for any officers on stakeout, she quickly ran the quarter-mile distance to Wilson's home. Moments later, she knocked on his back door.

Wilson opened the door, cup of coffee in hand, and stared at her in surprise. "Get in." He grabbed her arm and pulled her into the kitchen, closing the door behind her. "What on earth are you doing here? That idiot cop Manuelito has been watching me since late last night. I can't even look out the window without seeing him in the distance with his binoculars on the house."

"Is he still out there?" Ella thought she'd checked the area thoroughly.

"No. Well, at least I didn't see him." He led her into the hall, away from the windows. "I've been really worried about you."

"I couldn't get in touch, it was just too risky. But now things are finally coming together." She handed him the tape. "It's imperative that Big Ed or Blalock get this. This has evidence that will be substantiated once the PD picks up Lupe Dearman at the hospital and she makes a statement."

"I'll hand-deliver it to them."

"Be careful that you don't get into trouble. Say that you found it in your mailbox this morning."

"Where are you going?"

Ella hesitated. If she didn't make it out in one piece, she wanted someone else to know what she'd done and why. She told him the story as quickly as she could.

"You can't be seriously considering going out there alone."

"I don't have a choice. I'm still a fugitive."

"But the tape—"

"Is inadmissible. All it can do is give Big Ed and Blalock an edge they can use to pressure Lupe if she changes her mind about making a statement. Once Lupe signs her statement, it'll be a different story. But I've got to move out now. If Paul gets wind of this, he may decide to make a run for it. Of course, bringing Paul in will be easy in comparison to what I can expect from Jeremiah. He's the mastermind, and a lot more dangerous."

"Nothing can bring his boy back. Why is he doing this? It makes no sense."

"Jeremiah wants revenge against the Navajo police. He blames us for stirring up the gangs and getting his son killed. It's that simple. Everything comes in second to that one goal. Even Paul's expendable. I think Jeremiah's going to go down fighting hard—if I find him at all."

"Let the cops find Paul and Jeremiah then. You're walking into a situation that could get you killed."

"If I wait, and Lupe manages to warn Paul or Jeremiah, they'll take off. Then, in essence, they will have gotten away with what they've done, and continue to be a threat to me and my family. I can't live with that. Take the tape in and talk to Big Ed. I left word for him already to pick up Lupe."

"Let me tell him where you're going. At least you'll be able to get eventual help that way."

"They'll know when they hear the tape. But it's imperative that

I get there fast and have time to work. If Lupe has lied, or I don't have Paul in custody as well as enough evidence to convict him by the time they get there, they could end up trying to arrest me instead. In the confusion, Paul will get away. I need your word that you won't say anything, Wilson. I'm counting on you."

"All right."

Ella headed back to the door. "Once this is over. I owe you the best dinner around."

"Back to the fried-chicken place?"

She laughed. "Well, that *is* the best food around." Ella stood at the window, checking out the area for several moments. "I better go," she said at last. Moving quickly, she opened the door and raced back to her pickup.

Ella got under way, trying to swallow back the bitter taste of fear at the back of her throat. She wasn't kidding herself. There was a lot of risk in what she was doing. If Jeremiah happened to be with Paul when she arrived, there'd be shooting for sure. And Jeremiah, she suspected, would be armed to the hilt.

Ella worried about an officer pulling her over as she drove through the community of Shiprock again this time of the morning. She knew from the police scanner that Manuelito hadn't be able to read the plate before, but he still had a general description of the truck.

She decided to "low-ride" and drive slowly, throwing off suspicion by doing the opposite of a fugitive in a hurry. Using the directions given to her by Lupe, Ella headed west on Highway 64, hoping she wouldn't encounter a patrol car at all before she left the main highway near Rattlesnake. A mile out of Shiprock she saw a tribal unit parked beside the road ahead, so she assumed the scrunched-down driving position of a "low rider," and slowed to under the speed limit. Rolling down the windows, she turned up the radio so the music blared.

With the bill of her cap shading her face, and careful not to make eye contact, Ella cruised past the parked unit. Two minutes later, well down the road, she sat up again, turned off the radio, and listened on the police scanner. The cop hadn't given her a second glance, apparently.

More than an hour later, after she'd driven along a well-traveled path into the piñon/juniper hills near Beclabito, the road abruptly disappeared into a thick stand of trees near a sandstone cliff.

She quickly parked off the track behind a cluster of junipers and slipped out of the pickup, carrying her rifle and extra cartridges in her pocket. Somewhere in the distance she could hear the faint chug of a small gasoline engine, but that was the only sign that the area had residents nearby. Moving forward very slowly, keeping low, she studied the area ahead with binoculars. Eventually, through a small gap in the trees, she saw a hogan with a sturdy-looking wooden door a short distance from the cliff. A cord of wood was stacked a few feet from the entrance.

When Lupe had warned her about video surveillance cameras, she'd expected one or two. Although the cameras were not in plain sight, she could make out at least three mounted on trees, with branches cleared away to give clear fields of view. Wires led down the trees, then disappeared at ground level, obviously buried and leading to a power source and monitor, the latter of which was probably inside the hogan.

Ella saw Paul Natoni come outside the hogan, take a look around using a pair of binoculars, then go back in. Though she waited patiently for at least an hour, she saw no sign of Jeremiah Manyfarms. The cameras didn't move, so they were either fixed to a single viewing area, or whoever was inside didn't care to put them into motion.

Ella circled around at a distance, coming to the edge of the cliff behind the log dwelling. There weren't any more cameras visible, though she searched for several minutes for mountings or wires before moving any closer.

As she drew near, she thought she heard Natoni speaking to someone inside, but she couldn't make out his words clearly. The sturdy structure made that impossible. To make matters even worse, whoever he was talking to hadn't answered at all. For some reason she couldn't explain, that made a chill creep up Ella's spine.

She searched the entire perimeter for another vehicle, trying to find out who was with him, but only Natoni's pickup was there, parked around back on the cliff side.

Ella crept even closer, trying to find the electrical generator from the sound it made. She finally spotted it right outside the entrance, screened from the front by the stack of firewood. Disabling it would be impossible without risking getting caught before she was ready. She searched again, but still couldn't find any additional cameras aimed toward the back. They must have had to exclude one area from scrutiny, and selected the cliff side with its natural barrier. If she approached carefully, she could stay out of the side cameras' viewing field.

Closer now, Ella realized Natoni was taunting someone. His voice has an annoying singsong quality. Ella clasped the badger fetish in her hand for courage. It was hot to the touch. Danger was close, something she already knew.

Heeding the warning, Ella decided to back off and take another look around the area, hoping to spot Manyfarms. She didn't want him to take her unawares, or come up the road and cut her off. As she climbed a bluff adjacent to the hogan and looked around from high ground, she saw a vehicle traveling toward them.

It took a few endless minutes before she recognized the SUV through her binoculars. It was Wilson Joe. Fear gripped her. The last thing she wanted was to be responsible for another person now.

Wishing he'd stayed in Shiprock and done as she asked, Ella circled around quickly and flagged him down before he came upon where she'd parked her pickup. Wilson parked his SUV, then climbed out of his own vehicle, carrying his hunting rifle.

"I turned over the tape to Big Ed, but then I realized that I couldn't let you face this alone," Wilson said softly. "What did you find?"

"There's a hogan ahead, protected by video cameras. I have a feeling that Manyfarms is nearby, but I don't think he's inside the hogan, and I couldn't find his vehicle. Paul Natoni is there, however. I heard him speaking to someone, but the person never answered." Ella exhaled softly. "You shouldn't be here, you know. You could get yourself killed."

Wilson ignored her. "Any chance that Natoni's talking to himself?"

"Maybe he has a radio or cell phone in there. It sounded to me like he was giving someone a hard time, though. Perhaps it's Justine's aunt Lena."

Ella heard another vehicle coming up the same road. In an area without traffic of any kind, sound traveled a long way. Probably the only reason her and Wilson's vehicles hadn't been detected inside the hogan was that the chugging of the generator drowned out the engine noise.

Ella climbed up on top of her pickup's cab and focused the binoculars toward the sound.

"You were followed! The first vehicle is Blalock's, I'm sure of it. No one else dares to drives a sedan out here in the sticks. The second is a tribal unit. My guess is that Sergeant Manuelito volunteered to back him up."

"Ella, I'm sorry. I don't know how I didn't spot them. I kept looking in the rearview mirror."

"Maybe Manuelito put a tracking device in your car." Ella jumped down and quickly searched the rear bumper and fenders of Wilson's SUV. She found the magnetically attached device immediately. "I need you to do something as quickly as you can."

"Name it."

"Drive to another spot beside the cliff and pitch this over the edge. Just don't let anyone see your vehicle from the hogan, and try not to let Blalock see you. If FB-Eyes and whoever else it is thinks they're going to have to drive back down to the bottom, it might buy me some time."

"What are you planning to do about Natoni?" Wilson asked. "You'd have to wait until he comes out or risk getting shot in a face-to-face confrontation. Maybe you should just let those guys find the hogan."

"I can't let that happen," Ella said, grasping her rifle firmly in her right hand. "When those cars come up to the hogan, Natoni will bolt, or start shooting. If he's got someone in there, maybe as a hostage, then that person will be dead. I still don't know what happened to Justine's aunt Lena."

Wilson got behind the wheel. "All right. I'll go. Watch yourself."

"Don't worry about me. Just get Blalock and Manuelito away from here a little longer."

As he drove off, Ella knew her luck was about to run out. With every passing second she was risking having Natoni hear the extra vehicles. She had to act now.

Ella returned to her vantage point behind the hogan and, after a quick look to make sure everything was as she'd left it, made her move.

She crept forward like a shadow, her footsteps light and silent, until she reached the hogan's log wall. Hearing the hogan's door open, she froze. Natoni stepped out casually, then waved at Jeremiah Manyfarms, who was just approaching the hogan with a pair of binoculars in hand. Natoni walked toward the other man.

She suddenly realized they'd come in the same vehicle, and Jeremiah must have been in the hogan earlier, or keeping watch outside where she hadn't been able to see him. Yet Natoni wouldn't have taunted Manyfarms. There was still a hostage to contend with.

She'd have to move fast. Manyfarms probably knew about Blalock and the tribal vehicle coming up the track. Noting that the lower half of the open door would be hidden from the two men by the stack of firewood, she crouched down low and slipped inside the hogan.

Ella's breath caught in her throat when she saw Paul and Jeremiah's prisoner. Justine was sitting on the floor, tied to the woodstove and blindfolded, but definitely not dead.

Ella recovered quickly and went to her side, removing the dark scarf that covered her eyes. "It's me," she whispered.

Justine, pale, bruised, and with her mouth swollen where someone had hit her, managed a lopsided smile. "Took you long enough."

TWENTY-EIGHT
——— ✖ ✖ ✖ ———

For a moment, Ella couldn't speak. Her cousin had been badly beaten, and one of her hands was wrapped heavily with bandages. The clothes she was wearing smelled like a PE locker and were much too large on her to be her own. But she was *alive*! "I'm so glad to see you!" Ella managed, her voice trembling with emotion.

"I don't think I'm going to be able to stand, Ella. They've been giving me painkillers. Strong ones. I almost fall over every time I have to pee. They make me use some kind of chamber pot."

Ella pulled out her pocketknife and cut through the ropes holding Justine's feet and arms. "Then let me help you. And stay as quiet as you can, partner," Ella warned softly.

"There are at least two men around somewhere, Ella. One of them is Paul Natoni. I've never seen their faces, but I recognized Paul even though he tried at first to disguise his voice. He likes to try and intimidate me by sneaking up close. It gives me the creeps. But it's the other one, the one who is always silent, who scares me the most."

"That's Jeremiah Manyfarms," Ella said, trying to support Justine as she got to her feet. "They're both outside right now, probably trying to figure out their next move. I think they know that help is on its way."

Justine swayed, and leaned on Ella for support. "I can't make it, Ella, I'm too groggy. I can't even shoot right-handed," she said, holding out her bandaged hand. "They cut off part of my finger."

Anger shook Ella. She wanted to rip out Natoni's lungs for this. "I'll explain later. But right now we need to get out of here. Help's still a long way off."

Ella went to the door to peek outside, but Natoni's abruptly stepped in, aiming a revolver at her chest.

"Stay where you are," he snapped. "Hand me your rifle, butt first."

Suddenly Blalock's sedan came roaring up, crashing through the brush to Ella's left. As the vehicle skidded to a stop and Natoni turned his head toward the new threat, Ella saw her chance. She stomped down on his foot, and at the same time knocked his gun hand to the side.

The pistol fired, and Natoni cursed, stepping back from Ella and whirling around to aim at the vehicle. He fired two shots into the windshield, but the occupants were already diving out both sides. Ella fired her rifle from the hip, catching Paul in the side. He collapsed to the ground, firing again as he fell, but the bullet went wild.

Big Ed remained behind the open passenger door, his pistol aimed at Natoni. Blalock was in the same position on the other side.

"Where's Manyfarms?" Ella yelled, stepping away from the hogan and looking to her right.

"He was coming around the other side of the hogan, but took off into the forest when he saw my car," Blalock answered. "What's going on?"

Justine came to the door, waved weakly, and leaned against the side of the hogan just as the tribal unit came roaring up with Sergeant Manuelito and Agent Payestewa.

Out of the corner of her eye, Ella saw Big Ed and the others staring at Justine as if they'd seen a ghost. But she had no time to enjoy her long-awaited vindication. Another vehicle was approaching, Wilson Joe's.

"Manyfarms was part of this too," Ella warned. "We need to catch him before he gets away." Ella tried to feed another shell into the rifle chamber, but it jammed. "Damn!"

"Don't worry about your rifle. We've got plenty of firepower now, and roadblocks and four-wheel-drive vehicles searching the entire area," Blalock said, shaking off his confusion over the quick firefight and Justine's appearance. He hurried to Natoni, who was on the ground, groaning. Blalock picked up Natoni's pistol by the grips and slipped it into his jacket pocket.

"Don't underestimate Manyfarms," Ella warned. "He could still hide out in this country. He's on foot, remember." Ella tried again to free the spent cartridge from the rifle chamber, but it was wedged firmly.

"We need to begin a search pattern to flush him out." She looked at Wilson, who was climbing out of his vehicle with a smile on his face. "In the meantime, Wilson can take Justine to the hospital. She needs medical attention."

Ella didn't want to say anything, but the bandage looked nasty, and her cousin had started bleeding again. Although there was no way for her to tell what Justine's condition really was, Ella knew her assistant was having a problem focusing her attention. Justine kept blinking her eyes as if trying to clear them.

Big Ed gave Wilson a nod. "I'll call in backup for you, Professor. They'll meet you on your way back to the highway. Don't stop for anyone you don't recognize as a police officer. Jeremiah Manyfarms is part of this, and he's armed and on the loose. Sergeant Manuelito can tend our wounded perp." He turned to Manuelito, who nodded, reached into his vehicle for a first aid kit, then walked reluctantly over to the wounded kidnapper.

As Wilson helped Justine toward the SUV, Ella looked up at the faces around her. Big Ed's chagrined expression was mirrored on Blalock's face. She looked at Manuelito, who was crouched over Paul Natoni, holding a bandage against the man's wound. The sergeant's face was stony, but he gave her a nod. "He'll live, unfortunately."

At least Ella knew that was one less nightmare she'd be having in the future. But in order to prevent another, they still had to catch Jeremiah before he could get to a vehicle.

"Let's track Manyfarms from the place you saw him run into the woods," Ella said to Big Ed. "Except we spread out on both flanks so he can't slip past us. Maybe we can trap him against the edge of the cliff."

"Good plan," Big Ed agreed. As everyone spread out to move

into the trees, a gunshot caught them all off guard.

Ella saw Wilson pulling Justine around the side of his SUV to get her out of the line of fire, but her injured cousin stumbled. Off balance, Wilson fell to the ground with her.

Ella hurried to help, then saw Manyfarms step out from behind some brush, trying to get into position to aim his rifle at the two on the ground. Ella dropped her jammed rifle, reaching around for her derringer as she ran, though she knew she was hopelessly outgunned and that a rifle bullet would surely penetrate her vest.

"Manyfarms!" she yelled, trying to deflect his attention away from Justine and Wilson. But it was too late. He fired quickly, then swung the rifle toward her, working the lever to put a new shell into the chamber.

"Duck, Ella!" Blalock's voice came from right behind her.

Suddenly Blalock collided with her from behind. She fell flat onto the ground, his heavy body bowling her over as if she'd been tackled.

Three or four shots went off at nearly the same instant, and Ella heard Blalock grunt sharply. "Damn!"

Rolling clear of Blalock, Ella scrambled to lift her derringer toward Manyfarms, but by then Big Ed and Paycheck were standing over him. Despite Jeremiah's curses and protests that he'd been shot, the Hopi FBI agent handcuffed the man after they discovered he was wearing a bullet-resistant vest.

Now on her knees, Ella turned her head and saw Blalock clutching his thigh and gritting his teeth. Blood oozed between his fingers, but when he saw her looking, he tried to smile. "My turn, huh?"

Remembering the other shots, she frantically turned and looked toward where Justine and Wilson had fallen. Wilson was helping Justine to her feet again, his arm wrapped protectively around her. "We're okay here," Wilson said.

"Blalock needs an ambulance," Ella shouted to Big Ed, then moved to help FB-Eyes.

"It's already on the way," Big Ed yelled back, holding up his cell phone.

Ella crouched next to Blalock as Agent Payestewa brought more wound dressings from Manuelito's first aid kit, then pressed them against the entrance and exit wounds on opposite sides of the FBI agent's thigh. "It doesn't look like you're bleeding from an artery," Payestewa reported. "But your slacks are a total loss," he added solemnly.

"Gee, you think?" Blalock muttered, fighting the pain.

It wasn't long before Ella saw the paramedic unit pull up, along with an SUV she didn't recognize. When Carolyn and Michael Lavery stepped out, Ella smiled. "I should have known you couldn't stay away."

"We'd stopped at Four Corners on the way back home when I heard on the police band what was going on. I came straight here."

Lavery treated Jeremiah's upper-arm wound as Carolyn went to help Blalock.

"You'll be all right," Carolyn assured the agent. "The bullet passed completely through you without damaging bone or major vessels. You'll be line-dancing in no time."

"A lifelong dream of mine," Blalock grumbled.

Happy to see Justine, Carolyn impulsively gave her a big hug, something that disturbed the other Navajo cops a lot more than it did Ella's shaky cousin. Carolyn studied the bandages on Justine's hand, then checked her vitals. Assuring Justine she'd be okay, she ordered Wilson to take her to the hospital ER immediately. They quickly left.

Soon the paramedics had loaded up Blalock and the two wounded kidnappers. Payestewa rode in the ambulance to keep an eye on the prisoners while Big Ed followed in Blalock's car as the injured were transported.

Ella retrieved her rifle, then stood with Carolyn and Michael Lavery as she finally cleared and unloaded her weapon.

"I know you two deserved your entire vacation, but I'm sure glad you got back when you did." Ella smiled at the two doctors.

"It's hard to enjoy a honeymoon when you're worried sick about a friend," Carolyn said with a shrug.

"What did you say?" Ella's jaw fell.

"I was worried about you," Carolyn said. "Don't look so shocked. We're friends, after all."

Ella saw the twinkle in Carolyn's eyes, but she couldn't tell how much of it was a joke. "The other part of what you said, Doctor."

Carolyn smiled. "There are two Dr. Laverys now. Only one is now known as Roanhorse-Lavery."

Ella hugged her friend. "I can't believe you two got married without telling a soul."

"Actually it was very unplanned," Michael joined in. "But some things are better that way. Right, dear?" He winked at Carolyn.

"Well, I want to hear every detail," Ella said, walking back with them to their vehicle. She wasn't officially a cop now, and the crime scene was someone else's responsibility for the moment.

"Where's your Jeep?" Carolyn said.

"I've got a borrowed pickup right now, and it's a couple of hundred yards back the way you came in. I'll accept a ride," she said, then settled in the backseat and listened to Carolyn chatter happily. Michael Lavery seemed content to nod and smile.

In all the time she'd known Carolyn, Ella had never seen her friend look happier. Ella sat back and relaxed for the first time since her ordeal had started. Carolyn had found love and Justine was alive and safe. Best of all, Ella knew she didn't have to run and hide anymore, and could go home to her daughter again.

"Is it true that you were suspended?" Carolyn asked.

Ella nodded. "But I'll be reinstated soon."

"I hope you'll allow all the ones who gave you a hard time to feel very guilty," Carolyn said, her tone now serious. "And if they try to make amends, don't be nice and try to save them the trouble. Make them suffer and have to find ways to earn your trust again."

Ella laughed. "I'll keep your advice in mind."

Ella showed them where she'd hidden the truck, and Michael stopped and parked. Once he got a clear look at Herman's truck, he whistled.

"That's a real muscle truck. Reminds me of an old El Camino I had."

Carolyn smiled. "Okay, fess up. That's not your mother's. Did you steal it?"

"Depends on who's asking," Ella answered, still protecting Herman Cloud. "I'll tell you about it later, but right now I want to get to the hospital. I'm really worried about Justine."

"Her hand's a bloody mess and I expect she's fighting an infection. Don't expect a quick recovery. They chopped off the end of her finger at the first joint, and she'll probably end up losing it down to her knuckle, maybe more. They had all the finesse of an apprentice butcher boning a chicken."

Ella slipped behind the wheel and started up the big engine. "I'm heading to the hospital. I'll see you two there."

Ella waited outside the Shiprock Hospital's emergency room, working on her third cup of what the vending machine had optimistically labeled coffee, when Big Ed came lumbering down the corridor with two pistols on his belt.

Anticipating his first question, she shook her head. "I still haven't heard anything about Justine. Any news on Blalock's condition? I know they took him on to the Farmington medical center."

"I just got a call. FB-Eye's going to be all right. The doctors say he should be able to regain full use of his leg after a period of recuperation. Probably not even limp."

"That's really good to hear." She was still trying to decide whether Dwayne had saved her from being shot by shielding her from the gunmen or knocked her down by accident. She was certain FB-Eyes would never admit to the truth either way.

Big Ed nodded. "While I'm here, there's something I need to give you."

The chief reached into his jacket pocket and handed Ella her badge. He then unhooked the extra holster from the right side of his belt buckle and gave her back her service weapon. "Accept these along with a very large apology. I've already made a statement to the press, so the story of what you did is getting around. I also got a call from Mrs. Yellowhair. She wants to speak to you whenever you have a moment. Who knows? She may even talk you into running for office."

"Not during this lifetime. I'm a cop. That's all I've ever wanted."

Seeing Dr. Rubens come out the emergency room doors, Ella held her breath.

He smiled, reassuring them instantly. "Officer Goodluck will need to rest and she'll be on strong antibiotics for a while, but she'll be fine. The drugs they'd been doping her up with are wearing off now, and should have no long-term effects."

"How long will she have to stay in the hospital?" Ella asked.

"It's too soon to tell. We need to see how she responds to the antibiotics."

Hearing footsteps rushing toward them, Ella turned her head and saw her cousin Angela coming up the hall. Ruth and Jayne were right behind her.

"I'll speak to them now," Dr. Rubens said, "but in the meantime, why don't you go in and see Justine? She asked for you."

Ella went inside and located the curtained area where her cousin was being treated. Justine lay in bed, her face pale and her arm linked to an IV.

"You're a sight for sore eyes, cousin!" Ella gave her a warm smile.

"I'm glad you're here, Ella. Wilson told me that you never gave up hope, although everyone else thought I was dead."

"It's long story, and a complicated one," Ella said. "I'll tell you all about it later. But how did Natoni and Manyfarms pull off the kidnapping? I haven't figured that one out yet."

"I stopped to help what looked like an old woman with a flat tire. I didn't even call it in, it looked so innocent. Somebody hiding in the dark apparently shot me in the leg with some kind of tranquilizer dart, because I went out like a light. When I woke up, I was in a house or trailer, tied to the bed with duct tape. My hand hurt like hell, and I passed out again. They kept me drugged so much I was out of it most of the time, but once when they thought I was sleeping I heard one of them talking. At the time, I couldn't figure out who it was, because he was in the next room. I know it wasn't Paul, so it must have been Jeremiah. His plan was devastating."

"What did you hear?"

"He had this strategy to get you arrested for my murder. Then while you were in jail, he was going to arrange for you to see a photo of me holding the current day's paper so you'd know I was really alive. After that, the photo would disappear and you'd never be able to prove a thing."

"And once I went to prison?"

"They would have probably killed me and gotten rid of my body. I'd already recognized Paul, and he knew it."

"And Jeremiah never planned to tell me who he was?"

"He wanted you to get convicted according to the white man's laws, and to know that you'd been set up. But he didn't want you to find out who was responsible. He figured that failure would haunt you and he'd end up destroying you—inside and out."

"I would have *never* given up trying to find out who he was," Ella said.

Tears suddenly filled Justine's eyes. "My trigger finger is gone all the way to the knuckle now. They had to cut the infected part off to try and save the rest. My career . . ."

"You'll just have to learn to shoot differently, that's all. After you requalify, you can go back to your job."

"Are you sure?"

Ella nodded. "You've already trained to shoot with your left hand in case of an emergency. You'll just have to get in some practice, and learn to use your right hand as it is. You'll have some adjusting to do all around, but you can learn."

Before Ella could say more, Justine's family came in, and Ella stepped back. Angela held Justine, then kissed her forehead. "We thought we'd lost you," she said, tears running down her face. "But you're here now. I still can't believe it."

Ella slipped out through the curtain, and was leaving the area quietly when Angela came out to find her. "Ella, it's thanks to you that I have my daughter back. I won't forget this."

"She's very brave, and the best cop I've ever worked with. You should be very proud of her."

"I am. And thank you for saying that."

As Angela returned to her daughter, Ella stepped out of the emergency room into the waiting area. Carolyn and Big Ed came up, Agent Payestewa following right behind them.

"We've been giving some thought as to who the dead person was. Nobody's reported any empty graves or stolen bodies," Carolyn said. "Do you have any ideas?"

Ella nodded. "My guess is that it's Justine's real aunt Lena, and she just hasn't been reported missing, living where she did. But short of documenting Lena's disappearance, I doubt we'll be able to prove it conclusively. A positive ID won't be possible, and Manyfarms isn't about to confess. Right now I figure he's probably working hard to come up with a way to avoid a first-degree murder rap, like Paul Natoni. But maybe the Manyfarms twins will plea-bargain and testify against them—if they can be located, that is."

"We have the Bureau looking for them in all the western states, and a bulletin has been sent to every police agency, large and small. They'll be picked up, especially if they stay together. Everyone remembers seeing twins," Payestewa said, notebook in hand. "Was Officer Goodluck able to fill in some blanks for us, like when and how they took her?"

Ella recounted everything Justine had said, knowing Paycheck would still have to interview her cousin later. "Jeremiah didn't complete his plan, but he still got some measure of revenge for the death of his youngest son. He put us all through the worst time of our lives."

"What do you say we go question him?" Big Ed asked. "With the vest he was wearing, he has only broken ribs and flesh wounds, so the doctors have already put him in a private room. I've assigned two officers to watch him full-time."

"He's not going to talk," Ella warned as they headed toward the floor where the prisoner was being held. "He's too smart to further incriminate himself. There's too much hatred in him, and he knows that in New Mexico he'll probably be out of jail before he's an old man."

"We still have enough to send him away for quite a while. Let's remind him of that, and see what else we can get from him," Big Ed said.

"I'd like to be in on the questioning, but first I have to call in some reports," Agent Payestewa said, stopping at the elevator. Can you give me a half hour or so before you see him?"

"Sure," Big Ed said. "He's not going anywhere."

Ella told Big Ed about her encounters with Harry Ute and Begaye, the fugitive he'd been after, then took the time to call her mother, even speaking to Dawn over the phone for a few moments. Rose promised to let Clifford know as well.

An hour later, the three sat in the prisoner's hospital room with the suspect.

Manyfarms was sitting up in bed, handcuffed to the rail. He regarded them with pure hatred in his eyes.

"You can have an attorney present," Ella reminded him.

"I don't plan on saying anything, so I don't need to waste my attorney's time."

The implication was, of course, that he was quite willing to waste Payestewa's, Big Ed's, and her time. Taking a deep breath, Ella pushed back her anger. No sense in letting him press her buttons.

"You're going to prison, Manyfarms. There's no doubt in anyone's mind about that—including yours. So why not tell us everything now?" Ella said.

"Finding answers is your job, not mine," Manyfarms said flatly. "I admit nothing."

"We could try and make things easier for you," Ella said vaguely, knowing that the truth was that the tribe would never cut a deal with him after what he'd done to a police officer, and probably Justine's aunt.

Jeremiah shook his head. "Nice try, but everyone knows about the corruption that's rampant in this department and in our tribal government. Your word means nothing and has no value."

"That's George Branch talking now. Was he working with you?" Payestewa pressed. "Do you rehearse your tirades together?"

Manyfarms smiled. "You'll never get an honest answer from me."

"It wasn't anyone I know who caught me from behind at the Farmington Mall, then pushed me in front of the van. Was it one of the twins?" Ella had spoken to Sergeant Neskahi on the phone, and although he'd seen all the mall security tapes, her assailant's face had been shaded by a cap. They had no leads on the perp.

"Why ask me? I wasn't there." Jeremiah smiled.

"You realize that you're only making thing look even worse for yourself," Ella pointed out.

He shrugged. "I might end up spending a few years in a New Mexico prison, watching TV and taking my meals from their excellent salad bar, but before your daughter's in high school, I'll be out." He held her eyes for a moment and added, "Maybe we'll meet again."

"You actually think you'll be out in a few years?" Big Ed's smile was almost feral.

"You can't prove I murdered anyone," Manyfarms said confidently.

"We won't have to," Payestewa said coldly. "Shooting Agent Blalock brings in a nasty federal rap, and that's just the tip of the iceberg. Add kidnapping and the attempted murder of various police officers, and you could end up with forty years to life in a maximum-security federal prison."

Manyfarms' expression changed into one of pure hatred. "You're still going to go down. Even if you get me out of the way, there are others who will take up the fight. The tribal government and its agencies are corrupt and will be disgraced. A new order will be established. It's inevitable. And you and others like you will be nothing more than the low point in Navajo history."

"Did you hear that on the radio or from the voices in your head?" Big Ed snapped.

Manyfarms smiled. "You'll see."

Forty-five minutes later, the questioning ended. As Manyfarms had promised, it had been a futile exercise. Payestewa, Big Ed, and Ella looked back and forth at each other as they walked down the hall.

"If he's not blowing smoke with his 'new order' propaganda, we solved one problem but can count on another waiting in the wings," Big Ed said.

Payestewa nodded. "A conspiracy."

Ella gave him a sharp look, but he seemed unaware of it. She forced herself to relax. "We'll face the battles that lie ahead when we have to, but in the meantime, let's enjoy this victory. And, guys, putting Manyfarms away is a *major* victory, seeing what was at stake," she added with a smile.

"Well said," Big Ed said as they reached the hospital entrance.

They left the building, separated, and headed toward their individual cars.

Long before she reached Herman's truck, Ella saw Kevin Tolino approaching from across the parking lot. Not in the mood to talk to him, she kept walking, trying to ignore him. Right now, all she wanted to do was go home and hug her daughter.

"Ella, I came to congratulate you," Kevin yelled, hurrying to catch her.

"Thank you," she said coldly, still not stopping to talk.

"I have some news of my own to share," he added. "I'll be running for the Tribal Council next election for sure. I have some major supporters behind me, and we think I can win."

Ella thought about what Manyfarms had said only a few minutes earlier. "Are you certain that's what you want? You'll be living in a goldfish bowl, and everything you do will be scrutinized—including your private life."

He nodded. "I realize that and it's why I'm here. I just wanted you to know I won't be able to visit with Dawn as often as I have been. My schedule is going to become very crowded. Once I'm elected, of course, we can go back to the way things were."

"Many things may change by then—including you," Ella said slowly, not bothering to mention that Kevin's visits to his daughter hadn't been "often" in any sense of the word, and that if he cut back much more in seeing her, he wouldn't be coming at all.

"No, not me. This is what I've worked for all these years. I've always wanted to be in a position to influence the future of our tribe. It'll just be the culmination of my goals."

So for Kevin, it was all about power, as she'd suspected all along. He was perfectly willing to choose the Navajo way of raising a child, with less paternal input and more help from her family, because it suited him to place his very Anglo personal ambition first. Part of her believed that two attentive parents were necessary, but that modernist influence wasn't going to make much difference without Kevin's participation.

He obviously had plans that excluded close family ties, and for that reason, she wondered if Dawn would be better off without him in her life. Either way, it was out of her hands now. "Good luck."

"Thank you. And I'll count on your vote."

"I wouldn't hold my breath on that if I were you, Kevin," she said, then walked away.

TWENTY-NINE
———— ✖ ✖ ✖ ————

Ella stirred the large kettle of pinto beans warming over the red-hot coals as their guests milled about the backyard. Big Ed and a majority of officers and staff from the police station had come, as well as family and friends from all around the reservation. A month had passed since Justine had been rescued, and this celebration was long overdue.

Herman Cloud came up to join Ella. "I have a feeling you're going to miss my old truck. Nothing except the police cars—maybe—run as well as mine." He winked.

Ella laughed. "You've sure done a great job with that engine! But that four-barrel carb sure eats up the push-toe," she joked, using an old Navajo term for gasoline.

"You can borrow it anytime, and long as you keep the tank full. I won't make that offer to anyone else."

"I'm honored!"

Wilson walked over as Herman moved away, and helped her reposition some of the charcoal in the fire pit below the grill, then turn over some hamburgers and place those that were done onto a large serving plate. "There's enough food here for an army," he said. "It's good to see that some things never change. Rose never likes to see anyone go home even remotely hungry." He smiled.

"There's more to it than that this time," Ella whispered. "Mom invited a lot of people, but only half—if that—showed up today."

Wilson grew serious. "That had occurred to me. You know the

stories about you and the legacy are still going around. A lot of people were convinced that you'd turned to evil, and they're having a hard time letting go of that belief even now. It's like one of those urban legends that takes on a life of its own."

"I had a feeling that would happen."

"Why aren't Clifford and Loretta here? Is Loretta still angry because he hasn't been giving much time to her and Julian?" Wilson asked.

"I honestly don't know. They were invited, but with the marital problems they're having, I'm not sure even he will come."

As Justine came out of the kitchen and into the yard, Wilson caught her eye, waved, and went to join her. Ella could see Justine respond to Wilson's presence, smiling brightly and allowing him to drape his arm over her shoulder protectively as they walked. Ella smiled. There was nothing that would please her more than seeing Wilson and Justine make a go of things. He'd been to see her every day recently, Ella had heard.

She looked around once more, wishing Harry Ute could have come, but understanding that his job had taken him elsewhere. It was odd how things worked out sometimes. She'd known Harry for a long time, and there'd never been anything between them. But something about Harry had changed, and now she found herself thinking about him a lot.

"Looks like those two have discovered each other."

"What?" Ella turned and found Clifford standing behind her.

"Our cousin and teacher friend," he explained.

Ella nodded. "Yes, they do seem to have found some chemistry, haven't they?" She pushed Harry out of her thoughts for the moment. "I'm so glad you came, brother! I was worried about you. How are things going?"

"My wife and I are together again," he said, gesturing toward Loretta and Julian, who was giving his grandmother Rose a hug. "But we still have a lot of problems to work out. We're taking it a day at a time."

"It's a good plan."

Clifford look past her, up onto the hill above the house. "I wondered how long it would be before that nonsense started up again."

Ella followed his line of vision. "What the—"

"Our family's watchers."

"That wasn't supposed to happen anymore," Ella said. Kevin and she had made an agreement shortly after Dawn's birth that he would put a stop to his family's intrusions.

"But it's not a complete surprise, is it?"

"No, I suppose not. The one up there now looks like the mother of my child's father." She paused. "I wonder how far the Bitter Water Clan would go to protect the tribe from what they *perceive* as evil."

"May we never know," Clifford said.

The party lasted on into the night, with people coming and going constantly. Seeing Dawn asleep on a big, fluffy comforter set inside her sandbox, Ella picked up her daughter and carried her inside.

"No bed. Not tired," Dawn protested, struggling to keep her eyes open.

"I'll tell you what. Would you like to lie down on *my* bed for a while?"

The idea went over well, and Dawn stopped fussing. Ella went to her own bedroom and set her daughter down, then covered her with the blanket her mother had crocheted.

"Stay!" Dawn protested as Ella started toward the door.

"All right. I'll work at my computer, but you have to close your eyes." Ella knew that her daughter would be sleep within a few minutes.

Sitting at her desk on the other side of the bed, Ella turned on the machine and logged on. She'd check E-mail quickly, then go back outside as soon as Dawn nodded off.

As she clicked on the icon for mail, an instant message came on the screen. It was from Coyote.

> Congratulations again on winning this battle. But the war
> is not over. The conspiracy against your tribe has not
> been dealt a lethal blow. Expect danger from almost any
> direction. They'll be challenging you again.

"Who's 'they'?" she typed quickly, hoping he wouldn't sign off like in the past without answering.

'They' are the unidentified power controlling Indian
gambling from behind the scenes. They'll stop at nothing
to get what they want on the Navajo Rez. Remain
vigilant. You're blocking their path, and that's not a good
place to be.

Before she could ask more, he was gone. Ella printed what was
on-screen, then placed the message in her desk drawer before log-
ging off.

For a few moments, she watched her daughter sleeping peace-
fully. She'd faced danger before and would do so again, but for
now, she was home and her family was safe. They would all walk
in beauty for a time.

Slipping quietly out of the room, she went to join her guests
outside.

MONROE CO. LIBRARY

BD

3 5001 43310776 7

FIC Thurlo
Thurlo, Aimee.
   Red mesa

MONROE COUNTY LIBRARY SYSTEM
MONROE MICHIGAN 48161